For John, my husband and best friend.
Thank you for sharing the dream,
every single step of the way.

Acknowledgments

"Thank you" seems inadequate, but I have to try. So, *thank you!!!*

...to my husband, John Clark, J.D., C.P.A, for helping with every part of this work—from the original concept to advising me on legal and financial matters in the nonprofit world to editing with the skill of a master. This book literally wouldn't exist without you!

...to my editor, Kim Moore of Harvest House Publishers, for opening the door and pulling me through into the amazing world of Christian publishing; and to my agent, Frank Weimann, for making the connection.

...to my father, Robert M. Starns, M.D., for medical information, clarification, and imagination.

...to my mother, Jackie Starns, for extensive proofreading (and cheerleading!).

...to my dear friend and research assistant, Shari Weber.

...to the best group of readers in the world: Alice Clark, Jennifer Clark, Mary Davison, Lucille Dickerson, Kim Farr, Kay Justus, Arline King, Shirley Morris, Dolores Perla, Suzanne Scannell, and Roberta Sullivan.

...to all who filled in the gaps of my knowledge: David Clark, Joyce Hammel, Eileen Hosgood, Mark Lampton, Sal Mannino, David Starns, Joey Starns, and so many others that I could fill this book with your names. You know who you are: Thank you!

...to fellow writers who willingly shared the wealth of their experience: Jeremiah Healy, for valuable instruction on creating a series character; Anthony Bruno, for an encouraging critique and review; and all of my lovely, ever-helpful Sisters in Crime.

...to Church of the Saviour in Wayne, PA, for Biblical guidance, theological clarification, and support.

...to my "e-mail posse," that long list of folks to whom I send out all kinds of questions in the middle of the night and they reply with clever, delightful answers and suggestions. Friends, I couldn't do it without you.

Finally, to my fabulous daughters, Emily and Lauren, for your constant love and support—and for giving mom "just five more minutes" at the computer. You're the best!

Brothers, we do not want you to be ignorant about those who fall asleep, or to grieve like the rest of men, who have no hope. We believe that Jesus died and rose again and so we believe that God will bring with Jesus those who have fallen asleep in him.

1 THESSALONIANS 4:13-14

One

The organization was legit. After three weeks of investigating, that was my final conclusion, the final report I faxed to my boss. After he reviewed my summary and gave me the go-ahead, I wrote out a check for $300,000, locked it in my briefcase, and headed for downtown Chicago. I had already reserved a flight home for later in the afternoon; now all that remained was to meet with these people and do what I had come here to do.

The place was called Transition Resources, and it was run by a friendly mother-and-son team. I had called for an "emergency" appointment, and they had readily agreed to see me, even though they didn't know who I was or the real reason I was there. All I had told them was that my name was Callie Webber and that I needed to have a meeting with both of them.

I'm sure they thought I was just another client wanting their agency's help. My showing up in a taxi, wearing a suit, did seem to throw them a little—probably because most of their clientele usually come by bus, wearing sweat pants or torn jeans. Nevertheless, they shook my hand and invited me down the hall of their cramped, somewhat shabby office building and into a room lined with stacks of papers and folding metal chairs.

"You'll have to excuse the mess," the woman said, motioning for me to have a seat. "There's a leak in the ceiling of the back room where we keep the files. We had to move everything in here."

"Quite alright," I said, smoothing a piece of hair back into the chignon at my neck. I always wore my long brown hair pulled straight back despite the nagging of my friend Harriet, who was forever urging me to visit her hairdresser. *He'll work a miracle on you!* she would say, insisting that my look was too severe and old-fashioned, that the right cut would bring out my blue eyes, my cheekbones. But I liked myself the way I was. The hairstyle that had served me for the last three years would continue to suffice.

"So how can we help you today?" the young man across from me asked, and I turned my attention to him. He was rather short and plain, but there was a sweetness to his face, a gentleness to his expression that reminded me of my brother. "Do you have a parent with a situation that needs our services?" he continued. "Because we do have to consider cases based on financial need…"

His voice trailed off as I placed my phenomenally expensive ostrich-skin briefcase on my knees and began working the gold-plated combination lock. The case had been a gift from my boss, who was generous to a fault and always spent far too much money on gifts. A thrifty person myself, I had never been comfortable with the briefcase, but I didn't return it for fear of hurting his feelings, knowing that somehow he would eventually find out.

"Tell me about your organization," I said as I clicked the first number into place. "I understand you're in three states now?"

"Four, as of last week," the woman answered. "We set up a little satellite office in Detroit, and already it's being swamped with applications."

She went on to tell me how their company was a nonprofit organization that specialized in the relocation of the elderly. Specifically, they helped older people with limited financial resources make the difficult transition from independent to assisted living, from their own homes into retirement villages or nursing homes. This organization helped find housing, do the paperwork, pack possessions, sell extraneous belongings—they even offered psychological counseling to guide their clients through the emotional experience of letting go and saying goodbye.

Of course, everything the woman told me I already knew. I knew that and much more.

It was my job to know.

"So are you a reporter or something?" the son asked, still eyeing my briefcase. "'Cause we've been trying to get some more exposure. We think we might stir up a few donations if we could get on the local news."

I finally got the lock undone. I opened the lid and reached inside the front pocket for the familiar rectangle of paper that was waiting there.

"Actually, I'm not a reporter," I said. "I'm from the J.O.S.H.U.A. Foundation."

It took a moment for that to sink in, but when it did the mother and son looked at each other in surprise.

"The grant!" the woman said. "I nearly forgot we applied for that. Are you here to get some more information?"

I shook my head and allowed myself a small smile.

"I'm here to present you with this check," I said, "from the J.O.S.H.U.A. Foundation to Transition Resources in the amount of $300,000."

I held out the check, and neither of them moved for a moment. Then suddenly they began jumping up and down and hugging each other and screaming and cheering and embracing me. It was one of the more jubilant reactions I had gotten in the last few months, and I allowed myself to relax and go with it, silently thanking the Lord for good people like these, people who had a gift for taking God's resources and using them in wonderful ways.

"We can buy a truck," the son said. "That'll cut our moving costs by 38 percent!"

"We can do a lot more than that," the mother said, counting off on her fingers the plans they had itemized in their grant proposal. "Extended counseling, bigger facilities, more caregivers…"

They listed ideas for the money, lobbing them back and forth like a tennis ball. They asked if they should call the local newspaper to have a photographer and a reporter record this event. I told them no, that our foundation preferred to do things in a more discreet manner.

"So what was it about our little company that caught your eye?" the mother asked, finally settling down into her chair and pausing to catch her breath. "We didn't think we stood a chance. We just did the paperwork and sent it out on faith."

I took a deep breath, wondering how I could ever explain the way our foundation worked. I wasn't exactly sure myself what the selection process was. I only knew how my part of it worked: I received a sealed packet from my philanthropist boss, a packet full of information about an organization or business to which he would like to make a donation. It was my job to verify the integrity of the organization as thoroughly as possible. Sometimes that meant digging around a little, examining records, talking to people—occasionally even posing as a client or infiltrating the ranks as an employee. My eclectic employment history as a private investigator and then an attorney had trained me well for my job, and I was very good at what I did. When my research was finished, I was the one who gave the red or green light, and thus far the boss had always relied completely on my recommendation. If I said the place was good, then he would commission me to write and deliver a check for amounts ranging as high as a million dollars.

The amazing part was that my boss stayed out of the picture, remaining completely anonymous. He kept such a low profile, in fact, that even I didn't know much about him beyond the basic facts. Tom and I had spoken on the phone hundreds of times, but we had never met face-to-face, nor did we have a need to. I left him to his privacy.

"It'll take days before this really begins to sink in," the son was saying now, still staring at the check in wonder and grinning from ear to ear.

"Whom can we thank for this money?" the mother asked. "I know a little about the J.O.S.H.U.A. Foundation, but is there someone in particular..." She let her voice trail off, looking to me for information.

I smiled, clicked my briefcase shut, and stood.

"The best way you can say thank you is to take that money and use it to further your mission as outlined in your grant proposal. The foundation believes strongly in what you're trying to accomplish, and we just wanted to have a small part in furthering your efforts."

It was a speech I had made many times before, but it still never failed to bring a small lump into my throat. There were so many unsung heroes out in the world, people who had decided to dedicate their lives to helping others. The fact that I got to be the bearer of such good news was the very best part of what I did for a living.

I caught the next flight back to Washington, DC, reading a magazine most of the way, closing it finally as we crossed over the Ohio River. I leaned back and looked out of the window, marveling at the gorgeous streaks of purple and orange that accompanied the sunset.

I was tired. Actually, I was exhausted. This was the fifth case I'd worked in a row without a break. Now I was ready to take a few days off, putter around the house, and catch up on things that needed doing there.

The seat in front of mine held a telephone in its back, and when the man sitting next to me headed to the rest room I took the opportunity to pull out the phone and dial. My boss liked to hear from me as soon as possible after a delivery; he would be expecting my call.

The connection was surprisingly good. I had dialed Tom's private line, the one I was supposed to use in case of emergency or at prearranged times. He answered on the second ring, his voice sounding deep and resonant as usual.

"Callie?" he answered.

"It's me," I said, feeling a smile creep into my voice. Though Tom and I had never met in person, we always had a certain rapport over the phone. I had an image of what I thought he looked like, though that image had evolved and shifted over time. All I knew for certain was that he was in his early 30s, like me, and that he had made his fortune in the computer industry. Otherwise, I did not use my investigative skills toward him. It was enough for me that he was my employer, that he valued his privacy above all else, and that he was a good man with a generous heart and very, very deep pockets.

"Callie, Callie, Callie," he said now, and I could hear the click of a computer in the background. "You traded in your first-class ticket for coach again."

"You know how I feel about flying first class," I said, rolling my eyes. "I got over $400 back."

"So keep the money as a bonus and spend it on yourself, then."

"It'll go back to the foundation," I said, "as always."

He exhaled slowly, but I could tell he wasn't exasperated, merely baffled. There were things I had no qualms spending money on—such as a good suit or a nice pair of shoes, because they were essential to the image the foundation wanted me to present. But to me, it always seemed silly to fly first class when coach was available. Either one got you where you were going, and wasn't that the point anyway?

"So tell me about our friends in Chicago," Tom said. "Were they pleased with our little contribution?"

I sat back in my seat and described their reaction, enjoying the vicarious pleasure Tom received from my description, wondering for the hundredth time why he didn't simply show up to deliver the money himself.

"As I was leaving," I said, "they got a phone call from a nearby hospital. Seems there was a 91-year-old woman who had been living with her son, but the son had died and the hospital didn't know what to do with the woman."

"Sounds like a case for social services."

"Social services was trying to locate a nursing home for her. But within five minutes Transition Resources had dispatched a counselor to go to the hospital and stay with the woman while they waited, and they even sent a volunteer worker over to her house to see about her cat."

"Nice."

"They're good people, Tom. You did a wonderful thing."

"As did you."

We chatted a little longer about nothing, really, the way we did sometimes. I always pictured Tom as a Quasimodo-type, alone in a vast castle, the world at his fingertips, but his life a somberly empty place. Of course, that image was probably way off. For all I knew, he was a dashing jet-setter with a gorgeous woman on each arm and a fancy home on every continent.

"Well, now that this case is closed, I have a different sort of assignment for you," Tom said finally. "This one is a bit of a departure from your regular routine."

"Oh?"

"The place is called Feed the Need. It's a worldwide hunger relief organization based in Philadelphia. I want you to make a delivery there tomorrow."

"Tomorrow?" I said loudly. A woman looked at me from across the aisle, and I lowered my voice. "You don't want me to check them out first?"

"The founder is an old friend of mine," Tom said. "Wendell Smythe. A wonderful man. I have no doubt his operation is everything it claims to be."

"Still, it wouldn't hurt to take a look—"

"The problem is that their need is fairly pressing. Seems that they want to put a bid in on a building that's up for auction, and they need a quick $250,000. I see no reason to delay."

I exhaled slowly, thinking about my immediate plans. I had been working so hard lately; I really didn't want to jump right into another case. I had things to do. I was going to get off this plane, make my way home to my little cottage on the Chesapeake, and spend the week winding down. My plans were no more ambitious than catching up on laundry, taking out the canoe every day, and tending to my personal e-mail. I hadn't been home for more than a few days at a time for the last month; even my poor dog, who lived with a neighbor whenever I traveled, was starting to feel like a distant memory.

"Callie," Tom said, interrupting my thoughts, "I know you miss your little Maltese. But it's only a one-day assignment, and the packet is already waiting for you at the apartment in the city. Spend the night there, zip up to Philly in the morning, and you'll be home by tomorrow night. Then you can take a whole week off if you want. Paddle down those little tributaries to your heart's content."

I smiled, wondering how it was that a man I had never met could know me so well.

"Everything I need is in the city?" I asked, thinking of the corporate apartment the foundation kept near the Watergate. It was nice, if a little sterile, and I did keep a toothbrush and an extra change of clothes there. I supposed a quick trip to Philadelphia wouldn't kill me. At least I knew my way around because of an internship I had done there one summer as a law student. Though I hadn't liked the law firm enough to accept their offer once the internship was over, I had kind of liked the city. It had a certain attitude about it, a traditional yet funky dichotomy I found intriguing. Though I didn't plan to stick around town a moment longer than necessary, it would be nice to drive through Philadelphia again. "Okay, I'll do it," I said finally.

We concluded our call, and I slipped the phone back into its holder. Once I got to the apartment, I would call Lindsey, the teenager who always kept my dog, and tell her she would need to keep her just a little bit longer. Then I would go through the packet of information about the agency in Philly and call it a night.

I leaned back and looked out at the sky, which was a dark purple now, the gray clouds silhouetted against the horizon. I felt at peace, satisfied with a job well done, eager to finish this one minor errand tomorrow so I could begin my little vacation.

It's a good thing I didn't know then how the following events would unfold, that my little trip the next day was going turn into something altogether different than either Tom or I could ever have predicted. In my years as a private investigator, I'd seen a few dead bodies, sure.

But I certainly didn't expect to run into one on this particular errand.

Two

⌒

According to the sign, Feed the Need was on the sixth floor. I pressed the button and then waited, checking my reflection in the silver elevator door.

I adjusted the stiff, tweedy fabric of my skirt, thinking that this was not one of my favorite suits but that it would do for this quick errand. I had hopes of getting in and out within an hour, something that probably wasn't possible. Once I had handed over the donation and the initial excitement had passed, the recipients almost always insisted on giving me a tour of their facilities, introducing me to some of their workers and taking me out to lunch or dinner. Usually, I didn't mind. Today, however, I just wanted to get out of there and go home. I wondered if they would think me rude if I begged off with a "prior commitment." Closing my eyes, I could just picture that prior commitment—all seven excitable, furry pounds of her, waiting for her long-absent mother to hurry home and give her a treat of beef jerky.

I got off of the elevator on the sixth floor and found myself facing an elaborate silk flower arrangement on an antique table. Subtly lighted on the wall above the flowers was a large brass plaque, directing me to turn left for Smythe Incorporated or right for Feed the Need. I turned right and walked through a glass door into a small but elegant reception area. The petite young woman at the desk was on the phone, but she caught my eye, gesturing to let me know she would be with me in a moment. As I waited, I looked around the small room and finally sat on a beautifully upholstered couch, picking up a brochure from the coffee table.

Smythe Incorporated and Feed the Need, the brochure said on the cover. *Two businesses, one leader, one heart.*

I was glad to read the brochure, relieved to find even a little bit of information about the place to which I was about to hand over a quarter of a million dollars. I hated this, showing up somewhere knowing nothing about a company. But it was, after all, Tom's money. If he said Feed the Need was legit, who was I to question that?

The woman was on the phone long enough for me to read the entire brochure. It was well written and professionally presented, and from it I learned that Tom's friend, Wendell Smythe, headed a clothing manufacturing business called Smythe Incorporated. Headquartered here in Philadelphia, Smythe's holdings included one domestic plant and sixteen foreign ones, and their clothes were distributed nationwide under several labels, a few that I recognized. The brochure went on to talk about the nonprofit part of the business: *It was on a visit to one of his clothing plants in Southeast Asia that Wendell Smythe first began to recognize the problem of world hunger,* the brochure said. Apparently, that led him to start a sister company called Feed the Need, whose sole purpose was to supply food, farming equipment, education, health care, and clean water to hungry children and their families throughout the world.

I wasn't unfamiliar with hunger relief organizations; I had done research on Save the Children and the Christian Children's Fund in the past. But Feed the Need was much newer and smaller than those organizations. According to the brochure, Feed the Need sponsored 75,000 children in 23 different countries and had an annual budget of around 30 million dollars.

Sponsorships of needy children provide the funds to change their lives, the brochure proclaimed above a line of black-and-white photographs of beautiful, exotic-looking children with dirt-smeared faces and big sad eyes.

It was slick, I would give them that. But I questioned the wisdom of operating a nonprofit business in such close proximity—both literally and figuratively—with a for-profit business. Even this brochure, touting both ventures at once, seemed nervy and inappropriate to me. Lines blur. Lines that should divide the two types of endeavors like night and day.

I tucked the brochure into my briefcase, standing as the receptionist hung up the phone.

"Sorry about that," the woman said. "May I help you?"

She looked to be about 19 or 20, attractive except for the wispy, too-long bangs that covered half of her eyes—fashionable, perhaps, but irritating nonetheless.

"Yes," I replied, handing her a business card. "Callie Webber, here to see Wendell Smythe?"

"Of course," she answered, taking the card. "I'll walk you back."

She came around the desk, revealing a slim-cut skirt and stylish, chunky-heeled shoes. She held the door for me as I stepped through into the offices of Feed the Need.

I looked around as we walked, surprised at the size of the place. It was huge, with a decor that seemed more appropriate for an upscale law firm than a charity. Still, the workers were quite busy, and there were a lot of them—milling around the cubicles, talking on the phones, typing into computers.

The receptionist explained the layout of the office space to me as we walked through. Apparently, the clothing business filled one side of the floor and the hunger relief business the other, hence the left-or-right choice in the hall by the elevator.

"And since Mr. Smythe is the president of both divisions," she said, reaching for a door on the left, near the back end of the giant room, "his office is right here in the middle."

She held open the door for me, then gave a little wave and left. I found myself stepping into yet another reception area; straight across from me was an identical door that was probably the entrance from the for-profit division on the other side.

The walls were lined with file cabinets, and at the massive oak desk in the center of the room sat an older woman, on the phone, with a tasteful brass plaque on her desk identifying her as Gwen Harding. She was neatly attired in a beige suit, and her only adornment was a pair of exquisite pearl earrings. She glanced up as I walked in, her manner radiating—above all else—efficiency.

"Out of the question," she said into the phone. "Mr. Smythe's surgery is scheduled for tomorrow morning. Perhaps a dinner session this evening?"

She pinched the bridge of her nose, briefly closing her eyes. When she spoke again, her voice was clipped and precise.

"But if you can't meet with him today, it'll be at least three or four weeks before he's available again. Hold on, please."

She pressed a button on the phone and then turned her attention toward me.

"Can I help you?"

"I have an appointment with Mr. Smythe," I replied. "Callie Webber? From the J.O.S.H.U.A. Foundation?"

"Yes, of course," she said, smiling politely and gesturing toward the door behind her. "Go right in. He's expecting you."

I knocked lightly on Mr. Smythe's door, then opened it to reveal a large and sunny office, the entire back wall lined floor to ceiling with windows. The view was a lovely cityscape of Philadelphia, that familiar skyline that I had grown to love during the three months that I had lived and worked in this city. At the center of the room was a huge gray marble desk, and the man behind it stood as I entered.

"Come in," he said warmly, extending a hand as he walked around the desk. "I'm Wendell Smythe. I know without you even telling me that you must be Mrs. Webber. Call me Wendell."

"And you call me Callie, please," I said, shaking his hand. "It's nice to meet you."

Wendell quietly shut the door behind me, then he took my arm and led me to a comfortable leather chair, offering me coffee, which I declined.

"That's an interesting name. Callie. What's that short for? Caledonia? Callista?"

"It's just Callie," I replied. "Not short for anything."

He returned to his chair and sat down, entwining his fingers and resting his hands on the ample bulk of his stomach. He was a stout man, perhaps 50 pounds overweight, attired in navy slacks, a blue-and-beige-striped tie, and a white shirt with rolled-up sleeves. He had a friendly face and smile. His head was about half-bald, his skin tinted a reddish-white. I could tell that at one time he must've been a handsome man, though the years and the pounds had blurred his features. Absurdly, I realized that he reminded me a bit of Santa Claus. Without much imagination, I could picture him in a red suit with white fur trim, giving away toys and belting out some hearty "Ho ho ho's."

"I can't tell you how much I appreciate you driving all the way up here to Philadelphia today," he said. "Tom tells me he had to twist your arm a bit to get you to do it."

I felt my face flush, but before I could respond, he continued.

"Oh, I'm sorry," he said. "I didn't mean to embarrass you. Tom and I go way back. I was giving him grief about not delivering the money himself, but he said he was sending his favorite emissary instead. Now that we've met, I can see why he talks about you so much."

"Oh," I laughed, "you flatter me."

"I've been hearing things about the 'wonderful Callie Webber' for a few years. I'm just glad we finally had a chance to meet. You're vitally important to our boy. I hope you know that."

"'Our boy'?"

"Tom, of course. He's like a son to me, you know. And anyone who is as dedicated to his foundation as you are is A-OK in my book."

The man had a certain energy that was infectious, and I decided right away that I liked him. He spoke in no-nonsense terms, cut straight and to the point. I decided to be blunt in return.

"I believe Tom told you this isn't our usual procedure for giving out money," I said, lifting my briefcase and resting it on my knees. "But it's his money. I'm sure he knows what he's doing."

"You may rest assured, my dear, that it will be repaid in full with ample interest. I only called Tom because I needed some cash *fast*. We're not very liquid around here right now, I'm afraid. I had a feeling Tom could help us out."

I hesitated, pulling the check from its slot in my briefcase and holding it in my hand.

"Repaid?" I said. "I was under the impression that this money was a grant."

"No, it's a loan. Most definitely a loan."

"In that case," I said, fingering the check, "I need to make a phone call first."

"Is there a problem?"

"No, no," I said, tucking the check away. "We've made loans before. But it's done differently, from a different account. I just need to speak to our accounting people to see if I can go ahead and give you this check or if it should be handled another way, like with a wire transfer."

"Of course."

"And I'll need to put together our standard loan contract. Shouldn't take too long; I have my computer with me. Still, if there's an empty office I could use somewhere…"

"Certainly," Wendell said, standing. "Come with me."

He led me back into Gwen's office, where she was just hanging up the phone.

"Mrs. Webber needs a telephone and a little privacy," Wendell said. "Can you help us out?"

"Of course," she replied.

"I'll be in here when you're ready," Wendell said to me. "Let me know if there's anything I can do."

"Certainly."

"Oh, and Callie?" he said, pausing in the doorway. "My wife's coming into the city in about an hour, and she'd love to give you a tour of our facility here and then take you to brunch over at Bookbinder's. A little thank-you for your trouble. This sounds terribly rude, but I'm just too swamped with all of this business today to join you."

"It's not necessary for her to take me out," I said, thinking of the long drive home that awaited me. As much as I liked Wendell, I didn't relish the idea of a long lunch in a fancy restaurant with his wife.

"I insist," he said, and I knew that he meant it. Companies always did this. They always insisted, and they always thought they were doing me a favor.

"That would be lovely," I replied finally, thinking it was easier just to give in and get it out of the way.

"Excellent. I know Marion will enjoy getting to know you. Though you have to watch out for her—she's a bit of a matchmaker where Tom is concerned." Wendell gave me a smile and a friendly wink and then returned to his office, pulling the door shut behind him. I felt an odd flush of some emotion I couldn't identify. A matchmaker for Tom? What did he mean by that? Tom was my *boss*. Besides, technically, we'd never even met!

"Would you like to use my phone?" Gwen asked, looking distracted. I noticed she had an appointment book open on the desk in front of her, and that it was marked all over with notations.

"Actually, it might take a little while," I said. "Is there an empty office around here with a desk I could use?"

"Let's see. There's nothing very private at Feed the Need. Let's take a look over here."

She led me through the opposite door into the Smythe Incorporated side of the building. It was similar to Feed the Need in size and decor and just as busy. Gwen led me around, asking two people before finding a vacant office.

"This is our VP of Production's office," she said, turning on the light. "According to his assistant, he should be gone for a while."

"This is fine," I said. The room was large and sunny with a full but organized desktop. Gwen showed me how to use the phone to dial out and then excused herself, pulling the door shut behind her.

Three

As I dialed the number of my home office I glanced at my watch and realized I was probably going to catch my coworker and dear friend Harriet in the middle of her morning goodie break. Our office was located in the embassy section of Washington, DC, two doors down from a French bakery where they made heavenly pastries each morning. Harriet said sometimes the smell of the baking breads was so strong, it was like the old cartoons where a puff of smoke would float into the room and take on the form of a human hand, beckoning the smeller like a temptress. Never one for resisting good food, Harriet usually followed the smell all the way back to the bakery, where she would buy something delicious before returning to the office and settling down with her bounty.

"J.O.S.H.U.A. Foundation," I finally heard in the clipped, nasal voice of our receptionist, Margaret. "How may I direct your call?"

"Hey, Margaret, it's Callie. Is Harriet in?"

"Just coming through the door," she said. "Hold on."

I waited, picturing Harriet heading to her desk to take my call, her hands loaded with treats. Though I usually worked either from my home or out on assignment, I tried to make a point of going into the office as often as I could. It was a two-hour commute each way, but it kept me involved with the regular goings-on there that a less frequent visitor might miss.

"Hey, Callie, what's up?"

"Hey, Harriet," I said. "Now don't get the phone all sticky."

"You just hush," she said. "It was sticky buns yesterday. Today it's a cheese Danish."

"Yum. I bet your arteries are so thrilled."

"My arteries are healthier than a horse on megavitamins. What can I do for you today?"

I told her briefly what was going on, and instantly I could hear her voice switch over to business mode. Harriet may have been a real character, but she knew her stuff. As the financial director of our little foundation, she was the one to make the decision in this matter.

We chatted for a while, Harriet putting me on hold occasionally to speak with the bank. Eventually, I pulled my laptop computer out of my briefcase and set it up in a clear area on the desk in front of me. While Harriet worked out the finances, I fiddled around with our standard loan contract, inserting the name of the company and the principals and amending a few clauses. Together, it took us about 20 minutes to work everything out, but in the end Harriet and I were both satisfied that we had managed to set up a simple low-interest loan from the J.O.S.H.U.A. Foundation to Feed the Need.

After that, I headed down to my car to get my little printer from the trunk. Back upstairs, I returned to the empty office I had been using, connected the cable from computer to printer, and set it to work. As the loan contract slowly printed, I sat back in the chair and looked around the office, wondering what exactly a Vice President of Production for an international clothing company did. Posted on a giant bulletin board that lined one wall were sketches of clothes, swatches of fabrics, and a world map covered with marks and scribbles. The stacks on the desk were mostly contracts and faxes. The only personal item in the entire room was a framed 5x7 photo of a man who looked handsome but fake, like the photo that comes with the frame when you buy it.

Then, like a mirage, the fake man suddenly appeared in real life, swinging open the office door and stepping inside. He was tall and immaculately dressed, with fine blond hair and chiseled features.

He didn't see me behind the desk at first, but as he turned, he drew up short, catching his breath.

"Hi," I said. "Sorry to startle you. I was just borrowing this office for a minute."

He seemed out of breath and disheveled, with something like anger or irritation on his face. I didn't blame him. He didn't know who I was, and I felt sure he wasn't happy coming in to find a total stranger at someone else's desk.

"I'm Callie Webber," I said, coming around the desk and extending my hand. "From the J.O.S.H.U.A. Foundation."

He hesitated, obviously taking in my Ferragamo shoes, my ostrich-skin briefcase, my Donna Karan suit. He, too, was well dressed in an Italian suit and what looked like a Hermes tie.

"Alan Bennet," he answered finally, proffering a smile and shaking my hand. "VP of Production for Smythe. How do you do?"

"So this is *your* office," I said, wondering what kind of man kept a photo of himself on display on his own desk.

"Yes," he said. "I was just out running some errands. Bank, post office, things like that."

I nodded, explaining that Gwen had offered me the room while he was out, but that as soon as my printer was finished I would be able to get out of his way.

"No hurry," he insisted, gesturing for me to take a seat again behind his desk. He took off his jacket and hung it on the back of his door then came and sat across from me, loosening his tie and unbuttoning his cuffs, flashing me a sudden grin in a manner that suggested instant intimacy. Somewhat disquieted, I averted my eyes. I'd been a widow for three years, and I was not at all comfortable with the rhythms of casual flirtation.

"I take it you're here on business?" he asked, glancing toward the printer. There was something a little too aggressive about the man, and I was glad suddenly that my printer pages came out from the machine in a face-down position.

"I'm here meeting with Mr. Smythe," I said evasively.

"For Feed the Need business or Smythe Incorporated?"

I felt strangely reluctant to answer his questions. As an experienced "snoop," I always hated when someone tried to turn the tables on me. I ignored his question, changing the subject.

"VP of Production, huh?" I said. "I imagine you travel a lot."

"A fair amount," he replied. "But I don't mind. It's an exciting job, full of—"

We were interrupted by a knock, and then a young woman stepped into the room, looking toward Alan Bennet adoringly. I recognized her from the Feed the Need office next door.

"I've got the budgets for Haiti and the D.R. that you asked for," she said, holding out a small stack of papers. He took the papers from her and asked her some questions about them, the woman smiling shyly at him as they spoke. He was stunningly handsome, I'd give him that. But with his blond hair, bulging biceps, and model-perfect jaw line, he wasn't at all my type. I preferred the quiet, understated good looks of my late husband, Bryan. He was the kind of man you didn't double take on the street for, but when you looked into his eyes and listened to him speak, you knew he was good-looking through and through.

"Sorry about that," Alan said after she left. "I've been helping out with Feed the Need's finance department. Their CFO's on maternity leave."

I was surprised, thinking again of the blurry line between these two ventures. It was bad enough that they already shared a building and a brochure. Crossing over to share fiscal responsibilities was *really* pushing it!

"Nonprofit accounting is quite different from regular accounting, isn't it?" I asked evenly.

"Somewhat," he replied.

Somewhat?

I thought of my own introduction to nonprofits, from a class at law school. "What you have to remember," my instructor had said, "is that while a for-profit's goal is to *make* money, a nonprofit's goal is to *spend* money, seeing that when all is said and done there's none left over except the minimum required to keep it going." I had found it an odd mind-set to get used to, though of course nowadays I worked with nonprofits almost exclusively.

"So you said you're from a foundation?" Alan asked.

I nodded, glancing toward my printer. Glad to see it was on the last page, I stood and let it feed directly into my hand.

"Yes, though I'm not much of a number cruncher," I said. "I leave that to the experts. I deal more in legalities."

"I see. Is there something I could help you with around here?"

I could tell he was dying to know exactly who I was and what I was doing. Though I doubted the J.O.S.H.U.A. loan needed to be kept secret, you never knew who was privy to what information in any given company. I had learned a long time ago to keep my mouth shut and keep myself out of it.

"No thanks," I said simply. "I'm all done here now."

I gathered up my papers, put away my computer, and unplugged my printer. Once I was loaded up and ready to walk out, I thanked the man again for the use of his office.

"No problem," he said warmly. "But here, let me help you."

Despite my protestations, he took the printer from me and then insisted on carrying it to Wendell's office.

We headed there side by side. I glanced at the clock on the wall, surprised to see that I had been working for nearly an hour. Mrs. Smythe would be here soon, I realized, ready to give me a tour of the office and take me to brunch. Then I could head out into the Pennsylvania sunshine, maybe take one nostalgic stroll around Independence Square, and head for home. Hallelujah.

When we reached Gwen's office, she was back on the phone. She flashed us a quick smile and waved us through to Wendell's door. Alan knocked once and opened the door just as I had done earlier. This time, however, the office appeared to be empty.

"Wendell?" Alan called.

There was no response except for a muffled "thump" from behind a closed door to the far left. Looking mildly embarrassed, Alan turned to me, lowering his voice. "Ah," he said, "I believe he's indisposed for the moment. I'm sure he'll be right out."

"Of course."

Apparently, Alan intended to wait there with me for Wendell to come out of what I assumed was his private rest room. I put down my briefcase and computer and reached out for the printer.

"Well, here," I said, taking it from him. "Don't let me hold you up."

"Oh, okay," he replied, having no choice then but to go. "But don't leave without stopping in to say goodbye."

He flashed me another luminous smile, his teeth straight and perfectly white. Once he had stepped out the door, I set the printer on the chair and let out a long, slow breath.

My hope was that Wendell and I could wrap this up in a matter of minutes. All I needed to do was go over the contract, get some signatures, and present the check. As I waited, I glanced around the room, noting the healthy ficus tree in the corner, the obligatory diplomas on the wall. To my right was a lovely portrait painting I had noticed earlier, and I walked over to it to get a better look.

The painting was exquisite, though somewhat dated. It featured a fresh-faced young woman in her early 20s, a half smile on her lips and a twinkle in her eyes. She sat in a wicker chair, a fuzzy kitten curled in her lap. Judging from her clothes and hairstyle, the painting must've been from the early 1950s.

As I was turning away from the painting, I froze, my heart suddenly in my throat. On the floor, nearly hidden behind the massive desk, Wendell Smythe was sprawled facedown across the floor.

I ran to him, grabbing his shoulder and turning him toward me. His eyes were open, his skin the odd pallor of a dead man.

"Wendell!" I yelled, shaking his shoulders. When he didn't respond I put my fingers on his neck and then his wrist, feeling for a pulse.

There was none.

I ran to the door and threw it open, startling Gwen, who was still on the phone.

"Quick!" I said. "Call 911! It's an emergency!"

She stood, dropping the phone, one hand to her mouth. I dashed back into the room and over to the lifeless man. She followed me into the room and used the phone there, yelling in a frantic voice to the paramedics, "Hurry! Please hurry!"

I started CPR, even though I felt sure it was in vain. As I worked—15 pumps, two breaths, even and strong—I noticed that the trash can was on its side, its contents scattered on the floor beside him. Among the balled-up papers and pencil shavings were a syringe and some medical-looking implements. Glancing toward the bathroom door, I called out, but there was no reply.

I looked at Gwen as she hung up the phone. Her hands were visibly trembling, her face as pale as the pearls on her ears.

"Who else was in here besides him?" I asked her, breathing hard as I pressed rhythmically against Wendell's chest.

"No one," she rasped. "W-why?"

"Because someone's in there. Is that a bathroom?"

"Yes. It has an exit out the other side, though."

"Do you know CPR?"

"Y-yes."

"Take over."

She was frozen in shock. I grabbed her wrist and pulled her down next to me—that seemed to jolt her into action. She leaned forward over Wendell's body and slid her hands into place on his chest, taking over my rhythm. I got up and ran to the bathroom door, knocking loudly. There was no reply, but I thought I could hear movement from the other side. I tried the knob, but it was locked.

"Is someone in there?" I yelled, pounding on the door. There was no answer, just the faint sound of another door opening and then closing.

I stepped back and tried kicking the door open, but it wouldn't budge. I pulled my shoes off and was about to try a harder kick when Gwen called out.

"Wait!" she said, still pounding in vain on Wendell's chest. "A pencil...the hole in the doorknob..."

I pulled a pen from my pocket and poked it into a small hole in the center of the doorknob. I heard a click and twisted the knob.

"Got it."

The door swung open to reveal a very large and elaborate executive bathroom. It was empty. Across from me was another door, and I stepped through it to find a long, narrow hallway. I ran down the hallway to a metal door marked Exit—a door that was only now slowly falling to a close. Swinging it open revealed a stairwell, and from below I could hear the brisk patter of feet going down the cement steps. I looked down through the center of the stairwell but couldn't see the person running.

"Stop!" I called out, my voice echoing in the cement chamber. There was no reply except the hastening of the footsteps on the stairs. Glad I had already kicked off my high heels, I started my descent in stocking feet, hiking my narrow skirt high enough to allow my legs full range of motion.

I had gone down about three floors when I heard a door somewhere below me open and then close. Then all was silent except for my gasping breath and the pounding of my heart. I continued down three more flights, then burst through the door into the busy first-floor lobby.

There were plenty of people there, heading in all directions, though no one that looked suspicious or out of place. Glancing around, I could find no doorman or security guard. It was just a typical downtown office building, anonymous and vaguely chaotic.

Still in my stocking feet, I ran out of the front door and looked up and down the street, hoping to catch sight of someone running away, but again there was no one running, nothing unusual. There was a cab parked in front of the building, the driver leaning lazily against the hood.

"Excuse me," I said. "Did you see someone come out of this building just a moment ago?"

He looked down at my bare feet, then back at my face.

"Why ya wanna know?"

"It's an emergency," I rasped. "Did someone come running out of here ahead of me?"

He shrugged.

"Lotsa people been in and out. Nobody running."

"Out of breath, maybe? Sweating?"

"Not that I noticed. Say, what happened? Somebody steal your shoes or something?"

I didn't bother to reply. I returned to the lobby and walked around it, trying to decide which way I would've gone if someone had been pursuing me. There weren't that many choices, really, just the elevators, the front doors, or the stairwell on the opposite side of the lobby. I opened the door to that other stairwell and listened, but I couldn't hear any movement overhead.

I closed the door to the stairs and walked around the lobby one more time, looking for some sort of video surveillance cameras, but there were none that I could see. Finally, I gave up, stepping into the stairwell just as I heard sirens drawing closer in the distance.

Wearily, I started back up the stairs. There was always the chance that what I'd heard was not the person getting out of the stairwell at the first floor, but at the second. When I reached that door, I stepped through and let the door fall shut behind me.

It was a quiet hallway, lined on each side with small offices. I walked slowly down the hall, peering into each office door. There were a variety of businesses, all of them calm and quiet and seemingly normal. Nothing out of the ordinary on this floor.

Finally, I gave up and returned to the stairwell, slowly walking up the remaining five flights to where I had begun.

When I reached Wendell Smythe's office, my shoes were right where I had left them, though now the room was filled with people and commotion. I pulled the shoes on as I observed the paramedics working over Wendell's body, cops milling about the room, curious onlookers crowding in the doorway. There was a buzz of nervous energy—almost panic—and things seemed on the verge of getting out of control when one of the cops took charge and herded the crowd away, finally closing the door in their faces.

Gwen hovered in the corner, sobbing.

"Oh no! Oh no!" she kept saying, two dark black streaks of mascara running down her wrinkled cheeks. I went to her and kept a comforting arm about her shoulders as we watched.

Wendell was dead, that was for certain. The paramedics had already checked for vital signs—feeling his pulse, pulling back his eyelids, flexing his stiffening fingers. Now, taped to his chest were wires that led to a small machine. As they studied the machine, one of the cops pulled out a notebook and began jotting down some notes.

"Estimated time of death?" the note taker asked.

"Not too long ago," one of the paramedics answered, reading from a piece of paper that had printed out from the machine. "Body's still warm. I'd say he's been dead 'bout 30 minutes. An hour at the most."

I could've told them the same thing: Wendell Smythe had met his end during the brief period of time I had sat in another man's office, talking on the phone, typing on my computer, tinkering with a stupid loan contract.

"Anybody call the coroner yet?" the cop asked, scribbling into his notebook.

"He's on his way."

I took a deep breath and let it out slowly, turning my gaze from the man's body to the lovely view out of his window.

The man was *dead*. Incredible.

I felt a lump lodge in my throat, a lump I couldn't seem to swallow away no matter how hard I tried.

Four

I felt guilty, but there it was: All I really wanted to do was go home. The whole time the police questioned me, I had to work hard not to picture my dog, my house, my little hand-hewn canoe sitting forlornly in my shed, just waiting for me to slide it out into the water and climb aboard. How I longed to be out on the water, paddling away the knots in my shoulders, breathing in the scents of peace and quiet and wilderness, falling into the rhythm that comes over me like a trance—wiping away all other pain, all other feelings except a oneness with myself and my Creator.

Instead, I sat in a spare office of Feed the Need in my itchy wool suit, describing for the fourth time exactly what had transpired from the moment I entered Wendell Smythe's office until the moment the paramedics arrived. Even as I spoke, I felt overwhelmed with a pervasive sense of sadness and loss. I had spent no more than five or ten minutes with Wendell Smythe in total, but even in that short time I had found him to be a charming and vibrant man. The fact that his life had ended at some point during the one hour we were apart boggled my mind.

"So not only were you one of the last two people to see Mr. Smythe alive," Detective Keegan said, "you're also the one that came back and discovered his body an hour later?"

Detective Keegan was a short man, his aged but boyish-looking face topped by coarse, reddish hair that bristled out over his ears. Though I knew what he was insinuating, I wasn't worried about being incriminated in any sort of crime here—if, indeed, a crime had even been committed. Wendell's secretary, Gwen, had seen me leave Wendell's office while he was still perfectly alive and well. She could attest to the fact that I hadn't returned for an hour—as could any number of people in the Smythe offices, including Alan Bennet, who had found me working away at his desk.

As we talked, the detective seemed to figure out that I wasn't someone of whom to be suspicious, but in fact quite the opposite—someone who could provide valuable information about the entire situation. Though the medical examiner still hadn't identified the cause of death, it seemed as if the detective suspected foul play, particularly when I described the sounds from the bathroom and my subsequent pursuit of someone running from the office. All in all, we seemed to agree: Something just wasn't quite right about the death of Wendell Smythe.

Luckily for me, having grown up surrounded by cops, I knew the lingo of an investigation, not to mention the fact that I was a licensed private investigator myself. I made sure to mention my lieutenant father and my detective brother more than once. I didn't bring up my own experience in investigations or my law degree. You never knew how information like that might go over with cops; I thought it would be best to just coast along on my family's laurels for the time being.

When Keegan was finished with his questions, he thanked me for my cooperation.

"Of course, I'm sure we'll be speaking with you again," he said as he swung the door open. "So you'll understand why we have to ask you to remain in the area, at least for the next few days."

I had known it would be coming, but that still didn't make it any easier to hear.

"I live near DC," I said, feeling guilty and selfish even as I pleaded with him to let me leave. "Surely I can go on home and then come back up here if necessary."

"I'm sorry, ma'am," Keegan replied. "For the time being, I'm afraid I must insist that you remain nearby."

"But I don't have any clothes, I don't have anywhere to stay, I don't—"

"Excuse me, Detective," a woman interrupted, suddenly standing before us. "Mrs. Webber will stay with me. There's plenty of room."

I looked at the woman, wondering why she seemed familiar to me. She was petite and attractive in a well-preserved sort of way, with expensive hair and clothes, a meticulous manicure, and a rock the size of Gibraltar on the ring finger of her left hand.

"I'm Mrs. Wendell Smythe," she said to me, holding out her hand. "Marion."

Of course. The portrait on the wall in Wendell's office. She had been striking in her 20s and was now an elegant beauty in what I guessed to be her late 60s.

"Thank you, Mrs. Smythe—" I said, shaking her hand.

"Call me Marion, please."

"Marion. But I couldn't possibly impose. I'll get a hotel room—"

"Nonsense," she interrupted. "My house is huge, with tons of empty bedrooms. Sticking you in a hotel after what you've been through today would be unspeakable. I won't take no for an answer. And Wendell wouldn't have had it any other way."

I had a feeling she was right about that. I studied the woman in front of me, wondering how she could be so strong. Then I noticed the shaking of her fingers and the pale face beneath her carefully applied makeup. Something told me to accept her gracious offer, that the kindest thing I could do under the circumstances was to become a temporary guest in her home.

I thought about that as we drove through the city. She had a large beautiful Cadillac with a driver, and I followed behind in my Saturn, wondering if I could be of particular comfort to her because I was a widow, too. Though it wasn't a condition I would wish on anyone, I did have to admit that it gave me a certain empathy. Bryan had been dead for three years, and I still found myself sometimes awakening in the middle of the night, then gasping with pain when I became fully awake and realized he wasn't there next to me—and wouldn't ever be again.

Now I tagged along as Marion's Caddy sped westward out of the city under a gray cloudy sky. We drove for about half an hour before turning onto local roads that wound through suburbs dense with new housing developments. Once we reached a more rural area, I realized that the terrain itself was lovely, with rolling hills and thick trees bursting with the colors of autumn. We finally began passing what could only be called "estates"—gorgeous properties with beautiful stone houses and acres of fence-lined pastures. We slowed and then turned into a long winding driveway that led to one of the most beautiful estates of all. From what I could see as I parked the car, there was a huge main house, several other smaller buildings, a pool, a greenhouse, and, around back, what looked like a barn and some pastures.

It was all a little much, considering the fact that half of their business was supposedly the *non*profit kind.

I reached the front door just as the driver of Marion's car was helping her up the front steps. He was a huge man, tall and quite heavy, though I couldn't tell if his bulk was mostly fat or muscle. He had dark eyes and hair, with a neatly trimmed beard and a slightly stooped posture. Once inside, Marion dismissed him with a thank-you and then took my arm, leaning on me for support as we headed through the foyer, the elegant, antique-laden decor not unlike that at the Smythe offices.

I learned a long time ago not to be impressed with money—how much a person made, how much a person owned. It seemed to me that the Bible had a lot to say about the things of this world, and I really did believe that the only important treasures were the ones we stored up in heaven. On the other hand, I wasn't immune to the aesthetic pleasures that money and good taste could provide, and I looked around at our gracious surroundings as we walked.

Marion continued to lean on me as we went past a handsome study on the left and through the formal dining room to a small drawing room off to the right. As she settled onto the couch, she explained that just as her husband, Wendell, had had his study across the way, this was her little "getaway" room, her personal sanctuary. Though it wasn't exactly my style, I found the delicate laces and the pale blue-and-yellow floral patterns oddly soothing. After I made sure she was comfortable on the couch, I allowed myself to sink down into an especially cushy armchair on the side.

"I just have to say how sorry I am that you've been caught up in all of this," she said, placing her hand on mine. "I feel terrible, especially now that they won't let you go home."

"Please," I said quickly, "don't apologize. It's just one of those awful things that can't be anticipated. Right now the last thing you need to be worrying about is me. I'm more concerned for you."

She was silent a long moment as tears slowly filled her eyes. She was reaching into her purse for a handkerchief just as a young maid came bursting through the doorway, speaking with a hint of an Italian accent.

"Mrs. Smythe, I am so sorry! I just heard the news on the radio, coming back from the grocery store!"

"Angelina," Marion said, suddenly overcome with emotion, "can you believe it?"

The young maid came into the room, seemingly oblivious to my presence. She was very distraught, and she went to the couch and wrapped her arms around Marion. This attractive girl appeared to be in her early 20s. She wore a black, slightly-too-large maid's uniform with a white apron, her straight dark hair twisted into a tight braid on the top of her head.

"Such a good man," the young woman cried. "Such a good, good man!"

"I know, Angelina, I know," Marion sobbed as the two women held each other, rocking slowly back and forth. Though I was a little startled to see a woman of Marion's class and generation interacting so intimately with a member of the household staff, I was glad. I thought it was telling of the kind of person Marion Smythe must be.

I was also glad she had someone with whom she could share her grief. I still remembered that horrible feeling after Bryan died, that there was no one left to hug me, to cradle me. His funeral was filled with polite cheek kisses and somber handshakes when the whole time what I really needed was a pair of capable arms around me, holding me as tightly as possible, whispering that it was okay to let myself go.

The young maid did this for Marion, rubbing her back as she cried. Unsettled by the depth of their grief, I closed my eyes and did the only thing I could think of to do: I prayed for them, prayed that the Lord would fill their minds with understanding and their hearts with peace. After a while, the room grew more quiet, their sobs fading to a few shaky sighs.

"Wendell was a very devout Christian," Marion said to me, wiping at her eyes and trying to pull herself together. "That's my only consolation, that I know right now Wendell is with God, in heaven."

I felt the same about Bryan, and Angelina voiced similar thoughts about her beloved grandparents. Finally, the young woman excused herself, returning a few minutes later with some hot tea and promising to have the cook whip up some soup. Marion and I drank the tea, rehashing the events of the day. She bemoaned the fact that had she arrived an hour earlier to her husband's office, she would've been able to see him while he was still alive. I felt badly about that, knowing she had set her timing to coincide with mine so she could take me to brunch once my work with her husband was finished. Now, instead of coffee and soup at Bookbinder's Restaurant, she and I were sharing tea and tears in her drawing room, and Wendell was dead.

"I only spoke with your husband for a few minutes," I said, "but he seemed like such a nice man, such a pleasure to be around."

"Oh, he was. Warm. Funny. Genuine. And so smart, so capable. Now all I have for my last memory of him is the quick kiss he gave me this morning as he left for work. Typical morning rush, you know. 'I'll see you at the office,' he told me. Those were his final words to me."

We sipped tea silently after that, and as she sat on her lovely sofa and stared off in the distance, I started to feel restless, wondering what I was going to do about clothes and toiletries. Finally, as if reading my mind, Marion put on a brave smile and said it was time for Angelina to show me to my room, insisting that I borrow some of her daughter's clothes until I could pick up a few things of my own.

"It's our fault you're here, Callie," she said against my protestations. "Please let us make you feel at home."

I thanked her and then followed Angelina through the dining room, back to the foyer, and up the main staircase. As we climbed the stairs, I asked the young maid how many people lived here.

"Well," she said, counting off on her fingers, "there is Mr. and Mrs. Smythe; their daughter, Judith; their son, Derek; his wife, Sidra; and their son, Carlos. Oh, and my brother Nick and me. That's eight." She faltered a bit, then continued sadly, "Until today, of course. Seven, now that Mr. Smythe is gone."

We reached the second floor, and she led me past a cozy alcove and down to a room at the end of the hall, a lovely bedroom/bathroom combination decorated in muted peaches and greens.

"I will be back in a minute with some clothes for you," she said after opening the curtains to reveal a nice view of the expansive grounds. "If you need anything else, just let me know."

Once Angelina was gone, I sat on the edge of the bed and pulled out my cellular phone. While dialing Tom's private line, I wondered if he had already heard the news about his friend Wendell or if I would have to be the one to break it to him.

He answered on the first ring.

"Looks like he was probably murdered," Tom said after he realized it was me. "I just got off the phone with a friend in the Philadelphia police department. Wendell's death has been tentatively classified as a homicide. I don't have all the details of how he died, but it looks like someone gave him an overdose of insulin. Wendell had really bad diabetes, you know. Apparently, he died from insulin shock."

I sat back on the bed, my head reeling. Here I was in the middle of things, and yet somehow Tom had more information about the situation than I did. Typical for the man who always seemed to know everything about everyone.

"Couldn't it have been an accident?"

"Not likely," said Tom. "The full coroner's report should be released in the morning, but the police seem fairly certain that it was a premeditated act. Between the condition of the body and the fact that you chased someone from the scene, the cops are fairly certain: Someone gave him a lethal dose of insulin."

"I thought diabetics usually gave themselves their own shots."

"Not Wendell," said Tom. "He had a needle phobia. Had other people do it for him whenever he could. Apparently, this particular injection was in a spot he couldn't reach, so it had to be done by someone else. They're thinking that whoever did this came into his office through the bathroom entrance—the same way you chased them out."

"Do the police have any suspects?"

"Right now," he said, "they're not ruling out anybody. Coworkers, business associates. Family, which is of course ridiculous. But it's a big list."

"Incredible," I said.

"It seems that the coroner found the injection sight clean and straight, with no sign of a struggle. Wendell willingly let whoever did this give him the injection. I think that's telling."

"I think so, too."

Because Tom wanted to hear my version of all that had happened, I went through the entire story once again, pausing only when Angelina came into the room with an armload of clothing. She put it on top of the dresser and then left, closing the door softly behind her.

"That's about it," I said, finishing my tale. "Now I'm stuck here until the police decide I can leave town."

"What did you do with the J.O.S.H.U.A. money?"

"Still have it," I said. "The check is in my briefcase."

Tom told me to hang onto it for the time being, to wait and see whether they planned to proceed with the purchase of the building before we handed over the money.

"Sure."

"I can't imagine what could possibly have happened to lead to Wendell being murdered," he said somberly. "If you had known him, Callie, you'd understand my shock. He was my mentor, my hero. I'd have bet the farm he didn't have a single enemy in the whole world."

"All it takes is one," I replied softly, picturing the man's lifeless form lying on the floor in front of me.

"You know, of course," Tom continued, his voice suddenly resolute and business-like, "we'll have to run our own concurrent investigation. I'm sure the Philadelphia police department is competent, but I want to take things a step further. No expense spared here, Callie. Wendell Smythe was my friend. If he was indeed murdered, I want you to find out who killed him and why."

I had had a feeling this would be coming. My head throbbed as the image of my little canoe, my beautiful tributaries, receded further still from my mind.

"I don't have any contacts," I said halfheartedly. "The Philadelphia police aren't exactly going to open their files to me. They'll only think I'm in their way."

"I'll take care of that," he replied, and I couldn't help but roll my eyes. In other words, he knew someone who knew someone—and with probably one phone call the whole homicide department would be laid out at my feet. Tom's world always seemed to work that way.

"I'm not licensed in Pennsylvania, Tom."

"Already looked into that. Takes at least 30 days to get a license there, so you'll have to work under someone else's. I've already contacted an old friend of mine, Duane Perskie of the Perskie Detective Agency. He says it's just a formality, that as long as you keep him posted, you can work on your own. You know the drill, Callie; we've done it plenty of times before."

"But not in a *criminal* case, Tom. I haven't done any criminal investigating in a long, long time."

Tom knew that I had begun working for a private detective when I was in high school. I loved that job, and I had stayed with it through college and law school. I still kept my PI license current. But the day I passed the bar was the day I unofficially "resigned" as that type of private investigator. The next morning, I had traded in my Nike sneakers for a pair of Dolce & Gabbana pumps and headed for my new position with a law firm. My career had taken a few twists and turns in the eight years since then, but I still had no desire to go back to the gritty, full-time PI world of liars and murderers, coroner's reports and crime scene photos.

"What are you talking about, 'a long, long time'?" he asked. "You do investigations for a living."

"I investigate *businesses*, Tom," I said. "I check out their programs, their finances, their legalities. I'm not equipped to handle a murder case anymore."

He was quiet for a long moment.

"Callie," he said finally, "you are better than anyone I have ever known at ferreting out information, at getting down to the truth of things. What difference does it make whether it's a murder or a business? It's still an investigation."

"I don't—"

"I'm not even asking as your boss anymore," Tom said. "I'm asking you to do this for me, as a friend. Though of course I'll pay you extra. I'll pay you very, very well to do this for me. Please."

I blew out a deep breath, frustration gripping like a headache at the back of my mind.

"My reluctance has nothing to do with money," I said, thinking that the minds of the rich always seemed to go that way first.

"Of course not," he replied quickly. "But you know what I mean."

"What will Marion say to all this, Tom? She won't want me snooping around here. Her husband just died, for goodness' sake!"

"I'll speak to her," he said. "I'm sure she knows as well as I do that time is of the essence. It's crucial you act now, before any evidence is lost."

I closed my eyes, wondering how it was, exactly, that I had ended up in this position. Despite the fact that Wendell Smythe was a kind man, a decent man, I selfishly didn't want to stay here. I didn't want to investigate his murder. But I also didn't want to disappoint Tom, who had never been anything but good to me, who had never once asked me for a personal favor before.

"Of course," Tom said, "your safety is my uppermost concern. It is a *murderer* you'll be looking for, after all. If at any point you feel you are in any danger whatsoever, I would want you to pull out of the investigation immediately. I don't want you in any personal jeopardy. I just want Wendell's killer found."

When he put it like that, I really had no choice.

"Alright, I'll do what I can," I said finally, bidding goodbye to the images of my home, my canoe, my dog. "But only until the police allow me to leave."

"Thank you, Callie," Tom replied, the gratitude evident in his voice. "You've no idea what this means to me."

Five

I hung up the phone, tucked it back in my briefcase, and turned to the pile of clothing Angelina had placed on the dresser. After going through the lot, I finally chose some slightly loose navy slacks, a tan blouse, and a large but comfortable pair of sneakers. Though it seemed pointless to change just now, I couldn't stand the tweed suit any longer; I just had to get it off. Once I was dressed, I helped myself to the basket of toiletries in the bathroom, washing my face with scented soap, brushing my teeth with a stiff new toothbrush. I would still need to pay a visit to a dime store for some underwear and other necessities, but this would do for now.

I pulled my hairbrush from my purse and redid my chignon, catching sight of my face in the mirror. I looked worn out, I decided, with dark circles just starting to show beneath my blue eyes. *You're not as young as you used to be,* I thought as I stared at my reflection. At 32, I was beginning to realize that my body couldn't bounce back from this endless activity the way it once had.

Turning from the mirror, I exhaled slowly, wondering where to begin with my investigation. I usually started in a rather meticulous way (or, according to my friend and coworker Harriet, an overly obsessive way)—by setting up my files, going through the initial paperwork given to me by Tom, gathering what information I could from the internet and other sources. This time, however, I wasn't investigating the legitimacy of an organization but rather the murder of a human being. Undoubtedly, this case would require an altogether different approach.

Still, no matter what type of investigation it was, step one was always the same: Set up an information database on the computer. Using my laptop I quickly installed the framework, creating the necessary categories but leaving most of them blank for the time being. As I gathered information, I would load and organize the data into this framework. Then, as the investigation proceeded and I needed to double-check, cross-reference, or sort facts, I could use the computer to help organize my data—and my thoughts.

Once the database was set up, I saved what I had done, then shut down my computer and carried it to my car. I had decided to start the official investigation by returning to Wendell Smythe's office. There were a few things I needed to know in order to begin.

As I got in the car and started it up, I prayed for insight and for the stamina to see this thing through. My prayer continued as I drove toward the city, retracing the route we had driven earlier. If I were to be successful in this investigation, I knew I would have to put it completely into God's hands, trusting Him to reveal things to me in His way, in His own time.

∽

I stopped by the Perskie Detective Agency first, eager to get going on the case but knowing I couldn't do this at all without the proper authority. Duane Perskie turned out to be a big ex-football player-type of guy with an easy smile and a heavy Midwestern accent. As we chatted in his office, I found myself laughing at his jokes, wondering how he knew Tom, what their connection was. I had long ago ceased to be impressed by the variety and extent of my boss' connections. It often seemed that no matter where I was going or what I was doing, someone somewhere who knew Tom was there to help me out.

By the time I reached the Smythe building, it was just after one in the afternoon. The parking garage was full, but I finally found a spot on the very bottom level, at the end of the row. Glancing at my watch as I headed for the elevator, I tried to calculate just how long the police had been here. My hope was that their investigation of the crime scene was finished and that it was no longer secured.

I rode the elevator to the sixth floor, seeing the familiar signs for Smythe Incorporated and Feed the Need in the hallway as I got off. I turned right and stepped into the reception area, pleased to find the desk there empty. Without missing a beat, I opened the glass door into Feed the Need and strode purposefully through. The place was much more subdued than it had been during my visit earlier that day. Now instead of the busy hum of an office at work, there were only small clusters of employees speaking in hushed tones around their cubicles.

No one seemed to notice me as I reached the door to Gwen's office and stepped inside. Unfortunately, several people were in there, all of whom looked up as I came in. I recognized Detective Keegan, the man who had interviewed me earlier. He was standing next to a tall, familiar-looking man and a woman I hadn't seen before.

"So anyway," the woman was saying, "about three hours and I should have some preliminaries."

She was holding an opened-topped box that was filled with lunch-sized paper bags—evidence, no doubt. Carefully carrying the box, she headed out the door, the other man holding it open for her.

"I'll catch a ride with Michelle," he said to Detective Keegan. "See you back at the station."

The two of them left, and Keegan turned to me inquisitively.

"Can I help you?" he asked, squinting his eyes as he studied me. "Oh, you changed clothes. Sorry I didn't recognize you right off."

"I couldn't stand that stiff suit any longer," I said, smiling. "I don't mind dressing up, but sometimes I get a bit claustrophobic."

He didn't laugh but merely raised one eyebrow and continued to look at me.

"I was just wondering if the crime scene has been released."

"Just finished," he said. "I think I'm the last one here. Is there something you need?"

"No," I answered lightly. "I just wanted to take a look around."

I could tell he wasn't going to let me off that easily. I took a deep breath, exhaled slowly, then lowered my voice.

"I've been...retained," I said, "to look into Mr. Smythe's death."

"Retained?"

"As an investigator."

"When I questioned you earlier, you said you were an attorney and that you worked for a foundation."

"That's correct. But I'm also a licensed PI. My boss seems to think I might be of some use around here now that Mr. Smythe's death has definitely been classified as a homicide."

Detective Keegan didn't look very pleased.

"You're licensed in Pennsylvania?" he asked.

"Maryland," I said. "But I'm working here with the Perskie Detective Agency. I can give you the number of Duane Perskie, if you need to verify it."

He waited a beat, studying my face.

"No, I know Duane," he said. Then, with a final nod, he picked up his jacket from the back of Gwen's chair, slipped it over his shoulders, and headed for the door.

Once he was gone, I turned and went into Wendell's office. I didn't blame Detective Keegan for his wary attitude, and I wished there was some way I could assure him that I knew what I was doing, that I was fully aware of the principles of chain of evidence and the like. In time, I supposed, he would see that I wasn't some incompetent Nancy Drew wanna-be, but a finely trained and meticulous detective. I smiled as I thought of Eli Gold, the man who had taught me everything I knew about investigations. Though he was now retired and living in Florida, he would always be very much a part of my life. Sometimes it almost seemed as if Eli were still looking over my shoulder, interpreting the facts and calmly explaining what I should do next.

Welcome back to the scene of the crime, I thought now as I walked around Wendell's desk and looked down at the floor where his body had lain, dead, this very morning. The police had left a bit of a mess behind with fingerprint dust on walls and furniture and vivid white chalk marks on the dark blue carpeting. It looked as if they had been very thorough—as one would expect in a high-profile case of a wealthy man such as this.

Still, that didn't mean there wasn't more to find. I thought of Eli's "crime scene checklist"—the 30 things I was supposed to try to ascertain right up front, beginning at the scene of the crime. Eli had made me memorize all 30, in alphabetical order, from Age of Victim to Wound Patterns. As I mentally worked my way through the list now, I knew that there were still a lot of unanswered questions.

Silently, I padded around the room, looking for things the police might've missed, reconstructing the events of the morning in my mind. From what I could remember when I first found the man on the floor, nothing had been amiss with either the victim's clothing or his office. The only thing askew was the trash can, and its contents had since been removed by the police. The papers that had been on Wendell's desk were gone now, too, as were his appointment calendar and the hard drive from his computer. I went through his drawers but found nothing unusual. I flipped through his Rolodex and noted that he did seem to have a lot of medical-type phone listings, from drug supply stores to dialysis centers. I made a note to ask Marion about any chronic medical conditions that he might have had other than his diabetes, knowing these numbers could either be work-related or personal.

Because I needed to see an appointment calendar, I headed back out to Gwen's office and easily located hers. It was still open on the desk, the notebook-sized pages heavily penciled on, scribbled through, and otherwise edited. Flipping back a few days, I could see that previous entries were much neater. Turning back to today, however, which was a Monday, I saw that this entire week was kind of a mess. Though Wendell had had appointments scheduled every day this week, Gwen had drawn a large "X" on each day after today, and there were notations next to many of the names, like "left message," "appt. cxed." and "resched." Obviously, she had been canceling and rescheduling his appointments for the week. I remembered her saying something earlier on the phone about Wendell going in for surgery. I wondered what the surgery was for, and I made a note to ask Marion about it later.

Reading Gwen's calendar, I jotted down names and numbers that I thought might be relevant. When I had gleaned all I could from the calendar, I put it back on the desk the way I found it; then I turned and went through Wendell's office to the private bathroom that was attached. This was where the killer had been when I first arrived, but there was nothing notable about the room now; it was just a nice bathroom. Police had dusted thoroughly for fingerprints in here as well, especially around doorknobs and the sink and faucets.

I looked at the door I had run through earlier, the door to the short hallway that led to the stairs. I retraced my steps now, wishing that this sort of work could be easier, wishing that killers dropped calling cards on their way out. I stepped into the stairwell, leaned over the rail, and looked down the center of six flights of stairs, all the way to the ground floor. Something about that frantic chase down the stairs was bothering me, but I couldn't put my finger on what it was. I closed my eyes, trying to recall sights, sounds, smells. Nothing in particular came back to me.

I returned to the hallway and headed back to the bathroom, but as I opened the door and stepped through, I could hear a noise in Wendell's office. I hesitated just inside the bathroom.

Someone was out there, looking for something. I chanced leaning forward to take a glimpse, and I saw the back of a smartly dressed woman who was digging through the files in Wendell's desk. I stayed where I was, listening as she finally slammed the drawer and then picked up the telephone.

"I don't see anything here," she said into the phone after only a moment's pause. "It looks like the cops took anything of any importance."

She was quiet for a moment, listening.

"But they took the hard drive, too."

I wondered who she was and what she was looking for. Her demeanor was more than simply concerned; she seemed nearly frantic.

"What do you mean, 'cross that bridge when we come to it'? Don't be stupid."

She hung up the phone and continued to poke around the desk. Deciding to make my presence known, I softly shut the door, then flushed the toilet. When I came out of the bathroom, she was standing only a few feet away, hands on hips.

"Who are you?" she demanded. "And just what are you doing in my father's bathroom?"

I swallowed hard, feeling my face surge red in spite of myself.

"My name is Callie Webber," I said. "I'm from the J.O.S.H.U.A. Foundation. You're Judith, I take it? I'm so, so sorry about your father's death. I know this must've been a shock for you."

She nodded, her expression softening just a little, though she remained there, immovable, in front of me.

"What are you doing here now?" she asked.

I hesitated, studying her. She was quite striking, probably in her late thirties, dressed in an elegant but understated navy suit, her hair cut and colored in an expensive, up-to-the-minute fashion. Even standing perfectly still, she radiated nervous energy, like a hot engine giving off steam.

"More questioning by the police," I hedged. "I'm the one who found him, you know."

"Do you think he felt any pain?" she asked suddenly. "I mean, it's kind of a relief, in a way, that he's gone. But I'd hate to think he suffered."

"A relief?"

She nodded, turning away.

"His health was failing fast. His death wasn't much of a surprise."

"What was wrong with him?" I asked, coming around the desk.

"What *wasn't* wrong with him?" she asked, rolling her eyes. "Diabetes, kidney failure, heart disease, you name it. Daddy was a mess."

I thought of him, dead, his overweight frame in a heap on the floor.

"Kidney failure," I said. "Was he on dialysis?"

"Three times a week," she answered. "He was trying to line up a kidney transplant, but the doctors were about to pull the plug on that idea."

"Why?"

She shook her head, as if suddenly my questions were just a bit too pushy for her.

"I've got to get back to work," she said. "Can I walk you out?"

Though it was posed as a question, I could see I had no real choice in the matter. I nodded, letting her lead me through Gwen's office and into the Smythe Incorporated side of the building. As we walked through, I realized that it had the same hushed and concerned atmosphere as Feed the Need. We passed a small group of whispering employees who dispersed the moment they saw Judith.

"The natives are restless," Judith said disdainfully under her breath as we walked past.

"I'm sure they're upset about your father's death."

"The show must go on," she replied curtly. "They've all got more than enough work to keep them busy."

"But the shock of it all," I said. "You've got to expect them to be thrown a bit."

"What shock?" Judith snapped. "I'm his daughter, and you don't see me whimpering about it. Daddy's been living on borrowed time for years. My only surprise is that he lived as long as he did."

I was so stunned by her callous attitude that I know it must've shown on my face. After a moment, she stopped and looked at me, swallowing hard.

"You probably think I'm a heartless monster," she said quietly. "I'm not. I just won't let this get to me. He was a good man, and he had a good life. But now he's dead. That's it. Finito. Over and out."

"But you must be in pain from this. The loss of such a good man—"

"Oh, I am. I loved my father, Ms. Webber. Make no mistake about that. I'll miss him. But I can't change what happened. My guess is that either his heart finally gave out or his blood sugar just went crazy. Either way, we can't bring him back. So we move on."

"At least you can take comfort in the fact that he was a Christian," I said, but I was surprised when she waved my comment away with the flip of her wrist.

"That's my family's thing, not mine," she said, walking again toward the door. "I don't believe in heaven. Don't believe in God."

"Not even now, in the face of your father's death?"

"We live, we die. End of story, far as I'm concerned."

My heart lurched for her, and I wanted to stop everything and try to convince her how wrong she was. How could anyone not know God was real? How could anyone get through life without the daily presence of the Holy Spirit?

"God *is* real, Judith," I said. "I know that as surely as I know I'm standing here, in front of you. The miracles He's worked in my own life—"

"Thanks, but no thanks," she said. "Save your sermons for someone else."

We reached the doorway, and she held it open for me, dismissing me not only from the building but from our conversation as well.

"Well…" I said, grasping for something to keep us talking. "I'm sure I'll see you later, at the house."

"Whatever," she replied, and then she turned and walked away, the door slowly swinging to a close behind her.

Six

Dumb, dumb, dumb, I thought as I pressed the button for the basement. Not Judith, but *me.* I was just *dumb.*

How many times in life did I have to be reminded that you don't bring people to God by arguing or pleading with them? It takes love and support, living the right kind of life, meeting them where their needs are. The elevator door shut and I was alone, staring at my reflection as I headed down.

Judith didn't come across as needy, I knew, but that tough exterior certainly masked a hurting soul—and my desperate preaching had probably done nothing more than push her further away from a decision for Christ. I would have to back off and change my approach. Surely, I didn't need to be beating her over the head with a truth she wasn't able to see!

Putting Judith out of my mind for the time being, I reached the basement, retrieved my car, and headed out into Philadelphia traffic. I went back over my conversations with Tom and then with Duane Perskie, thinking about what we knew of Wendell's death so far—not much, but enough to draw a few conclusions.

Wendell Smythe was a diabetic who had been murdered with an overdose of insulin. That meant someone had snuck into his office through the back way, given him a lethal injection, watched him die, and then almost been caught by me in the rest room before making a getaway.

Not that unusual of a scenario for murder, of course, but this one had a catch: There had been no struggle. This murder had been committed cleanly and quietly, with only a dead body and an upturned trash can to show for it. Even the secretary, Gwen Harding—who claimed she was at her desk, on the phone nearly the whole time—said she had heard no unusual sounds whatsoever coming from Wendell's office. Assuming she was telling the truth, I thought that whoever killed Wendell must have been someone he had known and trusted, someone who could pop in through the back way and give him an insulin shot without causing any sort of disturbance.

My thoughts, of course, went to coworkers, family members, and household employees. If anyone that Wendell Smythe knew and trusted could've waltzed in there, offered to give him his insulin shot, and then waltzed back out, then all it would've taken was an extra-big dose of insulin, and he was history. Wendell was used to getting his shots from other people; he could've easily been tricked into sitting still for this one.

The next step, then, was for me to try to find out who in Wendell's world usually gave him his shots. If he had a needle phobia and hated giving the shots to himself, then he had probably trained quite a few people to do it for him so that he would never be caught in a bind. I wondered who was on that list and what would be the quickest way to find out their names.

In a moment of inspiration, I pulled out my notes and dialed the home number of Wendell's secretary, Gwen Harding. We had "bonded" a bit this morning, having gone through this crisis together, and my hope was that I could finesse a conversation with her to get the information I sought. Unfortunately, a man answered the phone, and when I asked to speak with Gwen, he told me she was indisposed.

"Who is it?" I heard her ask softly in the background, and I realized that she was probably overcome with emotion and exhaustion.

The morning had been extremely difficult for her. I gave my name, and after a moment's hesitation, she came onto the line.

"Callie?" she asked, her voice slightly muffled. "What's going on?"

"I got your number from the office," I said. "I hope you don't mind. How are you holding up, Gwen? Are you doing okay?"

"How sweet of you to ask," she said. "I was just lying down." She went on to tell me that her husband had come home from work to be with her, and that her doctor had prescribed a sedative.

"I just took one a few minutes ago," she said, and I could hear the slight slur in her voice. "I'm going to take a little rest now."

"That's a good idea," I said. "Before you go, I wonder if you could tell me something."

"What, dear?"

"Would you be able to provide a list of names of the people who regularly gave Wendell Smythe his insulin injections?"

"Again?" she moaned. "I just told this to the police."

I took that as a positive sign—the police and I were on the same track.

"What I told them," Gwen continued, "was Wendell's family, the household staff, me, and Alan Bennet. That's it. Why does everyone need to know, anyway?"

"No telling," I said, thinking, technically, that wasn't a lie; I did know, I just wasn't telling. "Are you sure that's everyone?"

"Positive," said Gwen. "We were all trained at the house, at the same time. We all learned together."

"And all of you gave Wendell his shots?"

"From time to time. At the office, it was usually me. At home, it was usually Sidra."

"Sidra?"

"His daughter-in-law. She's a nurse."

"How about Alan Bennet? Why him? I mean, isn't he a vice president or something?"

"He's also a close friend of the family. And he and Wendell traveled a lot together on business. Alan always did it when they traveled."

"How about any other nurses? I understand Wendell had a bunch of medical problems. Was there no regular nurse on staff?"

"Again, Sidra handled his dialysis and everything. Wendell did have some night aids a few months back, but none lately."

"I see."

I could hear the slur in her voice growing more pronounced and, feeling guilty, I let her go, telling her I hoped she felt better once she got some rest.

I put away the phone, thinking of Gwen's list. If I was going to continue with my current theory, then there was a good chance the killer was either a member of the family, a member of the household staff, Alan, or Gwen.

I thought about the Smythe family, knowing that Tom would have a fit if he knew I was looking in their direction first. He was close to them and probably would feel the killer couldn't possibly be any of them. But I didn't know the family at all, which was to my advantage at this point. A good detective never assumes anything— and in a case like this one, the family is the most logical place to start, statistically speaking. Marion's grief at her husband's passing had seemed genuine, but even that wasn't always a clear sign of innocence. As I headed to the house I resolved to keep an open mind, hoping I would have a chance to meet and get to know the entire family a little better.

When I was nearly there, I stopped at a large strip mall to pick up some toiletries and makeup, a bathing suit, and a few office supplies. I didn't feel like spending time trying on any clothes and just grabbed some things that looked like they would fit, hoping for the best.

By the time I reached the house, it was early afternoon, and the place was quiet. Realizing I hadn't eaten since breakfast, I stashed the bags in my room and set off for the kitchen, hoping to catch a quiet interview with the maid, Angelina, and maybe find something to eat at the same time.

I was in luck. I peered around the corner of the kitchen to see Angelina sitting at the kitchen table, snapping some beans. The chauffeur was standing behind her, now dressed in a white cook's jacket, kneading some dough on the counter, then pausing to stir a pot on the stove. They were speaking softly as they worked, delicious smells filling the room.

Angelina stood when she saw me, her features offering a guarded smile.

"Mrs. Webber," she said. "Can I get something for you? A cup of coffee, perhaps?"

"Sit, please," I said, heading toward the table. "I didn't mean to bother you. I was just hoping I could maybe make myself a little sandwich or something. I never had lunch."

"Perhaps a bowl of soup?" the man suggested. "I just made a pot of cream of potato with scallions and peppers."

"Sounds wonderful."

Angelina gestured toward the man behind her, introducing him as her brother Nick, the cook.

"You will excuse me if I don't shake hands," he said, waving to show me that his palms were covered with flour.

"The cook?" I asked. "I thought you were the chauffeur."

"The chauffeur?" he replied sharply. "I am the *chef!* I just drove Mrs. Smythe into the city this morning as a favor."

"I see."

Our eyes met, his almost challenging me. Obviously, this was a man who took great pride in his work. I realized I had insulted him.

"My mistake," I said apologetically. "No offense intended." After a moment, he spoke again, his tone warming.

"It is quite alright. Have a seat. Angelina, get the lady a bowl."

She fluttered around, gathering bowl, spoon, gourmet crackers, and a glass of lemonade. I made a great show of tasting the soup and pronouncing it heavenly—which it was. Nick beamed proudly.

"So where is everyone?" I asked, taking another sip. "Is Mrs. Smythe okay?"

"She had a light meal in her room," Angelina answered, resuming her place at the table, "and now I believe she is taking a nap."

"Soup, hors d'oeuvres, dinner," Nick said, counting off on his fingers. "Good thing you did that big grocery shopping trip this morning, Angelina. Who knew we would need all of this food?"

I continued to eat as Angelina explained that Marion's son, Derek, was in the den, returning phone calls from friends, family, acquaintances, and reporters.

"The phone has been going crazy," she said. "I did not know what to tell people. I hardly understand what has happened myself."

"I'm sorry for your loss," I said, "for all of you." Angelina nodded, closing her eyes.

"Mrs. Smythe will be accepting visitors around six," Nick said. "Things should be quiet around here until then."

He continued to cook, and Angelina snapped her beans. As I ate, I began to watch Nick's movements with interest; there was something oddly soothing about his hands working the dough, rolling it out onto the floured counter, cutting it into perfect rings, which he then pressed into the little cups of a muffin pan.

"Pecan tarts," he said when he finally noticed my interest. I nodded, wondering how long he had been a chef. He moved in a professional, efficient manner throughout the kitchen just like the chefs in cooking shows on TV.

"Have you been cooking for the Smythes for a long time?" I asked.

"I met the Smythes about ten years ago when they came into my uncle's *ristorante* in Florence."

"Florence, Italy?"

"Yes. That is where I grew up. The Smythes took one bite of my pan-seared lamb steak on linguini with garlic and a light pesto sauce and then offered me this job, on the spot."

"Goodness."

I listened as he described the meal that had so impressed them, thinking that some people might find his arrogance a little off-putting. I found it sort of charming, particularly because I was in the middle of a bowl of the most delicious soup I'd ever tasted. Like any great artist, he perhaps had the right to be a bit egocentric.

"I had always thought about coming to America," he continued. "And to get a chance like that, to have the freedom to cook what I wanted, to have as my audience people with educated palates—I did not hesitate. I said yes, packed my bags, and flew to America within the week. Of course, at the time I had no idea that my employers would become like family as well. I love it here. I never looked back."

"That's wonderful," I said. "I take it the Smythes get along well? One big happy family?"

Nick and Angelina shared a glance, and I realized suddenly that my seemingly innocent question had somehow touched a nerve. I let the question hang there, eager to see who would answer it, and how.

"They…have their problems," Angelina said finally. "But then, who does not?"

I nodded, thinking that she had skillfully deflected the question. So things weren't all hunky-dory on the home front. That didn't bode well for any of them, particularly since the head of the household had now been murdered.

"Marion and Wendell? How was their marriage?"

"Like a rock," Nick said defensively, giving Angelina an angry glance. "You never met two people so totally in love."

"I see. What's the problem, then? Parent-child issues?"

They both seemed uncomfortable, and I didn't blame them. Here I was, a complete stranger, grilling them about their beloved employers.

"Their son and his wife are separated," Angelina said finally. "It makes things a bit tense sometimes, especially because she still lives here."

"She lives here even though they're separated?"

"She and her son moved into the cabana a few weeks ago," Nick said, his voice tight.

"Sidra is Wendell's dialysis technician," Angelina added. "So even though she's living in the cabana now, she is still in the house a lot."

"Dialysis in the house? I thought that type of thing was done at a dialysis center."

"Not if you are rich," Angelina whispered. "Mr. Smythe has a whole dialysis room upstairs. The chair, the machine, the supplies. It is really something."

I nodded, wondering if the supplies upstairs included syringes and extra insulin.

"So why are Derek and Sidra sep—"

"This is really not any of our business," Nick interrupted, and I could tell the subject was closed. I decided to take things in a different direction.

"So how about you, Angelina?" I asked lightly. "How did you end up here, working for the Smythes?"

"When I finished *scuole media*—high school, I guess you would call it—Nick convinced Mama to let me come to America, to live and work with him."

"She is a good girl," Nick said paternally. "Works hard for the Smythes, and they appreciate her."

"Do you like it here as much as Nick does?" I asked.

"The Smythes have been very good to me," she replied evasively. I wondered about the two of them, brother and sister, living in the Smythes' house, the servant class in residence. Angelina was an attractive girl, but something in her seemed unsettled, as if her life here was as ill-fitting as her uniform. I thought perhaps I should speak with her later when her big brother wasn't there watching over her shoulder. For now, I would wrap up this conversation before either of them realized that I was more than just a nosy houseguest.

"I think I'll wander around a bit," I said when I was finished eating, carrying my dishes to the sink. "Everything is so lovely here."

"It is beautiful, isn't it?" Angelina said. "You must see Mr. Smythe's rose garden, he was always very proud of it. The white roses are probably finished blooming for the season, but the pinks and especially the yellows are still coming out..."

Her voice faltered, and her eyes grew red and brimmed with tears. Without speaking, Nick turned and placed a calming hand on her shoulder. She leaned her head against his arm and closed her eyes, seeming to draw strength from his very presence.

"The pool is nice, too," Nick said to me even as he continued to comfort Angelina. "It is heated, so it will be warm enough for you to take a dip if you're so inclined."

I nodded, offering again my condolences for the death of a man who obviously meant a great deal to both of them.

"We will miss him," Nick answered sadly. "He was a great man. A great friend."

Angelina dabbed at her eyes with a tissue, nodding.

"A kinder soul I never knew," she said, blowing her nose. "Like a second father to me."

Finally, Nick removed his hand from her shoulder, leaving a faint white handprint against the dark cotton fabric.

Seven

~

Leaving Nick and Angelina in the kitchen, I wandered through the first floor of the house, peeking into rooms that were open. Passing by the door of the den, I heard a man's voice inside. I realized it must be Derek, the Smythes' son, talking on the phone. The house was large, but not so big that I wasn't able to get a handle on the layout of the rooms. Another day, perhaps when everyone was off at the funeral, I would attempt to explore the upstairs as well as the small wing off of the kitchen where I assumed Nick and Angelina lived.

For now, I headed silently across the dining room to the study I had glimpsed earlier, pushing the door open to find a dark paneled room lined with books and filled with exquisite leather furniture. I stepped inside, shut the door behind me, then turned on the light.

This was Wendell's office, certainly. A beautiful desk filled one end of the room, the chair behind it a duplicate of the chair he had in his office at work. I looked around, observing the neat stacks of papers on the desktop and the dormant computer on the side arm. Unlike the office at work, there had been no police activity here, no dusting of fingerprints or confiscating of papers. I sat at the desk and quietly flipped through everything on it and in it, but nothing jumped out at me as being important. With a tiny jolt of adrenaline, I flicked on the computer, a little afraid that it might make too much noise starting up, particularly with Derek in the room next door. But it whirred to life quietly, and once it was up and running, I took the liberty of taking a stroll through the hard drive—looking for what, exactly, I wasn't sure. I opened files, read letters, scanned data. But nothing jumped out at me as being of any particular interest.

I shut down the computer and walked over to the bookshelves. The books there formed an eclectic collection, and I could tell they were well used and not just for show. Many of the bindings were cracked, and a few books held little slips of paper sticking out of the top, marking some unknown place. I felt a twinge of sadness as I thought about that. The man who had read these books, who had found some passages worthy of marking, was now dead and gone. Bookmarks or not, he wouldn't be back to take another look.

On a coffee table next to a wingback chair, I saw the most important book of all, and I paused to pick it up and flip through it. It was Wendell's Bible, more dog-eared and page-worn than any of the other books in the room. I loved seeing a Bible that looked like this, for it was obvious that its owner had dedicated himself to studying it and delving into its truths. There were verses highlighted in neon yellow, notes scribbled in the margins, question marks next to confusing passages. I felt comfort just looking through it, but also a sadness that this man hadn't been able to pass along the richness of his Christian faith to his own daughter, Judith. Finally, I put the Bible back where I had found it and moved on.

The far end of the room held a large locked glass case; inside were three shelves covered in black velvet. On the shelves were neatly arranged but very old pieces of clothing. It wasn't until I had finished looking at all of them that I saw the list, typed neatly and resting on the top right corner. It was an identification key, describing each piece. As I read it I realized that this was a collection of antique clothing, with items like "Tall-crowned man's felt hat with curled brim, circa 1770," and "Double-breasted frock coat with lined pocket and bound edges, circa 1855." I smiled, thinking that collecting antique clothing was a clever hobby for a man who had made his fortune in the clothing industry. I wondered what some of the pieces were worth. Judging by the lock on the side of the case and the security wiring that ran discreetly around the perimeter of the glass, I decided that this must be a fairly valuable collection.

I was just scanning the room for signs of a safe when I heard sounds coming through the wall. I listened to the muffled rise and fall of angry voices from next door, and though I couldn't make out any of the words, I realized that Derek was no longer alone in the den.

Silently, I went to the door, turned off the light in the study, and let myself out. I hesitated in the foyer, looking toward the door of the den. It was too exposed, too out in the open, to risk standing there with my ear pressed against it. Instead, I headed out of the front door and around the outside of the building, pacing off the distance until I was just about even with the den.

I could hear the angry voices much more clearly from here, and I took a step closer to the open window, crouching down on the grass beneath it. I could now make out nearly every word that was being said, and I quickly discerned that there were just two people in there—a man and a woman.

"…considering what's happened today," the man was saying, "that you'd lay off. Just lay off for one day. But no. Not you. The old tricks just keep coming."

"Look who's talking!" the woman replied, her words tinged with a slight accent that sounded vaguely Hispanic. It wasn't the Italian lilt of Angelina; this was a different accent, a different voice. "The master of dirty tricks. Don't tell me it wasn't you who put those dead roses at my door."

"Here you go again. Sidra, do you really think anyone believes you when you make these ridiculous claims? Anyone?"

"Your father believed me."

"My father's dead."

"And isn't that just so convenient for you?" she retorted.

The man gasped.

Then there was a long, weighty silence. I held my breath, wishing I could chance a peek through the open window. I heard no movement or speech, but after a while the man spoke in a soft, controlled voice.

"I won't even dignify that with a response."

More silence, and then the woman spoke.

"I'm changing the locks on the cabana. Carlos is starting to have nightmares."

"If he's having nightmares," the man responded furiously, "it's because of all the crazy ideas you're putting into his head!"

I heard a door open and then slam shut, and I quickly glanced in the window to see the back of a head of curly grayish hair. The man, Derek, was standing in the center of the room, facing the door, fists clenched at his sides.

Silently, I moved away from the window, wondering why Wendell Smythe's death could possibly be "convenient" for his son. I headed around back, hoping that the woman, Sidra, was going now to the cabana. As I rounded the far corner, I heard the back door open, and I hurried along the building so that I "accidentally" almost collided with her.

"Excuse me!" I said, taking a step back. She looked at me, startled, her face a study in agony. In spite of the red eyes and wet cheeks, she was strikingly lovely in an exotic sort of way. Her features reminded me of old portraits of Spanish royalty; she had dark, almond-shaped eyes, straight black hair, and a perfect olive complexion.

"Sorry," she said with the same slight accent I had heard through the window. "I wasn't looking where I was going. Who are you?"

"I'm a houseguest here," I said, watching as she swiped angrily at the tears on her face. "Are you okay?"

"It's just…the death and all," she said. "It's been a difficult day. I'm sorry."

With that, she continued onward in the direction she had been heading. I turned and watched as she circled around the pool toward the cabana—a large, understated building with a row of French doors facing the pool. She opened the door on the end, stepped inside, and pulled it tightly shut behind her.

I could hear a car starting in front of the main house, and I jogged along the side of the building in time to see a navy blue Jaguar pull out from the long driveway onto the road, Derek at the wheel.

Without hesitating, I pulled my keys from my pocket and climbed into my own car. I started it up and also headed down the long driveway, pulling out onto the road in the same direction he had gone.

I caught up with him a few blocks away, and I held back, letting one and then two cars slip between us. I didn't know what I hoped to accomplish by following him, but I felt it wouldn't be prudent to let him drive off like that, unobserved. I thought of one of Eli's favorite sayings, that sometimes it is in anger that we reveal our truest selves. I wondered if that would be true of Derek Smythe, if there was anything I could learn by following him now.

After only a few turns, the Jaguar slowed down, its right blinker flashing. I was surprised to see a brown wooden sign indicating a state park. I watched as the car turned into the parking lot, and then I drove on past, waiting until I was out of sight around a bend before I pulled into a driveway and turned around.

I got back to the park in time to see Derek climbing from the driver's side of the Jaguar and slamming the door. Without even a glance around, he headed off toward the park. I pulled into the parking lot and slid my Saturn into a space at the other end of the row. Once he was around the first bend and out of sight, I quietly climbed from the car and took a look around.

I realized that this wasn't a park in the usual sense—there was no playground or baseball diamond. Instead, it featured a walking and biking trail that wound alongside a broad, shimmering river— probably some branch of the Schuylkill. Through the dense autumn foliage I could see the man I was following; he was walking briskly up the path, arms swinging at his sides. Though it was probably still a good half hour before dark, the sun had already reached the horizon, and it seemed especially dark among the foliage. Nevertheless, I took off after Derek, staying as far back as I could without losing sight of him altogether. He walked for a while, and I had just begun to wonder if he was simply doing his evening exercises when he finally stopped walking and stepped off of the path, moving toward the water.

I quickly glanced behind me and then ducked into the trees myself. As quietly as possible, and without looking too suspicious in case someone happened upon me, I advanced. There was a broad tree about ten feet behind Derek, and I thought if I could reach the base of that tree, I could scramble up out of eyesight and shimmy my way down a big branch far enough to be able to see what he was doing by the water.

I moved slowly but steadily, and by the time I had reached the high point of the tree, I had a sudden image of myself—Callie Webber, dignified widow, Director of Research for the J.O.S.H.U.A. Foundation, all-around straight-laced attorney—hanging from a tree limb in the middle of a state park, trying to spy on a man who may or may not be pertinent to my investigation.

It wasn't a pretty sight.

I heard the laughter of some children, and through the trees I spotted a family walking up the trail in our general direction. I waited until they were about even with my tree to make the last scooting movements down the limb. They had a dog with them, and his playful barking provided enough of a distraction for me to get where I was going without being heard by the man beneath me.

I lay against the rough bark, peering down at my target. He was sitting at the edge of the water, staring off into the distance, absently tearing a leaf into tiny pieces and tossing them into the current. He was talking to himself. He was crying.

"...falling apart, it's all just falling apart."

I couldn't understand everything that he said, but I certainly got the gist of what was going on. He was sobbing. Sobbing and trying to pray. This was a man in pain, come to a place where he could be alone and grieve the death of his father. I listened as he moaned, calling softly for "Daddy," praying for help with his pain. He prayed also for God to change the angry heart of his wife, and I knew instantly that he was talking about Sidra, that here was a man whose life was falling to pieces before his very eyes.

I swallowed hard, shame burning my face. This man deserved to be alone in his grief. He had come out to this place in the country, this quiet, empty, riverside park where he could find solitude for his thoughts and prayers. As carefully as possible, I made my way out of the tree. When I reached the ground, I crept away until I was nearly out of sight, then I took off running, and I ran all the way back to the car, the darkness finally enveloping me as I climbed inside. *Shame on you for being so persistent*, I thought as I started my car. *Shame on you for having to butt into his business at all.*

Eight

By the time I arrived back at the house, it was almost completely dark outside. As I turned into the driveway, I saw that it was filled with cars, and I realized this must be close friends and family come to offer their condolences. I parked my car around back, near the garage, and got out, glancing around at the lovely estate that surrounded me. The pool was still and inviting, its dark calm water suddenly irresistible to my exhausted soul. I decided that perhaps later I would come back out and take a quiet dip before bedtime.

I glanced toward the cabana next to the pool, noting that there were several lights on inside. I took a chance and headed there now, despite the fact that I wanted to get into the main house while Marion's visitors were still there and perhaps mingle and meet a few of them.

Still, this seemed a good time to question Sidra. I hoped she would be alone; I wondered where the child, Carlos, was and why I had neither seen nor heard him thus far.

I reached the door of the cabana and rapped on it lightly, and after a moment the door swung open to reveal a sobbing Sidra. If she had been crying before, right now she seemed positively hysterical. Though I didn't know her, I felt the urge to wrap my arms around her and tell her it would all be okay.

"What do you want?" she asked, not unkindly. She stood in the doorway, clutching a handkerchief to her cheek, her shoulders shuddering from stifled tears.

"I just wanted to see if you were okay," I said. "Obviously, you're not."

She seemed to sense my honest concern, and after a moment recognition came into her face.

"You're the woman Marion invited to stay here, the woman who found Wendell's body."

"Yes."

"I didn't realize that earlier. Come in."

I stepped up into the cabana and pulled the door closed behind me. I looked around, noting the tasteful but subdued beige-and-brown decor of the living room/kitchen. The place looked like what it was, a poolside cabana that had been converted temporarily into an apartment.

"I know we don't know each other," I said, "but I was worried about you. You seemed so distraught earlier. And now, even more so."

That set her off. She let out a sob, catching it in the handkerchief pressed to her lips.

"I'm sorry," she said, "but I'm just so frightened, so confused. So many things have happened, and then the roses and now the picture…"

She pointed toward a shelf of photos, and I stepped closer, taking them all in. There were several photos of Sidra, as beautiful in pictures as she was in person, along with quite a few small framed photos of a handsome little boy.

"Is this your son?" I asked.

"Carlos. He's away at a soccer tournament."

Looking down, I realized that one of the photos was on the floor, a lovely family portrait that had been shattered, a knife bored into it through Sidra's face.

I gasped, kneeling down to get a better look. It was a framed 8x10 photo of the Smythe family, a nice professional shot like the kind people send in Christmas cards. In it, the family was posed artfully around a fireplace with Marion and Wendell seated at the center. I recognized Judith to their right and Derek and Sidra to their left with Carlos standing in front of them.

"Who did this?" I asked. The knife looked like an ordinary steak knife, but it had been driven right into the photo, broken glass radiating out from there like a spiderweb.

"I don't know," she said. "But it's one of my knives. From in there."

She gestured across the bar to the kitchen area. I stood and walked closer to where I could see a small butcher's block with knives sticking out of little slots in the top. One of the slots was empty.

"When did this happen?" I asked.

"I don't know. I guess it could've been any time in the last day, but I didn't notice it until just a few minutes ago."

"Did you call the police?"

She let out a small sob.

"They won't let me," she wailed.

"*They* who?"

"The family. Derek. His mother. They refuse to involve the police at all."

I looked at Sidra, realizing suddenly that this wasn't the first time something like this had happened to her.

"Why don't you tell me about it?" I said, leading her to a chair. She sat, crying so hard that she couldn't talk. She began growing hysterical, but I took her face in my hands and told her sternly to calm down. That seemed to surprise her enough to swallow back the rest of her sobs and stare at me with frightened eyes.

"What's going on, Sidra?"

"Things like this," she replied, her voice shaky. "They happen all the time now. Someone wants me out of here. Someone wants me dead."

"Why won't Marion and Derek let you call the police?"

"They don't believe me," she said miserably. "They think I'm crazy, that I'm doing this myself."

"What?"

She was about to speak further when we heard a loud pounding on the door and both jumped. I left Sidra on the couch and went to open it myself. It was the maid, Angelina.

"I am sorry to bother you," she said, looking from me to Sidra, confused. "But the school is on the telephone for you, Sidra. Something about the bus."

"Are the kids okay?" Sidra asked, her eyes suddenly wide with terror.

"They are fine. It is just some sort of delay. They want to speak with the mother or the father, but Derek is not home. So I came to get you."

"Thank you, Angelina."

The maid turned and walked away. Sidra blew her nose, tucked away her handkerchief, and started for the door.

"I'll wait here for you," I said, frustrated that our conversation had been cut short.

Sidra shook her head.

"I shouldn't have bothered you with this," she said, waiting until I had stepped outside to pull the door shut behind us. "I don't want to talk about it anymore."

I hurried to stay with her as she strode quickly around the pool and toward the house.

"What about the knife?" I asked. "Don't you want it dusted for fingerprints?"

Sidra stopped walking and looked at me.

"How would I do something like that?"

"I'll do it. Let me have it. I'll get it checked out for you. No police. I promise."

She hesitated, glancing toward the house.

"You won't tell them?" she asked, indicating, I felt sure, Marion and Derek.

"That I checked it for fingerprints? No. This is just between you and me."

"Go ahead then," she replied, opening the back door. "But don't ask me any more questions. I can't talk about it."

She stepped inside and let the door fall shut behind her as I turned and walked back to the cabana.

Nine

I tried the doorknob on the cabana, surprised to see that Sidra had left it unlocked despite the act of vandalism that had so terrified her just moments before. I went straight for the kitchen where I dug around until I found an empty grocery bag. Then I went to the photo and knife on the floor and carefully slid the whole thing into the bag. That done, I went to the window and peeked out, glad to see that Sidra wasn't yet on her way back from the house.

Because Sidra was Wendell's nurse and thus a prime suspect, I decided to do a quick search of the apartment. I headed down a short hall, going first into the bathroom, which was perfectly neat and clean. A quick scan of the medicine cabinet revealed a large supply of prescription drugs, most of them tranquilizers, sleeping pills, and antidepressants. Carefully, I removed a wide pink comb from the bottom shelf, hoping it would have some clear prints of Sidra's for comparison.

I went into the first bedroom, which obviously belonged to the boy. On the twin bed was a racing car bedspread, and posters of soccer players adorned the walls. I didn't bother to search, though I did grab a plastic dinosaur by the tip of its tail from the dresser, again for fingerprint confirmation.

The two bedrooms across the hall were empty, though one of them held some cardboard boxes. I peeked inside a few, noting that one of them held a number of medical books, mostly about kidney disease, dialysis, or transplants. Glancing at my watch, I left the books there and headed for Sidra's bedroom. Heart pounding, I rifled through her closet and her drawers, knowing she could return any moment. There wasn't much to find, just some old family photos in one drawer and a pile of what looked like love letters in another. The letters were tied together with a purple satin ribbon, and on impulse, I grabbed the whole pack of them.

Knowing I was out of time, I headed back to the living room and slipped the comb, the toy dinosaur, and the pack of letters into the bag. Then I carefully folded down the top, picked up the bag, and headed out of the door, passing Sidra as we met near the pool.

"You got the knife?" she asked, looking oddly at the bag I carried.

"I took the picture, too," I said. "You never know."

"Okay."

She headed on, her mind obviously occupied with other things.

"Is your son alright?" I asked, calling after her.

"He's fine. The bus broke down in Lancaster," she said. "They won't be home till tomorrow."

"Do you need someone to go and get him tonight?" I asked. "If you gave me directions, I wouldn't mind making the drive—"

"Thank you," she said, "but no. This'll give him one more day before he has to face the news of his grandfather. Tomorrow will be soon enough."

She continued walking, letting herself into the cabana. I turned and headed for the house, slipping into the back door and up the stairs before anyone saw me and asked me what I was carrying.

Up in my room, I searched for a hiding place for the bag. I set it on the bed, then slowly walked around the room, thinking, peeking in drawers, feeling under furniture. Nothing really struck me as a good hiding place in either the bedroom or the bathroom until my eyes came to rest on the radiator covers along the wall, under the window.

The covers were made of beautifully stained wood, fronted by an elegant sort of bronze mesh. I had seen these types of covers before, though not as fancy, and I knew they fit down over the radiators like boxes. I grabbed one on each side, and it came up easily. Underneath was an old-fashioned radiator—with plenty of room between it and the wall for my stash. Carefully, I slipped the bag in place, then slid the cover back down over the whole thing. As I looked from each angle, I could see that I had chosen a perfect hiding spot. As long as the temperature outside stayed relatively warm and the radiator never actually kicked on, it would be okay.

I hurriedly put on some makeup and changed into my new dark slacks and top, which fortunately fit just fine. I fixed my hair, pulling a few twigs and leaves from it as I went, then glanced at my watch. I probably only had a few minutes or so before the guests downstairs would begin to leave.

I could hear the low murmur of voices as I reached the bottom of the stairs. From the doorway of the living room I could see Marion dressed elegantly in black, holding court from her perch on the couch, a white handkerchief clutched tightly in her hand. There were about ten people there, their voices hushed and respectful. I joined the small crowd, mingling around, listening as they all spoke of Wendell Smythe in glowing terms, expressing their shock at his sudden death. Marion saw me and proceeded to introduce me as a friend of the family. I was glad; I would've hated being known either as a visiting philanthropist or, worse, as the woman who discovered Wendell's body.

Alan Bennet was there, hovering solicitously around Marion, looking as handsome and perfectly put-together as he had that morning at the office. He seemed to know everyone there, and I realized that he acted almost like a member of the family himself, keeping a comforting hand on Marion's shoulder, accepting people's condolences on behalf of the widow. Considering that Derek and Judith were conspicuously absent, I supposed Alan's presence was helpful. At one point, I overheard him chatting with the family's minister, Reverend Quinn, giving suggestions for the eulogy.

That, in turn, made me think of my husband Bryan's eulogy, and I wondered suddenly how I was going to get through the events of the next few days. I hadn't been around death since Bryan died. I wasn't sure I could do this without somehow falling apart. It was already hard, I realized, just standing here among these somber, dark-suited guests in the comfort of the Smythes' home. How would I ever survive at a funeral home, much less a cemetery?

"Hello again."

Startled, I turned to see Alan Bennet at my elbow, a friendly glint in his eye. *He certainly knows how to work a room,* I thought. I seemed to be the only person left he hadn't yet had a conversation with.

"Callie, right?"

"Yes," I said, shaking his hand. "Quite a day this turned out to be, huh?"

"You said it. I still can't believe what has happened. What a shock to us all."

He spoke softly, his tone and manner implying familiarity. Looking at his handsome face, I thought, *Oh yes, I can definitely see how this man works his magic.* He was stunningly handsome, though I sensed a certain emptiness behind the charming facade.

"So where are Marion's children?" I asked, knowing that Derek must be back from the park by now.

"Haven't seen Derek," Alan said. "Judith's still at the office. She asked me to come tonight and look after things since she couldn't be here until later."

"Her father just died today," I said, remembering my conversation with her at the office. "How on earth can she still be working?"

"She's the boss," he said simply. "Lots of loose ends to tie up if she wants to be free for the next few days."

I mulled that over, thinking I wouldn't be surprised if Judith begrudged her father the time she would have to take off from work for his funeral. To me, she'd seemed just that callous.

"This morning we were talking about the traveling you do for work," I said, changing the subject. "I would imagine a clothing manufacturer must have to go all over the world."

"Oh, yes," he replied. "Wendell and I have logged so many frequent flyer miles, I think we set some kind of record. Though once he went on dialysis, he had to cut down a bit, of course. It was a lot of trouble."

"I would imagine it would be kind of difficult," I said. "Going into foreign countries with all of his medical problems."

"The hardest part—even a bigger pain than the dialysis—was that horrible nephrotic syndrome diet he was on," Alan said. "He had to monitor every single bite and every ounce of fluid that went into his body. Just awful."

"How about his diabetes?" I asked. "Was it under control?"

"Well, no, but that was all part of it, the reason for the kidney failure and everything."

"He used insulin?"

"Oh, yeah. Hated testing his blood, hated giving himself the shots. You'd think you'd get used to something like that, but he never did."

"I don't think I could ever give myself a shot," I said, shuddering. "I'd probably have to have other people do it for me."

We were on dangerous ground here, but if Alan had reason to change the course of this conversation, he didn't show it.

"Wendell was the same way," he said, nodding. "He wanted all of us to learn how to give shots. We had to practice on oranges until we got it right."

"Oranges?"

"Yeah, Sidra taught us—the family and staff, Gwen, and me. We sat around the table one day, injecting water into oranges. It seemed funny at the time, but then that was Wendell's way, turning his tragedy into a big laugh."

"I see."

"And I didn't mind giving the shots. Hey, if it made his life a little easier, what the heck?"

What the heck, I thought, studying the man in front of me. He looked back at me with handsome, piercing eyes, and I knew: If it were he who had administered that final, fatal injection, he certainly was one cool character about it right now.

Ten

Alan was the last guest to remain, but he turned down Marion's offer to join us for dinner, citing other plans. Once he was gone, Marion took my arm as we turned from the door. I didn't think I would be very hungry after that late bowl of soup, but delicious smells from the kitchen began to whet my appetite.

"We'll have a drink in here before dinner," Marion said as we walked, and before I could reply we were standing in the doorway of the den, looking in at Derek, who knelt in front of the fireplace, poking at the burning logs.

He glanced our way, and I could see that he was wearing the same dark slacks and white shirt as before, his tie now loosened around his neck. Derek seemed to be in his early 40s with short grayish-blond hair and wire-rimmed glasses. Though I wouldn't exactly have called him handsome, there was something fairly engaging about his face and demeanor. He stood as we approached.

Our eyes met, and though I feared some glint of recognition or even scorn, he merely smiled and extended a hand, oblivious to the fact that less than two hours before I had clung to a tree over his head and eavesdropped on his private grief. I studied his face for a moment, not surprised to see his eyes looking puffy and tired.

"Derek Smythe," he said, giving my hand a firm shake. "How do you do?"

His mother began to explain that I was "the one from the foundation" and he immediately looked at me with a painful grimace.

"You're the one who found him, then," he said sympathetically. "I'm so sorry you had to go through that. How traumatic for you."

I didn't reply that I had long ago learned to deal with dead bodies. In fact, I had seen plenty during the years I spent in investigations, encountering my first dead body at the age of 19 when I tagged along with Eli to take notes on a missing persons case. The woman, a heroin addict, had tried to fly off of her second-story balcony and ended up impaling herself on a decorative wrought iron fence post. Compared to that—as well as plenty of other grisly scenes we had worked on—today had been a walk in the park.

Marion stepped toward the fireplace, holding out her hands to warm them.

"Thank you for fixing the fire, Derek," she said. "I know September's a little early in the season, but I just feel so chilled this evening."

"Fireplaces are nice," I said noncommittally, thinking that the room *was* a bit warm. Outside, I hadn't even needed a sweater.

"Mother's always cold," Derek said to me, smiling. "We put up with it."

They exchanged banter while I studied the man in front of me, the man I had heard arguing with Sidra in this very room only a few hours before. Now he seemed calm and collected, the picture of hospitality as he went to the bar and offered me a drink from a glass pitcher of red liquid.

"Thank you, no," I said.

"It's not alcohol," Marion said. "It's juice. What's it tonight, darling? Mango?"

"Cranberry mango," he replied, holding a small glassful toward me. "Try it."

I took a sip, surprised at the delicious tangy flavor. I usually hated cranberry juice.

"Mother's into nutrition," Derek explained. "A glass of juice before dinner is one of her prescriptions for health. Kicks up the blood sugar, you know."

"We always have juice, except of course for Wendell," she said. "With his diabetes, he can't—" Marion stopped herself, suddenly realizing what she was saying. "*Couldn't*, I mean…"

She seemed suddenly pale and tired. Looking at her, I remembered it all well: the confusion, the shock, the assumption that the man who had always been there would still be there. Even after three years I still sometimes caught myself referring to my late husband in the present tense.

Derek quickly took his mother's arm and led her to the nearest chair.

"Why don't you have Angelina bring dinner to your room?" he asked her softly as he sat beside her, stroking her hand. "Callie and I can make do here. And Judith should be home soon."

"No, no, I'll be fine. I'd rather not be alone right now, anyway."

At that moment, Angelina appeared in the doorway, announcing that dinner was served. Marion let Derek lead her to the table, which was set for five. Derek seemed surprised; once he had seated his mother, he rang immediately for Angelina.

"Yes?" the maid asked, appearing silently in the doorway.

"Angelina, I'm afraid Sidra will be taking all of her meals in the cabana from now on. Didn't she tell you?"

The girl shook her head, her face a blank.

"No, sir. Nobody said anything to me."

She quickly set about removing the extra place setting as an uncomfortable silence settled around the table.

"Shall I say grace?" Derek asked, glancing at his mother. She nodded. The three of us bowed our heads as Derek said a short prayer of thanks for the food.

"I met Sidra earlier," I said when he was finished, hoping to see what sort of reaction I could get. "She was very upset. Apparently, someone had vandalized a photograph in her apartment."

Derek and his mother stopped eating and looked at each other.

"You've got to speak with Dr. Bell about Sidra's medications," Marion said to him. "I'm afraid things are escalating."

"She said that someone has been doing things to her," I continued. "That someone wants her out of here—or wants her dead."

"She told you that?" Derek asked, a pained expression on his face.

"I'm sorry, Callie," Marion said, shaking her head sadly. "I'm afraid Sidra's delusional."

"Delusional?" I asked. "She was upset, of course, but she seemed perfectly lucid to me."

They again shared a long look and were silent as Angelina entered carrying a tray filled with small plates of salad. When she was gone, Derek stood and put his napkin beside his plate on the table.

"If you'll excuse me," he said vaguely, "I'm afraid I've lost my appetite."

As he left the room I felt my face flush. Hadn't I learned anything from my stint up in the tree? This was a man in pain, a man who didn't deserve to be prodded and pushed. And yet Sidra seemed to be in genuine pain as well. Whether she was delusional or not, she deserved to be protected—from herself or someone else.

"Sidra's in danger," I said softly, ignoring the salad in front of me. "If things are escalating, then it's time to bring in the police."

"The police are the last thing we need," Marion said, her face pale. "Goodness, Callie, I appreciate your concern, but I'm afraid this is a family matter."

I pressed on.

"Why not call the police?" I asked. "Are you afraid of what they might discover?"

"I'm afraid they'll take her away!" Marion exclaimed. "I'm afraid they'll commit Sidra to some sort of institution. Better she remain here, among family, and get the help she needs. We're handling this problem, Callie. She's under the care of a psychiatrist. Beyond that, I'm afraid you'll have to accept that this is family business."

The room was silent, echoing with Marion's outburst. I thought about Sidra, about the medicines I had seen in her bathroom.

Certainly, she was being treated for something. But whether she was delusional or just depressed, I wasn't sure.

"I'm sorry," Marion said after a long moment. "You may think us heartless, but we're not. I couldn't love Sidra more if she were my own flesh and blood. But I'm afraid we've had to take a hard line on this. She's always had problems. It's just lately they seem to have manifested themselves in this way."

"If you really think she's crazy," I challenged, "then why let her keep Carlos out there with her? And why let her care for your husband and his dialysis?"

"I didn't say she was psychotic," Marion snapped. "She just has some emotional issues."

I let the matter drop, knowing I would reserve judgment for the time being. Marion and I ate our salads in silence, and after a few minutes we were joined by Judith, who strode purposefully into the room.

"Evening, Mother, Ms. Webber," she said, nodding in turn toward each of us. She came to the table and took the chair Derek had just vacated and dug immediately into his salad.

"Judith!" Marion exclaimed. "Where have you been? There were people here. I needed you."

"I know, Mom. I'm sorry. I was tied up at work."

"How could you work with all that's happened today?"

"Well, I figured I'd probably have to take the rest of the week off. If I'm going to do that, I had things to take care of first. I'm sorry."

She didn't sound at all sorry, merely irritated. I looked at her, amazed that a brother and sister could be so different. Where Derek was sweet and vague and sort of gentle, Judith was brusque and direct and almost masculine.

"You could've called," Marion said, putting an end to the matter. "I was worried."

"Sor-ry," Judith replied sarcastically, and I couldn't help but think she sounded for a moment more like a 12-year-old kid than a grown woman.

The three of us ate silently, tension hovering around the table like a fog. I finally spoke, my voice sounding loud in the quiet.

"I didn't think to ask you earlier, Judith, about your position at the company?"

"I'm CEO of Smythe Incorporated. The for-profit division."

"I thought your father ran things."

"Daddy was the president. The big decisions, the overall vision. I implement the day-to-day. Just like Derek does for Feed the Need on the nonprofit side."

"I see," I said, feeling a surge of frustration over my lack of knowledge. Usually, by the time I approached a company with a donation, I knew them inside and out. But this assignment had been so hurried, so different from my usual procedure. I had only the vaguest idea of how the Smythe enterprises operated, and most of that information I had gleaned from the brochure I had read in the reception room that morning.

"How about you, Callie?" Judith asked. "What do you do exactly?"

I eyed her cautiously for a moment. There was something odd about her demeanor, and I wondered if she had checked me out after finding me in her father's office that afternoon and knew exactly what I did.

"I work for the J.O.S.H.U.A. Foundation," I said. "I'm the Director of Research."

"I told you, dear," Marion added. "She works for Tom."

"Director of Research?" Judith asked. "What exactly does that mean?"

I put down my fork, glancing at Marion.

"I verify the integrity of charitable organizations," I said, "to see if they're spending their money wisely and if their programs really do what they say they will do. Basically, I make sure they're everything they claim to be."

Judith looked at me, truly interested now.

"And if they are?"

"Then we give them a grant."

"And if they're not?"

I shrugged.

"Depends. Most of the time we just reject their grant proposal. In a few odd cases, we've actually helped bring out fraud or criminal charges."

"What were you doing here?" she asked. "Did Feed the Need apply for a grant?"

I hesitated.

"Different situation," I replied finally. "Seems your father had an 'in' with our president, Tom. The usual rules didn't apply."

"What are the 'usual' rules?" Marion asked. "I mean, how do you judge a nonprofit organization? How do you 'verify its integrity,' as you put it? I assume it has to do with how the money is spent—administrative and fundraising dollars versus program dollars and all that."

"That's only part of the picture," I said, "though overhead versus outlay is the first thing we look at. All nonprofits file a Form 990, information that they are mandated by the IRS to provide to the public."

"That's good," said Marion.

"It is. That way, I can know, going in, the sort of percentages we're talking about."

"What's a good percentage to look for?" Judith asked. "I mean, if a nonprofit spends 50 percent of its income on expenses, is that bad?"

"Fifty percent should certainly raise some red flags," I replied. "But it really depends on the organization and how it classifies its expenses. Newer companies are going to have higher start-up costs. And certain types of nonprofits have more administrative expenses than others."

"So how do you know whether a nonprofit is really legit or not?" Judith asked. "I mean, I'm sure there are companies that play with the figures to make them look better than they are."

"We use a lot of different criteria," I replied. "There are voluntary watchdog groups, for example. Nonprofits can sign up and hold themselves accountable to these stricter guidelines. That's always a good sign."

"Feed the Need belongs to more than one, I'm proud to say," interjected Marion. I nodded, remembering that several accountability groups were listed in the fine print on Feed the Need's brochure.

"What else?" Judith asked.

I hesitated, taking a bite of the shrimp cocktail that Angelina had just placed in front of me. The shrimp was perfect, the sauce a tangy complement to the seafood.

"It's kind of hard to say," I answered after swallowing. "If the foundation is considering a sizeable donation, we try to get a look at the books and redo the calculations ourselves."

"So basically it's a matter of mathematics?"

I speared another shrimp, hesitating.

"No," I said. "The math is just the first step. Once things check out on paper…"

I stopped, stalling with another bite of shrimp, wondering how much to say.

"Go on," urged Marion. "Once things check out on paper…"

"I don't usually talk about this," I said finally.

"Oh, come on," Judith urged. "It's very interesting."

I looked from one to the other and finally smiled, wondering if these two rich women could even comprehend my criteria.

"Once the math checks out, more often than not it's simply a 'mentality', if you will. A way of thinking, of doing business."

Marion and Judith both studied me, their shrimp cocktails ignored.

"I usually start by reading their mission statement, then I look to see if they really seem to be living by it. I mean, I hate to call it intuitive, but in a way, it is."

"You've been doing this a long time," Marion replied. "I would imagine your instincts are fairly good."

"It's not just that," I said. "Really, anyone could do the same."

"You've lost me," said Judith.

"It's the salaries," I said. "The benefits. The decor, even."

"The decor?"

"For instance, is the office fancier than it needs to be? Are the salaries too far above the norm? When the executives travel, are they staying in Holiday Inns or Ritz Carltons? When an employee needs to go to a training session, is she going to one in the next state—or one in Hawaii?"

"What's wrong with staying at a Ritz Carlton?" Marion asked. "Those are lovely hotels."

"But they're very expensive," I replied. "Nonprofit organizations should have a pervading mentality of saving money, of cutting corners. Of using their resources for the things that are important."

"So if you work for a nonprofit, you should suffer?" Judith asked.

"No," I replied. "But in a way you should be *giving* more than you're *getting*. Most really good nonprofits all have one thing in common: They have a sort of 'service' mentality. The people work there because they want to make a difference in the world, not for personal gain. They work tirelessly and selflessly, even though it usually means few perks and lower-than-average incomes."

"That doesn't seem fair," Judith said.

"Put it this way," I continued. "People in the nonprofit sector work just as hard as people in the for-profit sector, but they do it with the understanding that they will never be compensated at the for-profit level. But because they derive so much personal satisfaction from the work itself, they're usually okay with that."

"I think I understand," said Marion.

"I reviewed a company in California once," I said, "a nonprofit health care organization. On paper, it looked very good. But something about the place bothered me."

I took another bite of shrimp, thinking about all of the nonprofits I had examined, both good and bad.

"It took some digging," I said, "but I finally found a few disgruntled former employees who were able to point me in the right direction. Turns out, the head of the organization liked to travel. Within five years he had gone to 12 international conferences in places like Zurich, Singapore, and Monte Carlo."

"But if these conferences were necessary for doing his job—"

"They weren't," I replied. "They were all only marginally related to his work."

"But legal?"

"Yes, legal. And it turned out that he brought along his wife, four children, and their nanny on each of the trips. They stayed in some of the nicest hotels in the world, dined in some of the fanciest restaurants, took in all of the sights—and the entire tab was always picked up by the agency."

"Wow."

"Needless to say, that man was getting more than he was giving. Classic case of financial abuse. They were denied the grant."

"I should hope so," Marion said.

Angelina came in and removed our shrimp dishes, replacing them with a small plate of Waldorf salad. I was glad when Judith turned the conversation to other matters, asking her mother about flowers for the funeral.

I ate as they talked, and by the time the main dish arrived I was already full and mostly just pushed the food around on my plate with my fork. Apparently, I wasn't the only one overwhelmed by the sheer volume of food; when Angelina entered the room with a covered bowl of hot homemade breads, Marion held up one hand, delicately wiping the corner of her mouth with her napkin.

"Angelina, please," Marion said. "We're about to explode here. How much more food is there tonight?"

The maid smiled, setting the bowl on the sideboard.

"I told Nick you would be yelling at me soon if he did not stop," she said. "But you know how he is. When he is upset, he cooks. If I had not put my foot down, you would be getting three different desserts tonight, too."

"Well, tell Nick to find some way to drown his sorrows other than spoiling us with food. We are a hunger relief organization, after all. How does he think it looks to our guest—children starving all over the world while we sit here with this feast?"

Judith caught my eye across the table and grinned sardonically. Obviously, her mother had taken my little lecture to heart.

"Yes, ma'am. I will tell him that is enough for now."

Angelina ducked out as Marion reached out and put a hand on my arm.

"Wendell and our cook were very close, Callie. I'm sorry about this."

"Oh, please, I—"

"I'm sure you noticed my husband was a very…ah…abundant man. Before his kidneys began to fail, his favorite part of the day was always the evening, eating these delicious meals, or sitting in the kitchen later with Nick, sharing some forbidden dessert and debating current events. That cursed diabetes! I'm afraid Wendell's love of rich food may have proven to be the death of him after all."

"We don't know that for sure, Mom," Judith corrected. "The police still haven't released cause of death."

I looked at my plate, surprised that they didn't yet know the truth. Was the Philadelphia Police Department really that slow at getting the word out to the victim's family?

"His death was imminent regardless," Marion said miserably. "Only a matter of time. You know what a disaster his health was, especially here at the end."

I held my tongue, thinking of the unseen intruder I had chased down the stairwell. Whether Wendell's death was merely a matter of time or not, I thought, someone had helped speed things along just a bit.

"I suppose we should ask Nick to be a pallbearer," Judith went on matter-of-factly. "Have you thought of the others?"

I was struck by the casualness of her tone, as if she were choosing the right scarf for her blouse rather than choosing the men who would carry her dead father to his grave.

"I've had a few thoughts," Marion answered sadly, going on to discuss some tentative ideas for the funeral. I glanced at my watch, wondering if it would be impolite to excuse myself now that the discussion had turned in this direction. I certainly didn't need to be involved with any of this, and I felt myself growing uncomfortable. Bryan's funeral had been three long years before, but Wendell's death was stirring up some very unsettling memories.

"Anyway," Marion said suddenly, "we can discuss these matters later. For now, I wonder, Callie, if you would join me in my study. There's something I want to discuss with you."

I glanced at Judith, but she seemed absorbed in buttering a steaming roll she had dug from the bread bowl.

"You guys go ahead," she said, gesturing toward her plate. "I'm going to finish up here, and then I have a ton of paperwork to do."

"Thank you, dear."

Marion and I rose from the table, and she walked over and planted a kiss on her daughter's head.

"Your father would be glad to know you've stepped in and taken control of things today. He always said that no matter what problems are besetting a company, anything can be surmounted as long as a strong, united front is presented to the employees and to the public."

"I agree 100 percent. Things are in good hands, Mom."

"I know, my dear, I know."

With that, Marion walked from the room, shoulders high, leading the way to her study.

Eleven

"My husband was murdered," Marion said softly after we were seated in her drawing room, the door closed. "The children don't know yet. I'm not sure how to tell them, or when. But I know that you know, because I've spoken with Tom."

I sat back and exhaled slowly, impressed with Marion's Oscar-winning performance at the dinner table. *You know what a disaster his health was,* she had said to her daughter Judith, *especially here at the end.*

"They're going to find out, Marion. The story will probably be featured on tonight's news."

"I know," she answered, shaking her head sadly, "but poor Derek is struggling so with his own problems. And Judith has the responsibility of the company on her shoulders…" Her voice trailed off. "I want to protect them for as long as I can."

I nodded, thinking that no matter how old a woman's children grew, to her, they would always be her babies.

Marion stood and walked to the window, which was dark against the night sky. Absently, she traced a pattern in the condensation of the glass, and I could tell that she was taking a moment to form her words.

"According to Tom, the one blessing in this whole thing is that you're here. He says that you're the type of person who can find out anything about anyone."

"Oh?"

"He told me he asked you to solve this murder."

I took a deep breath and let it out slowly, knowing that I should just let her talk. She obviously had something important to say.

"I don't mind telling you I was against the idea at first," Marion continued, still facing the window. "The whole notion of someone nosing around in our affairs, poking through things—I didn't like it."

She turned to face me.

"But then Tom pointed out that the police will be doing that anyway. Better to have someone with our own interests at heart, someone whom we can trust to keep things in absolute confidence."

"Of course."

"I guess what I'm trying to say is, I *do* want you to investigate, Callie, to find Wendell's killer. I want this over and done with—the killer caught, my poor husband's memory laid to rest—as soon as possible."

"I'll do my best," I said, thinking that, unbeknownst to her, I had already put in a full afternoon and evening of investigating.

"Though I'd rather not upset the family, as I'm sure you understand. We can keep this between us, can't we?"

I nodded solemnly.

"No one besides you needs to know, for now at least."

"Good."

She came and sat across from me. I studied her for a moment, knowing full well that there was more on her mind than she had said.

"What is it you're not telling me, Marion?" I finally asked. She colored, then looked down.

"Am I so transparent?"

"Obviously, there's something else you need to say. Do you think you have an idea of who may have killed your husband?"

She shook her head.

"Oh, no, dear, nothing like that. It's just that…well, that there were some things going on here, at the end. Wendell was concerned. For the business."

"The business?"

"Feed the Need, specifically," she said, lowering her voice. "I'm so very afraid. The money you came here to deliver, it wasn't—"

Her voice stopped as she looked up. I turned to follow her glance and saw Derek standing in the doorway.

"Derek!" she said loudly. "You startled me."

"Sorry, Mother," he replied, stepping into the room. "I just wanted to come and apologize for ducking out of dinner like that. It was rude of me."

I hesitated, finally standing.

"I'm the one who was rude," I said. "Open mouth, insert foot. I shouldn't have asked so many questions."

"No, no," he answered. "I'm afraid my wife and I are separated, and it's gotten rather messy. She just, she doesn't…" his voice trailed off as he brushed a hand back through his hair. "The whole thing is sort of bizarre. Then we had a big fight today, which has only made a bad situation worse."

"I understand you have a son. I saw some pictures of him in the cabana."

He looked at me and smiled a sweet smile that cut through the pain and exhaustion on his face.

"Carlos," he said, beaming. "Great kid. He's at a soccer tournament. They were supposed to get back tonight, but they had trouble with the bus. So now—"

"Trouble with the bus?" Marion asked. "Was it an accident? Is Carlos okay?"

Derek held out a hand to stop her from talking.

"Calm down, Mother," he said. "It was a mechanical problem. Water in the gas line or something. Anyway, they're spending the night at a Ramada Inn in Lancaster. They should be back in the morning in time for school."

"Does Carlos know about his grandfather?" I asked.

Derek shook his head sadly.

"We decided to wait until he's here, with us, to tell him."

"I think that's best," Marion said.

"Anyway, Mother," Derek said, turning toward her, "I'm feeling a little better now. I'm wondering if this would be a good time to discuss the funeral, to make some specific plans."

Marion glanced at me then back at Derek.

"Of course," she said. "Much as I hate the thought, I know this is something we need to do."

Then she stood and took my hand, giving me a meaningful look.

"We'll speak at breakfast?" she asked and I nodded, knowing I had been dismissed, wondering what she had to tell me that she hadn't wanted Derek to overhear.

Twelve

⁓

No doubt about it, I thought as I sat in my room. I had come to realize there were certain supplies I would need in order to do this job, not the least of which was a fingerprinting kit. The paper bag with the knife and photo was still stashed under the radiator cover, and I left it there as I reached for my phone and dialed the Perskie Detective Agency. Duane was gone for the day, of course, but I left a message in his voice mail, asking if he might be able to supply me with a fingerprinting kit or at least tell me where I could get one.

Once I hung up the phone, I sat back and thought again how odd it felt to be working on a criminal investigation with someone other than my dear friend and mentor Eli Gold.

Eli had been an old police force buddy of my father's, and when I was a teenager looking for a job more challenging than selling shoes at the local mall, he had suggested I come to work for him. He needed a part-time secretary for his new private investigation firm, and my after-school-and-on-weekend hours seemed to fill the bill. Little had I known when I started the job that it would shape my life and indeed my entire future. As Eli began teaching me the tricks of his trade, I grew to think of him like an old kung fu master or something, filled with an incredible store of knowledge, doling it out carefully as I learned each new lesson. Even my mother, who had objected to the job at first for fear it would be too dangerous for me, slowly came around as she began to see how much I loved it. Over time, Eli began to say that I had a unique gift for the work itself. When I turned 18, he hired another secretary and made me his assistant, and I knew he had hopes that I would take over his business once he retired. My father, on the other hand, wanted me to follow in his footsteps and head to police academy after college. But I had surprised everyone by opting for law school instead, touching off an endless but good-natured debate between them about cops versus private investigators and "who needs more lawyers anyway?"

Eli and I still kept in touch, though he was now retired and living in Florida. We had always been close, but since Bryan's death I had come to rely on him in ways that I couldn't rely even on my own father. My dad was a sweet but plain-talking, shoot-from-the-hip kind of guy who thought the world was a black-and-white, right-and-wrong sort of place. He still harbored a complete unforgiveness for the man who had killed my husband, albeit accidentally, and his anger was nearly palpable at times—too palpable, I think, for me to be around.

Eli, on the other hand, was a more objective thinker than that, seeing many shades of gray in life, and rarely ever just black-and-white. He refused to let me wallow in my own anger and grief for very long, steadfastly insisting that I must simply turn the matter over to God and allow Him to use it as He saw fit. I tried, and it was hard, but Eli was my own personal cheerleader, watching from the sidelines, building me up, encouraging me to forgive and get on with my life. I treasured our friendship more than anything.

Unable to resist the urge, I picked up the phone and dialed his familiar number. It took nine rings before he answered, and for a moment I worried that I woke him up. His voice was distant, the line crackling.

"Eli?" I said. "It's me, Callie."

"Sally?"

"Callie!"

"Hold on."

A few clanks and bangs later, Eli spoke again, the line much clearer now.

"Sorry about that," he said. "The battery's dying on the portable phone. Who is this?"

I smiled to myself.

"Callie."

"Oh, goodness, Callie, why didn't you say so? How the heck are you doing?"

I told him that I was in Pennsylvania, staying as a guest in the mansion of a recently murdered millionaire.

"And I thought my life was exciting now that we've signed up for tango lessons!" he exclaimed.

"I'm on a case, Eli. I need some guidance. You got a minute?"

"For you, sweetie, I've got all night."

I could picture him settling in near the phone, pen and paper in hand, as I told him a bit about Wendell Smythe and the case thus far. He listened intently, asking for occasional clarification, pointing out details I might've missed. As usual, I felt myself growing more relaxed and confident as we spoke. To Eli's way of thinking, there was almost no such thing as an unsolvable mystery; it was merely a matter of hard work, patience, and the occasional lucky break.

"I'm putting together a package for you first thing tomorrow," he said. "No need for you to waste good time running around trying to collect all this stuff."

"Don't worry about it," I said. "I've got the resources of a local agency this time. But thanks."

"Whatever. Why not let's talk about you now? You holding up okay?"

"I'm fine," I said. "Though it's kind of hard, you know, being around a family where there's just been a death."

"I can imagine. Brings it all back to you, huh?"

"Yeah. The conversation turns to pallbearers and casket designs, and I start to hyperventilate."

I was exaggerating, but he knew that.

"I got something for you," he said. "Saw it just today. Hold on."

I could hear him put the phone down, then pick it back up a moment later.

"Here we go. Had to get my Bible."

I smiled. Eli was a devout Messianic Jew and a true scholar of both Testaments. Having him as a friend was like having my own personal biblical reference; I hadn't found a situation yet where he couldn't offer a pertinent verse.

"It's in Paul's second letter to Timothy," he said, the sound of pages turning in the background. "Chapter 1, verse 12. Hmm, here we go, 'I know whom I have believed, and am convinced that he is able to guard what I have entrusted to him for that day.'"

"Yeah, I know, Eli. 'His grace is sufficient,' and all that."

"No, not 'all that,'" he scolded. "Listen: He will guard *what you are entrusting*. Have you entrusted this situation to him?"

"I suppose. I've prayed about it."

"Don't just pray about it! Hand it over completely! Let Him guard it for you! Paul's in prison here, Callie, knowing he's probably about to be beheaded, yet he can say those words. Can we look at our comparatively petty lives and do any less?"

I felt properly chastised, and after a moment I let out a deep breath, nodding to myself.

"I understand," I said softly.

"Good, because Stella's putting on another album of tango music and I gotta go. You gonna be okay?"

"Of course."

"Alright. Then take care. And call me if I can help you any more."

I continued smiling long after I had hung up the phone. I couldn't help but picture Eli and Stella doing the tango. *If ever a man deserved to live out his golden years dancing with a rose between his teeth,* I thought, *it was Eli.*

Thirteen

⌒

I dove into the black water, bracing myself for the cold. Instead, the water was wonderfully warm and welcoming, and I let myself glide down to the bottom, my muscles relaxing almost instantly. Still holding my breath, I swam to the other end of the pool, finally surfacing near the steps to fill my lungs with fresh air.

What a place! The sky was pitch dark and the grounds were mostly silent, but I hadn't been able to resist the urge to swim away the tensions of this day. After hanging up with Eli, I had tried to muster some enthusiasm for going through the love letters I had swiped from Sidra's bureau, but my brain was just too tired. Knowing they would keep for the night, I decided instead to go for a swim. I had changed into my new dime-store bathing suit and had stolen out here to the pool, slipping into the water without even turning on any of the lights. Luckily, the rain clouds that had seemed to be threatening earlier had passed, leaving the sky clear and full of stars above me.

I tilted my head back and floated in the water, looking up at the house, which was now dark except for a few softly lit windows. What a day this had been! Though it was late, I was glad I had decided to come out here to unwind. Now I could swim some laps, then head back to my room for a good night's sleep.

Time and worries faded from my comprehension as I swam, and I was grateful. Sometimes I could find the same mind-numbing rhythm in swimming that I always got from rowing. Now I was one with the water—stroke, stroke, breath, stroke, stroke, breath, back and forth, one end to the other, again and again. When I completed my fiftieth lap, I flipped over and slowed my pounding heart rate with a gentle backstroke, five more laps, finally coming to a stop in the shallow end.

I rested near the concrete steps, the back of my head tilting against the cold cement edge of the pool. Though I had never been one for conspicuous consumption, I did have to admit that I had often toyed with the notion of installing a pool at my house. Now as I let my body gently rock and float in the water, my toes just breaking the surface, I wondered what it would cost, exactly, and how long it would take to have one put in.

I was designing the shape and placement in my mind when I saw the final lights click off in the Smythe house, and I realized I should probably go inside. After this warm water, the air was going to feel twice as chilly. I was just bracing myself to stand up and climb out when I saw movement along the side of the house.

My heart skipped a beat as I quickly ducked back down, my chin just above the surface of the water. Looking out across the dark yard, sure enough, there was someone moving from the house diagonally across the lawn. Though I supposed it could've been just another late-night swimmer, something about this figure's movements suggested actions a little more circumspect.

As the person drew nearer, I realized it was Judith, and that she had changed from her earlier business attire into a more casual outfit of black jeans and a dark shirt. I was wondering whether I should call out to her when suddenly she turned toward the back of the property and quickened her pace. I watched her go, trying to remember what was back there. From my earlier walk, I seemed to recall some kind of outbuilding, like a shed or a small barn.

As quietly as possible, I stepped out of the pool, grabbed my towel from a nearby footstool, and wrapped it around me. Silently, I slipped on my shoes, then I quickly padded off after Judith, keeping enough distance so she wouldn't see me, but still following closely enough behind so I wouldn't lose sight of her in the dark. *Here I am again*, I thought, *following one of Wendell's children into the woods.* I could only hope I wasn't being foolish this time, too.

I followed her across the wide expanse of grass, and as we neared the far building, I could see that there was a low light coming from one of the windows. It was a barn, I could tell now, though since the Smythes had no livestock, I doubted it housed anything more than lawn-cutting equipment. As Judith reached the door, I stepped behind the shelter of a tree and watched. She tapped once, lightly, and it swung open. I could see a man step out, and I ducked my head behind the tree just as he craned his neck to look toward the house.

"Anybody see you?" he asked softly, and I recognized his voice almost instantly. I dared to take another glance to make sure, and I was right: It was Alan Bennet.

"No," I heard Judith whisper, and then they both stepped back inside and pulled the door shut.

I hesitated, suddenly feeling the cold for the first time since slipping out of the pool. I was soaking wet, the towel around me was also soaked, and I was freezing! Still, I took a few running steps toward the barn, hoping I would be able to hear them.

What are the two of them doing out here? I wondered as I inched along the rough boards of the barn's side. I finally found a gnarled hole that seemed to go all the way through to the inside. Pressing my ear against it, I could hear a low murmur. When I looked through the hole I realized that Judith Smythe and Alan Bennet held each other in a tight embrace, kissing. Near them was some sort of makeshift bed, and it didn't take much imagination to figure out where things were going from here.

I stepped back from the barn wall, wondering how Alan had even gotten on the property. Peering around in the darkness, I could see that we weren't that far from a quiet road that ran along the side of the estate. He must've parked there, among the trees.

Interesting, I thought to myself as I jogged back across the lawn, toward the pool. Though I would've liked to stick around and see if there was anything else on the agenda besides a lovers' tryst in a barn, I didn't exactly feel like waiting them out, damp and cold in the darkness. I gathered up my things, glad to see that my wet footprints leading from the pool had already nearly dried.

Back in my room, I was still shivering from the chill even though I had rinsed off in the shower, changed into a dry nightgown, and climbed under the covers. All the relaxation of my swim had been wiped away, my head filled with the image of their secret encounter, my mind racing with questions. Why the secrecy? Was Alan married? If so, why were they meeting in a filthy barn rather than in a nice hotel room somewhere? It wasn't as though they couldn't afford it!

Pushing those thoughts aside for now, I tried to lure my mind back to the steady, soothing rhythm of my swim. Between climbing a tree this afternoon and traipsing around in the dark in a wet towel tonight, I realized that this hadn't been one of my finer days. *It'll serve me right,* I thought as I finally drifted off to sleep, *if all I get from this is a terrible head cold.*

Fourteen

I awoke to the sound of ringing. I reached for an alarm clock, only to realize it was my portable phone, chiming from inside my briefcase. By the time I got the case open and the phone out, I was awake enough to sound relatively coherent.

"Callie!" I heard Tom say. "I was just about to hang up."

"Sorry about that," I replied, sitting up on the bed and stretching my legs out in front of me. They were a little sore from my swim the night before, but not too bad.

"Just wanted to see if you were able to make any headway in your investigation yet. I know it's only been a day, but I'm anxious to hear."

I hesitated, thinking of what I knew thus far, the impressions I'd had of the people I'd met, the odd goings-on around the house.

My short list of suspects, at this point, extended to those people who regularly gave Wendell his shots. That meant four family members, two staff members, and two employees. Eight people in total, half of whom Tom would immediately rule out simply because they were members of his dear friend's loving family. Despite the things I had thus far seen and heard, I didn't think Tom would appreciate the direction my investigation had already taken.

"I'm narrowing things down," I replied evasively. "But at this point, it's more a matter of watching, listening, and, above all, not jumping to conclusions."

"Of course."

I wondered how I could pump him for information about the different members of the Smythe family. Though I didn't want him to know that I was including family members on my list of suspects, I also needed to find out what his impressions were of Marion, Judith, Derek, and Sidra.

"The Smythes' home is so lovely," I said finally. "Do you get to come here often yourself?"

"From time to time," he said. "Now that Wendell's dead, I realize it wasn't nearly often enough."

Without much prodding, Tom began to reminisce a bit, telling me that he had first met Wendell and Marion when he was 18 and a freshman at the University of Pennsylvania. He described his first lonely week at college in Philadelphia, hundreds of miles from friends and family. One Sunday he and some fellow students went to a large church near the campus.

"They had a wonderful program there," he said, "where church members would 'adopt' new students for a semester—taking them out for Sunday dinner, showing them around the city, sometimes inviting them over for a home-cooked meal. The Smythes adopted me. We hit it off so well that we made it a permanent arrangement. We've been friends ever since."

"And their children?" I said. "Are you close to them?"

"I always liked Derek," he replied. "Decent fellow, kind of shy and quiet back then. I never really got to know his wife, Sidra."

"How about Judith?" I asked, and to my surprise Tom laughed.

"Back then, Judith terrified me," he said. "Because we weren't that far apart in age, Marion got it in her head to fix the two of us up on a date."

"Oh?"

"Judith was very direct, very aggressive. We went dancing, and I think she even led on the dance floor. When it was time to order dinner, she did it for both of us. I felt as if, given the chance, she could grind me into the ground with her two-inch heels."

I chuckled, trying to picture the laid-back Tom on a date with the older, more overbearing Judith.

"Our disappointment in each other was mutual, I think. We ended the date as friends, though we never exactly palled around."

"She's an attractive woman," I said. "She never married?"

"Nope," Tom answered with a laugh. "I guess she could never find anyone willing to love her, honor her, and obey her."

~

I found Marion alone at the breakfast table. She wasn't really eating, merely pushing around a small pile of eggs with her fork. In the morning light, I could see the heavily etched lines in her face; her eyes were swollen, and despite the artfully applied makeup I could tell she probably hadn't slept all night.

"You made it through the first night," I said gently as I pulled up a chair across from her. "It can only get better from here."

"Oh, I hope so," she said, her eyes filling with tears.

"I remember the first night after Bryan died," I said. "I woke up screaming. I couldn't stop. They finally had to bring in a doctor to sedate me."

"I know how you felt."

"But the next night I didn't scream, I only cried. The night after that, I cried again. But each night it got a little better and a little better, and eventually I was able to go to sleep at night without praying I would die before morning."

Marion pushed her plate away and rested her head in her arms.

"I didn't know it would be so hard."

"No one ever does."

"I mean, we weren't spring chickens, you know. Wendell's health was very bad, Callie. Between the diabetes and the dialysis, I'd been preparing myself for his death for some time."

"Oh, you can prepare for death, Marion. You just can't prepare for your life after his death."

One tear slipped down her cheek, and she dabbed at it gently with her napkin.

"You're very wise for one so young," she said.

"It's taken a lot of heartache to get me this way," I answered. "I'd rather have been spared the pain and remained naive."

Angelina entered, bringing Marion a fresh cup of coffee.

"Good morning," she said warmly. "Would you like some breakfast? Eggs? Waffles?"

I looked over at Marion's plate, which by now looked rather unappetizing. My usual breakfast of poached eggs and toast didn't seem appealing at all.

"Maybe just a muffin or a bagel, something like that?" I answered.

"Of course. Right away."

She took Marion's plate and left the room.

"How did your husband die, Callie?" Marion asked once we were alone. "Tom only said that it was an accident."

I took a deep breath, wondering how long it had been since I shared this particular story with anyone. I didn't like talking about myself or my problems—especially not the saga of my late husband's death.

"We were on vacation," I said reluctantly. "A boating accident."

"Oh, my."

"Bryan was water-skiing. I was his spotter, and—"

"His what?"

"His spotter. I watched him from the boat while his brother was driving."

"I see." She listened earnestly, her eyes glued to my face, almost as if she hoped to find comfort in my sad story.

"Anyway," I continued, "Bryan was a good skier. But it was getting near the end of the day and he was tired. He gave me a wave and let go of the rope. We were turning the boat around to swing back and pick him up out of the water when another boat came around the bend—one of those big, expensive cigarette boats. The guy driving it was drunk, going much too fast, not even watching where he was going. Before we could do anything about it, he drove that boat right into Bryan. Killed him instantly."

"Oh, my."

"By the time we reached Bryan, he was—" I stopped. The sight of my husband, floating dead in our wake, was an image I would live with the rest of my life. "He never had a chance."

"You poor dear."

"In any event," I said, shaking my head, shaking the picture from my mind, "I survived. As you will survive."

"I suppose we have no choice, do we?"

Angelina entered with a warm blueberry muffin and a glass of milk, which she placed in front of me. I ate slowly, remembering the pain of those first days of mourning. I wondered why the Lord saw fit to put me in a situation now where I was having to revisit so many of those feelings.

"I have a question for you," I said finally, changing the subject. "I've been wondering about Alan Bennet. Has he worked at Smythe for very long?"

"About a year and a half. Judith has been pleased with his work."

I know, I thought. *I saw how pleased she was with him last night.*

"Is he married?" I asked.

Marion shot me a wry glance.

"Handsome fellow, isn't he?" she said. I colored, knowing that she thought I was interested in him personally.

"Just curious."

"He's single," she replied. "Though there never seems to be a shortage of beauties in his orbit."

"I can imagine."

Alan was single. Judith was single. So why were they keeping their affair a secret, having a midnight rendezvous in a barn? I tucked that question away, determined to find the answer later.

"Last night, Marion, you were about to tell me something important about Feed the Need. About the company? You said Wendell had concerns?"

Marion glanced around then lowered her voice.

"I don't know much," she said. "But I do know Wendell was very upset about certain financial matters there. If you're looking for his killer, you might turn your attention in that direction."

I sat back in my chair and looked at her, wondering if she was insinuating something about her own son. He was, after all, the head of Feed the Need.

"You started to say something about the money I came here to deliver," I said softly. "The loan from the J.O.S.H.U.A. fund?"

Marion nodded.

"I know that loan was extremely important to Wendell, that the J.O.S.H.U.A. money was his last desperate hope to put things right."

I was about to question her further when we heard the sound of childish laughter coming down the hall. Marion's face suddenly lit up, and she turned in her seat just as a young boy bounded into the room, followed by Sidra. As he came in, I was struck not just by his enthusiasm, but also by his sheer physical beauty. About 11 or 12 years old, he was a gorgeous child, with what was obviously his mother's dark eyes and hair and perfect almond skin.

"Carlos!" Marion cried happily as the child came to her and gave her a hug.

"Gosh, where is everybody?" he said, dropping a big backpack and sleeping roll on the floor. "I gotta show you what I got."

He bent down to dig in the backpack, and Marion glanced at me with a wink.

"Carlos, you haven't met our guest. This is Callie Webber, she's—"

"Hi," he said, flashing me a friendly grin, cutting her off. "Here it is!"

From the bag, he pulled a small trophy, a wood-based golden statue of a young man holding up a soccer ball.

"Second place," he said. "Isn't it cool?"

"Your mom must be so proud," Marion said, glancing at Sidra and taking the trophy from Carlos. She studied it carefully.

"You get to keep the team's trophy?" I asked.

"Nah," he answered enthusiastically. "The team got a giant one, to go in the case in the front hall at school. The players each got these little ones."

He chattered on, and I realized suddenly that he hadn't yet heard the news that his grandfather was dead. I could see a somber look come back into Marion's eyes, and I knew she, too, was hesitant to destroy the happiness of this ebullient child.

"Is that a soccer star I hear in there?" Derek called excitedly from the hallway, and then he was in the room with Carlos in his arms. I took a final bite of my muffin, then pushed away from the table.

"We'll talk later," I whispered to Marion, touching her hand as I stood to go. She nodded, distracted by the loving scene between father and son. Sidra had taken a step back and was waiting somberly in the corner.

"It was so cool, Dad," Carlos was saying as I left. "The bus broke down, and we got to stay an extra day! The driver was really mad 'cause somebody from the other team put water in our gas tank and—"

"Carlos, we have something to tell you," Derek interrupted. "Let's go in the living room where we can sit down and talk about it."

"Why?" Carlos said. "What's wrong?"

"I'm sorry, son," Derek answered. "It's about your grandfather."

Fifteen

~

I headed upstairs, picked up my keys and my briefcase, and then came back down and went outside, away from the emotional scene that was taking place with Carlos. I went out through the kitchen and walked along the rear of the house, beside the pool. I passed the greenhouse and had just reached my car when I overheard two angry voices speaking in a foreign language. It sounded as if the voices were coming from the back side of the garage. I put my briefcase in my car and then quietly shut the door and followed the sounds.

My intention was to eavesdrop and try to make out what they were saying, but I was spotted before I could get close enough to listen. Just as I rounded the corner, Nick came striding out from behind the garage, gesticulating wildly in the air.

He stopped short when he saw me, his face turning red.

"Are you alone?" he asked.

"Who is it?" a female said from behind him. Angelina stepped out and looked at me. "Is anyone with you, Callie?"

I shook my head, wondering what could possibly be going on.

"What is it?" I asked. The two of them looked at each other, then motioned for me to follow them. Apprehensively, I walked around behind the greenhouse, past a row of trashcans, to the back side of the cabana.

"Nick saw it when he was putting out the garbage," Angelina said, gesturing toward the trash cans nearby. "He wants to alert the family, but I say this is not the right time. They are in the house now, telling Carlos that his grandfather is dead. I do not think they need to know about this right now, too."

We stopped walking when we reached the cabana, and I stared, stunned, at what I saw. The back side had four windows across the wide expanse of the building. There was nothing remarkable about the architecture or the landscaping, nothing remarkable about the building at all, except for one thing: The sills of each of the four windows was now coated and dripping in a dark, red liquid that looked very much like blood.

I gasped, taking a step closer.

"It is not real blood," Nick said. "Just food coloring in Karo syrup. Derek had it tested the last time."

"The *last* time?"

"Yeah. A few weeks ago, they found this stuff all over the side of Sidra's car."

"I don't understand," I whispered, shaking my head, thinking of the knife in the photo last night and now this. I felt a wave of nausea rising from the pit of my stomach. If Sidra really had done this herself, then she truly was one messed-up girl.

"It is kind of hard to explain," Angelina said softly. "Things like this—they have been going on for months. Stupid vandalism, usually targeted at Sidra."

"Like what?" I asked, pretending I hadn't already heard part of this story before from Sidra herself.

"Dead roses at her door. Fake blood on her car. Torn up clothes. Angry notes."

"Do you have any idea who's doing it?"

I walked over to the window sill and leaned forward, smelling the oozing substance that dripped from the wood. Nick was right; it smelled like syrup.

"No," Angelina said, shaking her head. "Sidra thinks maybe Derek is doing it. Derek swears Sidra is doing it."

"Who do *you* think is doing it?" I asked, looking at them both. But neither would reply. Nick only shrugged while Angelina stared at the ground.

I turned and leaned closer to the window, looking through the half-drawn shade at Sidra's room inside. It was perfectly neat, the bed made, the lights off. Right now, Sidra and Carlos were obviously still in the main house with Marion and Derek. Looking into the cabana, I shivered, thinking that if it wasn't Sidra herself, then whoever had done this must've come in the night while she was inside this very room, sleeping.

"Sidra's in danger," I said simply. "Call it 'vandalism' or whatever you want; this kind of wacky behavior can only escalate from here."

"And we should tell her about this, right? Tell all of them?" Nick asked. Angelina rolled her eyes, but also looked to me for the decision.

"Wait until you can get Derek or Sidra alone," I said. "They both have to know. But you're right. Carlos really doesn't need this right now."

~

I sat in my car for a long time, thinking about the fake blood on the windowsills. It had been a terrifying sight, more frightening still because it was so odd. Food coloring in Karo syrup, painted on the windows like blood? Why would someone want to do that? I was still in my car when I saw Derek and Sidra emerge from the house with Nick. He led them around to the back of the cabana, and a moment later I could hear Sidra's muffled scream. I assumed Angelina and Marion were distracting Carlos in the house.

I started my car and pulled out, turning right from the driveway and then right again on the first road. It ran alongside the Smythes' estate, and I followed it almost to the end where a low wire fence marked the back boundary of the Smythes' property. I parked my car and got out, examining the shoulder of the road for tire marks where Alan Bennet might have parked his car among the trees the night before. There weren't any telltale tracks, but as I headed for the barn I could see where he had crossed over the fence. There was a patch of tall grass bent down from footsteps, a bend in the wire where almost any full-sized adult could have easily climbed over. I did so now, making my way across the grassy field to the barn.

I opened the door to the barn and stepped inside, propping open the door to let in the sunlight. It was a dark building, two stories tall, with an empty loft spanning half of the upper level. Along the wall to my left was a huge green John Deere tractor. On my right was an old couch with the same blanket I had seen spread across it the night before now neatly folded at the end.

It was just a creaky old barn, filled with the smells of dirt and mold and damp hay. Though I didn't exactly know what I was looking for, I stepped further inside and began poking around among the tool boxes and lawn clippers, hoping that something might turn up. In the back of my mind, I was wondering if a little mischief had been the ultimate purpose of Judith's meeting with Alan out here the night before. It was just a hunch, but as I poked around, I hoped to find a bucket with traces of the fake blood or perhaps whatever had been used to wipe the blood on the windowsills. But my search turned up nothing, and finally I gave up.

I exited the barn, sliding the board into place along the front of it. I realized that I had made an error in judgment last night by going to bed when I did. I should've gone into the main house, gotten out of my wet bathing suit and into some warm, dry clothing, and then come back out here to wait them out, to see what was on the agenda besides their little bout of hanky-panky. Now all I could do was wonder if their meeting here had been connected with the fake blood on Sidra's windows.

From where I stood, I could see Nick in the distance, alone now, hosing down the back of the cabana, the red liquid pouring from the windowsills, diluted by the hose water until it ran clear. About halfway between us I noticed a tree house built high into a large oak tree. I decided that if it was sturdy, it might be a perfect spot for surveillance. Tonight, I knew, I would come back there and man my post, watching to see if any new mischief was afoot.

Without question, I wouldn't be caught sleeping on the job again.

Sixteen

~

Traffic into the city was light, so despite all the delays back at the house, I still managed to arrive ten minutes early for my meeting with Duane Perskie, the local PI supervising my case. I took the exit for Independence Mall, then found a parking place nearby, right on the street—a miracle in Philadelphia, to say the least.

We were supposed to meet at the Liberty Bell at ten o'clock; Duane had said he had a 10:30 meeting nearby. I glanced at my watch, slipped some change into the parking meter, and decided I would just have time for a quick stroll around my favorite part of town before meeting up with him.

As I headed toward Independence Square, I thought of how much I loved everything about the historic district. Visiting the sights of Philadelphia always made me swell with a sort of patriotic pride—even more so, in a way, than the monuments and landmarks of Washington, DC. Though DC was certainly impressive and awe inspiring, I always found that whenever I passed the Library of Congress or the White House or the Senate buildings, I saw the hundreds of people in them working hard to keep the wheels of our nation's capital turning. Philadelphia, on the other hand, was like a moment frozen in time, a turning back of the clock, a preservation of some of the greatest events in our nation's history. I loved touring the Graff House, where Thomas Jefferson wrote the Declaration of Independence, and Independence Hall, where the Declaration and the Constitution were signed. I didn't have time to go there now, so I contented myself with walking along the blocks of the square, pausing to enjoy the gorgeous sun and perfect blue sky above me.

I made my way back to the Liberty Bell a few minutes before ten and found a spot on a nearby bench. Despite the beautiful weather, the area wasn't very crowded. There was just a smattering of tourists and the occasional businessperson out for a stroll. I tilted my face toward the sunshine and scanned the group of people that surrounded the bell until I saw the man I was looking for.

"Duane!" I called, giving him a wave.

He responded instantly, walking toward me, a large Styrofoam cup in each hand.

"Hey, Callie," he said in his distinctive Midwestern twang. "Thanks for meeting me down here. You really saved me some time."

He offered me one of the cups, which turned out to be coffee. I accepted gratefully, drinking it black.

"So how's it going?" he asked. "Have you made much headway?"

"I've got a theory," I replied. "And a few suspects to go with it."

I told him about the insulin and the lack of a struggle, about my guess that the fatal injection had been given by someone Wendell Smythe knew and trusted.

"I've been talking with the coroner," Duane said, reaching into his inside pocket to produce a rolled-up manila file folder, which he handed to me. "Cause of death was definitely overdose of insulin by injection. The injection site was neat and clean. According to him, the man would've gone into a hypoglycemic attack almost immediately after that, which would've made him weak, dizzy and confused."

"Why was he on the floor?"

"The coroner thinks he was trying to go for help, stood up, and passed out. Apparently, just three cc's of regular insulin can take a diabetic's blood sugar level down into the 20s. All alone like that, he didn't have a chance. Probably died while he was passed out, some-where between 10 to 30 minutes after his insulin shot."

"I see."

"I believe you discovered the body soon after that."

"Yes," I answered, remembering the odd pallor of Mr. Smythe's face and the startling feeling of a wrist that held no pulse. "And the stuff around him on the floor?"

"All diabetes-related. He had a little kit he used to test his blood sugar."

"Prints?"

"They got a partial off the syringe. Not very clear, but they're working on it at the lab. They also got a hair, which they're testing for a DNA match. Speaking of prints, here's the fingerprinting kit you asked for."

From another pocket, he produced a small box, which I accepted gratefully and tucked away in my briefcase. I opened the report he had given me, scanning it as he continued.

"The final blood sugar reading in the tester machine's memory said 44, which is extremely low. The coroner thinks Smythe was given the insulin injection, got to feeling woozy, tested his blood sugar and saw that it was only 44, tried to go for help, fell down, passed out, and died."

"So who did it?"

"From that back door, through the bathroom, it could've been anybody. Secretary says no one except you went in or out through her door all morning."

"No one?"

"Mr. Smythe had a lot of work to do and didn't want to be dis-turbed. He left strict orders that he was to be interrupted only for the lady from the foundation with the money. That was you."

"Yes."

"Anyway," he said, "I guess that's all I have to tell you."

I closed the file. I would go over it more carefully later when I was alone.

"Right now," he said, "they're looking to the beneficiaries, family, business associates, you know the drill. 'The usual suspects,' as they say."

"Has the will been read?"

"Standard stuff," he said, nodding his head. "Most of Smythe's fortune was divided evenly between his wife and kids. A few bequests to charities and things. No big surprises."

"What's your impression, Duane? Who are they really looking at?"

He leaned forward, resting his elbows on his knees.

"Their search field is still fairly wide," he said. "But I think you're on the right track where you are now. If you've got eight or nine close relatives and employees who you know for a fact regularly gave the man his insulin, then I would stick with them. Look for motives, check out their alibis—process of elimination. I wouldn't be surprised at all if the killer is on your short list."

I thanked Duane for his help, tucking the file beside the kit in my briefcase.

"No problem," he said. "Happy to help. Though from here on in, you'll be dealing directly with the police. I'm sorry to say you won't need to see me much unless there's a problem."

We stood and shook hands, then he took our empty coffee cups and tossed them into a nearby trash can.

"I'm familiar with the police detectives handling this case," he said. "Good guys, both of them. Very competent. They're happy to cooperate—as long as it's mutual. They'd like you to stop by and see them this afternoon."

I smiled, thinking of the reluctant Detective Keegan. Rarely was an arrangement like that ever truly mutual.

"Sounds good," I said.

"Anyway, I guess that's it for now. May I walk you to your car?"

I nodded, gesturing towards Sixth Street.

"Tom probably told you that he and I go way back," he said amiably as we headed off. "We were in college together."

"Here at Penn?" I asked. Tom's alma mater was one of the few facts I knew about him.

"Yes," Duane said. "Though I've got to tell you, you're a lot different from the gals Tom went for back then."

I felt my steps falter for a moment.

"I don't understand," I said, regaining my footing, keeping my voice light. "What do you mean, 'went for'?"

"I mean, you know, Tom always dated real flashy types. You're very beautiful, of course, but in a subtle way. More classy."

"Duane…"

"Oh, don't worry. I'm not making a pass at you. Tom already told me that you're all his. Strictly hands-off for me."

I stopped walking and turned to face him.

"He said *what?*"

"That you were hands-off. 'Just give her the facts,' he told me. 'No dates, no flirting, no trying to run the ball to the end zone.' So don't worry. I got the point."

I felt a red flush creep into my cheeks.

"I'm not 'all his,'" I said, confusion pounding in my brain. "It's none of Tom's business who makes a pass at me. My relationship with him is purely a business one."

"That's not the impression I got," he said, grinning. "But if you say so."

"I say so."

I opened my car door, climbed in, and shut the door. I had just put the key in the ignition when I heard Duane tapping on my window. I started the car and rolled it down.

"So how about it?" he asked, still grinning. "Since you're fair game after all, would you like to go out while you're in town, maybe have some dinner?"

"No," I said sharply, then, hearing my tone of voice, repeated it again, more kindly. "No. But…thanks for asking."

I put the car in gear and drove off, leaving him looking after me, confused. Though I wasn't sure why, my hands were shaking by the time I finally reached the Smythe building and turned into the parking lot. *Tom was just being protective,* I thought as I slid my car into a narrow space and pulled to a stop. *Like a big brother.*

Or was he?

I leaned back in the seat and closed my eyes for a moment, thinking back on all the long nights Tom and I spent talking on the phone, on all the exciting events we had shared, albeit via long distance. We were so close in so many ways—and yet, in many other ways, we barely knew each other.

Now he was insinuating to his friend that I somehow was "taken"? That I in some way belonged to him? It was too much to think about.

Tucking my keys in my purse, I decided I would put Detective Perskie's words behind me for the time being and concentrate on the task at hand. There was too much going on already. I would have to sort out my relationship with Tom later.

I got out of the car and headed for the garage elevator, stepped inside, and pressed the button for the sixth floor. The doors slid closed in front of me, and I studied my distorted reflection in the metal, wondering if I would ever know how Tom really felt about me. After all, when it came down to it, there was just one issue here: How could a man lay claim to a woman he'd never met face-to-face?

Seventeen

~

By the time I got off the elevator, I felt reasonably calm and in control. As I stepped through the doors of Feed the Need, I couldn't believe that only yesterday I had come here expecting to deliver a check and then leave unencumbered. What a difference a day makes!

I approached the receptionist, but before I said a word, she was on her feet, coming around the desk.

"Mrs. Smythe called," she said, motioning for me to follow her. "She said to give you full use of any and all office equipment. Computer, fax, phones, whatever. I'm Kristy, by the way. With a K."

"Kristy, hi," I answered, following as she headed into the main area of the office. Marion and I had decided that we would say I was here using their facility for foundation business, that it was the least they could do considering the police wouldn't let me leave town. Hopefully, that way people wouldn't be on their guard around me, and I would be able to dig around a little and see if I could learn anything.

Kristy led me to a nice cubicle in the far corner. It had an L-shaped desk with a computer and phone, but otherwise it was empty.

"How's this area?" she asked. "I wish I could give you a private office, but they're all full."

"A cubicle will be fine," I answered, glad that a private office wasn't available. This way I'd be visible and thus much more able to assimilate into the office quickly—not to mention that this would be a better spot for eavesdropping. It had long been my observation that office cubicles tend to lead people into a false sense of privacy—much like e-mail, cellular phones, and other deceptive accoutrements of modern office life.

I settled into the desk and opened up the file Duane Perskie had given me. It was a little after 11 A.M. My intention was to work busily for an hour or so, letting the office staff see me and pass the word around about who I was and what I was doing there. Then I would amble into the office break room and hopefully share my lunch hour with a few chatty secretaries.

I read the file slowly, thinking about my theory that the killer was someone Wendell trusted, someone who regularly administered insulin to him. My list of suspects was a good one, with a few exceptions. I knew for a fact that the person I had heard in the bathroom off of Wendell's office couldn't possibly have been Alan Bennet or Gwen Harding because they were with me at the time. Of course, one of them could've been working with someone else; at this point, I wasn't eliminating anyone as a suspect.

I closed the file, deciding to read the rest of it later. For now, I would go onto the internet and see how Feed the Need checked out as a charitable organization to the outside world.

I worked for a while, scanning through Guidestar, digging up financial statistics, calculating the reported ratio of administrative dollars versus program funding. I checked out a copy of their 990 form, pulling out some helpful information.

Overall, I decided that things seemed fairly normal for a hunger relief organization, though I e-mailed one of the more complicated sets of financial data to Harriet back at the office. She would go over the numbers with a fine-tooth comb, I knew, and tell me if anything at all seemed amiss.

At noon, I sent off one last quick e-mail; then I shut down my computer, grabbed the sack lunch Angelina had prepared for me that morning, and set off looking for the lunch room.

I found it on the other side of the building, a large, sunlit area tucked away behind a conference room. There were about six or seven tables surrounded by chairs, a small kitchen area with sink, fridge, and microwave, and a row of soda and candy machines against the wall. All in all, it was a pleasant place to have lunch.

Most of the tables were full, but I found one with only two women sitting and quietly chatting.

"Is this seat taken?" I asked, feeling suddenly like I was back in the eighth grade, and all eyes were on me.

"Oh, please, join us," one of the women answered, pushing the chair out with her foot. I sat, putting my lunch sack on the table in front of me.

The women introduced themselves as Beth and Tina, saying that they knew who I was, but not my name.

"You're the woman from that charity, right?" Beth asked.

"The J.O.S.H.U.A. Foundation. Yes. You can call me Callie."

"Callie, you discovered Mr. Smythe's body, didn't you?" Tina whispered, and then I could see her jump as Beth must've kicked her under the table.

"It's okay," I said, pulling a sandwich out of my bag. It looked like tuna on whole wheat with lettuce. "I didn't know Mr. Smythe personally, so it wasn't quite as awful for me as it would've been for one of you."

"Yeah, I guess you're right."

They had a few questions about the whole incident, and I spoke freely, trying to give the impression that I was just a regular gal, warm and friendly, ready to chat about anything and everything. What I got from them wasn't much: It was a pretty good place to work, management was okay (with a few exceptions), and Wendell Smythe had been a beloved boss and friend.

"I hope they let us all off work for his funeral," Tina said, "because I know everyone's going to want to go and pay their last respects."

"So were a lot of people close to Mr. Smythe?" I asked.

"We all respected him, if that's what you mean."

"I mean, whom did he confide in? Who were his closest associates?"

Beth shrugged, and for a moment I was afraid I had crossed the line with my questions. But they didn't seem suspicious, only thoughtful.

"Besides his wife and kids, you mean?"

"Yes."

The two women looked at each other.

"His secretary, Gwen," Beth answered, and Tina nodded in agreement. "She's been with him for, like, a hundred years."

After lunch, I stepped into Gwen's office. A brief flash of *déjà vu* brought me back to the day before when I first came into this room, seeing her behind the desk in her beige suit and pearl earrings, talking on the phone. Now the desk was empty, the office oddly silent.

I decided Gwen must've taken the day off—not that I could blame her. Yesterday had been incredibly traumatic for her; seeing her dead boss was more than the woman had been able to handle.

I thought I might take another peek around Wendell's office, but a quick turn of the knob told me that this time it was locked. I jiggled the handle to no avail, but then suddenly the door swung open from the inside, and I found myself face-to-face with Gwen. She looked much different than she had the day before. Now, instead of a suit, she had on jeans and a light yellow sweatshirt. Her hair was a mess, and her face was pale without makeup.

"Callie!" she said, startled. "Goodness. I didn't know who that was, trying to get in. What are you doing here?"

"I was just looking for you," I said quickly. "I wanted to make sure you were okay."

She hesitated a moment, then finally stepped back and let me in. Once we were both inside Wendell's office, she closed and locked the door behind us.

"I'm not really here," she said. "At work, I mean. I took the day off, but then I was going crazy around the house. I came up the back stairs into Wendell's office. I tried to do some filing, but it's no use. I can't seem to concentrate."

She did look genuinely distraught, I decided. I made my way to the couch along the wall and sat, tucking one leg under me, knowing that this might be a good time to throw a few questions at her.

"Why don't you tell me about your boss?" I said warmly. "It seems he was very much loved. What was it that made him so special?"

Gwen seemed eager for the conversation. She settled tiredly onto the couch, leaning back against the cushions.

"I assume you've known him a long time," I added.

"I met Wendell Smythe almost 40 years ago," she said. "He and I started working at the same company on the same day—I in the steno pool, he in the distribution department. Textiles, it was. Wendell was fresh out of college, full of energy and big plans, very popular. All of us stenographers loved it when we were assigned to him. Six months later, he had worked himself into an administrative position, and he asked me if I would like to transfer out of the steno pool to become his personal secretary."

"Was he married then?" I asked.

"No, but I was." She glanced at me and frowned. "I know what you're thinking, but it was nothing like that. Wendell and I were always just friends—like brother and sister, you know. My husband was never jealous."

"I see."

"Of course, that was a lot of years ago. Eventually, Wendell left the textile company to begin his own business. A year later, he came back and hired me to be his office manager."

"For Feed the Need?"

"Oh, no, that happened much later. We were just a clothing manufacturer in the early days. Very successful. Made a small fortune."

I told Gwen that I had already read their brochure and that I had recognized some of their labels.

"We're all over the place," she replied, nodding. "From Kmart to Macy's and everywhere in between."

"So where did the nonprofit side of the business come from?" I asked.

Gwen sat up and stretched her legs out in front of her, exhaling slowly. She told me about a buying trip Wendell had taken to Southest Asia about ten years before. On his way to a meeting, his limo had broken down in the center of Seoul, and he had to sit on the side of the road for two hours until the company could send out another car. According to Gwen, those two hours changed Wendell's life. As he sat there amid dozens of poor starving children, he wondered how it was that he had been to that city dozens of times and never really noticed the squalor of the row houses, the protruding, malnourished bellies of the children. He decided right there to do something about it. By the time all was said and done, he had formed a sister company—a nonprofit organization—dedicated to the eradication of hunger throughout the world.

"We've done so much, so very much," Gwen said, standing and pacing excitedly. "If you could hear about some of the lives we've touched, the children we've saved. Building wells, planting crops, teaching Third World communities about irrigation and sanitation—it's just been incredible."

"And Wendell's son Derek is the CEO of the hunger relief fund?"

"Yes."

"Is he a brilliant businessman like his father?"

"Like Wendell?"

Gwen hesitated, a bemused expression crossing her face. She reached the edge of Wendell's desk and leaned against it.

"Just between you and me," she said softly, "comparing Wendell to his son Derek would be kind of like comparing the sunshine to...to a light bulb."

"I see."

"Don't get me wrong—Derek's good at what he does, perfectly suitable for heading up Feed the Need."

"Light bulbs do give light," I replied, carrying along her metaphor. "But..."

"But Derek is not the visionary his dad was. What Derek has to offer is good 'people skills,' enthusiasm, compassion. As long as he has a competent staff working for him, which he usually does, things are fine."

"What do you mean?"

"Derek's not particularly strong in finance or public relations. But he's good at spotting top talent and bringing it in. He's got a fantastic PR person. And as soon as his chief financial officer gets back, he'll be at a hundred percent."

I thought about what Alan Bennet had said that first day, that he was helping out because Feed the Need's CFO was on maternity leave. I asked Gwen about that.

"Nancy started having complications about four months ago," Gwen said, "so I guess you could call it an extended maternity leave. The baby was just born last week. She'll be back soon."

"And Alan Bennet's been handling the finances while she was gone?"

"Oh, partly," she said. "The accounting department runs pretty smoothly anyway. Since Nancy left, it's sort've been a mix of Alan and Derek and even Judith. They've managed to muddle through."

"So how is Judith as CEO of Smythe?" I asked. "Another light bulb?"

Gwen smiled and shook her head.

"Well now, that's a different situation altogether. Judith inherited her father's brains, his moxie, and his talents. Now if she could just temper all that with a little of his kindness and compassion, she would be as crackerjack as her father."

"She does seem a little brusque," I said.

Gwen laughed.

"To put it mildly," she replied. "It's funny, but Judith was always very headstrong, very no-nonsense, even as a child. Her parents were both so sweet, so mild mannered. They never could quite figure out how to handle Judith."

"She told me yesterday that she doesn't even believe in God," I said. "That must've been hard for such a devout man as Wendell."

"Terribly," Gwen said, nodding. "He carried a special burden for Judith's salvation. They talked about it from time to time, of course, but her heart was just never ready to hear the truth."

"How sad."

"He never gave up hope," she said. "Maybe now, with his death, she'll begin to see the light."

"Perhaps."

Gwen stood and walked some more, pacing as she spoke.

"You know," she said, "with Wendell gone now, I hate to admit it, but I'm not very worried for the company itself. I believe it will do fine under Judith's direction—and Derek's. We may stumble along the way a bit, but I think we'll get our feet back under us soon enough."

"That's good."

"My greater concern is with the big picture. I mean, with Wendell gone, who will steer this giant ship? Who will lead our way in the years ahead?"

Gwen was so emphatic that I felt a brief flash of pity for her. Had she been born in a different generation, one where women had the same opportunities as men, she might have risen to the helm of such a mighty ship herself.

"Surely there was a plan in place for the succession of leadership here," I said.

"Oh, yes," Gwen replied sadly. "Wendell knew the end was in sight for him. He made provisions. But, truly, there's no one that could ever be big enough to fill his shoes."

She blinked back tears, and I realized that she held Wendell in the same high esteem Tom did.

"So his death didn't come as much of a surprise?" I asked gently. She thought about that.

"A surprise? No. Difficult? Yes."

"I'm sure."

"Then I heard on the radio this morning that they're calling it a murder. You have no idea what that does to me, Callie. It tears my heart out."

"Any suspicions of your own, Gwen? You were, after all, right on the other side of that door when it happened." *Or in here, doing it yourself,* I thought, but did not say.

"No," she whispered after a long pause. "Everyone loved Wendell. I can't imagine who would want him dead."

She looked as though she was about to burst into tears, so I quickly changed the subject.

"Tell me about the money I came here to deliver, Gwen. Apparently, there was a building Wendell wanted to buy? What's happening with that?"

Gwen seemed to hesitate, her face clouding over with something I didn't recognize.

"I'm not sure," she said evasively, looking away. "Wendell had a lot of projects going on at once. I don't know much about that one."

I wondered why the sudden change in Gwen's demeanor. I decided to press it a little further.

"Two hundred and fifty thousand dollars?" I said. "And you don't know anything about it?"

Gwen shrugged.

"Sorry," she said.

"I thought your office was sort of the pulse of the company. I thought you'd know everything that was going on around here."

"I do!" she said. "It's, ah, I—"

Her voice sputtered to a stop.

"I'm sorry, Callie," she said. "I'm afraid I've got a terrible headache. You'll have to excuse me."

With that she walked to the door and held it open, waiting expectantly. I counted to five, slowly, then finally unfolded myself from the couch, stood, and headed for the door.

"You should take something for that headache," I said dryly as I walked past her. "It seems to be affecting your memory."

She closed the door behind me without replying, leaving me with one burning question: *What does Gwen know about that money that she isn't telling me?*

Eighteen

~

I headed toward my little cubicle, thinking about Gwen's words and her suddenly befuddled manner when the subject came up about the money I had been sent there to deliver. Obviously, there was something fishy about that $250,000 loan. *Was* there really a building they wanted to buy? And, if not, had Wendell lied to Tom—or had Tom misled me?

I knew the place to start answering those questions was with a phone call to Tom, but I hesitated. Our relationship depended on an enormous amount of trust on both sides: him, trusting me to analyze our grant recipients carefully; and me, trusting him enough to take all that he presented to me at face value. Perhaps my questioning of him would cause bigger problems later than the ones it would solve now.

No, I needed to approach this from some other direction first, analyzing the less disturbing possibility that Wendell Smythe had lied to Tom. Perhaps there was no building. Certainly, Gwen knew more than she was telling.

I changed direction, strolling toward the desk of Tina, one of my lunchroom companions. I had seen her earlier closer to the front, and I went there now, nonchalantly pausing at the entrance to her cubicle. Scattered along the fringes of her desk was a collection of lady bugs—figurines, stickers, little toys. Though a few might've been cute, the collection as a whole was a little distracting.

"Hey, Tina, you got a minute?" I asked.

"More like a second," she answered, opening a drawer and pulling out a blank pad and a pen. "Staff meeting at two o'clock."

I glanced around, noticing the abundance of empty desks and the clusters of people heading toward the conference room.

"I'll make it quick," I said. "I just need some help."

"What's up?"

"When your company buys a building or a piece of land or something," I asked, "who handles that for you?"

"What do you mean?"

"Is there a lawyer on staff here, or are legal matters like that handled outside? I need a quick opinion about some of the foundation's real estate. I thought maybe if you had a lawyer working here...?"

She shook her head.

"No, we use a firm downtown. On Walnut. Coach, Croatz, something like that—a small group. I don't know. Let me look."

She flipped through her Rolodex and pulled out a card.

"Here you go," she said, scribbling on a Post-it note. "Coates, Dillon, and McGruff. Good firm—even if I can't ever remember their names." I took the paper from her casually and gave her a big thanks.

"No prob," she said. "You're just lucky you caught me before I headed off to the meeting. We'll probably be in there for hours."

She lowered her voice and leaned toward me conspiratorially.

"I think they want to talk about Mr. Smythe's dying and how we'll have to carry on without him and all of that stuff. They're saying now that he was *murdered*. Did you hear?"

I nodded, startled by the tinge of excitement in her voice. The human desire for the titillation of tragedy never ceased to amaze me.

"Yes, I heard," I replied evenly.

She nodded before turning toward the conference room and bringing up the rear of the last small group. The door closed behind her, and I was alone in the outer office.

I took the long way around back to my cubicle, making certain that I was, indeed, the only person here who wasn't in the staff meeting. Then I returned to my desk, ready to make some calls.

It wasn't until I sat down and went to pull out my papers that my heart gave a little start: Someone had been rustling through my briefcase while I was talking with Gwen.

To anyone else it might not have been noticeable. But to me there was no question: The order of papers in my briefcase was always, always the same—calendar, then organizer, then certain files, all in a row. The order was still the same. But now the files, the calendar, everything was flipped. Someone had emptied my briefcase, then put it back together again—upside down.

I stood, glancing around, but the office was completely empty. I sat back down, heart pounding, angry at myself for not locking the case while I was gone. I dug through each pocket of the lid, but everything seemed to be in place—including the undelivered $250,000 check to Feed the Need. The file from Duane Perskie was there, too, right on top. When I was confident that nothing had been stolen, I snapped the case shut and placed it on the ground next to my chair. I would have to be more careful from now on. Though there wasn't really any information in there that would compromise my case should it get out, it still bothered me greatly that someone had been audacious enough to take such a chance. Somebody was getting way too curious about me and what I was doing here.

Putting the briefcase matter out of my mind for the time being, I picked up the phone and dialed the law offices of Coates, Dillon, and McGruff. The receptionist answered promptly, then put me through to Coates' secretary, a woman with a deep Southern accent despite the fact that their office was in downtown Philadelphia. I introduced myself as "Callie over at Feed the Need." She didn't question it.

"I need a favor," I said warmly. "I'm trying to pull together some information about our current and future development plans. I was wondering if there's any way you could fax me over copies of our current file."

"You're kidding, right?" she said. "Y'all have three current files, each one of them at least an inch thick."

"Oh, gosh," I said, reaching for my pen to doodle along the edge of the page. "Let me narrow it down for you. How about just the documentation regarding any real estate closings that are pending."

"Pending?" she said, and I could hear the shuffle of papers in the background. "You've already closed on Taipei...Manila...and Tegucigalpa. I think that about covers it for active real estate matters. Nothing else pending."

"We've already paid in full?" I asked. "For all of these properties?"

"Paid?" the woman drawled. "Heck, no, y'all *sold*. The people that bought the places paid."

"Oh, of course," I said. "I'm sorry, I don't know what I was thinking."

"Which department did you say you're with again?" she asked, her voice suddenly turning suspicious.

"I'm sort of a consultant, really, just heading up this one project. I was told that we were about to buy a building, and that the information would be relevant to my work."

"Well, ma'am," she said, "I don't know what that would be. There isn't anything being done through *us* anyway."

"No title searches or surveys or anything?" I asked.

"No, ma'am," she answered. "Far as I know, the last piece of property you people *bought* was over a year ago. The three properties you *sold* were in the last few months, but other than that I haven't heard of anything new."

"Well, thanks anyway," I said, ready to hang up the phone. "Guess I'll have to go back to Alan and see what he was talking about."

"Alan Bennet?" the woman said. "Is he your supervisor?"

I hesitated, berating myself for tossing off his name just to make myself sound legit. Ah, what a tangled web we weave...

"Well, no, not really," I said finally. "I just thought I overheard him say something about a new building."

"If anyone knows about it, he probably would," she answered. "At least, he was fairly involved with the last three sales. I'd talk to him if I were you."

"I sure will," I said, eager to hang up before she asked any more questions.

"I don't know about you," she continued, lowering her voice, "but if I worked over there at your company, I'd look for any and every excuse I could find to talk to that man."

"Excuse me?"

"He's *so* gorgeous. Around here, we call him 'The Hunk.'"

"Yes, well, he is good looking," I said lamely. I was usually lost when it came to silly girl talk, even now when I was just trying to fake it. "Thanks for your help."

I hung up the phone and sat there for a moment, thinking about what she had said. Unless they were using another lawyer, which apparently was unlikely, then there was no pending building purchase. So what had the money really been needed for? Tom had sent me here urgently, I thought as I recalled our conversation from Sunday, on the airplane. If not to buy a building, then just what did Wendell Smythe have in mind when he called his old friend Tom and asked him for a quarter of a million dollars?

I found the possibilities very disturbing. Wendell Smythe was by all accounts a forthright, honest, Christian businessman. What would make someone like that tell a lie to one of his dearest friends—a *quarter-of-a-million-dollar lie*, no less? I knew there weren't going to be any easy answers to that question for the time being, but I would keep it at the forefront of my mind.

For now, I got up from my desk and headed for the Human Resources department. In the main cubicle, I found that the file cabinets were low and under a counter, all locked. Turning to the desk, I rummaged around in some of the drawers, finally finding a key in one of the small compartments of a desk organizer. Sure enough, it unlocked the filing cabinets. So much for office security.

I quietly slid out the drawers and and easily located the personnel files on Alan Bennet, Gwen Harding, Derek Smythe, and Judith Smythe—four of the people on my list of suspects. I pulled the files, closed and locked the drawers, and returned the key to the desk. I strode to the Xerox machine, then began making copies of each of the files. They weren't very long. Still, by the time I was finished, I wasn't sure if I should risk returning the files to the Human Resources area or not. I hesitated, glancing at the closed conference room door.

Quickly, I popped open my briefcase and slid the photocopies in. Then I headed back to Human Resources, slipped the key from the drawer, and opened the filing cabinet.

I started with Bennet, then filed away Harding. I was just looking for Smythe when I heard voices and realized the meeting had adjourned and people were headed my way. Taking the chance, I quickly flipped through until I found Smythe. I slid the last two files into place and then closed and locked the drawer, but before I could put the key back in the desk, a woman came around the corner.

"Oh!" she said, stepping back. "You scared me."

"I'm sorry," I said, my mind racing. "I was just wondering if you had any blank W9 forms."

She hesitated a beat, looking at me thoughtfully with two dark brown eyes. She was an attractive woman in her early 30s wearing a tan silk pantsuit.

"Is that that new Burmese washable silk?" I asked, reaching out to finger her sleeve. "That's *beautiful*."

"Washable?" she answered, "Um, no. The tag says 'dry clean only.'"

"Still," I replied, "it's lovely."

"Thanks."

Her suspicion seemed to have passed. She crossed in front of me, pulled open the bottom drawer of her desk, and rummaged around a bit.

"Don't think I have any W9s," she said, flipping through some tax documents. "Maybe you can get one from accounting."

"Oh, okay."

She closed the drawer.

"Or nowadays, you know, you can go to the IRS website and download almost any form you need."

"Good idea," I said, the key feeling hot in the palm of my hand. "Thanks."

I walked out of her cubicle, praying she wouldn't need that key any time soon. I headed for Tina, who was back at work at her desk, surrounded by her ladybug collection.

"Sorry to bother you again," I said in a low voice, "but can you tell me, what is that woman's name, the one in personnel?"

"Debra?"

"Debra," I said. "Yes. Sweet lady."

"Yeah, she is. Did you need her for something?"

I shook my head, smiling.

"No, I just couldn't remember her name."

I walked on back to my cubicle, picked up the phone, and rang the front desk. The receptionist answered on the first ring.

"Hey," I said quickly. "Would you buzz Debra and ask her to come back to the conference room for a minute?"

"Sure. Who is this?"

I scratched my fingernails on the phone receiver, as if there was something wrong with my phone.

"Thanks," I said. I hung up and walked back toward personnel, timing it so that I was just coming around the corner as Debra was heading out of her cubicle, walking with her back to me.

I slipped right into the cubicle behind her, opened the drawer, neatly dropped the key in its slot, then closed the drawer with a quiet thud. Mission accomplished, I left the cubicle and looped around toward the conference room, where Debra stood, puzzled, in the doorway. She stood there for a moment, then rolled her eyes and turned back toward her desk.

"Oh, these people," she said, shaking her head as she walked away. "I don't have time for all their foolishness."

Smiling, I headed back to my desk to get a look at the files I had worked so hard to acquire, hoping that something in one of them might lead me to the murderer.

Nineteen

~

I flipped through Judith's file first, not really looking for anything, just trying to get a better idea of who she was. Not surprisingly, her background was direct and impressive—a B.A. (summa cum laude) from Rutgers College, an M.B.A. from Wharton, and a stellar rise through the ranks at Smythe Incorporated.

Derek's file was equally impressive, though more colorful. He had a degree in Divinity from Eastern Theological Seminary, a Masters of Social Work from the University of Pennsylvania, and apparently he had worked for a while as a missionary. He had spent time in Central America and had, in fact, only been working for Feed the Need for a few years.

That surprised me. Most of the missionaries I knew were fairly adventurous, the hearty type. But Derek seemed so soft, so genteel—certainly not the kind of guy who would live in a Third World country without modern amenities.

I put his papers aside and took a look at Gwen Harding. Her work history was just as she described it, though I did a double take when I came to her salary classification. With her long tenure and regular, steady pay increases, she was making nearly as much as the executives. Rarely did secretaries earn what they deserved, but I would say this was an exception. I thought about Gwen and those gorgeous pearl earrings she wore, and I realized that she very likely had bought them for herself.

Alan Bennet, on the other hand, was definitely not making enough money to be going around in Armani suits and $200 ties. His salary was perfectly respectable, but it certainly wasn't on a par with his spending. I saw that he had only been at Smythe for about a year and a half, and that good semi-annual reviews from his boss, Judith, had led to two six-percent pay increases.

A copy of his resume was there, and I took a moment to study it. Prior to working for Smythe Incorporated, he had been with three other clothing manufacturers. Under Education, he had listed a B.S. in Accounting from a small private college in the Midwest that I had never heard of.

According to my discussion with Gwen, Alan had basically been running Feed the Need's finances for the last four or five months or so while the regular accountant was out on extended maternity leave. Even though I knew it wasn't him I had chased from the bathroom two days before, I still felt that he was worth a little more research.

I tucked all of the papers away in my briefcase, then closed it up and turned to my computer, typing out a quick e-mail to my office, giving them the information I had and asking them to look into Alan's history a little more closely.

The police department was only a few blocks away, so I took advantage of the gorgeous weather outside and walked. The men I sought were in a cavernous downtown building, at the end of a long hall. A handwritten sign taped to the door said "Keegan and Sollie." I knocked, thinking the two names sounded more like a dog and pony show than a pair of police detectives.

"Come," a voice barked from inside. I swung open the door to find a tiny office with two desks crammed in a space barely big enough for one. Behind the first desk sat Detective Keegan, tufts of reddish hair still poking out over each ear. He gave me a broad smile, unexpected after his gruff greeting, not to mention his attitude at our previous meeting the day before.

"You made good time," he said warmly, rising halfway and then sitting again.

"Hi, Detective," I said, shaking his hand. "Nice to see you."

He gestured toward a chair and I took it, turning my knees to the side so I could fit.

"Kind of a tight squeeze in here," he said, smiling. "Not that I have a problem with it. But some folks complain."

"I'm fine," I replied.

"Sollie just went out for a soda. He'll be back in a few. Can we get you anything? Coffee?"

I shook my head, wondering at the change in his attitude. Tom had obviously worked some magic here. I had no doubt that some higher-up had told Detective Keegan to be on his best behavior with me; I couldn't have asked for a warmer reception.

Keegan grabbed a file from the piles on his desk and skimmed through it for a moment before looking at me.

"Okay," he said, lowering his voice, "we got some of the lab results here, though not everything."

"Okay."

"I don't know who you know, Ms. Webber, but I've been given explicit instructions to be as forthcoming as I can within the bounds of the law."

"I know."

"That's why I'm gonna leave this file right here and go get myself something to drink. Understand?"

"I understand."

Then he stood and walked out, leaving me to flip the file around and gather what information I could.

I skimmed the updated coroner's report, noting that the lack of a struggle had been confirmed. The needle had gone straight in and come straight out; there were no other significant bruises or trauma. The injection site had been the back of his left arm. Wendell's fingernails had been clean and revealed no skin scrapings. Under "Other

Findings" there was a long list of abnormalities, including "fistula in upper right arm," "severe ischemia of the toes and feet," and "nephritis." Though I felt certain these were diabetes-related conditions, I pulled a pen and notepad from my purse and wrote it all down.

Fibers collected in the office and bathroom were numerous, though mostly unidentified. There was one hair found on Wendell's arm *under* his shirt, near the injection site, described as "Blond, chemically compromised." I thought immediately of Alan Bennet, who seemed just vain enough to have his hair colored, just blond enough to hint at foil highlights.

There wasn't much more information than that, so I glanced toward the door and began flipping back through the other things in the file. I stopped near the back at a long list of suspects. Many of the names had alibis penciled in next to them.

I looked for the names I was interested in, jotting them all down as quickly as possible:

Wife—shopping at Desmond's dept. store. Confirmed by salesclerk and cook.

Son—working alone in office. Unconfirmed.

Daughter—working alone in office. Unconfirmed.

Secretary—working alone in office, on phone. Confirmed by telephone records—see list and confirm at other end.

Bennet—running errands, then back in office. Errands unconfirmed. Return to office at approx. 11:15 conf. by receptionist.

Cook—shopping with Mrs. Smythe.

Maid—shopping at grocery store, confirmed by checker.

Daughter-in-law—Bible study at St. James Church. Unconfirmed—pastor out of town. Try again."

There were plenty of other names on their list, too, but I concentrated for the time being on the ones that matched my own list of suspects. I wrote everything down without thinking much about what I was writing, knowing there would be time to sort through it all later. I was on the last one when I heard loud voices in the hall, and I knew that was my cue to put the file back.

I was inserting my notepad into my purse when the door opened and two men came in, each carrying a can of soda. Keegan was first, followed by the tall black man I had seen him with in Gwen's office the day before. I stood so that they could get past me to their desks, then we all sat down again at once.

"This is Detective Sollie," Keegan said, waving toward his partner. The man nodded at me coldly.

"Ma'am," he said.

"Sollie," I said, giving him my most charming smile. "That's an interesting name."

"Slang for 'Solomon,'" he answered gruffly.

"Solomon because he's so, so wise," Keegan teased. That seemed to break the man's reticence. He balled up a piece of trash and tossed it at Keegan's head.

"Mrs. Webber, you said on the phone that you had some information for us."

"Yes," I replied, nodding. "I don't know how pertinent it might be, but I doubt it's something you've turned up so far."

"Go on."

I hesitated, hating to give out any information at all. But the police wanted this relationship to be "mutually cooperative." The least I could do was throw them a bone.

"Judith Smythe and Alan Bennet are involved in a clandestine affair."

Sollie grunted. Keegan didn't react at all.

"Judith, the daughter, and Bennet, the employee?" Sollie asked, consulting his notes. "How do you know this? Somebody told you?"

"I, ah, happened upon them by accident. They don't know that I know."

"What do you mean by clandestine?" asked Keegan. "Neither one of 'em's married, far as I know."

"All the more reason that their secretiveness is so odd. I saw them meeting late at night in an old barn on the back of the Smythe property. And, believe me, they may have been in a barn, but they weren't out there discussing tractors or hay."

"I see," Sollie said, forming a tent with his fingers. "Anything else you'd like to tell us?"

I thought about the vandalism incidents involving Sidra, of Marion's pleas not to involve the authorities. More importantly, I thought about the $250,000 that I had been told was for buying a building—but apparently was not. For now, I decided, I would keep these bits of information to myself.

"No, nothing else to report," I replied.

"Then thank you for coming in," Sollie said politely. "Do give us a call the next time you have any information."

I thanked them both and then stood to leave.

"Don't give the girl a hard time," Keegan said, throwing the ball of trash back at Sollie. "She's just doing her job."

I glanced back at Sollie, who finally allowed himself a small smile.

"Just so long as *her* job doesn't interfere with *my* job," he said.

I met his gaze for a long moment.

"I'm very good at what I do," I told him earnestly. "I'll make it a point not to interfere with your job."

Twenty

I walked back to the car, deep in thought. I was glad for the police list of alibis; it saved me a lot of time and trouble. Though I would verify each of the alibis myself, at least this list provided a good starting point.

I passed several department stores as I walked, the windows decorated colorfully for autumn, most of the clothes the colors of the changing leaves. I thought about the small stack of clothes back at the house—the things Judith had loaned me as well as the few things I had picked up for myself—and I wondered if there was anything suitable for a funeral in any of that. Passing a lovely dark gray suit in a store window, I hesitated, wondering how much it cost and if they would have it in my size. I turned back to take a better look.

From the corner of my eye, I could see that someone else also stopped about 30 feet behind me and was looking into a window there. My heart skipped a beat. Was someone following me?

Heart pounding, I started walking again, then stopped abruptly at the next window. I glanced back to see the person behind me also stop. A man—I couldn't discern more than that without being conspicuous.

I wasn't sure what to do.

If the person meant me harm, then I needed to lose him. But if this was just someone keeping tabs on me, then I would do better to let him trail along for now and only lose him when I got to something important. Either way, I needed to get a good look at him to figure out who I was dealing with.

I headed off again, this time at a more leisurely pace. At the next corner, I saw my opportunity: I turned right, then quickly darted into the first door on my right. It opened into a long, narrow, musty-smelling jewelry store with faded velvet material draped in the window displays.

Fortunately, the only salesperson in attendance was with a customer at the far end of the counter. I stayed near the door, facing a glass case filled with wristwatches, watching the window.

Sure enough, after a moment, my pursuer rounded the corner and then stopped. He was in his mid-20s with an angry face and short brown hair. He had a slight widow's peak at the top of his forehead, and his inch-long bangs stuck straight up from there like a little flag. He was dressed in a gray sweatshirt and jeans, his physique showing the bulging arms and shoulders of a serious weight lifter. He certainly looked threatening. He stood there in front of the window for nearly a full minute, hands on his hips, scanning the street in front of him. When I saw that he was about to look inside the store, I crouched down beneath the glass case and counted to 20 before peeking to see that he was gone.

"May I help you?" I heard from the salesman behind me, and I jumped, startled at his close proximity.

"No, thank you," I mumbled, and then I walked out of the door and trotted across the street to peek around the far corner.

There he was. I could see him standing a few yards away, talking into a cellular phone. I couldn't hear everything he said, but I did catch bits of "lost her" and "nothing I could do." For a moment, I toyed with the idea of confronting him once he got off the phone. Surely, out in the open like this, he couldn't harm me. In the end, however, I thought it might be wiser to turn the tables and follow him to see where he might go.

It didn't take long to find out. His destination was the parking garage of the Smythe building. I watched from a safe distance as he took the stairs down to the first lower level. He headed straight for a red pickup truck, let himself in, and then just sat there.

He was waiting for me, I felt sure. My car was parked in view of his, across the row and down a ways. Though I had no intention of getting caught alone in here with him, I inched my way along the back wall toward his truck until I could just make out his license plate number. I memorized it, returning to the front of the parking garage.

I didn't have time for this. There was still much to do today in a short amount of time. The last thing I needed was to try to wait this guy out. For all I knew, he was settled in for the night, complete with a Thermos full of coffee and Port-A-Potty jar.

Suddenly, the elevator dinged, echoing sharply in the cement garage, and the doors opened to let out a small group of businessmen. Seizing the opportunity, I crossed over and fell into step with them, walking safely to my car without incident. After I got inside, I cracked the window, then started it up, listening for the sound that was sure to follow. Within an instant, I could hear the truck start up as well. *Here we go,* I thought as I pulled out and headed for the exit. Just what I needed. A tail.

Reaching the exit of the garage, we headed out into the five o'clock gridlock of downtown Philadelphia. After a few blocks, I pulled out my cellular phone and dialed Harriet. I got her machine, so I left a message describing the car that was following me, complete with license plate number. I felt sure she would have no trouble taking it from there. And if something unfortunate should happen to me, at least they would know where to start looking.

After going six slow blocks with the truck two cars behind me, I felt just antsy enough to try to lose him. We were in a long line of traffic trying to funnel onto a bridge over the Schuylkill River in an area I was familiar with from my summer at the law firm there. I waited until I was even with an empty one-way street, then suddenly turned right and zipped down it the wrong way, to the sound of several different honking horns. I turned right again once I reached the next intersection.

I went about a block, then turned right again, essentially doubling back behind the truck that had been following me. There were other routes out of the city, and I considered my options as I checked my rearview mirror for signs that the guy had succeeded in following me. With no glimpse of him, I crossed over the road I had started on, then continued in a perpendicular direction for a few miles before finding another bridge over the river and out of town.

I had lost him; I was sure of it. Letting out a long, slow breath, I settled into my seat and tried to put the entire thing out of my mind. Someone was keeping tabs on me, and I wondered who it could be. Perhaps once Harriet ran the plate, I'd have a better idea.

Traffic grew heavy again once I was on the Schuylkill Expressway, and I glanced at my watch, knowing that the wake for Wendell Smythe was in two hours. It would be my first good chance to be alone in the Smythe's home, and I planned to work my way through the bedrooms I hadn't yet seen. I knew I would have to move quickly; I couldn't be too late for the wake.

As I sat in stop-and-go traffic, I got out my notes from the meeting with the police and went back over the alibis of all of my suspects.

According to their notes, Derek and Judith had both been at work at the time of their father's murder, supposedly at their desks, though no one had yet confirmed that they actually were where they said they were.

Gwen was also at work, using the phone. Though phone records did show a number of outgoing calls during the time that Wendell was killed, I didn't think this was much of an alibi. With private access to Wendell's office, she could've easily put someone on hold, gone into Wendell's office and given him the lethal injection, and then come back out again. Of course, there was still the fact that Gwen wasn't the person I chased down the stairwell. If she was the killer, she certainly wasn't acting alone.

Ditto for Alan Bennet, who was "running errands" at the exact time of death. I remembered how impatient and out of breath he had been when he first came into his office and found me sitting there. I wondered if somehow he and Judith had been working together to murder her father, if it was Judith I had chased down the stairs.

The maid, Angelina, had been at the grocery store; apparently, the checker remembered seeing her. Her brother, Nick, had been busy in the city, helping Marion Smythe with her shopping.

I supposed with Nick and Marion out shopping, that gave either one of them opportunity, of sorts. One or the other of them could've slipped away at some point, dashed over to the Smythe building, and done Wendell in. I decided to reserve judgment on Nick and perhaps look more closely at him for some sort of motive. As for Marion, my gut told me that her grief was too genuine, her sorrow too real, for hers to have been the hand that killed her husband.

That left Sidra. Supposedly, she had been attending a Bible study at the time of Wendell's death, though that was thus far unconfirmed because the pastor wasn't available.

I looked up the address of St. James Church, seeing on the map that it was near the Smythes' home. Depending on how long it would take to get through all of this traffic, I decided to stop there on the way to the house, knowing that if I skipped dinner with the Smythes I would just have time to squeeze it in.

Twenty-One

~

The front doors of the church were locked, so I walked around the building and tried each one. The place was modest in size, though very lovely, and I wondered if there was a parsonage nearby. I was just about to walk away when I heard someone calling from the window of a building across from the church.

"May I help you with somethin'?" the man's voice called. I crossed the quiet street and walked closer to the window.

"I'm looking for Pastor Quinn," I said. "Does he live here?"

"He lives here, yes."

"Is he here now?"

"Right now? Well, yes. Right now he's lookin' out the window at you."

It took me a moment, and then I laughed.

"Come on in," he said, pointing toward the door. "I'll meet you in the dining room."

I walked to the door and turned the knob, stepping into a warm, roomy kitchen. It had an industrial dishwasher and double ovens, and through a large doorway I stepped into a room with seating for about 20.

"This is nice," I said when he came in. "I bet you can feed a lot of people in here."

"Even more than you'd think, lass," he answered. "Have a seat. How can I help you?"

I pulled up a chair at the corner table and sat.

"My name is Callie Webber," I replied. "I'm here on an investigation."

"An investigation?" he asked. "A policewoman, are you?"

I shook my head.

"It's a private investigation," I said. "But if you're Pastor Quinn, you can really help me out."

"I'm Ian Quinn. You got somethin' to ask me, child?"

"Sidra Smythe," I said. "Do you know her?"

"Do I know her?" he cried. "She's one of the Lord's angels, she is. Comes to church almost every day, helps out in the church office, even cooks with the soup kitchen in here on the weekends."

"My."

"A lovely girl. So what is the problem?"

"I need to know if she was at Bible study here on Monday morning. Around 10:30 or 10:45."

He sat back and squinted intelligent blue eyes at me.

"Same time of day that her father-in-law was murdered, is that what you're asking?"

I hesitated for a moment, startled by his bluntness.

"She's not necessarily a suspect," I finally replied. "Right now, it's still sort of a process of elimination."

He leaned forward and rested both elbows on the table, looking at me earnestly. He seemed to be in his late 60s or early 70s, robust and healthy, with a tinge of a suntan on his face and the wiry body of a runner.

"Well, about fifteen other parishioners and I can tell you that Sidra Smythe was here for ten o'clock Bible study on Monday morning. She led the prayer. Got here well before ten."

"What time did she leave?"

"Around noon—not until after she had helped straighten up after the service and helped us set up the tables for our Wednesday night prayer meeting."

"Good."

I could tell he was feeling defensive, and I felt bad that I'd had to challenge the integrity of one of his beloved parishioners. I was quiet for a moment, wondering how I could keep him talking, maybe get him to shed a light or two on Sidra's relationship with Derek. I wondered if he knew about the "incidents" at the house. Finally, I made a big show of pulling my notebook from my purse, flipping to the list of suspects, and scratching off Sidra's name.

"Thank you so much," I said. "That's one down at least."

"Glad I could be of help."

"It's my understanding that Sidra and her husband are separated," I said. "In your opinion, is she—"

"That's enough questions," he said abruptly, standing.

After a moment's hesitation, I stood as well.

"I'd like to know who 'tis exactly that you're working for," he said as he escorted me toward the door.

"The family," I said. "Well, Mrs. Smythe, in a way."

"Don't tell me Marion suspects her own daughter-in-law of murder?"

"Goodness, no!" I said, hoping I showed enough shock at the question to get back in his good graces. "I'm working on behalf *of* the family. I'm just establishing ironclad alibis so there won't be any questions further down the line."

"I see. Well, good luck to you then."

"Though I would appreciate it if you wouldn't mention this conversation to Sidra. Marion doesn't really want the rest of the family to know that I'm investigating, and for the time being I need to keep it that way."

"As you wish."

"The police will probably contact you soon with the same questions that I had. Just tell them what you told me."

"Of course," he said, and then he opened the door and held it as I stepped out.

"Pastor Quinn—" I started, turning back around.

"Good day," he replied, cutting me off. Then he shut the door, just as Gwen had earlier, telling me in no uncertain terms that our conversation was over. *That is the second time today*, I thought as I headed for my car, *that someone has ushered me out of somewhere and then closed the door in my face.*

Twenty-Two

The wake was scheduled to run from seven to nine at the Morrison Funeral Home, though the family was expected to arrive about a half hour early. I got to the house just as they were gathering in the foyer to leave, which was perfect timing as far as I was concerned. Now I had a good excuse for being late: I still had to get ready.

"Oh, Callie, there you are," Marion said, pinning a small gold brooch on her black lapel. Despite the somber occasion, she looked lovely in black, and for a moment I could glimpse in her face the portrait of the young woman that hung in her husband's office at work. "Would you like to ride in the car with us?"

"Thank you, Marion," I said, "but I need to freshen up first. I passed the funeral home earlier, so I know where it is. I'll come along as soon as I've showered and changed."

"Alright, dear," she said, distracted by the arrival of Judith, who was dressed smartly in what looked like a Versace suit and matching coat. Black, yes, but perhaps a bit too stylish for such a somber occasion. "It's the Morrison Home, you know, just up the street."

"I know."

I watched as the family grouped up and left, Nick driving Marion, Judith, and Angelina in the Cadillac. Sidra and Carlos climbed into the Jaguar and waited as Derek showed me how to lock the door and engage the alarm when I left.

"I've heard that people look in the paper for wakes and funerals so they can rob the house while everyone's gone," he said. "That's just what we'd need—somebody digging through all our stuff while we're not here."

If you only knew, I thought as I assured him that I would, indeed, set the alarm before leaving. Carlos gave me a wave as they drove off, and then I pulled the door shut and locked it, turning to face the Smythe home alone for the first time.

I would start with the rooms downstairs that I hadn't yet seen— namely, Nick's and Angelina's. Though I found it hard to suspect either one of them, I dared not leave even one stone unturned—or, in this case, one insulin injector unexamined.

I headed for the kitchen, knowing that their rooms must be in the back wing. I found Nick's room first, and I knew immediately that it was his because it held an entire bookcase filled with cookbooks. The furnishings were modest, with a queen-sized bed flanked by two bedside tables, a small sitting area by the window, and a great big dresser. Scanning the room, I could see that Nick was interested in golf— there was an unopened pack of tees on the dresser and several dirty pairs of golf shoes in the closet.

Nick wasn't very organized or neat, so going through his things took a bit of time. He apparently liked science fiction novels, and he had a few of them in the drawers of his bedside table along with several clunky pieces of gold nugget jewelry. There was nothing else of interest there or in the closet. I was amazed at the size of his clothes, and I pulled out one pair of pants just to hold them up to myself. I realized my entire body could fit inside one of his pant legs. I wondered what he weighed.

It wasn't until I got to the dresser drawers that I hesitated. In one drawer, among the paper clips and hard candies and Kleenex packs, I found a small bottle of injectable insulin.

Gingerly, I lifted the bottle by its metal lid and held it up to the light. It was about half full with less than an inch of clear liquid in the bottom. I memorized the words on the label and wondered if a coroner could determine if this was the same brand that had been injected into the body. Heart pounding, I put the bottle back where I found it and slid the drawer shut.

Angelina's room was next. It wasn't nearly as cluttered as Nick's, nor as large. It was a simple room, painted an airy light blue with a white bedspread on the bed and a few knickknacks on the dresser. The closet held surprisingly few clothes—so few, really, that I flipped through the lot of them, counting three uniforms, two dresses, two pair of jeans, and about four shirts, finally coming to a huge navy blue overcoat at the very end. I pulled the coat out and held it up, wondering what it was doing in there. Checking the collar, I saw that it was a woman's size 24—much larger than Angelina, who was about a size eight. I looked in the pockets, but they were empty.

I put the coat back and turned to Angelina's dresser, a smaller, more feminine version of the one in Nick's room. The drawers were all half-empty, though neatly organized with a small collection of socks, stockings, bras, slips, and nightgowns. The top right drawer held hair clips, bobby pins, and, in the back, several empty purses. There was a wad of cash tucked inside one of them; I counted out the money, realizing it added up to more than four thousand dollars!

I put back the cash and closed the drawer, looking, finally, at the row of photos she had clipped to the side of her mirror. One was of an Italian-looking family, all smiling, clustered in front of a *ristorante*. There were several school-type photos of dark-haired, dark-eyed children with "to Aunt Angelina" scribbled on the backs. I looked closely at the next photo, showing Angelina wearing jeans and a T-shirt, leaning against the base of some sort of monument, grinning seductively at the camera. With her hair down, she looked very carefree and sexy. On the back of the photo she had scribbled some hearts and written "our special place." I wondered who the other half of "our" could possibly be. Judging from the way she gazed at the camera, whoever took the picture was definitely the object of her affection.

I tucked that photo back into place and then pulled down the last one. It was of a heavy girl with a chubby face and Angelina's features. Thinking at first that it might be a sister, I did a double take when I realized that it was a picture of Angelina herself. She used to be overweight, I recognized with a start. That explained the ill-fitting uniform, the relatively small number of clothes in the closet. The size-24 coat must be hers, I thought, saved as a reminder of heavier days.

I put the picture back, then left Angelina's room and headed up the stairs.

I wanted to start with Wendell's dialysis room, but I wasn't exactly sure where to find it. Opening a door near the end of the hall that I had originally assumed was a closet, I discovered a huge, sumptuous-looking black leather reclining chair next to a machine that was obviously the dialysis unit. Behind the chair were shelves filled with tubes, bandages, syringes, and other medical supplies. In front of the chair was a sturdy built-in cabinet holding a nice television, a VCR, and stacks of video tapes.

I walked to the shelves of medical supplies, poking around until I found a small refrigerator containing two entire boxes of injectable insulin bottles, the same size and brand as the one I'd found in Nick's room. At least I knew now that the killer, whoever it had been, wouldn't have had any trouble procuring the murder weapon. All they had to do was come in here and take a bottle from the box.

I closed the door to the dialysis room and crossed the hall to Derek's suite. *No wonder he still lives at home,* I thought after I had opened the door to a gorgeous living room with a fireplace, comfortable furniture, and a wide-screen television discreetly tucked into the top half of a giant armoire. Two doors opened off of this room— one into what had obviously been Carlos' room before his mother moved him out to the cabana, and one that had been the master bedroom for Derek and his wife. Now, I noticed, one half of the bed looked as if it hadn't been touched. On the other half, the covers were pulled up but ruffled, as if Derek had sat there just a while ago, pulling on his shoes or fixing his tie. This room would be harder to search, I realized, because it was so big and held so many chests and cabinets and closets and drawers. Perhaps I could come back tomorrow, during the funeral, and dig deeper. For now, I did a cursory search, stopping for a double take at the shower/tub in the master bathroom, which was huge and so elaborate it came complete with a CD player and television.

This is how the other half lives, I thought as I closed the door to the bathroom and scanned the interior of the walk-in closet. The right side was Derek's, and I saw that his clothes were neatly organized by style and color. The left side had obviously been Sidra's—it looked stripped of all but her heaviest winter clothes. There was a box on the top shelf, and I glanced at my watch before climbing up to peek inside. What I found startled me: It looked like a fur coat, sable if I wasn't mistaken, but it had been cut into shreds. I folded the box shut and stepped back down, wondering if this was an example of the vandalism that had been plaguing Sidra.

I returned to the bedroom and quickly slid the drawers of the bureau open and shut. I was starting to feel worried now, knowing that soon I would have to give up this search and head for the funeral home. Though I didn't know what I was looking for, I hesitated at a printout of medical data that was tucked away among some other papers. It was a medical workup of Derek, though much more thorough than a normal physical. The bloodwork listed the usual things like white blood count, red blood count, and cholesterol, but there were two pages of other tests, including a section about antigens and liver function. The whole thing showed probably ten pages of medical results, from bloodwork to EKG, but it wasn't until I got to the end that I realized what I was looking at. The last page was a psychological profile of Derek, and at the top of the page, someone had written, "Pre-transplant Workup."

Transplant. I thought of Judith in Wendell's office the day before, talking about her father. *He was trying to line up a kidney transplant, but the doctors were about to pull the plug on that idea.* I had assumed Wendell was waiting for an organ donor to die, but now I remembered that a kidney could come from a live donor as well. Had Derek been planning to give his father one of his kidneys?

I quickly scanned the psychological profile. Derek was described as "a stable man with a strong Christian faith, a bit indecisive, but eager to help his father in any way possible." At the end of the report, the psychiatrist had given Derek what essentially amounted to the transplant seal of approval.

I put the report away and slid the drawer shut, then headed from Derek's room to the opposite end of the hall and Judith's room. Her suite was identical to Derek's, though she had turned the second bedroom into an office. The desk itself was neat but functional, with the computer surrounded by stacks of papers. Next to the phone was a small blank pad of paper, the top page clearly indented, and I slipped the pad into my pocket. I was going through the other stacks of paper and looking in drawers when I first heard the noise. My heart stopped and I froze, listening. There it was again. Someone else was in the house and coming up the stairs.

I darted into Judith's living room and over to the door, peeking out. The hallway was dark, and all I could see was the foot of someone slipping into my bedroom, down the hall.

This person, whoever it was, had come here for me. I wondered if it was the same guy who had been following me earlier in the city. Heart pounding, I scanned Judith's room, desperately trying to think of a good hiding place. If her closet was as big as Derek's, I decided, then that would probably be my best choice.

Silently, I ran to the closet and stepped inside, glad to see that both sides were filled to overflowing with clothes. Pushing my way between two coats, I climbed up on a small shelf about six inches high and flattened myself against the back wall, pushing the coats back into place in front of me. My face just peeked over the top of the hangers, so I crouched down, quietly removed a jacket from a hanger, and draped it over my head, covering everything but my eyes.

I stayed there a long time, listening, wishing I had thought to arm myself with something before I hid, some sort of blunt instrument. There was a rack of shoes to my left, and I snaked my arm out through the clothes and ran my hand along the shelf, feeling among the shoes for the highest, sharpest pair of heels I could find. Near the back of the shelf, my fingers closed over something else, something that felt like a handle. I pulled it out, surprised to find myself holding onto a wide paintbrush. I paused, confused, then shoved it into my pocket and reached out again, this time grabbing a satin stiletto-heeled pump. I held the shoe close to my chest, knowing it wouldn't offer much defense but feeling it was better than nothing.

I could hear noises again, moving closer, and I knew that the person was in Judith's living room and then her bedroom. I poised myself for action. If he did catch sight of me in the closet, my best move would be to spring out at him, immobilizing him with a heel to the face before running away.

Finally, a shadow fell across the doorway to the closet.

"Callie?" I heard. "Ms. Webber?"

It sounded like the voice of Nick, the chef. I hesitated, trying to decide what to do. He was supposed to be at the wake; what was he doing here? Did he mean me harm?

He stepped closer, and I knew I had a decision to make. Should I reveal myself to him, or keep hiding? I was certain only of one thing: If he did indeed mean me harm, there was no way I would ever gain the upper hand in such a confined space. He was just too physically overpowering.

He had just turned to leave when I heard a distinct crack beneath me. In time that felt like slow motion yet was only a split second, the shelf under my feet split in two, causing me to lose my footing and tumble forward, through the clothes, onto the floor. Nick yelled, backing away as I landed at his feet on the ground. My heart pounding, I looked up at him in fear.

"Callie!" he exclaimed. "What are you doing? Are you okay?"

He leaned over to help me. I let him lift me to my feet, and then I took a deep breath, letting it out slowly.

"You scared me to death!" he said. "Are you alright?"

"You scared me!" I said, my mind already racing for an explanation. "You know I've been borrowing Judith's clothes, so I came in here to find something to wear, and then I heard someone in the hall. I guess I just panicked. I hid."

To cover my burning face, I bent down and examined the shelf that I had broken. It wasn't a real shelf, I realized as I looked at it, but just a plastic box, filled with heavy sweaters. The lid was pushed in where I had been standing and I pressed it back out with a snap.

"I am sorry I frightened you," Nick said. "Marion wanted me to come back and check on you because you never showed up. She was worried."

I looked at my watch, startled to see that over an hour had passed since they left the house.

"I...I fell asleep!" I said stupidly. "I thought I'd rest my eyes for just a minute, and I ended up falling sound asleep. Then when I woke up, I came looking in Judith's closet for something to wear. You know, because I don't have many clothes here."

I made myself stop talking, knowing that whenever I lied I always ended up babbling. *You know a person's lying,* Eli always told me, *when they give you too much information.*

Nick studied me for a moment, an odd look on his face.

"Well," he said finally, "that explains it."

"Yeah."

"Sorry I frightened you."

"Sorry I frightened *you.*"

He waited as I hastily gathered an outfit suitable for the wake. Then we walked together back through Judith's bedroom and living room and into the hall. When we reached the top of the stairs, Nick paused.

"I will just wait for you down here, in the foyer," he said. "You can ride with me."

"Sure," I said, heading for my room.

Once there, I stepped inside and closed the door behind me, leaning back against it, my knees trembling so badly that I could hardly stand. Quickly, I removed the paintbrush and the pad of papers from my pockets and, as quietly as I could, tucked them behind the radiator next to the paper bag. Later, when I had more time, I would examine both items more closely. For now, I had no choice but to pull myself together and get ready for the wake.

Twenty-Three

We reached the funeral home at eight o'clock. The parking lot was so full we had to park on the street. On the way over, Nick told me proudly of some of the people who had already come, including a congressman, one minor TV star, and a famous clothing designer.

Once we were inside, Nick went off without me, and I hesitated in the front hall. I still hadn't gotten a handle on my fright back at the house, and I took a moment to gather my wits about me. The problem was that I was going from one trauma to another: Since Bryan's death, I had managed to avoid funerals and funeral homes. Now, standing here, the smells and sounds of the place assaulted me, and I felt my lungs growing tight, my head suddenly dizzy.

"You don't look so good."

I turned to see Carlos, strikingly handsome in his little suit and tie, his hair slicked straight back with some sort of shiny gel. He was standing in front of me, a worried expression on his face.

"I don't feel so good," I said lamely, wishing I could get some control over myself. Without speaking, I let him lead me around the corner, away from the crowd, to a nearby couch.

"On TV, they put their head between their legs," he said, and so I sat and leaned forward, suppressing a smile even as I felt my heart pounding wildly out of control. A moment later, there was a small hand on my back, and I sat up, accepting the cup of water that Carlos held out for me.

"Thank you," I said, taking a sip. I closed my eyes and prayed for peace. I thought of the Bible verse Eli gave to me, and I repeated it to myself now. Within moments, I felt the calming of my heart, the amazing stillness that only the Holy Spirit can provide.

"I think I'll be okay," I said finally to Carlos, who was still looking at me with concern. "Thank you for your kindness." He nodded and sat back on the couch next to me, swinging his legs in front of him. "So how's it going?" I asked.

He shrugged.

"I'm okay now. When we first got here, they were fighting over whether to have the casket open or closed. That wasn't too cool."

"Did you see your grandfather's body?"

"He looked like an old wax dummy. It gave me the creeps."

"That gives me the creeps, too," I said. "When my husband died, I insisted the casket stay closed." I didn't bother to add that, given the nature of his accident, there really wasn't much choice in the matter.

Carlos looked at me in surprise.

"Your husband's dead? Gosh, you're not that old. I mean, you're old, but not *that* old."

"Not old like a grandmother, you mean?"

He nodded.

"My husband was in an accident," I said. "He would still be alive if it hadn't happened."

"Wow."

"This is the first wake I've been to since then."

"Is that why you got sick when you came in?"

"Yeah," I said, "that's why I got sick."

We sat there in companionable silence for a while, until finally Sidra came out and joined us.

"There you are, sweetie," she said softly, sitting on the other side of Carlos. "You holding up okay?"

"I am, but she wasn't," he said, pointing at me. "She was sick. I got her some water and made her put her head between her legs."

Sidra glanced at me with concern.

"I think you've got a little doctor here," I said, smiling. "He was very professional."

"That's the kind of boy he is," she said, wrapping an arm around his shoulders and pulling him in for a hug. "Always taking care of everyone."

"Sidra," Derek said suddenly, appearing in the doorway. I could see Sidra's shoulders stiffening as she released Carlos from his hug.

"What?" she answered, not meeting Derek's eyes.

"The Hansens are here. I think you should come out and say hello."

"Of course," Sidra said softly. She gave Carlos a pat on the knee and then stood and went with Derek.

"I'm sorry your parents are having problems," I said suddenly to Carlos, once they were gone. I wasn't sure if it was a subject he would be willing to discuss, but I knew most kids were pretty aware of the things going on around them.

"It'll all work out," he said breezily. "I have a few ideas."

"Ideas?"

He glanced at me, then turned away.

"Never mind."

I could see from the set of his jaw that he wasn't going to say any more. I wondered what possible impact a child his age could have on his own parents' failing marriage. But then I thought of the blood on the windowsills—painted the night he was off on his soccer trip—and I knew there were other forces here, other elements to this mix besides just two adults who couldn't get along.

"Your mother is so beautiful," I said, steering us toward more neutral territory. "Is she Spanish?"

"From Honduras."

"Wow," I said. "How did she end up in Pennsylvania?"

"My dad."

"Ah."

"She lived near one of Grandpa's factories there. That's how they met, when Dad went with Grandpa on one of his trips."

"How romantic."

"Yeah, I guess. My dad says he fell in love with her at first sight. Then, when he became a missionary, he got them to send him there so he could marry her."

"I see." The story was fascinating, but it was in the shorthand of an 11-year-old boy. I wanted the long version.

"Anyway, I've been there a few times. It's a long plane ride, but really fun. My other grandparents live there."

"Cool."

Carlos stood and walked to the door.

"Guess I better go inside," he said. "You think you'll be okay?"

I stood, smoothing my skirt in front of me.

"I'll be fine," I said. "Just fine."

The place was packed, the crowd spilling into every available space. I gave Marion a hug and apologized for my delay, then positioned myself near the front of the receiving line, listening as everyone who came through spoke about the wonderful Wendell Smythe and what an amazing man he had been, not to mention their shock at learning his death had been a murder. I began to appreciate the extent of his popularity when the mayor of Philadelphia came through, addressing Marion by her first name, talking with her as though they were old friends.

After a while I grew tired of the crush of the crowd, and I made my way back out to the guest book in the front hall. There were pages and pages of signatures, most of which would mean nothing to me. Next to the book was a laminated copy of Wendell's obituary, and I picked it up and read it with interest.

Apparently, though Wendell had made his fortune in clothing, he was going to be remembered mostly for his contributions in human rights. I was surprised to see that besides Feed the Need, he was on the board of several other charitable organizations and in fact had sponsored the passage of quite a few humanitarian laws in Honduras, where his largest clothing factory was located.

He was also described as a generous supporter of his church as well as a few museums and the arts. "An avid collector of antique clothing," the article said, "Smythe has bequeathed the remainder of his private collection to the Philadelphia Museum of Art. The museum already houses quite a number of pieces previously donated by Mr. Smythe and his wife."

According to the article, he was survived by his wife, one sister, and his children and grandchild. Two brothers had preceded him in death.

"He was quite a man, wasn't he?" I heard over my shoulder. I turned to find Gwen standing behind me. She was immaculately attired, the pearls on her ears now replaced with a pair of square-cut emeralds.

"You go on in, dear," she said to the man next to her. "I'll be there in a minute."

The man patted her shoulder and walked away; I assumed that was her husband, Frank.

"I just wanted to apologize for being so brusque with you at the office today," Gwen said to me, taking hold of my elbow. "I didn't mean to be rude. I was just a little overwhelmed."

"I understand," I said, though I didn't. I still thought she was holding out on me regarding important information about the need for the J.O.S.H.U.A. money.

"Have you been inside yet?" she asked.

"Yes. The family seems to be holding up well," I replied. "So far, anyway."

"Poor Marion," Gwen said. "I don't know what I'll do when Frank dies. I only pray I go first."

Still holding my elbow, she led me with her into the main room where we joined her husband in the long line that snaked almost to the door.

"So, Gwen," I said after she made the necessary introductions, "I was wondering if you could tell me a bit about the hunger relief business. I don't know much beyond what I've seen on those late-night TV commercials."

She enthusiastically launched into an explanation of how needs were identified and then how the money they raised was distributed. As we slowly worked our way up in the line, she talked about Feed the Need's efforts toward education regarding proper health and hygiene, nutrition, farming, and medical care, all of which helped improve a needy community's standard of living. As she spoke, I recalled a mission trip I once took to Haiti as a teenager with my church. The need there was so great, and our group's resources so limited, that I had spent most of the time on the verge of tears, aching for the suffering that could've been so easily alleviated with a little money from other, more prosperous countries. That trip had overwhelmed me with despair, and it had taken me years to come to grips with the devastating poverty I had witnessed there.

"Do you really bring in enough money to these countries to make a difference, though?" I asked. "It seems to me that the suffering is just so tremendous."

"We can't look at it that way. For every water pump we install in a village in Africa, for every well we dig in Korea, for every health worker we place in Mexico—we've made a difference. We've changed someone's life for the better."

"I suppose it all helps the giver, too. Gives them a feeling of altruism, of making a difference themselves."

To my surprise, Frank grunted and turned his head.

"Oh, you hush," Gwen said to him. "Yes, Callie, it does help the giver. We live in such a wealthy country; we should all be sharing that wealth."

"Frank?" I said. "You have an opinion here?"

He grinned and shook his head.

"I respect what they're doing there," he said. "I just don't agree with the means."

"How so?"

"It's an ongoing debate in our house," Gwen explained. "Frank has a problem with the whole starving-child angle."

"It's exploitation, it is," he said. "You show me a picture of an emaciated child and tell me my $20 a month or whatever will change her life. Of course I'm going to send you money."

"Doesn't the money go to help the child?"

Gwen hesitated and then spoke, lowering her voice.

"For the most part, the money is pooled. One person's donation won't go very far, but the combination of lots of donations can help pay for schools, food, health care, and so on."

"Yeah," Frank said, also lowering his voice, "but with some of those hunger relief organizations, the things your money's paying for aren't even in the same village as the child you're sponsoring— sometimes not even in the same country! I give my $20 to help little Jose in El Salvador, and unbeknownst to me, it's used to pay for an irrigation system in Mozambique!"

"But people are still being helped," Gwen said. "Regardless of where the money is ultimately being used."

"Exploitation," he insisted, shaking his head. "I'm getting these cute little photos and sweet letters and patting myself on the back for making a difference in the life of this child. In reality, this child's life hasn't changed at all. Maybe an extra sack of rice at Christmas time. Other than that, he's still living in squalor, and my monthly donations haven't helped him one bit. And it's not just Feed the Need. Almost all the hunger relief organizations work that way."

"Charity is charity," Gwen countered in what I could tell was their well-worn debate. "Your money still goes to help the needy one way or another. And at least with Feed the Need, the majority of the money goes into the program and not to support some exorbitant CEO's salary."

"Yeah, the money is spent wisely. But they're still using the innocent little faces of children to get that money out of my pocket. I have a problem with that."

The three of us were silent for a moment. I could see both sides of the argument equally. Though in my heart I agreed with Gwen, as a nonprofit professional I had to side with Frank. One of the basic tenets of good stewardship is that "all statements made by the organization in its fund raising appeals about the use of the gift must be honored by the organization." In other words, the money you raise should always go to the exact cause you stated that it would go for in your money-raising efforts. Anything else was fraudulent.

"What you really should have a problem with," Gwen said softly to her husband, "is the American people. As a whole, they don't respond to intellectual information. Tell them some remote village somewhere needs a well or an irrigation system, and forget it. But show them a hungry child, and they're there. They give their money based purely on emotion."

"Yeah," Frank agreed. "You know what they say in this business, Callie? They say, 'You wanna build a well? You won't collect a dime until you've given that well an adorable face with pouting lips and big sad eyes.'"

Twenty-Four

I was heading outside for some fresh air when I happened to glance at Marion. Our eyes met through the crowd, and she waved me over, so I abandoned my plans for a moment and went to join her.

When I got there, I was surprised to see her standing with her pastor, Ian Quinn.

"Pastor," I said, my surprise evident. He nodded at me.

"Ian was just asking about you," Marion continued. "He didn't realize you were with the J.O.S.H.U.A. Foundation."

"You should've told me you worked for Tom this afternoon, child," he said, taking my hand. "I might not've kicked you out quite so abruptly."

"You're familiar with Tom and the foundation?" I asked.

"You have no idea!" he cried, beaming. "Let me tell you what you people have done for us. And call me Ian, please."

Glad to see that the pastor and I had connected, Marion excused herself and then turned to face another grouping of people.

"I'd love to hear about it," I said, "but if I don't get some fresh air very soon, I'm afraid I'll pass out."

"It is a bit crowded in here," he replied, taking my arm. "What do you say we go for a walk outside?"

The warm air soothed me like a balm. I breathed it in slowly, feeling my heart return to a steady, even rhythm. So far, I had been holding up very well, but I didn't want to push it too far. I took Ian's arm, and we walked through the parking lot and out onto the sidewalk beyond. It was a clear night, full of stars. Light from bright street lamps spilled down onto the strip of closed shops surrounding us.

"Is it safe here at night?" I asked.

"Absolutely," said Ian. "I think we can walk to the end of the streetlights and back."

That we did, strolling the blocks with ease. Ian told me all about his soup kitchen, about the money from Tom that got it all started. I listened with interest because this had taken place several years before I came to work for Tom.

"Of course, he didn't head an official foundation back then," Ian said. "He was just a wealthy man with a yen for giving to needy causes. Wendell put the two of us together, and even though Tom didn't know me from Adam, once he took a look at my business plan for the soup kitchen, he pulled out his wallet and wrote me a check for $5000."

I smiled, knowing that sounded exactly like something Tom would do.

"Of course," Ian continued, "I know that must sound like a piddling little sum to you, considering the amounts you people dole out these days. But it was a godsend for me, I'll tell you. That money made the difference that got us off and running."

"I'm so glad."

We chatted about his soup kitchen until we reached the end of the lighted sidewalk. As if prearranged, we both stopped and turned around and headed back toward the funeral home.

"My late wife loved strolling at night," he said wistfully, out of the blue. "Especially on an evening like this when the temperature is pleasant and the sky is so clear."

"My late husband was the same way," I replied. "Loved being out at night, loved looking at the stars."

We glanced at each other and smiled, acknowledging without words that we were both members of the same club—a club that neither of us wanted to belong to.

We were silent for a moment after that, each of us lost in our thoughts. My mind drifted from memories of my own happy marriage to that of Derek and Sidra and their current marital disaster.

"So, Ian," I said, forming my words carefully as we walked, "I assume you are aware of the odd things that have happened to Sidra lately."

"Yes, I am."

"What can you tell me about it? Obviously, she's in a lot of pain."

"It's an awful situation."

"How did it start?"

Ian looked at me, apparently deciding how much he should say. As the family's pastor, he surely had some confidentiality issues. On the other hand, he knew that I was an experienced professional on an investigation. Anything he told me might help to unravel this mess.

"I'm here to find out who murdered Wendell," I said softly. "I think this business with Derek and Sidra might be related to it."

He nodded, finally coming to a stop at the edge of the parking lot. If he was going to tell me this tale, I assumed, he was at least going to do it where we couldn't be overheard.

"I can tell you things that I learned from Marion because she asked me to. But anything that I may have heard from Sidra is of course confidential."

"Of course."

"It all started a few months ago," he began, "following an argument between Sidra and Derek. Apparently, Derek had bought Sidra a sable coat as a gift, but when she learned what it cost, she had had a fit. Despite the fact that they could well afford it, she accused him of having changed, of having becoming materialistic and wasteful.

He was hurt by her accusations, not to mention her rejection of his gift, and they went to bed angry. The next morning when they got up, the coat had been slashed to ribbons."

I realized that was the coat I had discovered earlier, in the box at the top of Sidra's closet.

"That, however, was just the beginning," continued Ian. "Derek blamed Sidra; Sidra blamed Derek. A few weeks later, Derek found his good leather briefcase, filled with important papers, submerged in a bathtub full of water. The next day, there was a bouquet of black roses waiting on the front step. The envelope was addressed to Sidra, and the card said, 'Black is for death. I wish you were dead.'"

"Oh my goodness," I whispered.

"Sidra was so frightened she wanted to move back to Honduras. But Derek refused to let her take Carlos with her. With Sidra's history of mental problems, she knew he had her over a barrel and that she had no choice but to stay. She's been suffering in silence ever since, but I know she's got to be at the end of her rope. Out of the whole family, I think only Wendell truly believed that she wasn't doing these things to herself."

"And now he's dead," I said.

"Yes. Now he's dead."

We began walking again, across the parking lot toward the funeral home.

"Let me ask you a question," I said. "What do you really know about Sidra's mental state?"

"Sidra had…some problems, a few years back. She's much, much better now. But for some people, I think it's easier to blame her 'condition' than it is to consider that this might be something else entirely."

"So, in your opinion, she's not doing these horrid things herself?"

"In my opinion, no, she is not."

"Do you fear for her safety?"

"I fear more for her marriage, not to mention her child's sense of security. I think if someone were out to harm Sidra, they would've done so by now. This stuff is all so juvenile, so theatrical. I don't see it so much as a threat to her physically as it is a threat to her emotionally."

"But now Wendell's been murdered!" I exclaimed. "Don't you think it's possible that someone has upped the ante and gone over the edge? That Sidra might be next?"

He was thoughtful for a moment, one finger pressing nervously against his chin.

"I hadn't thought if it that way," he said finally. "I suppose perhaps we all should take it more seriously now."

"Even before Wendell's murder," I said, "I just don't see why the Smythes wouldn't contact the police. At the very least, you'd think they would've installed a better security system."

We reached the door of the funeral home. Ian hesitated, pausing thoughtfully.

"As for Marion," he said, "she's so completely convinced that it's Sidra that she won't even consider any other possibility. She's terribly afraid that calling the police or hiring a security company will only prove her daughter-in-law's precarious mental state. Maybe even force them to commit her, like before."

"Like before? Sidra was in a mental institution?"

Ian colored, looking uncomfortable, and I knew he felt that he had outstepped the bounds of confidentiality.

"I'm sorry," I said quickly. "I'm just trying to get a better handle on what's going on."

"I think it's all perhaps best expressed in the words of John Donne," he said, accepting my apology with a nod. "'As states subsist in part by keeping their weaknesses from being known, so is it the quiet of families to have their chancery and their parliament within doors, and to compose and determine all emergent differences there.'"

"In other words, it's a family matter, and they'd like to keep it that way?"

"Exactly, my dear," he replied, opening the door. "That's it exactly."

Twenty-Five

~

Back at the house once the wake was over, the remaining friends and family members seemed reluctant to disperse. Even Sidra didn't head immediately to the cabana, but instead came into the den with everyone else and sat on the couch in the corner with Carlos. It seemed as if they all needed to be together, to rehash the events of the evening, and though I was exhausted, I was glad. My head was also spinning with the sheer quantity of people who had been there. I wanted to sit back and listen to what everyone else had to say.

I also was interested in watching Alan Bennet and Judith Smythe. They were friendly but not too personal, their relationship seemingly befitting a boss and her employee. I looked around at the others and wondered if anyone besides me knew they were romantically involved.

It wasn't long before Angelina came into the room with a tray of delicious-smelling hot hors d'oeuvres. Marion, eyes closed in her chair next to the fireplace, reached out and took the girl's hand.

"Angelina," she said in a tired voice. "This is not a night for serving us food. You and Nick come, join in, and relax with everyone else. It's been a hard day."

"No, no," said Angelina, placing the tray on a low table in a central spot. Carlos came over and began snacking immediately. Having missed dinner, I, too, was hungry and would've loved to dig in, but I didn't want to appear too overeager. "This is time for family."

"Callie's just a friend," Marion said, waving toward me. "So is Alan. And Ian. Please. I insist."

Angelina hesitated in the doorway and then smiled.

"Nick is heating up a couple of different things. When he is all done, we will bring them in and join you."

"Good."

"And I expect every one of you to eat some," Angelina added. "Everybody just picked at their dinner. You do not want to hurt Nick's feelings."

Next to me, Derek chuckled as Angelina left the room.

"She's right about that, Mother. You haven't been eating much."

"Who can eat, darling? My heart is broken."

The conversation went on from there, and I listened quietly, eating a few of the heavenly hors d'oeuvres as they were brought in. At one point, I offered to help with the coffee and Angelina accepted; together we brought in a large bubbling coffeepot, a tray of cups and saucers, and the sugar and cream. Once everyone was served, she and Nick sat on a low bench along the wall and joined in the conversation.

Despite the somber occasion, things did begin to lighten up somewhat after that. I think it started with Carlos trying to eat the cheese from around an hors d'oeuvre, which made Marion giggle, which in turn made us all laugh. We were punchy and exhausted and in need of a release.

Everyone began tossing out memories of Wendell—good memories of happy times. Obviously, this was a man who had been loved by those close to him. I listened to their stories, thankful that this was a family who believed in the Lord. Though they were mourning Wendell now for their own loss, behind the mourning was a joy, a complete assurance that he was with his Maker. I wondered how it would feel to mourn the death of a man who *hadn't* had the assurance of heaven?

The only odd thing about the whole evening was that no one mentioned the fact that Wendell had been murdered. To listen to them, one would think he had gone in his sleep or suffered a heart attack. I suppose that was probably how it felt because his health had been so bad. Still, I thought it odd. If my father had been murdered and the killer had not been caught, that would be the *only* thing on my mind.

After about an hour, the conversation began to die down and the small crowd dwindled somewhat. I carried the cold coffeepot back into the kitchen, then headed for the pantry to put away the sugar. I just had my hand on the doorknob when I heard a noise from inside, and I hesitated, listening. I heard it again—a distinctive whisper coming from behind the pantry door. Carefully, I pushed it open without a sound, just far enough to peek inside. The room was small and narrow, the size of a walk-in closet, with shelves lining each of the walls, floor to ceiling, which were stacked with cans and dry goods. Down at the other end, I could still hear whispering, and I strained to listen.

"Nick will kill me," the voice said, and I recognized it immediately as Angelina's. "You know that he will."

A man responded but I couldn't hear what he was saying. Heart pounding, I pushed the door a little farther and dared to stick my head far enough in so that I could see.

What I saw nearly made me gasp. There, in the back corner of the pantry, was Angelina in a fervent embrace with Alan Bennet—the very same man I had seen about to make love to Judith the night before!

"He does not want us to be together," Angelina moaned, eyes closed, as Alan slowly ran a trail of kisses down her neck.

"But *I* want us to be together," he whispered urgently. "I *need* us to be together."

"I know," she cried. "I know. But Nick will kill us if he finds us!"

She offered Alan only slight resistance, and soon his hands were working the buttons down the back of her blouse. Watching, I thought of the photo in her bedroom, of the scribbled hearts and the notation "our special place." The other half of "our," I realized, must be Alan Bennet. I pulled the door closed and then stood for a long moment in the hall, heart pounding. Surely it was only a figure of speech; the girl didn't really fear for her life, did she? Nevertheless, this new development was shocking. I wondered if Judith had any idea about Alan and Angelina.

On the other hand, I wondered if Angelina knew anything about Alan and Judith.

Twenty-Six

I awoke with a start, and it took me a minute to figure out where I was. The lights were off, but the faint glow of the moon spilled in through the window, and slowly I could make out the four walls of the guest bedroom in the Smythes' home. The clock said 12:35 A.M. I must have fallen asleep.

I sat up, rubbing my eyes. I remembered coming up here and sitting on the bed, thinking I would rest my eyes for just a moment. Now I had a stiff neck and two bobby pins stabbing me in the back of the head.

I reached up and massaged my scalp. Letting my hair loose, I shook it out and then caught my breath. *My dream.* In my dream, I had taken down my hair from a ponytail, shaking it slowly while Bryan watched from the doorway. He had loved my long hair, had loved running his fingers through it. In the dream, he had come to me and taken my hand, pulling me outside into the dark night to look at the stars.

It seemed so *real.*

I stood and went to the bureau, reaching for a brush, stroking it through my hair vigorously. I hadn't dreamed about Bryan in a long,

long time. Why now did this have to happen, this awakening of my memories, this eclipsing of time?

My heart pounded with the memory of the dream. It had been this way in the beginning, in the weeks after his death when all I'd wanted to do was to sleep, to hide, to disappear. Bryan came to me in my dreams sometimes, and I had spent those early days in a tranquilized stupor, waiting for the sleeping visions where he was still alive and life was back to normal.

In the years since, of course, I had moved past all of that, and in fact most dreams of him these days were almost always odd, disjointed, and blurry. Yet the dream I'd had this time was as clear and memorable as in the early days, as if he had really come to me, as if it really happened. *Please, Lord,* I prayed, *why this? Why now?*

I put down the hairbrush, turned on the lamp, and retrieved my Bible from the bedside table. *It isn't fair,* my mind cried as I flipped through the pages for some sort of verse, some sort of message to comfort me.

There was solace there, but I was too agitated to find it, and finally I set the book aside and got down on my knees, pleading with God to heal my aching heart. How could a wound tear open after three years, a wound as fresh and painful as it had been that first day? *I want my husband back! I want Bryan in my life again, as alive and real and happy as he was in my dream.*

My plea felt unheard, though I knew it wasn't. In the end, I simply recited the Lord's prayer, letting its familiar rhythm soothe my aching heart. Once my prayer was over, I wiped the tears from my face and stood, going over to the window and gazing out across the wide expanse of lawn. It was a beautiful night, crisp and clear.

I felt a little more calm, but still there lingered an infinite sadness. I sat in the chair next to the window and counted the stars and thought about Bryan and how much he had loved the night sky. He knew the names of hundreds of stars, and when we were first married, we would take our sleeping bags out into the backyard and look up at the sky and make up names for the ones he didn't know. We called one CB220—for Callie and Bryan and February twentieth, the day we were married. I tried to find CB220 now, and as I did I felt an ache of pure loneliness, a pain so agonizing that it made me double over.

"I miss you," I whispered, the tears starting up again. "Bryan, how I miss you so."

I cried, as quietly as I could manage, but still I cried. After a while, I wasn't even crying for me anymore; I was crying for Marion, for all the women I knew who had loved their husbands and then lost them. I cried for the babies Bryan and I would never have. I cried for myself, for the lonely life I had carved out of a little house on an isolated stretch of the Chesapeake, with only a few close friends and a dog to keep me company. I cried until I didn't have any more tears. I cried until the sharp pain of loss turned to a dull ache. Then I sat for a long time, staring out at nothing, wishing this job could be finished and I could return to the peace and quiet of my own life, to the safety of a place that didn't make me continuously confront my own unspeakable loss.

Twenty-Seven

Despite my own personal sorrow, I had a job to do. At 2:00 A.M., I knew it was time to put on my surveillance gear and get on out to my hidden perch in the tree house. I dug through my pile of clothes and pulled out black pants and a black sweater. The only shoes I had were my good Ferragamo pumps and a pair of sneakers on loan from Judith. I put on the sneakers and then pulled a pair of black socks on over them. I knew I would ruin the socks, but I also knew that it wouldn't do if my bright white feet were spotted as I made my way across the lawn.

Once I was finished with the shoes, I turned my attention to my hair, fashioning it back into its tight chignon. Grabbing a blanket from the bed, I tightly rolled it up and tucked it under my arm, then stealthily headed out into the night.

It was quiet and cooler outside, and I closed the back door with only a faint click. The nearly full moon was both a blessing and a hindrance, and I knew that the sooner I got up into that tree house, the safer I would be. I made a wide arc around the garden and headed toward the back of the property along the fence. Once at the end, I saw there was no car parked there in Alan's spot, no fresh footprints on the grass. Nevertheless, I crept to the barn and took a peek through the knothole, but the barn was quiet and dark.

Nearly running now, I crossed the lawn and reached the tree, quickly finding a ladder of boards nailed at 12-inch intervals up the side of the trunk. I climbed carefully until I reached the platform. Pulling myself through the hole and into the tree house, I looked around the small area, relieved to see that it was devoid of any nocturnal creatures and in fact held nothing more than an old faded comic book and a few spider webs.

I folded up the blanket into a square and used it as a cushion against the hard wooden floor. The tree house seemed sturdy enough, with room to sit fully upright beneath the child-sized ceiling. It certainly provided me with an excellent view. It was built almost like a watchtower, with window openings on all four sides. By shifting around, I could see the house, the barn, the poolside cabana, and nearly everything in between.

I settled down and waited, watching the house, listening to the night sounds, wondering if this lost night of sleep would be in vain. As I peered across the quiet lawn, I wished I had a good pair of binoculars. I knew Eli would never have set out on a job like this without first stocking up on the necessities: binoculars, camera, tape recorder, Thermos full of coffee, and a little food.

I thought about Eli now, tangoing his way across his living room in Florida. The last case he took before his retirement had been to track the movements of a wealthy widow, helping her children to prove that the woman was mentally unfit and ought to be declared incompetent. Instead, he found himself falling in love with the woman, who absolutely had all of her faculties and was just a bit eccentric. After the trial, during which she succeeded in putting to rest any and all questions of her mental capacity, she asked Eli to marry her. They now lived in a condo in a retirement community, deliriously happy, taking long walks on the beach every morning and playing cribbage at the local Senior Center on Tuesdays.

I shivered, thinking that I could do with a little Florida sunshine right about now. It felt as though it was getting colder up in the tree house, and it didn't help that the wind was poking its way down my back and chilling my neck. I was just adjusting the blanket so I could half sit on it, half use it as a covering, when I spotted some movement near the cabana.

With a shock, I realized it was Carlos. He was climbing out of his bedroom window—one of the windows that had earlier that day been coated with fake blood, but had since been washed clean. He was wearing what looked like army fatigues, and he carried something small and black in his hand that looked like a boom box or a radio. With my heart pounding, I watched as he quietly pulled the window shut and then set off across the lawn.

He was coming straight toward me! As he got closer, I peered down at him, wondering what he could possibly have in his hand. A *camcorder*, I finally realized. Carlos was carrying a camcorder, and he was heading for the tree house.

I didn't know what to do. My gut feeling was that he had come out here to do a little surveillance of his own. Why else would he be bringing a video camera? Unfortunately, if he climbed up in the tree, pulled himself through the hole, and came face-to-face with me, he might nearly scream his head off, alerting the entire family to our presence here.

With no other choice, I silently positioned myself next to the hole across from the tree trunk, so that as he emerged into the room his back would be toward me. Kneeling, muscles taut, I waited until he was almost completely through the opening, and then I grabbed him, clamping one hand over his mouth and wrapping the other around his chest, pinning his arms to his sides. I jerked us both backward, safely away from the hole, as his camera dropped onto the wooden floor. He thrashed about wildly, trying to get loose, trying to kick me, but unable to make a sound. I held on tight, surprised at the strength of an 11-year-old boy, whispering as urgently as I could, over and over, "It's Callie; I won't hurt you…calm down." When he finally stopped thrashing and began listening, I spoke more softly.

"It's Callie. Don't make any sound. Do you understand?"

He nodded, my hand still firmly over his mouth.

"I'm not going to hurt you. I'm an investigator, Carlos. I'm out here on surveillance. Do you hear what I'm saying?"

Again, he nodded. Under my right arm, I could feel his heart pounding against his chest. I had very nearly scared the poor boy to death.

"I'm going to let go now," I whispered. "Don't make any noise."

I did as I said, releasing him from my grip and sliding back against the wall. He scampered across the wooden platform to the safety of the tree trunk, which he held onto like a shield. But he didn't climb back down; he merely stared at me around the tree with wide, terrified eyes.

"Are you okay?" I asked.

"You're an investigator?" he finally whispered. "You mean, like a spy?"

"Yes," I said. "I wasn't going to hurt you. I just didn't want you to scream."

It seemed to take a few minutes for him to digest this information, but when he did, he seemed to relax somewhat. He reached out for his camera and busied himself by examining it, making sure it hadn't gotten damaged in our scuffle.

"A spy?" he asked finally. "Like James Bond?"

I shrugged.

"Not exactly," I replied. "More like the Hardy Boys." He looked at me blankly so I added, "Sherlock Holmes?"

That one seemed to ring a bell. He scooted closer toward me.

"Are you trying to find out who's been doing all those things to my mom?" he asked.

I nodded, not bothering to add that primarily I was trying to find out who killed his grandfather.

"That's why I'm here, too!" he whispered. "I got the camera and everything."

"You're certainly prepared."

"I have to be," he said, taking a seat next to me on the blanket and peering through the camera lens toward the house. "This time, I've just got to catch her on tape."

"Her?"

"My Aunt Judith. She's the one who's doing it."

I sat back and exhaled slowly, remembering my conversation with Carlos at the funeral home. *I have some ideas,* he had said then. Apparently, I realized now, he really did.

We sat there side by side in the darkness, watching the house and grounds, while Carlos gave me his version of all that had been happening. He told me about the incident with the sable coat that started it all and the other weird things that occurred as the situation escalated. Carlos described how, as the incidents continued to happen, the family slowly began to take sides. Wendell thought Derek might be the one doing these things; Marion thought it was Sidra who was doing them and then trying to make everyone think it was Derek. Though everyone in the family seemed to blame either Derek or Sidra for all of the hateful incidents, Carlos had felt certain that neither one was involved. Finally, Carlos had had an idea: He decided to stay up all night and try to catch the person himself.

It had taken a while, but finally he did it: Waiting in the tree house one night last week, Carlos had watched in shock as his Aunt Judith snuck out of the house, right about this same time, and placed a bouquet of black roses on the doorstep of the cabana before running back in. Knowing no one would believe him, Carlos didn't say anything to anyone. Instead, he decided to wait until after his weekend at the soccer tournament and then catch her on videotape. That was what brought him to the tree on this night. As he talked, I thought of the paintbrush I had found in Judith's closet, and I knew unquestionably that it must've been used to paint the fake blood on Sidra's window sills.

"I have to wait until Mom is asleep before I can sneak out," he said. "Tonight she was up really late."

"What makes you think Judith will do something tonight?" I asked.

He shrugged.

"I don't know," he said. "Just a hunch."

I waited with him, thinking how difficult this must be for a young boy. Despite Ian Quinn's elegant quote about families keeping things private, I couldn't understand why the Smythes—as moneyed as they were—hadn't set up some surveillance cameras of their own. I finally decided their reasoning was twofold: For one, the perp was surely some member of the family; sometimes it seemed better *not* to know things like that. The second reason was more complicated; for Derek, at least, it probably felt easier to let the marriage slip away than to get out there and do something about it.

"Callie, look!" Carlos whispered. I followed his gaze to see someone stepping out of the door of the house—someone who looked a lot like Judith. She was dressed in black, and in her hand she carried some sort of bottle.

She crept past the pool and the cabana until she was no longer in our sights.

"Go, go, go!" Carlos said as he struggled to slip through the hole of the tree house with the camcorder in his hand. He jumped the last five steps and then ran; I followed more carefully, just catching up to him as he passed the greenhouse and rounded the corner near the garage. We both froze along the side of the building, catching sight of Judith as she stepped inside the garage.

There was no way to see inside the garage without being seen, no windows except a small one on the door. I took a chance and peeked inside, but in the darkness all I could see was Judith standing at the far corner of the four-car garage, waving her arms, her back to me.

"What do we do?" Carlos whispered, the camera still whirring quietly in his hands. We crept back to the shadows together.

"Just film the door," I said quietly. "We'll get in there once she's gone."

It didn't take long—maybe a minute at the most. From our hidden spot along the wall, we watched as Judith stepped back out of the garage and then quickly sprinted across the lawn toward the house. Once she was inside the house, we headed into the garage.

We smelled its scent before we could see it—paint thinner or nail polish remover.

"Callie!" Carlos whispered, waving me over as he stood filming the hood of a pale green Mercury. As I got there, I realized that Judith had poured the chemical all over the hood of the car, and that the paint was slowly bubbling up, ruining the finish.

"That's my mom's car," Carlos said, lowering the camera. He looked at me with wide dark eyes, stunned at the destruction created by his own flesh and blood.

I couldn't think of a word to say that would comfort him.

Twenty-Eight

~

"No way!" Carlos said, a forkful of pancake headed for his mouth. "They actually shot at you? With a real gun?"

I smiled and nodded and told him to keep his voice down.

"When it was all over with," I said softly, recalling one of the more exciting cases in my investigative past, "they found a bullet in the wall, only three inches from where my head had been."

He let out a low whistle.

"Did you dig it out? Did you keep it?"

I responded by taking out my car keys and setting them on the table between us. The spent bullet was encased in Plexiglas and hooked to my keychain, a farewell gift from Eli, who told me I should always carry it around as a reminder of how close I had come to danger.

"Awesome," Carlos said for about the hundredth time. He held up the bullet and studied it closely, twisting it back and forth in the light.

I had been regaling Carlos with stories of my investigative past for the last hour. We were sitting at a corner table of a nearly empty diner, the sun just coming up outside. After the incident with Judith, I knew neither one of us would've been able to sleep, and so I had

Carlos leave a note for his mother saying that we had gone for an early breakfast and would be back later. Then he and I had gotten in my car and headed here. What Carlos didn't know was that while he was changing his clothes and getting cleaned up, I had also taken a moment to run into the main house and sneak into his father's room; I had left a message for Derek propped against his mirror, asking him to please meet us here as soon as he woke up.

Carlos had been an engaging breakfast companion, pumping me eagerly for information about "spy tools" and exciting assignments. I didn't tell him that most of my investigations these days rarely involved much more than sitting at a computer, poring through legal data. Let him think I was the next 007 if it would get him to cooperate with me and keep my identity a secret. In time, I would find the murderer of his grandfather, and then his life could return to normal—or as normal as could be expected, under the circumstances.

As we talked, I found myself watching the door. Then finally, at about 7:30, it swung open and in walked Derek. He came straight to our table, his face stern.

"What the heck is going on?" he asked, thrusting my note at me. It said, *Please meet us at the Town and Country Diner as soon as you get up. Don't tell anyone. Come right away.* I had signed it, *Callie Webber and Carlos.*

"I think you should sit down," I said calmly. "Carlos and I have something to tell you."

Concerned, he slid into the booth next to his son. In the light from the window, I could see that he hadn't shaved or even brushed his hair.

"Are you okay?" he asked Carlos.

Wide-eyed and excited, Carlos nodded back.

"Callie's a private eye, Dad," he said. "Did you know that? She's here on an investigation!"

Derek looked at me.

"Not exactly," I said. "I came here to deliver some money to Feed the Need. Then your father was murdered. I *stayed* for an investigation."

"Okay, take it back a few," Derek said. "You've both caught me totally off guard."

A waitress appeared then and poured Derek some coffee. Once she was gone, I tried to explain everything in terms that were simple and direct.

"I do investigations for the J.O.S.H.U.A Foundation," I said. "Programmatic investigations. Verifying the integrity of nonprofit organizations, making sure they do what they say they do, seeing that they spend their money in a responsible way. As you know, I came here to deliver a grant to your organization."

"A grant? To Feed the Need?"

His question threw me.

"Of course," I said. "You mean you didn't know about it? But you're the CEO."

He shook his head.

"I knew you were here on some sort of business with my father, but I never thought to ask what it was."

"But your mother told you that I work for Tom, for the foundation."

"I guess I just never put two and two together. I've been a little distracted."

"Your father asked us for $250,000. He said it was for a building you all wanted to buy."

"I can't imagine that," Derek said. "There's no building that I know of. My father never breathed a word of this to me."

"Is that unusual?" I asked.

"I would say so," he replied indignantly. "I should know everything that's going on with Feed the Need."

"Well," I continued, "anyway, when your father was killed, Tom asked me to investigate the murder. My background is in criminal work."

"Is that why you're staying at the house?"

"Partly," I answered. "The police won't let me leave town because I'm a material witness to your father's murder. But your mother knows that I'm investigating."

"What does my son have to do with any of this?" he said. "Why have you brought him into it?"

I smiled at Carlos.

"Well, as it turns out, Derek, Carlos has been doing a little investigating of his own. Why don't you tell him about that, Carlos?"

Suddenly shy, Carlos recounted the story of how he had seen Judith with the black roses and then set about trying to catch her mischief again on videotape.

"I got it on tape this time," he said, holding up the dark cassette for his father to see, telling him about the damaged car. "Now everybody has to believe me."

"It's Judith alright," I added.

Derek seemed truly stunned, and I felt for him as he looked from me back to his son. I told him that we needed to keep this information to ourselves for just a bit longer. Of course, if he wanted to go ahead and let Sidra know, that was up to him.

"Okay, buddy," he said, finally reaching out to squeeze Carlos' hand. "Thanks for telling me. Now Ms. Webber and I need to talk. You want some quarters for the game room?"

"Sure!"

Derek gave Carlos a ten-dollar bill and sent him to the cashier for an entire roll. Then Carlos ran to the little room at the back of the diner where we could watch him playing video games through a glass door.

"Unbelievable," Derek said finally, resting his head in his hands. "I couldn't imagine what was going on here this morning, but I can say this was the very last thing on earth I expected. Judith. My gosh, why?"

I wanted to trust Derek, but I still had some reservations.

"I have to ask you a question," I said, thinking back to the argument that I overheard that first afternoon. "Why did Sidra say that your father's death would be 'convenient' for you?"

He looked at me, confused.

"Your big argument. The day he died?"

"You heard us?"

I shrugged.

"It wasn't hard," I said. "You were practically yelling."

Not to mention the fact that I was hovering right outside the window, straining to catch every word.

The waitress came with more coffee, and Derek paused to order a full breakfast. When she was gone, he shook his head.

"We were about to file divorce papers. My father was going to testify on Sidra's behalf. No big surprise—he always had a soft spot for Sidra, especially once she took over his dialysis. He thought I was doing all of these nutty things and then trying to make it look like she did them."

"I see."

"I guess when he died, she lost the one person in the family who believed in her."

He looked out of the window, his mind a million miles away. I sipped my coffee, leaving him with the quiet of his thoughts, wondering if he was the murderer, if he had killed his own father.

"How does it all get so far offtrack?" he said finally, softly, more to himself than to me. I didn't respond, and after a moment, he spoke again, his voice distant and lost.

"The first time I saw Sidra, she was sitting in the doorway of her mother's *hacienda*, embroidering a shirt collar. She was so beautiful—and only 17. I was 20."

"In Central America?" I asked. He nodded.

"I went there with my dad," he said. "I liked going, liked the scenery and the culture. But I was changed after that trip. I wanted to get back. I wanted to get back to her."

"You finished seminary first."

"I'd always felt the call to be a missionary despite the fact that Dad wanted me to come into the business with him. Once I met Sidra, my mind was made up. I knew the Lord wanted me to be a missionary to Honduras. Sidra and I started writing, and we fell in love through our letters."

After graduation, Derek explained, he worked things out with the mission board and headed south, where he and Sidra were soon married. They lived in her small village and built up a church and a school there.

Their life was fulfilling but not always easy. A devout Christian, Sidra was the perfect helpmate for Derek's ministry. But as a woman of relative privilege who had been educated in Buenos Aires, Sidra found labor conditions in her homeland simply appalling. She often railed against the huge holes in the local labor laws that created sweatshops, holes that allowed children to work 12-hour days and women to spend seven days a week hunched over their sewing machines.

"She verbally attacked my father the first time they met, calling him a capitalist pig," Derek said, smiling at the memory. "Once he got her to calm down, they had a real conversation. After that, Smythe Incorporated became a humanitarian leader in the clothing industry, a leader in eradicating poor labor practices. My father and Sidra found a common ground, and together they accomplished a lot. They even managed to have some laws made there."

"Your wife strikes me as a very capable woman."

To my surprise, tears suddenly filled Derek's eyes.

"I seem to have lost sight of that lately," he said.

"So why were you so convinced it was her doing all of this crazy stuff, Derek? What's the big secret in her past that made you and your mother convict her without even a trial?"

"There's no big secret," he said, shaking his head. "Sidra's manic depressive. When she was pregnant with Carlos, she quit taking her medications and ended up having a nervous breakdown. I brought her up here to Pennsylvania to have her treated."

"Is that when you moved back to the states?"

"No," he said. "We took a year's sabbatical and stayed here until Carlos was born. After that, she was able to go back on her medications, and it wasn't long before she was fine again. When our year was up, we returned to Honduras. We stayed another six years after that."

"Has she had any other episodes like that?"

"No. As long as she stays on her medication, Sidra is fine."

"So what made you finally give up missionary life, Derek?"

He wiped at his eyes and looked off in the distance.

"I don't know exactly," he said. "Restlessness. Frustration. To be honest, I think I began to question whether it was *God* who had led me to be a missionary or just my own adventurous leanings. By then, Carlos was of an age where I found myself wishing for him the things *I* had had as a child. Soccer teams and American movies and horseback riding. I realized I didn't want the life of a missionary any more. I wanted the life I had grown up with. I wanted the life of privilege."

"So you moved here and bought the Jaguar and the fur coats and all the things you'd been missing out on."

"Hey," he said, frowning, "it's not like I sold out. I'm head of Feed the Need. We're doing wonderful things all over the world."

"I know."

"And coming here permanently gave Sidra the chance to go back to school and get her nursing degree."

"That's good."

"With my father in such poor health, I knew I would be needed here anyway," he continued, sounding even more defensive. "Just because I happen to prefer indoor plumbing to a hole in the ground doesn't make me a bad person."

"No," I said, "it doesn't."

The quiet settled between us as Derek angrily ate his breakfast. After a few minutes, Carlos stuck his head out of the door and called to us.

"Hey, Dad!" he said enthusiastically. "I got the high score on Death Match!"

Derek gave him a thumbs up, and Carlos went back to his video game.

"He's thriving here," Derek said, looking after his son.

"Something tells me he'd thrive anywhere," I replied, wondering if Derek was so deep into reacquainting himself with his "life of privilege" that he couldn't even see the danger zones for a boy living in modern-day America, the areas where his child needed his father's guidance and protection—and censorship.

Beyond all of that, though, I couldn't help but imagine the gulf that had been widening between this man and his wife since they came to the States. As Derek accumulated and experienced the finer things, his wife must've felt as though she was looking on from a vast distance, wondering where the selfless, dedicated man she once knew had gone.

Derek looked at me, his fork paused in midair.

"What is it?" he asked. "Obviously, you want to tell me something, something more than just the fact that it's my sister who's been ruining my marriage and my life. What is it?"

I sat back, wondering myself. What did I want to say? That his marriage was worth saving? That he was lucky that the person he loved was still alive, still around to patch things up with? I lowered my voice and leaned forward.

"Your problem is solved, Derek. Sidra isn't the bad guy here, and neither are you. Now what are you going to do about it?"

"Too much damage has been done," he said, shaking his head, looking down at his plate. "She's perfectly sane, and I've been treating her like she was nuts."

"You can make it up to her."

"It's too late."

"Why won't you fight for your marriage?" I demanded, but he wouldn't reply.

I felt my stomach lurch, and I was angry with him, angry with myself for even caring.

"Three years ago," I said, my voice a furious whisper, "I watched my husband—the husband I loved and cherished and promised to be with until death do us part—get *killed*. Killed in a senseless accident by a drunken boater who wasn't paying attention. When it was over, I held my husband's lifeless body in my arms."

Derek's eyes were wide with surprise.

"So don't look at me," I whispered, "and tell me 'it's too late' for anything. My husband is *dead*, Derek. *That's* what you call 'too late.' Everything else is just an excuse."

I picked up my purse, pulled out a twenty, and slapped it onto the table. Then I stood and walked out of the restaurant and to my car as quickly as my trembling legs could carry me.

Twenty-Nine

By the time I reached the house, I didn't feel like seeing or speaking to anyone. Fortunately, the place was quiet, and I made my way up the stairs and to my room without encountering a soul. Once there, I threw myself across the bed and tried to clear my mind of every thought and every emotion. Instead, all I could see was Bryan. Bryan, grinning at me as we climbed on our bicycles for a bike ride. Bryan, stepping from the shower and teasing me with a shy smile. Bryan, losing himself in concentration as he studied the paperwork in front of him.

Bryan. Three years might as well have been three days for all my heart had managed to let go. I pressed my hands against my eyes and tried to wrench myself away from the images that filled my head. I wondered, not for the first time, if I would ever get through a single day without thinking of him, without missing him. I told myself, as I always did, how lucky I had been to have him in my life. Better five years in a wondrous, near-perfect marriage than 30 years in a miserable one. *Still,* I thought, *I'm ready to bargain; maybe a little less happiness and a little more time? How about that, God? Do we have a deal?*

I sat up, shaking my head. When you try to strike a deal with God, it's time to change the subject.

I headed for the bathroom and a hot shower, letting the water pound away the thoughts from my brain. I knew that part of my problem was sheer exhaustion, and I thought back over the most recent run of cases I had worked. While my canoe sat mostly unused and dusty in my shed at home, I had jetted off to five different states in the last three months. Usually, extra work like that gave me an escape, a way to distract my mourning heart. But I think this time I had pushed it all too far. Between my fatigue and the events of this particular case, I was near the breaking point. The only place I really wanted to be right now was out on the water with an oar in my hand, paddling along the Chesapeake. Instead, I was a prisoner of Pennsylvania with an ongoing murder investigation as my only distraction.

After my shower, I took extra care applying my makeup, fixing my hair. Going through the motions was somehow soothing, and I felt myself lulled into a sort of numbness, my best defense when all else failed.

Once I was done, I looked at the clock and realized I still had nearly two hours before it was time for the funeral. After my sleepless night, a nap would've been a good idea, but I knew my brain was spinning far too much to let me fall asleep. What I really wanted was to spend that time doing something physical like swimming or jogging. I decided, instead, to use this time to take a look at the things that were stashed behind the radiator. I pulled out the paper bag from Sidra's cabana and the blank pad of paper and the paintbrush that I had swiped from Judith's suite.

It was a normal brush, about four inches wide, and I studied the base of the bristles for any trace of red fake blood. Though I couldn't see any, I went into the bathroom, filled the basin with a little water, then pressed the brush under the water, working it against the side of the sink. After a moment, my suspicions were confirmed: The water turned from clear to vaguely pink.

I wrapped the brush in a towel, then carried it to the closet and stuck it down among my dirty clothes. Carlos, Derek, and I knew that Judith was the one doing these things to Sidra. The question that remained now was *why?*

I reached for the blank pad from Judith's room, wishing I had access to an ESDA. Electrostatic Detection Apparatus was just a fancy name for an instrument that let you analyze sheets of paper for writing indents, sometimes as deep as 20 sheets into the pad. Instead, I would have to rely on the old-fashioned method—a pencil rubbed lightly across the paper.

It didn't take long, and what I found was rather disturbing. Once I was finished, I held the paper in front of me and read it again, to be sure: It was information, jotted in a row down the page, about *me.* It started with my full name. Under that was my license plate number, and under that was the make, color, and model of my car. I continued reading my age, my job title and place of employment, where I went to college and law school, and my current home address. That was it, all in a row, Callie Webber in a nutshell.

I was still studying the page when I was startled by a knock at the door. I shoved the pad into the paper bag, slid it under the bed, and went to the door.

I opened it to see Angelina holding out a big FedEx box.

"Hi, Callie," she said. "You have a phone call. And this came for you."

I took the box and put it on the bed, seeing Eli's return address in the corner. The old rascal had sent me a box of goodies despite my telling him not to. He must've called Harriet at the office and gotten my current address from her.

"Where should I take the call?" I asked.

She motioned for me to follow her, and she led me down the hall to the lovely sunlit alcove at the end. It held an upholstered window seat, and next to the seat was a recessed shelf in the wall, with a telephone.

"Thanks," I said, taking my seat. As I picked up the receiver, Judith came out of her room and headed for the stairs, giving me a vague smile and a wave as she passed by.

"This is Callie," I said into the phone.

"Callie Webber?"

The voice was muffled and high pitched, though I couldn't quite tell if it was a man or a woman.

"Yes?"

"I need to speak with you."

"Who is this?"

"That's not important. Can you meet me in an hour?"

I hesitated, and after a moment the person spoke again.

"I have information that you'll be interested in. Something important I need to tell you."

"Why do we have to meet?" I asked. "Why can't you just tell me now over the phone?"

"I have to show you something. One hour. Meet me in the cemetery, next to the Smythe family plot."

Now my interest was piqued. What could this person possibly need to show me there?

"The funeral's today," I said. "There will be people around."

"Funeral's at 11:00," the voice said. "Meet me at 10:00."

"How will I—"

"Just be there."

The line clicked and my caller was gone.

I hung up the phone and returned to my room, sitting on the side of the bed. I should leave now, I decided. If Eli had taught me anything, it was that you don't ever head into a situation like this unaware. If we were meeting at 10:00, I would get there at 9:15 and scope the place out first.

I thought about calling Duane Perskie for backup, but I hated the thought of taking up any more of his time. I would be fine, I decided. In a place that public, what could happen?

Bending over, I slid my stash from under the bed and returned it to the better hiding place behind the radiator. Then I went to the closet, pulled out the same black clothes I had worn to the wake the night before, and slid them into a bag with some shoes and stockings. I grabbed Eli's box and headed out, knowing I could change clothes in the bathroom of the funeral home after my meeting at the gravesite of Wendell Smythe.

Thirty

It was another gorgeous day with the sun shimmering in every direction and the new fall colors just peeking from the trees. The cemetery wasn't far from the funeral home, and I found it easily, turning between two large marble posts at the entrance. The place was lush and expansive with the rolling hills dotted with memorials and tombstones that ranged from the incredibly ornamental to the tastefully simple and everywhere in between. It looked as if Wendell's wasn't the only funeral here today; there were several funeral awnings set up throughout the cemetery. Wendell's, however, was the only one teeming with activity at this time. A funeral home van and a florist's truck were there, and about five men milled about the gravesite setting up chairs and bringing out flowers.

I drove past the site and continued on as the road looped around the far side of the cemetery and back again. When I was near a mausoleum, I turned my car around and pulled over to the side. I could see Wendell's gravesite in the distance, though I was far enough away that I doubted any of them would notice me. I turned off the car and reached for Eli's box, slicing the tape with the point of my key. Knowing him, there would be a pair of binoculars in there—just what I needed. I finished ripping the tape, flipped the lid open, and looked inside.

"God bless him," I whispered, reaching inside, pulling out the items one by one. Eli had sent a pair of binoculars, some handcuffs, a miniature camera, and a tape recorder. For my protection he had also included a billy club and a can of pepper spray, but no gun. Despite my training and proficiency, Eli knew I didn't like handling guns and hadn't since my brother had been shot in the line of duty years ago. Michael's accident had totally thrown me for a loop, and though he eventually recovered, I found that I was never comfortable around guns and ammunition after that. Besides, I swung a pretty mean club. For now that would have to be enough. *Leave it to Eli*, I thought, *to take care of me from a thousand miles away.*

I put everything back in the box except the binoculars, which I pulled out and pressed against my eyes. They were small but very powerful, and through them I could easily observe the goings-on at the gravesite. I studied the men who were there, watching as they went about their duties without much conversation. Mostly they just went back and forth, back and forth, pulling out chairs, setting them up, going back for more chairs. I put the binoculars down and just watched them with my naked eye until about ten minutes before ten, when I saw a new car pull into the cemetery.

I put the binoculars back up to my face, watching as the car came to a stop near the gravesite. It just sat there for a long moment, though I couldn't see inside because the sun glared off of the windshield. Finally, a man got out and I gasped, recognizing him as the same fellow who had followed me through Philadelphia, the young man with spiky hair who lost me outside of the jewelry store.

He wasn't driving the red pickup now, but a plain blue sedan of some sort. As I watched, he crossed over to talk to one of the workers and handed him a piece of paper. When he was finished, he got back in his car and drove off.

I waited until ten o'clock sharp before I started up my car and drove it to the gravesite. I got out and made my way over to the green AstroTurf that had been spread on the ground under the awning. I hesitated, wondering what to do next, when the same workman I had seen interacting with "Spike" came over and asked me if my name was Webber.

"Yeah," I said, my right hand cradling the canister of pepper spray deep in my pocket. "That's me."

"I got a note. Some guy left it here for ya."

He handed me a piece of paper, which was folded with my name scribbled on the outside. I took it gingerly and opened it.

It said, *Too many people here for us to talk. Meet me at the first canopy, by the big tree.*

I slid the note into my pocket, glad that Duane Perskie had given me a fingerprinting kit.

I got back into my car and headed toward the front of the cemetery. I knew the place the note was talking about—it was another funeral site, with the requisite green awning and ground-covering AstroTurf, but this one was devoid of any activity. I parked nearby, grabbed the billy club and the pepper spray, and then walked down the hill toward the awning, noting the absence of the blue sedan and the man who had been in it.

I reached the awning and stepped onto the carpeting, looking around cautiously. Something about this bothered me, perhaps the fact that this spot was so much more isolated than the other had been. I stood in a sort of valley, hidden from the Smythe gravesite by a short hill that rose up between us. I was wishing now that I had called Perskie after all, and I walked the place off, headed for the relative safety of the big tree that bordered the cemetery plot.

I had to walk past the freshly dug gravesite to get there, and as I went past, I couldn't help but glance inside. *Graves are always so much deeper than we expect them to be,* I thought absurdly. Then, before I could even take another step, I heard sounds and saw movement, and suddenly I felt a body thrust against me and fling me forward. Then I was flying down, through the air, into the empty grave. I screamed as I fell, hitting the dirt at the bottom with a heavy thud, pain searing into my right side.

I opened my eyes, looking up to see dirt walls—dirt walls a mile high, with blue sky beyond. Then I closed my eyes, waiting for more dirt to fall in on me, for me to be buried alive. But nothing came. I stilled my breathing and listened, but I couldn't hear a sound.

"Help!" I yelled. "Help!"

I felt terror rising up in my throat as I realized that no one could hear me. The dirt walls simply sucked in all the sound I could make.

I was in a grave. A freshly dug grave. Pushed in here by the same man who had been following me the day before.

"Stupid!" I yelled at myself, then I grimaced at the pain that my outburst caused. I had let myself be ambushed, I realized, by a man who had been hiding behind a tombstone. A lot of good my weapons had done me; I'd never even had a chance to use them. Carefully, I sat up, reaching around to feel my right side with my left hand, running my fingers down my arm, pressing gingerly against my ribs.

I didn't think anything was broken. I tried leaning forward, leaning to the left, and though it hurt like heck, I could still do it. I pulled myself up to my knees and tried to catch my breath, forcing away the panic that sat at the back of my throat.

I don't know how long I sat there before I saw the paper on the ground. It was a plain sheet of white paper, pressed into the mud as if I had landed on it when I fell. Hands trembling, I lifted it by one corner and turned it over. It was a note, typed, to me.

Welcome to the grave, it said. *Drop this case and go home, or next time you'll visit one of these in a casket.*

I let go of the note, watching as it softly fell to the ground. Whoever had done this had made a big mistake. Little did they know it, but they had crossed the wrong person now.

I stood carefully, feeling an aching throb in my back. Looking upward, I analyzed my situation, wondering how I was going to get out. I pressed my hands against the walls, testing the dirt, finally deciding that the only choice would be to dig some hand- and footholds out of the wall and climb up. I used the billy club to start digging, gouging out holes at two-foot intervals. When I had dug as high as I could reach, I tested the holes. I pulled myself up a few feet before the dirt collapsed and I landed back on the ground. Ouch.

I tried again, making the holes deeper and farther apart. This time, I was able to pull myself up higher and then stand there while I dug more holes.

It would be slow going, I knew, but eventually I felt sure I could reach the top of the gravesite. I looked at my watch—there were only 15 minutes until the funeral would begin. I knew I'd never make it.

I climbed up to dig a higher handhold and suddenly felt the dirt crumble under my foot again. I landed on my behind with a thud and let out a scream of pain and frustration.

"Hello?" I heard. "Is someone there?"

"Down here!" I yelled, as loudly as I could. After a moment, I saw the face of a young man peer nervously over the edge of the grave.

"Ahhh!" he screamed when he saw me. "What are you doing in there?"

He peered down at me in horror. I looked up at him, trying to remain calm, afraid he would bolt and I'd never get out.

"Help me!" I said. "I fell in."

"Are you hurt?" he asked.

"No. But I can't get out. I need a rope or something."

"Just a minute."

He disappeared, and while I waited for him I brushed the dirt from my clothes, picked up the threatening letter from the ground, and put it into my pocket.

I wondered if Judith was responsible for this. If so, then whom had she gotten to do the dirty work for her? Was Spike on her payroll? Had he pushed me in here on her orders? I reminded myself that just because Judith was the one who had been vandalizing Sidra, that didn't mean she had also murdered her father—or that any of my other suspects were off the hook.

Finally, my young warrior returned, clutching what looked like a bright orange extension cord.

"Don't have any rope," he called down to me. "Think this'll do?"

I told him to tie his end around the tree then toss the rest on down to me. He did as I asked, and soon I was using my footholds and the cord to half climb, half drag myself out of the hole. When I neared the top, I could feel him pulling me up as well. In the end, I landed in a heap on top of him, both of us gasping and exhausted. I sat up and looked at him. He couldn't be a day over 16. He was wearing a gray uniform with Bud's Rentals stitched over the pocket. Parked next to my car was a gray van with the same name, and I could see that the back doors were wide open, metal chairs piled high in the back.

"We did it!" he exclaimed excitedly. "We did it!"

"Thank you," I replied. "I don't know what I would've done without you."

"That was like *Silence of the Lambs* or something," he said, his eyes still wide with excitement. "You know, the way he kept that woman down in that pit?"

"Afraid I didn't see that one," I said, feeling grateful that I hadn't. I stood, brushing off my pants, and then thanked him one more time before heading to my car. If I hurried, I'd still have time to get cleaned up, change my clothes, and make it late to the funeral.

Then I'd sit back and watch to see just who looked surprised to see me.

Thirty-One

I cleaned myself up in the bathroom of a nearby service station. I had planned to change at the funeral home, but once I looked in the rearview mirror and saw the dirt and mud streaked in my hair and on my face, I knew I'd better not chance running into anyone. I did the best I could, washing my face and rubbing my hair with damp paper towels. I repaired my makeup as quickly as possible before pulling on the outfit I had brought along.

By the time I arrived at the funeral, Ian was well into his eulogy. I hesitated inside the doorway, debating whether to slip quietly into a seat in the back row or head closer to the front where I might have a better chance of being spotted by the person responsible for my little trip into the grave. In the end, I compromised: There was an aisle seat, about a third of the way up, and I headed there, knowing I could watch the faces of the people as they came down the aisle when the service was finished.

In the meantime, I sat back in my seat and tried to relax and listen to Ian. His voice was warm and melodic, but the words were lost on me. All that had happened so far in this day had left me more shaken than I wanted to admit. Now I sat with my hands clenched in my lap, feeling a tremble deep in the pit of my stomach while a dull roar vibrated inside my head.

My fingernails are dirty, I thought as I glanced at my hands in front of me. I had managed to clean my hair and my face. The fact that my nails were filled with dirt had escaped my attention. With a sort of odd fascination, I held my hands out in front of me and studied the effect. It looked like a French manicure, but with brown tips instead of white.

The funeral service ended with a prayer and then instructions on leaving the parking lot in the vehicular procession to the cemetery. The family would depart first, so we all stood at our seats as soft music played.

Marion led the way, Derek firmly supporting her arm as they headed up the aisle. She looked absolutely distraught. The black veil over her face did not hide her sorrow. I caught Derek's eye, and he acknowledged me with a slight nod.

Next came Judith, walking with two older gentlemen who I assumed were relatives. She also noticed me as she went past, though if she felt surprised to see me, it didn't show on her face.

Then came Alan Bennet. He headed down the aisle with the general crowd, deep in conversation with another man. As he neared me and then his eyes met mine, he seemed to visibly flinch. He stopped talking, his face suddenly pale.

Bingo.

"Callie," he said, trying to recover, forcing a smile. "Thank you for coming."

He reached out to shake my hand and I hesitated, feeling a strange calm sweep over me. It made things much better, knowing my enemies. I took his hand, debating whether to make some wry comment like, "Please excuse the dirt under my nails. I was doing a little digging this morning." But I didn't necessarily want him to know that I knew it was he. Instead, I remained silent, giving him an enigmatic smile before he moved on.

I drove myself to the cemetery, my little Saturn near the end of the procession. As I dutifully followed the car in front of me, I thought of Tom's exhortation that I remove myself from this case at the first sign of personal danger. *He should know me better than that,* I thought. *He should know that an attack like this would only strengthen my resolve. I'm not about to duck out on this investigation now.*

I just wouldn't mention to him what had happened.

The graveside ceremony was simple and solemn, the mood quiet and orderly despite the tremendous number of people present. Now that I felt sure I knew who was responsible for my earlier incident, I put it out of my mind and tried to concentrate on the proceedings at hand. I listened as Derek delivered a touching tribute to his father and then watched as a woman stepped up to the podium. She was about 20, slim with long blond hair, and she began singing in a beautiful clear voice to the accompaniment of a young man on a guitar. When I realized what song she was singing, I felt as if someone had punched me in the stomach.

"When peace, like a river, attendeth my way…" she sang, the first line of the first verse of the hymn "It Is Well with My Soul." It had always been my favorite hymn, but three years ago I had made the terrible mistake of choosing it to be sung at Bryan's funeral. Now, every time I heard it I was instantly transported back to that moment when I stood next to his grave, listening to the music, realizing that the only man I had ever loved was really and truly dead.

"When sorrows like sea billows roll…"

I hated that song now, hated it in the way a stubborn student hates his teacher, in the way a soldier hates his drill sergeant. I knew there were lessons in that song for me, lessons I needed very much to learn. But I wasn't even close to being ready to learn them. I knew the song had been written by a man whose life went from blessed to disastrous all in one year: First, he lost all of his money and nearly everything he owned in the great Chicago fire, then he lost his only son to sickness, then he lost his four remaining daughters when they were drowned in a shipwreck. As the man stood looking out at the ocean where his daughters had drowned, he had written this song, the refrain proclaiming that, in spite of everything, he would remain faithful to God and His will.

"Whatever my lot, Thou has taught me to say, It is well, it is well with my soul…"

But it is not well with my soul! I had wanted to scream at Bryan's funeral. *He's dead and I'm still alive, and all I want is one more chance to see him, to talk to him, to be with him.*

Now, remembering the moment that I buried my husband, I felt a purely physical ache, a visceral sort of rage and sorrow well up in me like a volcano. By the time the song was over, I knew that my face was covered in tears, that it was all I could do not to let out a strangled sob. I was glad I was in the back row, hidden from those few there who knew me. I had hardly known Wendell Smythe; to be weeping at his funeral might've seemed odd.

Blessedly, the ceremony ended soon after the song. The pastor said one final prayer, the family placed single roses on the top of the closed casket, and then they quietly made their way to their waiting limousines, the whole lot of them huddling together like mice in a rainstorm. I stayed where I was for a long time, walking to my car only after I realized that the crowd around me had begun to disperse. I think I might've stayed there all day, looking at the gravesite in front of me, reliving my own husband's funeral, if I hadn't been afraid to be there in the cemetery alone and unprotected.

～

When I got back to the house I avoided the gathering of people in the living room and instead made my way through the foyer to Wendell's study, closing the door behind me. I sat in his chair and wondered how on earth one person could so cruelly take the life of another. My Bryan had died in a horrible accident caused by a careless person; Wendell Smythe had had his life snatched from him by a deliberate action. But were their deaths really that dissimilar? Both were good men, men who loved their work and their wives, men who still had a lot left to give to those around them. The fact that Wendell was so much older at his death than Bryan had been at his still didn't alter the tragedy of either of them. I wanted to find this killer not just for Tom's sake, I realized now, but also for Marion's. Anything less would be unfaithful to the memories of the men we loved.

I don't know how long I sat there. I heard cars in the front drive, doors opening and closing, people talking in the front hall. Finally, as the noises died off, the door to the study eased open, and Marion peeked inside.

"Oh, it's you," she said, an odd expression on her face. "I saw the light on under the door and wondered. For a minute, I pretended it was going to be Wendell. But I knew better."

"I'm sorry," I replied. "I was just sitting here thinking."

She stepped inside and pulled the door shut behind her.

"Are you okay?" I asked softly.

She nodded.

"The doctor gave me some Valium," she said, no slur evident in her voice, but a strange calm in her eyes. "I don't know how I would've gotten through without it."

"I'm sure."

She stood quietly for a moment, her hands oddly still at her sides. She spoke again, after a moment, her voice sounding peaceful and resolute.

"Ian did a beautiful job with the eulogy," she said. "Don't you think?"

I nodded, not admitting I hadn't listened to a word.

"How about you, dear? You seem pale."

"I'm feeling sad," I admitted. "Your husband's funeral reminded me a little too much of my own husband's funeral, selfish as that sounds."

"Not selfish," Marion whispered. "Sorrow notwithstanding, we're also allowed a little self-pity now and then."

She came over to the desk and sat across from me. Looking at her more closely, I realized that there was an odd sort of excitement in her eyes.

"Right now," she said suddenly, "I have some things to show you, Callie. Big things. Do you feel up to hearing about it? Because I found them in here, this morning. I think they're important."

Thirty-Two

I sat up straight, giving Marion my full attention.

"You know I told you the other day that Wendell was concerned about Feed the Need, about the finances there?" Marion asked me now.

"Yes?"

"Well, it finally struck me to look inside Wendell's office safe. I thought he might have some papers or something, but I never expected to find all that I did. It's truly astonishing, Callie. I think once you've looked all of these things over, you might find our killer."

I watched as Marion went to a large portrait of Thomas Jefferson on the wall. She swung the painting out on a set of hinges, revealing a wall safe behind. She deftly worked the lock, opened it, and removed a cardboard box.

By the time she had carried it to the desk and opened it up, my curiosity was definitely piqued. Together we pulled everything out, and then Marion went through the various things, showing me what she thought each one meant.

She held out a handwritten sign containing a word I didn't recognize, and she told me that she remembered clearly the day Wendell found it.

"It was on a trip to the Philippines," she said. "We had an unscheduled stop in Manila, with a layover extended by several hours. There was a Feed the Need district office there, so Wendell and I decided to taxi over from the airport, drop in, and see everyone. Instead, all we found when we got there was this sign, written in Tagalog, hanging on the front door."

"What does it say?" I asked.

"It says 'closed.'"

"Like, closed for the night?"

"No, closed permanently. Out of business. The place was completely stripped, not a speck of furniture left, not a soul there."

"Without your knowledge?" I asked "I don't understand."

"Neither did we. Wendell was so furious he tore the sign down and took it with him. Once our trip was over, he told me it was just a mix-up, that he had dealt with it. But now I'm wondering if that was the truth. I'm wondering how many other district offices were closed."

I sat back, fingering the crude sign.

"Manila, you said?" I asked. Marion nodded, and I thought of my conversation with the attorneys' office two days before when I was trying to find out about any real estate deals that were pending. *We've already closed on Taipei…Manila…and Tegucigalpa*, the woman had told me over the phone. I had asked her if Feed the Need had already paid in full. *Paid?* the woman had drawled. *Heck no, y'all sold. The people who bought the places paid.*

Was it possible that someone was closing down Feed the Need district offices? If so, then why? To cut costs? To channel the money for those programs into some other direction?

"Look at this," Marion said, pulling out two file folders. "It took me a while, but I think I finally figured out what this is."

She opened the first file to reveal the black-and-white photo of a small Hispanic-looking child. The girl had dark skin and big round eyes, and she wore a wrinkled, knotty scarf and sweater that brought to mind the people of the Andes. Behind the photo was a profile; her name was Rosa Parmenta, and according to the profile she lived in a small village in Peru.

"Now this," Marion said, and she opened the second file. It held another black-and-white photo, this time of a group of children—three dirty but smiling faces, the two boys bare chested, the girl in a light Mexican-style embroidered dress. The profile with this photo listed the children as three siblings—Javier, Luis, and Martina Gonzales—and it said that they lived in the Mexican city of Guadalajara.

"Are these the children people sponsor through Feed the Need?" I asked. I thought of Frank's words at the wake, and I knew he was right—with these pitiful but adorable faces in front of me I definitely felt the urge to donate some money.

"When you agree to sponsor a child, you get a photo and profile, just like this," Marion said. "We have a team that prepares these things, that carefully monitors the database, that makes sure we track the progress of the children through the district offices."

"Okay."

She pulled out another piece of paper full of scribbled notes and lots of arrows and circles.

"This is Wendell's handwriting," she said. "This is how he brainstormed, how he worked through problems."

I tried reading the notes, but I couldn't make much sense of it until Marion interpreted for me.

"Right here," she said, pointing, "March 1, new database software. March 15, users trained, department reduced by 15."

"What does that mean?"

"It means last March, Feed the Need bought some new database software that was so good it allowed them to let 15 people go from the child-tracking department."

That sounded fishy to me; obviously, it must have to Wendell as well, because from that circle he had drawn several arrows with question marks and other notations.

"Spell it out for me, Marion," I said. "This is too confusing."

She pulled back out the two photos. She placed them side by side on the desk and then stood in front of me, her arms folded across her chest.

"Look at the pictures," she said. "What do you see?"

It didn't take long. The hair was different, the clothing was different, but the face was the same.

"This is the same girl!" I said, picking up the pictures of the two little girls. "Rosa Parmenta and Martina Gonzales are one and the same!"

"Exactly."

My eyes met Marion's, and she paused a beat before continuing.

"Think about it, Callie," she said softly. "Field offices are being closed. The children's photo records are being faked. Half the staff of the tracking department is laid off. All of this without the knowledge of the President or the CEO. What does that tell you?"

I hesitated a beat.

"That somebody somewhere is cutting costs. That somebody somewhere is up to something."

That hung in the air for a moment, and I thought that "somebody" was most likely Alan Bennet, the person who was responsible for having me shoved into a grave, the person who had had his hands in Feed the Need's finances for the last five months.

As far as I could tell, any way you looked at it, this was a man who was up to no good.

Thirty-Three

⁓

Upstairs, I hooked my computer to the phone line and checked my e-mail. Sure enough, the home office in Washington, DC, had finally responded to my request for more information on Alan Bennet. I downloaded the file and opened another e-mail that was waiting for me from Harriet.

It was a response to my phone call of the day before when I gave her the plate number of the man who had been following me around town. She had run the plates and come up with a name: Mitchell Ralston. There was no other information, and the name certainly didn't ring any bells with me.

I logged off and returned to my room before I opened the file and started reading. What I found was very disturbing. According to the research, the college Alan supposedly graduated from in the Midwest was now defunct. There was no way to check whether he had ever actually been a student there. More importantly, the three clothing manufacturers that he had listed in his employment history also no longer existed. Apparently, they had at one time been legitimate companies, but eventually they had all been closed down through bankruptcy or merger or something else. The details were unavailable.

On a personal note, though Alan Bennet was currently single, he had been married three times. The first wife, an heiress, had died in a car accident. The second and third wives weren't dead but merely divorced—with Alan receiving generous support payments in both instances! I thought of his dalliance with Judith Smythe and wondered if the stakes had been raised even higher now that she had inherited a large chunk of her father's fortune.

I closed the file and pulled out my cell phone to call Harriet back at the home office in DC. As I waited for her to come on the line, I reached into the box Marion had given me and pulled out the heavy set of accounting records from inside. A groan escaped my lips at the surge of pain from my side; my fall into the grave still resonated within my aching muscles.

Finally, I heard a click on the phone and then the warm familiar voice of my friend.

"Callie?" she said, and I was surprised at my own sudden rush of emotion. Sometimes I became so tired of being surrounded by strangers.

"Hi, Harriet," I said, sitting down on the bed. "Gosh, it's good to hear your voice."

We talked for a while. She caught me up on office happenings down there, and then I told her briefly about my work up here.

"I can't believe you got stuck in that mess," Harriet said, clicking her tongue. "Tom really got an earful from me. I let him have what for."

I smiled, knowing that even a little "what for" from Harriet was a formidable thing.

"At least I think the end's finally in sight," I said. "But I need your help."

"You got it."

I gave her an abbreviated version of my discussion with Marion about the financial funny business at Feed the Need.

"I've got two sets of books here," I said. "Looks like one is the public version and one is private, if you get my drift."

"Oh, I getcha alright."

"Do you think you can do your usual run-through?" I asked. "Sniff out all the discrepancies?"

"Like a bloodhound on the scent of a grouse," she said, and I smiled. Harriet was from Texas, and every conversation with her was filled with colorful similes and metaphors.

She agreed to come up on the first train in the morning. She put me on hold while she made her reservation, and then she came back on the line, gave me the time, and told me to meet her at the front entrance to the Thirtieth Street station.

After disconnecting, I called and reserved a small meeting room for the morning at a downtown Philadelphia hotel that my old law firm had used from time to time. That was about the most anonymous territory I could think of. I didn't want anyone to get wind of any of this just yet.

Once I had hung up the phone, I decided that it was time to get organized—first my thoughts, then my things. Now that Wendell's funeral was over, I felt sure the house would be quiet the rest of the day; I knew it was a good time to pause and take stock.

I clicked open the database on my laptop and pulled out all of my notes and the file Duane Perskie had given me. It was time to brainstorm, time to come up with some real theories for all that had been going on.

This was how I worked best—by digging around, unearthing facts, then sitting down and sorting out my thoughts until I came up with some plausible ideas. In the process, I would let my imagination fly, playing with every possible motive I could think up, no matter how far-fetched some of them might seem. Eli had taught me this method; he was a strong believer in the problem-solving power of the unconscious mind. "These things have been stewing around in your brain when you weren't even aware of it," he would say. "Now it's time to let your ideas out."

Following his lead, I typed in all of the information I had gathered thus far. Then I earmarked the names of the people I now suspected of killing Wendell: Alan Bennet and Judith Smythe. Because I couldn't positively rule them out yet, I also highlighted Derek Smythe and Gwen Harding, though I doubted either one of them had done it. Apparently, Angelina had a pretty good alibi; at the time of the murder, she had been seen grocery shopping at a local store, and the checker confirmed her presence there. I made notes to that effect, but did check off her brother, Nick, as a possible suspect just in case his alibi wasn't as airtight as the police thought. At the time of the murder, Nick had been in the city with Marion, helping her shop. Marion had been positively ID'd by a sales clerk, but I didn't know whether Nick and Marion had been together the entire time, or if he could possibly have had a chance to slip away for a while and pay a visit up the back stairs to Wendell's office. That left Sidra, who had the best alibi of all; she had been at a Bible study at her church, as attested to by her pastor.

To my mind, that left two strong suspects, Alan and Judith, and three weak-but-still-possible suspects, Derek, Gwen, and Nick. Wendell Smythe didn't seem to have any enemies. His will had already been read and held no surprises—everyone had been treated fairly. So what was it, what could've made someone want to kill him? I created a new category—motive—then typed in my best guesses.

For Alan Bennet, I knew, his motive would probably have been about money. I was suspicious of anyone who lived above their means, but Alan's marital history alone pointed to a man willing to go to a lot of trouble for the almighty dollar. I considered the ways he would benefit financially from Wendell's murder.

The most obvious way, of course, was taken in light of his relationship with Judith. Thanks to her inheritance from her father, Judith was now a much wealthier woman. If Alan's intention was to marry her, then I supposed it made certain sense to see that she was as wealthy as possible first. On the other hand, the timing seemed kind of dumb. After all, why not marry her first, *then* kill her father?

Of course, increasing Judith's wealth wasn't the only possible motivation for Alan. It could've been company related. Perhaps he had been diverting funds from Feed the Need into his own personal account, and Wendell had found out about it. Rather than facing the music, Alan could've killed Wendell to protect himself.

Or maybe it was less complicated than that. Maybe it was simply a matter of ambition. Perhaps Alan felt that with Wendell out of the way, Judith would move up to President and he could step in as CEO of Smythe Incorporated. It wouldn't be the first time someone had killed just to get ahead.

I scanned the screen and thought a bit about Judith. What did I know of her so far? She was heartless, direct, ambitious, and up to something. Her ridiculous acts of vandalism against Sidra might have nothing to do with the death of her father. But at least I knew now that she wasn't quite right, that she was acting out of some sort of desperation. Was it too much of a leap to imagine her committing a murder?

I might have believed she had done it if the family dynamics were different, if she had perhaps suffered from years of abuse or neglect, which was the usual pattern for patricide. But from what I could tell, Wendell had been an exemplary man and a wonderful father; the usual child-parent murder motivation just wasn't there. Despite Judith's vicious acts of vandalism, for some reason I just didn't peg her as the murderer—unless Alan Bennet had somehow pulled her in and twisted things around until she had become a party to something that ordinarily would've been unspeakable.

Derek's possible motivations seemed even further far-fetched. Could he have been involved in financial funny business within his own company? Perhaps his father discovered the mess, decided it was Derek's doing, and threatened to fire him or turn him in to the police. It just didn't fly for me, particularly when I thought about Derek's personality. Certainly, he had his faults; he was weak, complacent, and a bit confused spiritually. But he just didn't seem like a murderer. About the most likely scenario I could come up with regarding Derek had to do with the medical report I had found in his bedroom. Apparently, Derek was slated to donate a kidney to his ailing father. Was it possible that in a moment of fear—and knowing it was likely his father would die anyway and the whole thing would've been for naught—Derek had changed his mind and murdered his father instead? I doubted it, but I could think of no other motive.

Gwen Harding was a bigger mystery, though my gut told me she wasn't guilty. She had had the easiest access for committing the murder, but I knew she couldn't have done it alone because of the person I chased from the bathroom. I did feel that Gwen knew something, something she wasn't telling me. But I just didn't think she had any part in her boss's death. Her shock at the situation had been too great, her grief at his demise too genuine.

And then there was Nick. I thought about our conversation in the kitchen, his proclaimed affection for the Smythe family. Was he really to be believed? I remembered how offended he was when I mistook him for a chauffeur, and I thought that perhaps his tremendous pride might've played into some sort of motive for him. Beyond that, the only thing I could think of was what Alan Bennet had said, about Wendell being on a nephrotic syndrome diet. What torture it must've been for Wendell to sit back and watch his family eat Nick's heavenly cooking, only to have to deny himself of it completely! What if Nick had been slated to be let go—perhaps even sent back to Italy—now that Wendell could no longer enjoy his delicious cooking? To stay in America, to keep his job here—would that have been worth killing for?

I was stretching, I knew. A good chef could always find work in a gastro-oriented society like ours. I put down my notes, rubbed my eyes, then saved the file, closed the laptop, and stashed it in my briefcase. Brainstorming had its place, but now it was time to examine the physical evidence and see if it held any important secrets.

I went to the radiator and lifted the cover. I reached down to pull out my little collection, only to find myself grasping at air. Kneeling down to look, I was shocked to find the paper bag and its contents gone!

I stood, scrutinizing the room, a chill going through me. Everything seemed the same, though now that I knew someone had been here, I could see some subtle differences. A drawer that wasn't quite closed. The few items hanging in the closet pushed farther to one side.

My adversary, whoever it was, was smarter and more determined than I had originally thought. At the office, my briefcase had been rifled through. Was I really surprised that someone had now gone through my room? I berated myself for not finding an even better hiding place for my evidence.

I had made several mistakes now in this case, and I knew I was sorely out of practice for this type of investigation. I thought back to my conversation with Tom when he asked me to find Wendell's murderer. I had warned him then that my usual financial investigations were a far cry from a murder investigation. He had scoffed, insisting that my talents and instincts would prevail. *How wrong he was,* I realized.

I sat on the bed, trying to remember what had been in the bag that had been taken. I thought of the knife and photo from Sidra, along with the pack of letters, the comb, and the dinosaur from her apartment. There was also the pad of paper I had taken from Judith's room, scribbled on with a pencil to reveal the information about me. I walked to the closet and looked inside, digging through my dirty clothes. The paintbrush was gone, too. Whoever had been here had found it.

There was no way to figure out who might have done this. Because I had been the first one to leave this morning, it could've been almost anyone who lived here. Beyond that, someone could've broken in while we were all at the funeral—perhaps this Mitchell Ralston after he shoved me into the empty grave. Trying to figure it out was futile.

I felt the worst about the pack of Sidra's letters. If I hadn't taken them from her drawer, they wouldn't be missing now. I wondered how I could tell her what I had done, what had happened. Worse than that, I no longer even possessed the knife or the paintbrush, both of which assuredly showed Judith's fingerprints as final proof of her evil acts of vandalism.

I went to the window and looked out at the rich green lawn, exhaling slowly, letting my heart rate return to normal. I knew that if I was smart, I wouldn't let the invasion of my room here undermine my confidence as an investigator; instead, I would use my anger as a way to steel my resolve.

My room may have been rifled, but I still had the two notes from the cemetery. Perhaps one of them had a good print. I wanted an ID on the man who lured me there, to see if the fingerprints belonged to "Mitchell Ralston," the name that Harriet had given me from the car registration.

"You wanna play dirty?" I whispered. "Then let's get down to business."

Crossing to the door, I made certain that it was locked. Then I cleared an area at the desk and spread out my tools. The fingerprinting kit Duane Perskie had given me included the three most common types of fingerprinting powder: black for light objects, white for dark objects, and silver for glass and mirrors.

I pulled out the black dust and then went to work on the paper, using an ostrich feather fingerprint duster to swirl each of the notes in a fine coat of dust. I then carefully applied the special tape to the prints that showed up, lifting them right off of the page. Once I was finished, I got out my phone and called Duane. He said he could get someone to run the prints if I brought them right over, so I straightened up the mess I had made, locked everything in my briefcase, and headed out the door.

Thirty-Four

The trip to the Perskie Detective Agency was uneventful, but by the time I got back to the Smythes' house my side was aching and I was exhausted. It was around four in the afternoon—too late for a nap, too early to go to bed for the night. Wishing I could take a little canoe ride, I parked the car around back and headed for the house just as Sidra and Carlos came out of the cabana.

They were dressed in bathing suits, carrying towels. As I watched, they walked to the pool and set the towels on a wrought-iron table nearby. Suddenly, a dip in the pool seemed like the most wonderful notion in the world.

"Callie!" Carlos called out as he saw me walking up.

"Hi!" I said, pausing near the back door. "May I join you?"

"Of course," said Sidra. "Please do."

I headed upstairs, changed into my bathing suit, and came back down as quickly as I could. By the time I got back to the pool, Sidra was sitting on the side, her feet dangling in the water, and Carlos was doing cannonballs into the deep end.

I set my towel and my briefcase on the table next to theirs. I was going to offer an explanation about the briefcase by saying I thought

I might catch up on a little paperwork poolside. But Sidra didn't even seem to notice, and I was glad. From now on, I wouldn't risk having anything else taken from my room when I wasn't there.

"A lovely afternoon for such a sad day, isn't it?" Sidra said, adjusting her sunglasses.

"Yes," I agreed. "It is."

The sun was bright but the air was chilly, and I headed down the steps quickly, finding the warm water to be an invigorating counterpoint to the cool air. I slipped under the water and then surfaced, face upward, relishing the heavenly relaxation that came with a heated pool.

As I leaned back in the water, floating gently, Sidra stood and stepped into the water, easing down the steps. How stunningly beautiful she was. In a bathing suit, she could've been a contestant for the Miss Universe pageant.

"This feels so nice," she said, relaxing into the water. "Carlos and I couldn't quite figure out what to do with ourselves this afternoon."

"I know what you mean. Days like this are always tough."

She leaned back, letting her long brown tresses float out behind her. I did the same, thinking again how nice it would be to have a pool like this of my own.

"I just hope Marion doesn't think us disrespectful for coming out here," Sidra said softly. "But Carlos was going stir-crazy. I thought this would be a nice break for him."

"Of course," I said. "I'm sure Marion would understand."

I, too, felt a little guilty for swimming on such a somber day. But my shoulders were stiff and my side was still throbbing from my fall this morning. I knew the warm water would be the perfect antidote to my pain.

As Carlos played energetically in the deep end, Sidra and I languished in the shallow, floating and softly chatting. This was really the first conversation she and I had had when she wasn't hysterical or crying, and I found her to be a fascinating woman, very articulate. As we spoke, I asked about her life in Honduras, about what it had been like to move to the foreign culture of the United States.

"It's one thing to learn English, which I did as a child," she said, smiling. "Quite another to speak 'American.'"

She told me a funny story about her early days here when she was told they used napkins to wipe their mouths at dinner.

"In my village, 'napkin' is the word for—how do you say it?—a *diaper*. I thought we were all expected to wipe our mouths with diapers!"

I laughed out loud, trying to imagine this girl and her dinnertime *faux pas*. She talked about how much Carlos liked it here, how many friends he had made, how he was excelling in school. I avoided any talk of the knife in the photo, and she didn't ask. As for her disintegrating marriage, I had said what I had to say to Derek that morning; I could only hope that when everything came to light, he would be the one to take things from here. I thought it was his place to tell Sidra about Judith, not mine.

As Carlos perfected his back flip, our talk turned inevitably to Wendell Smythe and to the wonderful relationship he had shared with his grandson.

"Wendell would sit there," she said, pointing to a wrought iron chair placed beside the pool at the deep end, "for hours on end, coaching Carlos with his dives. He never raised his voice, never lost his patience."

"Did Wendell use the pool much himself?" I asked.

"Almost every day," she said. "He liked to wade in up to his waist, then climb on his inner tube and float around."

I smiled, trying to picture it.

"Of course, that was up until the last few weeks."

"Too chilly for him?" I asked.

Sidra shook her head.

"He didn't want to take his shoes and socks off," she said. "He was hiding his feet. Didn't want anyone to know."

I sat up in the water, remembering the notation I made from the coroner's report, *severe ischemia of the toes and feet*.

"Didn't want anyone to know what?"

"*Ugh*...Callie, it was awful," Sidra said. "Gangrene."

"In his toes and feet?"

"All the way up past his ankles," she said. "Apparently, at first it was just one toe. But Wendell knew what that meant. He was going to put it off for as long as he could. He wore the circulation stockings and everything, but in the end it didn't help."

"I don't understand."

"From the diabetes," Sidra said. "You can get gangrene. The toe starts to turn purple. Once it sets in, you have to amputate."

"Amputate the toe?"

Sidra shook her head.

"No, by the time Marion finally realized what was going on and made Wendell go to the emergency room Sunday morning, all ten toes and both feet were involved. He was scheduled to have both legs removed at the knee yesterday. That's the only blessing in his death, really—it happened before he had to go through the operation."

I was stunned. Why had no one mentioned this to me before? Worse than that, I realized, was that I hadn't ferreted out this information on my own. Was I so out of practice as a detective that I hadn't even thought yet to piece together the events of Wendell's final days?

"Go back a little bit," I said. "What happened Sunday?"

"Sunday morning, getting ready for church, Marion came into the bathroom just as Wendell was coming out of the shower. His feet were black, something he had managed to hide from her for several weeks."

"Ugh."

"As soon as she saw it, Marion called an ambulance and had Wendell taken straight to the hospital."

"I can imagine."

"The doctors said that the feet would have to come off. Wendell was very depressed and upset. We all were."

"Of course."

"They wanted to do the surgery on Monday," Sidra continued, "but Wendell refused to have the operation then. He scheduled it for Tuesday instead. He said he needed Monday to finish some important things at work."

Suddenly, I remembered Gwen on the telephone that first time I came into the office on Monday morning. She had been trying to reschedule a business appointment. *Mr. Smythe's surgery is scheduled for tomorrow morning,* she had said. *If you can't meet with him today, it'll be at least three or four weeks before he's available again.*

Why hadn't I looked into that further before now?

"The poor man," I said, trying to imagine how it would feel to know you'd be losing both of your legs the following day.

"Wendell was devastated," Sidra said, "and not just because he would be losing his legs. Until the gangrene set in, the doctors had been seriously considering letting him have a transplant. Now, all hopes of that had gone out of the window as well."

"A transplant?" I asked, feigning ignorance. "You mean a donor kidney?"

"Derek was going to give his father one of his kidneys," she said. "His antigen match was 4, which is excellent."

"Oh."

"But on Sunday, the doctors finally nixed the whole thing. Wendell's heart just wasn't strong enough for two such serious operations."

I thought about that, about a man who would've had both his legs and his new kidney essentially taken away from him in the same day.

"But I saw Wendell on Monday morning," I said. "He was bright and cheerful and very charismatic. Certainly not like someone who was in the middle of such a crisis."

"That was his way," Sidra said, shrugging. "Believe me, I was his nurse. I know. He could always put his adversity out of his mind, could always make you feel like whatever was happening with you was so much more important than any old thing that was happening with him."

"Amazing."

"He may have put on a smile for you Monday morning," Sidra said, "but I spoke with him at length on Sunday afternoon, and he was incredibly depressed—more than I've ever seen him."

"I can imagine."

"See, Callie, Wendell's mother had diabetes, too. Thirty years ago, she died of infection from an amputation. Poor Wendell saw all that pain and misery that his mother went through. He would've done anything to keep from going through that himself. That's why he was hiding his feet for so long."

"How sad."

I thought of my own Grandma Bessie's death from cancer. It had been long and painful and I, too, had spent much of my time there at the end thinking selfishly about myself, praying that I would never suffer the same fate. I knew how Wendell felt.

"The saddest thing to me," Sidra continued, "was that his murder was so pointless. He was such an ill man. There was a possibility that he wouldn't have survived the amputation anyway, what with his heart and his general condition and everything. Unless the murderer was a complete stranger, it makes no sense. Everyone knew there was a chance he would've been dead within a day or two regardless."

"How about Wendell himself? Do you think he knew he was dying? That he might not survive the operation?"

"I'm sure he suspected it. He had a pretty good handle on his condition."

I thought about Wendell Smythe, about a man racing with the clock to get his affairs in order before he had to become so horribly incapacitated or possibly even die. I felt a surge of pity for him, dealing with his physical condition on top of the betrayal within his own company. I thought about my phone call with Tom on Sunday, the call that had sent me to Philadelphia in the first place. As tired as I was from my previous case, Tom wouldn't even let me wait one day. Now I knew why: His dear friend Wendell urgently needed the money before he went back into the hospital.

Suddenly, a piece of the puzzle clicked into place.

Wendell Smythe didn't need the J.O.S.H.U.A. money to put a bid on a building. There was no building—and Gwen must've known that; it was why she had acted so strangely when I had asked her about it. No, Wendell's funds were all tied up in his business with no time to liquidate. He must have needed cash, and fast. That's why he called us: He told Tom the money was for a building, but in fact Wendell was going to use the J.O.S.H.U.A. money to straighten out the financial mess at Feed the Need. Even though it meant lying to his friend, Wendell must've felt the ends justified the means because he was determined to set things right before he went in for the operation.

The question that remained, then, was *who caused that mess in the first place? More importantly,* I thought, *was it worth killing for?*

Thirty-Five

Dinner was at six, and I was glad. Between missing lunch and taking the afternoon swim, I was starving. By the time I made my way down to the dining room, I was surprised to see that the entire clan was there: Marion, Judith, Derek, Sidra, and Carlos. We took our places at the table, and I was flattered when Carlos insisted on the chair next to mine.

Derek led us in grace, and then the meal was served, a sumptuous parade of cream of asparagus soup, Caesar salad, roast, vegetables, and breads. Angelina served skillfully from the background.

It was a good thing that the food was so delicious, because the conversation was stilted at best with Derek eyeing Judith suspiciously, Sidra avoiding eye contact with Derek, and Marion lost in her own thoughts. At one point, I felt Carlos slip a piece of paper into my hand, and I wondered with a start if he had something important to tell me. I unfolded it as soon as everyone else was distracted with a new course of food, but it was just a typed page of numbers and letters.

"It's my own secret code!" Carlos whispered enthusiastically. "I made it up this afternoon."

I winked at him, folded the paper, and tucked it into my pocket.

"It says, 'I want to be a secret agent, too,'" he whispered, and I gently kicked him.

Afraid that he might say something else, the rest of the meal seemed agonizingly slow. I just hoped Harriet and I could glean what we needed from the Feed the Need records tomorrow morning and then act before Carlos accidentally clued in the murderer that he was aware of my investigation. I didn't want him to be in any danger.

I was feeling more and more certain that the financial funny business that Wendell had uncovered at Feed the Need was the root cause of his murder. Someone had been stealing money from the nonprofit organization by privately selling assets, terminating staff, and cutting costs. Wendell had caught them when he realized they were selling properties around the world and then diverting the proceeds. The question was, who had been doing it, and where was that money now? I was working out a theory, but I needed more evidence to support it.

"Sidra," Marion said suddenly, raising her glass of juice, "I must tell you how pleased I am that you and Carlos have joined us for dinner tonight. We have been missing you at the table."

I could see Sidra color slightly before she replied.

"We're here out of respect for Wendell," Sidra said. "Family is still family, especially on the day of burial."

I glanced at Derek, who was looking at Sidra with deep emotion. She went back to eating, but Derek continued to watch her.

"Sidra," he said finally. "May I speak with you privately, please?"

She seemed about to protest, but she looked up at his face, hesitated, and simply nodded. Together, they rose from the table, and I could see him take her elbow as he guided her from the room.

"I wonder what that's about," Marion said once they were gone.

"Probably more of their shenanigans," Judith said, taking a bite of roast. I felt a surge of anger toward her, which quickly dissolved into disgust. Carlos jabbed me under the table, and I gave him a stern glance that I hoped would shut him up.

"So Marion," I said, grasping for something, anything, to change the subject. "I'm sorry I haven't yet extended condolences on behalf of my boss. I know he would've wanted to be here with you at this time if he could."

Marion paused in her eating, her face surprised.

"But Callie," she protested. "He was there."

"Who?"

"Tom."

"There where?"

"At the cemetery."

"*Tom* was at the *cemetery?*"

"Yes. He sat right behind me, dear. You mean you didn't speak with him?"

I was too embarrassed to admit that Tom and I had never actually met in person, that I wouldn't have known him even if I had seen him.

"No—"

"Of course, he did seem to be in a bit of a hurry when it was over. But still…"

I felt like an idiot. Tom and I were finally in the same place at the same time, and he hadn't introduced himself? He knew who I was, what I looked like. He could've—should've—spoken to me, even if he was pressed for time.

"I'm surprised you didn't see him. He came by helicopter with Congresswoman Brown. They were so late they missed the service at the funeral home. But they made it to the cemetery in time for the ceremony there."

"There was a helicopter at the cemetery?" Carlos asked.

"No, dear," Marion said. "The helicopter landed at the Pike Ridge Airport. I had a car meet them there and drive them to the cemetery."

I racked my brain, trying to remember the faces of the people that sat near the family. It was useless. I had been so thrown by the song the woman sang—not to mention my experience of being thrown into the empty grave—that I couldn't remember what the casket itself looked like. I felt my face flush red as I realized Tom must've seen me crying. He must think I was nuts, sobbing at the funeral of a man I hardly knew.

Congresswoman Brown? I knew who she was. I had heard a speech of hers once at a Philanthropy Now convention. She was an eloquent and intelligent woman, a divorced mother of two with a pretty face and short auburn hair. Formerly a nonprofit attorney, she was now actively involved in the legislation and regulation of non-profits. I wondered if she was also actively involved with Tom.

The rest of the meal passed in a blur with the four of us making uncomfortable small talk. Derek and Sidra never did return to the table, which I took as a hopeful sign. Obviously, he was telling her about Judith, perhaps even paving the way for them to work on their marriage. After dessert, I got out of there as quickly as I could; I wanted to be alone to think. My head was spinning, my stomach burning.

Tom had been at the funeral.

"Hey, Callie," Carlos called to me as I headed up the stairs. I came back down quickly.

"What?" I whispered, glancing around. Marion and Judith had gone on into the den after dinner, but I still didn't want to run the risk of being overheard.

"What's next?" Carlos whispered. "Are you on the case? Are we gonna spy on anybody tonight?"

My stomach lurched. Carlos and I needed to have a little talk. I took his arm and led him to the nearest door, which was Wendell's study. Swinging the door open, I realized the light was on and Angelina was inside.

"*Oh!*" she yelped when she saw us. She was at the far end, a bottle of Windex in her hand, cleaning the glass case that held Wendell's antique clothing collection. "You two scared me!"

"Sorry about that," I said, taking a step back. "We'll come back later."

"No, it is okay," Angelina said, folding the cleaning rag over her arm. "I am finished here."

She started to exit, then turned to speak.

"The museum people will be here next week to get the rest of the collection," she said to Carlos, an odd expression on her face. "I just wanted it to look nice. For your grandfather's sake."

"Thanks, Angelina," he said. "I won't touch the glass."

She left, pulling the door shut behind her. I headed for a chair so that Carlos and I could sit and talk, but he ran to the other end of the room, stopping just short of the glass case.

"Have you seen Grandpa's collection?" he asked me enthusiastically. "It's *so* cool."

I was surprised that an 11-year-old boy would find any interest in antique clothing, but I didn't say as much.

"You see this one here?" he asked, pointing to an old-looking white shirt. It had ruffles at the collar and wrists, and the neck was tied with a yellowed drawstring. "Grandpa bought that shirt for $10,000."

"That's a lot of money for an old shirt," I said, smiling.

"No, get this," he continued. "When he bought it, he thought it might have belonged to Thomas Jefferson, that it might even be the shirt in that painting. Then they did some tests and research and things, and now they're almost sure it did. That makes it worth ten times as much!"

Carlos pointed toward the portrait on the wall, a print of the famous portrait of Jefferson by Françoise Dumond. Unlike the more formal portraits of the era, this painting showed Jefferson deep in thought, leaning over a desk as he put pen to paper, composing the Declaration of Independence. I knew the original painting hung at the Smithsonian, but this copy wasn't bad. And, indeed, the shirt he wore in the painting looked identical to the one in the case.

"Wow," I said, meaning it. From $10,000 to a $100,000 was quite a return on an investment.

"But now," Carlos said, lowering his voice. "This is a secret. You see that dark spot on the sleeve?"

"Yes?"

"If it's what we think it is, that makes the shirt worth even ten times *more*."

I did a quick calculation, my eyebrows raising.

"What is it?" I asked.

"Ink," Carlos whispered. "They think that's a spot of ink from when he wrote the Declaration of Independence."

"*Wow.*"

"That's why we want to get it into the museum right away. We want everyone to be able to see it. Right now, only a few people know, but soon it'll probably be in the newspaper and everything."

I looked at Carlos, whose rapt attention was given over to the collection in front of him. He was such a beautiful child.

"We need to talk, Carlos," I said. He tore himself away from the collection and let me pull him back to the chairs across the room. We sat across from each other, and then I eyed the boy in front of me sternly.

"Now Carlos," I said. "You think this spy stuff is all a bunch of fun and games. But we're not kidding around here. This is serious, serious business."

I scolded him for a while, trying to impress upon him the fact that his grandfather had been murdered, and that the murderer had not yet been caught. He nodded, but I could almost see the wheels turning in his mind.

"This isn't the movies, Carlos," I said. "The hero doesn't always come out okay at the end. And the more you pass me secret notes and whisper about spying and poke me under the table, the more danger you put yourself *and* me into. Do you understand?"

He nodded, looking down at the floor, properly chastised. I was just glad he would be going back to school the next day. If Harriet and I found the proof we needed in the morning, I might be able to get the ball rolling with the police, and they could wrap up the matter before Carlos arrived at home at the end of the day.

"Sorry, Callie," he said, his eyes meeting mine. He looked suddenly tired, and I knew that he had been operating all day on even less sleep than I had.

"I think it's time we both went to bed, don't you?" I said.

"It's only eight!" he cried, glancing at the large grandfather clock against the wall.

"But you, my dear, were up all night on spy duty," I said, rising from the chair and walking with him to the door. "Even James Bond needs a good night's sleep after something like that."

Thirty-Six

It was 8:30 by the time I slipped under the covers, dressed in a loose cotton nightshirt, my teeth brushed, my alarm clock set. I was exhausted, ready to fall into a deep sleep.

Yet sleep didn't come. I kept thinking about Tom, about him being at the funeral, about him specifically not coming over to speak with me. Why hadn't he? I had always told myself we had never met because we were so busy, because we were never in the same place at the same time. But this time there was no excuse. Why had he avoided me? Was it because he was there with another woman? If so, why should that matter?

After tossing and turning for half an hour, I finally got up and got my cell phone. If he was home, he would still be up, probably hacking away at his computer. I climbed back under the covers and dialed, half hoping he wouldn't pick up the phone.

"Hello?" he said, his voice as warm and smooth as always. I tried to bring up the image I had created of his face, but it wouldn't come. Instead, all I saw were the backs of dark-suited people, sitting in a row at a funeral.

"Hey," I said, my voice soft.

"Callie!" he replied, pleasure tingeing his voice. "I was hoping this would be you. You've been on my mind all evening. I wondered how things are coming along with the investigation and if there's anything I can do to help."

I closed my eyes, wishing I could see through the phone, wishing I could see right now where Tom was and what he was doing.

"Getting closer," I said. "But that's not why I called."

"Oh?"

"I just had a little talk with Marion. From what I understand, you were there today. At the funeral."

There was a moment's pause, and then a quiet answer: "Yes."

I didn't say anything. I wasn't even sure how to ask it or if my question was even appropriate for our relationship. We were boss and employee, of course, but we were also something more. I thought we were something more anyway, something noble and special, the two of us in a fight to make the world a better place through his foundation. Our foundation.

"Why didn't you speak to me?" I asked finally. He didn't answer right away. I could hear him exhale slowly, and I imagined him leaning forward in his chair, maybe rubbing a hand over his forehead. Finally, when he did speak, his voice was soft and intimate.

"I was going to," he said. "I really was. I was going to surprise you and tell you it was me, and finally we were going to meet face-to-face."

"But you didn't."

"No," he said. "I didn't."

I closed my eyes, wondering why they had suddenly filled with tears. I just felt so sad. So sad and so very, very alone.

"I can't explain it," he added finally. "I stood there across the graveyard, and I looked at you, but you were crying. The expression on your face…I don't know. I thought you'd rather be alone."

"It was a hard day for me," I said. "It was the first funeral I've been to since—"

"Yes, I know," he answered. "That's why I didn't speak, in the end. I realized it wasn't the time and place for us to finally meet in person."

I thought about it, and I had to admit he was right, in a way. The longer we went without meeting, the more significance the event seemed to have taken on. When we finally did get together, it was bound to be an important time, with lots of laughing and talking. I could see why he had hesitated at the funeral of one of his best friends, particularly with me looking so distraught.

I blinked, sending the tears coursing sideways over my face and onto the pillow under my head. Why had I been doing so much crying lately? It seemed like that's all I had done since this case had begun.

"So what now?" I asked, the question seeming to pop out of nowhere. "For us, I mean. Will you and I ever meet, Tom?"

"Ah, Callie," he said, his voice warm and familiar. "Of course we will. I'm looking forward to that day more than you know."

I smiled, knowing that I also looked forward to it, much, much more than I had ever admitted to myself before.

"Trust me," he said. "It *will* happen, eventually. When it's right."

"When it's right," I echoed.

Suddenly, I was overwhelmed with exhaustion. I told him that I was meeting Harriet early in the morning and that for now I ought to get to sleep.

"Okay, Callie," he said, his voice growing serious again. "I really am sorry about today."

"You are?"

"It was tough for me, with Wendell gone. I thought you and I might've comforted each other."

"I'm sure you were comforted just fine by Congresswoman Brown."

He hesitated, and I mentally kicked myself for letting that slip out.

"She offered me a ride in her helicopter, Callie. It saved me a lot of time and trouble."

"Of course."

"She has nothing to do with this."

"Okay."

"It was you, Callie. Besides the crying, there was something in your face today…I don't know. An utter *sorrow*. I knew you were probably thinking of your late husband. I didn't want to intrude."

I was surprised by his comment. Tom knew about Bryan, of course, but he rarely brought him up in conversation.

"I think of Bryan all the time," I said, trying to make my voice light. "But thinking about him doesn't bring him back. My life has gone on."

"So it has," he said. "You are a very brave woman."

"There's nothing brave about accepting the inevitable." *Nothing brave about crying for a man a full three years after he's gone.*

We concluded our conversation, and just as we were about to hang up, Tom said my name once more.

"Callie," he nearly whispered. I pressed the phone to my ear, wondering what would come next. For a brief moment, I wanted to hear him say that when this case was over, we would plan a get-together of our own, that we would arrange the perfect place and time. I hesitated, knowing that the thought of that filled me with an odd mix of excitement and fear.

"I just wanted to say," he continued, "that in spite of everything else, you are even more beautiful in person than you are in pictures."

He disconnected the call then, and I sat with the phone in my hand for a long time, thinking about him, thinking about what we could, someday, be to each other. Outside, I could hear the soft patter of rain against the window. Half smiling, I turned over and closed my eyes. I was asleep in an instant, and slept through the night without stirring, my dreams for once the easy, pleasant dreams of the unencumbered.

Thirty-Seven

~

I awoke feeling surprisingly refreshed. I still ached, of course, from my big fall the day before, but my head was clear and I no longer felt tired. Mostly, I was full of unjustified optimism, ready to head out and wrap this matter up so I could go home.

Once I was dressed and ready to leave, I grabbed my keys and my briefcase and headed down the stairs and out the back door, grateful when I didn't run into anyone on the way. It was still early; I would stop for coffee and a bagel at the convenience store on the corner. I knew that would certainly be simpler and quicker than making conversation in the kitchen with Nick or Angelina.

It was a gorgeous morning, already warmer than the past few days. I was headed straight for my car when I noticed something odd about the pool. I hesitated, then took a step closer.

There were dozens of small sheets of paper floating in the water. Most were drifting here and there, but some of them had clumped into a wad in the deep end, around the drain, and a few had sunk to the bottom.

I took off a shoe and stepped down onto the first step, grabbing for the closest piece of paper I could reach. I knew what it was almost before I got a good look at it. It was onionskin paper, the kind of stationery Derek used to write to Sidra years ago when he was in seminary.

This was more of Judith's handiwork, I felt sure, another act of vandalism against Sidra. *I told him to go ahead and take the test,* I read, noticing the numeral 2 scribbled in the upper right hand corner. *I think he probably made about a C, but I have a feeling I aced it. Say a prayer that I did!*

I skimmed the entire page. The letter wasn't full of romantic platitudes by any means, but at the end, it was signed, *Counting the days, hours, weeks, minutes until I see you again, I remain faithfully and forever yours, Derek.* A love letter.

I exhaled slowly, a sinking feeling in the pit of my stomach. I would have to confess to Sidra that I had taken these letters and that they had then been stolen from me and ultimately dumped out here. As a sort of penance, I put down my stuff, removed the net from its hook beside the cabana, and dipped it in the pool until I had scooped every last letter out. Then I gathered up the entire soggy pile and knocked on Sidra's door. It was 7:20 A.M.

To my surprise, Derek answered. He was wearing a T-shirt and jeans with no shoes, and his hair was wet. He smelled pleasantly of soap and shampoo.

"Derek?" I said, unable to hide my surprise.

"Hey, Callie," he replied. "You looking for Sidra?"

"Who is it?" I heard in a soft voice, and then Sidra appeared next to Derek, her hair wrapped in a towel, wearing a peach-colored terry cloth robe. I felt my face flush in spite of the fact that they were married, in spite of the fact that this was a wonderful new development to their previously estranged relationship.

"We need to talk," I said to them both. "I just found these in the pool."

They both looked confused when they saw the dripping mess I clutched in my hands so I explained further.

"Letters," I said. "Old love letters. From you to you. It's a long story."

Sidra gasped, but Derek put a calming hand on her arm.

"Don't let it get to you," he said to her. "We know who's doing it now. The whole ball game has changed."

Sidra pulled the towel off of her head and held it out for me so I could drop the glob of letters onto it. I then grabbed my own things and came inside.

"We need to keep our voices down a bit," said Sidra as she motioned me toward a chair. "Carlos is still asleep. He doesn't get up for school until 7:30."

"I was just getting ready to head back over to the house," Derek said. "We don't want to…confuse him."

Derek's eyes met mine, and I knew he was telling me, in his own way, that he had taken my little lecture to heart. This *was* a marriage worth saving; it looked as though they had taken some first, important steps toward healing.

"Derek told me everything," Sidra said, coming to sit on a chair across from me, wet tendrils of hair sticking to her cheeks. "We know now that Judith is the one who has been doing these things. What we don't know yet is why."

"Have you had a chance to think about that? Both of you? Why she would want your marriage to break up?"

Sidra and Derek both shook their heads.

"Judith and I have always gotten along fine," Sidra said. "There was never any animosity between us."

"How about you, Derek?"

"My sister and I have a complicated relationship," he said. "Sort of competitive, I guess. Like a lot of siblings. But no, nothing in our history would've prepared me for this."

"Well, I'm afraid this latest incident was partly my fault," I said, looking toward the letters. I went on to explain how I had taken them from here a few nights before and that they had subsequently been stolen from my room.

"At the time, it was just a part of my investigation. But I'm sorry for taking them. Especially now that they're ruined."

Sidra was about to reply when we heard Carlos' alarm go off in the other room. She looked at Derek, who quickly slipped on his shoes.

"What's done is done," she said softly before rising. We all stood, and Derek and I headed for the door.

"Come back once Carlos has left for school," Sidra whispered to Derek, a sexy hint of promise shining in her eyes. He held her gaze, finally bending over for one more, slightly longer kiss.

"Till then."

"Hey, Mom!" Carlos yelled from his room. "Do you know if Angelina washed my new jeans?"

Sidra winked at us as we stepped outside, and she quietly shut the door. Derek and I walked a few paces together as I struggled for something fitting to say.

"You were right," he said finally. "There's no excuse for letting this marriage go. I want to thank you for banging me over the head with that fact before it was too late."

I grinned, picturing my fury of the morning before, slamming my money down on the table and marching out of the restaurant. At least my point had been made.

"Hey, Derek," I said, changing the subject, thinking of Harriet's e-mail, of the man who followed me around town and later pushed me into a grave. "Let me ask you something. Does the name Mitchell Ralston mean anything to you?"

"Rings a bell," he replied. "Let me think."

We reached the end of the pool and the point where the sidewalk made a T. We stopped walking because Derek was headed back to the house, but I was going to my car.

"Mitchell Ralston," he repeated. "If I'm not mistaken, that was the name of one of my father's night nurses."

"He had night nurses?"

"This was a while back. Dad was trying a different kind of dialysis where the cycler runs all night while you're sleeping, instead of during the day. Sidra didn't want him doing it unobserved; she thought it was too dangerous. So we tried hiring some night nurses, mostly for observation. But in the end, my father found he couldn't sleep well enough all hooked up to the machine anyway, so he went back to daytime dialysis."

"What happened to the nurses?"

"We let them go. But Ralston was fired before that anyway. He was bad news, almost from the day he started."

"Bad news, how?"

Derek pressed a finger against his chin absently as he thought.

"From what I recall, we made the mistake of hiring him without checking his references first. He had sticky fingers. Stole some cash from Dad's dresser, some jewelry from Mom. We let him go fairly quickly."

"How long ago was that?"

Derek shrugged.

"I don't know. Maybe six months ago. Why do you ask?"

I shook my head.

"Too complicated to explain," I said. "Why didn't you check his references before hiring him?"

"He came here on a recommendation. From Alan. Ralston had worked for Alan's aunt or something."

"What did Alan say when he found out the man was a thief?"

"He was mortified and furious, of course," Derek replied. "But what can you do? Sometimes things like that happen."

"I guess so."

I asked Derek to describe the man.

"Big muscles. Brown hair. Not too bad-looking. Funny haircut, though. Kind of spiked up in the front."

I thanked Derek for his help, then headed on to my car. As I drove, I thought about what I had just learned. A former nurse! By limiting my search to people whom Wendell would freely allow to inject him with insulin, I hadn't even considered *former* employees. Still, if this man had been let go under difficult circumstances, what would Wendell's reaction have been to the man now appearing in his office, slipping in through the back way? Somehow, I doubted that Wendell would've allowed this guy to inject him—unless, perhaps, it was done at gunpoint.

I pulled onto the Schuylkill expressway, knowing I needed to give this information to Duane Perskie because he was running the man's prints for me. I dialed his number on my car phone, expecting to leave a message on his voice mail. Much to my surprise, however, he answered on the second ring. I continued to drive as we talked.

"Callie!" he said when he realized it was me. "I was just trying to reach you at the Smythes'. What a mess I'm in here."

"What's going on?"

"Those prints you asked me to run? I was doing it on the QT just as a favor. But one of the names set off some red flags with Keegan and Sollie, not to mention the FBI. Now they wanna see you *and* me ASAP."

"Let me guess," I said. "The red flag was for Mitchell Ralston."

"Ralston, Rathbone...the guy went by several names. Real name is Monty Redburn. He's got a rap sheet long as my arm."

"Why was he flagged?"

"He's being sought in connection with Smythe's murder. Don't know how he fits in, exactly, but now I've got to explain why I was running his prints and where I got them. You've got to come in."

I glanced at the clock, thinking about Harriet. She would be at the train station in less than 20 minutes. So far, traffic was very light, but I knew I couldn't depend on that. Once I picked her up, we had lots to do, important work that might clear up the questions hovering over this entire investigation. I knew that if I went to the police station instead, I would be stuck there for hours, answering their questions, telling them everything I had done and been through since my investigation began.

"Duane," I said, "I'm really sorry and I owe you big on this one, but I'm not coming in. Not just yet."

"What?"

"You have to put off the meeting. I'll contact you in a few hours."

"But Callie, you can't—"

"Please, Duane. I'm sorry. I'll be in touch."

He was quiet for a long moment then finally exhaled loudly.

"Just a few hours," he said. "I can't hold 'em off any longer than that."

"I promise," I said.

I hung up the phone and was just slipping it into my purse when I heard the odd sound of a motor gunning.

I looked up, shocked to see a red pickup truck filling my rearview mirror; Mitchell Ralston or Monty Redburn or whatever-his-name was at the wheel.

Bang!

He rammed his truck into the back of my car! I felt the force of it thrust me forward, and I gripped the steering wheel tightly as I tried not to lose control.

I looked around frantically, trying to size up my situation, blaming myself for being so wrapped up in my phone conversation that I hadn't seen Redburn behind me.

Bang!

He hit me again, this time propelling me sideways into the cement median. He had chosen the place for this ambush well; we were driving along a several-mile strip of road construction, an area with no shoulders and absolutely no way to go but forward. On each side of the two lanes were four-foot-high concrete walls with only about a foot's leeway between them and the road.

I steered back from the median, yelling at the image in my rearview mirror. He kept coming though, so close that I could see the grin on his face. He was enjoying this.

I slammed my foot down on the gas pedal and managed to put a few yards between us. I tried to use that time to grab my phone and hit redial. But before I could press the "send" button, the truck slammed into me again. The phone shot from my hand, clattering to the floorboard on the far side of the car and out of reach.

"Stop it!" I screamed, racing through my options in my mind, desperately trying to figure out what to do. There were no other cars here, no choices but to go fast or faster. Still, my little Saturn was no match for his truck. I knew that if his intention was to kill me, he would more than likely succeed.

I thought about slamming on my brakes, but I felt sure that he would simply crush me from behind, making my car look like an accordion. We were already going about 85 miles per hour. One good impact into that cement wall and my car would be scrap metal.

I decided to take my foot off of the gas completely. As I slowed, he banged into me again, but I was ready for him. I steered against the push of his truck and then gunned myself ahead of him in a short burst. I tried that again, slowing until he almost hit me, then pressing down on the gas.

Bang!

He rammed into me hard. My head snapped back with such force that I thought I would see stars. Amazingly, my air bag didn't deploy, but I still lost all control of the wheel. I felt myself spinning, spinning out of control, then the next thing I saw was the cement barrier rushing closer. I would've crashed into it if I hadn't seen at the last moment a gap in the wall. I grabbed hard on the wheel and held on, suddenly steering to make a sharp right when I reached the break.

I didn't know where I was going as I turned, only that I was getting off of the road, away from the maniac in the truck. *With my luck, I'm driving off a cliff,* I thought as I pounded blindly down an incline, away from the road. When my car finally came to a stop, I was enveloped in a cloud of dust. I held my breath, eyes closed, praying that he was gone for good and that I was safe.

"You alright, lady?"

I opened my eyes to see six or seven men surrounding my car, looking in at me with concern. They were construction workers, all in jeans and hard hats. I nodded, opening my door with trembling hands.

"Somebody ran me off the road," I said, my voice hoarse.

"We heard the noise," one of the men said. "He was gunning right for you."

"Where am I?"

"Road construction," another one said. "We're widening the lanes."

I stood up on unsteady legs and looked around at the packed-dirt lot that surrounded me. There were cars parked in rows in the dirt, and I could see the cranes and other equipment of heavy construction in the distance. Fortunately, I seemed to have landed in the one part of the area that didn't have any vehicles in it. I realized that had I gone another 20 feet, I would've crashed into a group of workmen laying some cement.

I turned to look at my car, fear welling up in my throat when I saw what he had done. The car looked as though it had been through a major crash with paint scraped from the sides and the back crushed in like a cereal box. Only with God's grace, I knew, had I survived.

"You want we should call the police for you?" one of the men asked. I shook my head, knowing that the police were already looking for me.

"Just tell me if there's another way to get out of here besides the main road," I said, my voice sounding much stronger now than I felt. I knew my only choice was to pick up Harriet and get this mystery solved before I was as dead as Wendell Smythe.

The police would hear my story soon enough.

Thirty-Eight

Harriet was waiting when I arrived at the train station, a big tote bag clutched in each hand. As I pulled closer, I could see her face go from excited to appalled. She looked my vehicle up and down, her eyes wide.

"What in the world happened to you?" she exclaimed. "I guess Philly traffic is even worse than DC, huh?"

I got out and hugged her and then told her to lower her voice and get in the car as quickly as possible. She did as I asked, tossing her tote bags into the backseat before sitting down and slamming the door.

"Don't ask any questions just yet," I said. I put on my blinker, trying to pull back out into the line of traffic. "Please use your phone and find me the nearest car rental place."

"Were you in an accident?"

"Sort of."

"I've got a cousin here in town," she said. "Maybe we could run out there, and you could borrow her car. I was hoping to squeeze in a visit anyway."

"Harriet," I said evenly, "thanks for the offer. But I'd be more comfortable with a rental."

We found a nearby car rental agency, and I left Harriet waiting in my car while I went inside and asked for the biggest, safest, sturdiest vehicle that they had. They offered me a Lincoln or a minivan. I was about to decline both when the young man behind the counter volunteered that the Lincoln had a really strong V8 engine.

"Zero to 60 in about five seconds," he said, grinning, but when his boss flashed him a glare, he added, "Least that's what they say in the commercials."

I took him up on it, handing over my credit card and waiting impatiently as he did the paperwork. I had lost my pursuer in the red truck, and I had no intention of being found again. Once they got me all set up with my rental, the man recommended a body shop right up the block for my Saturn. I told them I'd rather just park it for the time being, so they let me have a slot on the end.

By the time Harriet and I got into our new Lincoln, she was bubbling over with questions, her face the picture of concern. I tried to convince her that everything was fine, or at least okay, but I knew she could tell from my trembling hands that it was not.

We headed into the city in our new rental, the interior as plush and comfortable as any I'd ever ridden in. I always had an odd affection for rental cars, for the pleasure of trying out different types of vehicles on a temporary basis. But I rarely went with the luxury class, opting instead for the more economical midsize. This was different, however.

This was war.

Glancing frequently in my rearview mirror, I tried to relax as we drove, finally giving Harriet a toned-down, modified version of what had happened. She seemed nervous after that, glancing behind us often, asking me twice to describe the truck that my attacker had driven. I realized too late that I should've just made up some story of a fender bender instead—Harriet was not the type who enjoyed or even endured danger or intrigue. The fact that the police wanted me for questioning would've only made her more upset, so I omitted that fact altogether.

Fortunately, we made it all the way downtown to the hotel without incident and without catching sight of the truck. I found the hotel's parking garage and claimed a spot on the first floor; then we loaded up all of our things and headed across the street to the hotel.

The place was huge, with a lobby spanning at least five floors in height. After we secured our meeting room with the sales office, I headed there while Harriet made a stop in the rest room.

"I would've gone at the train station," she said as she paused in the doorway, "but that place smelled worse than a hog's pen in Indian summer."

I laughed out loud, wondering how I had gotten through the week without her. Though Harriet was older than me by a good 20 years, she was a slightly eccentric, totally youthful ray of sunshine— her hair a vivid red pile of curls on top of her head, her glasses sparkling at each corner with rhinestones. And though she tried to wear nice clothes, she always seemed to be falling apart with shoes that didn't quite match her purse, lipstick smeared on her teeth, and hemlines that were perpetually crooked.

I found our meeting place at the end of a long hall, a pleasant boardroom-style setup with a huge conference table and seating for about ten people. I pushed the chairs around a bit so that Harriet and I would have access to the modem port and the electrical outlets; then I plugged in my own laptop and pulled out the box of records I had received from Marion—the ones she had discovered in Wendell's safe. The hotel had left a stack of notepads and sharpened pencils in the center of the table, and I helped myself to two of each, laying them in our working space.

"Here's your food setup," the hotel caterer said as she wheeled a cart into the room. On it was a coffee pot and a small stack of cups and plates alongside an artfully arranged pile of fresh fruit and pastries— the mandatory minimum catering service offered with the room.

"Looks wonderful," I said as she slid the cart against the wall. I had forgotten all about stopping for breakfast, and I felt a surge of appetite and a serious need for coffee. As soon as the woman left, I took a small plate and loaded it with fresh strawberries and watermelon before fixing myself a cup of the coffee, black and strong.

"Nice room," Harriet said when she finally came through the door. "But this table's big enough for line dancing!"

I smiled and pointed her toward the food and coffee. She got herself all set, then joined me at the table.

"Before we start," Harriet said, removing her glasses to study me carefully, "I wanna know how you're doin'. You really don't look so good."

I quickly swallowed a bite of a strawberry.

"I'm recovering," I said. "At least we're here now—we're safe."

"I'm not just talking about the incident this morning. I've been worried about you all week."

Glancing into her concerned face, I felt a surge of tears threatening behind my eyes. I looked away, rearranging the fruit on my plate.

"It's been a hard week for me," I said finally, softly. "The widow, Mrs. Smythe? She loved her husband very much. From what I can tell, they had one of those marriages…"

I let my voice trail off as I struggled for the right words.

"One of those amazing marriages, like you and your husband had?" Harriet finished for me. I nodded.

"But I've cried a little and worked some things through," I continued, "and now I think I'm going to be fine. No, I *know* I'm going to be fine."

"If you need to talk," Harriet said, "I'm ready to listen."

I smiled at her.

"Don't need to talk, actually," I said. "But I could use a prayer."

She nodded knowingly, and then we held hands and bowed our heads.

"Lord," she drawled, "I thank You for my dear friend, Callie Webber, the finest woman I have ever known. I just pray that You will come down and wrap Your lovin' arms around her and protect her from hurt and from harm. Bless us here today as we attempt to finish this job so Callie can come back home where she belongs. Help us to keep our eyes on You, God, and give me traveling mercies as I head back out this afternoon."

After her amen, I felt her squeeze my hands tightly before letting go. I said my own silent prayer of thanks for the blessing of a true friend. Then we turned toward the table, pulled out Harriet's computer and her adding machine, and got down to work.

Thirty-Nine

～

"You're telling me," I said to Harriet, "that there's a $250,000 discrepancy between these two sets of books?"

We had been working for nearly three hours as we compared the records and analyzed the cash flow from each set.

"Two hundred forty-nine thousand, seven hundred thirty-three dollars," she said, "that shows up in the public record, but disappears in the private one."

"Well, I guess that's not really a surprise," I said, tossing a grape up into the air and catching it in my mouth. "My bet is that Wendell wanted the money from J.O.S.H.U.A. to cover this debt. He wanted to straighten out this mess before he went in for his operation."

Harriet agreed. She had tried crunching the numbers several different ways, but it still came out the same. In the last five months, Feed the Need had drastically cut their costs, diverting the savings into a series of unrelated accounts. The surprise here was not that the money had been stolen, but where it had gone—not into someone's private account, as I had suspected, but into the business accounts of Smythe Incorporated. Whoever had stolen this money from Feed the Need had simply diverted it to the for-profit company. Of course, it wasn't quite that clear-cut on paper, but Harriet had brilliantly traced it out.

"I don't get it," Harriet said. "I mean, a quarter-mil isn't exactly a lot of money to a company like Smythe. They deal in multi-millions. I can't imagine why a measly $250,000 was worth all the trouble."

"Unless they're not done yet," I said. "What if whoever did this is still doing it, pulling out just a little at a time so they don't get caught?"

I stood and paced around the room, thinking of Wendell's secretary and wondering if she had had any part in this. I doubted it. She so truly valued Feed the Need; I doubted she would've done anything to hurt the good works they were doing. It had to have been Judith and Alan.

"This is so awful," I said. "Not to mention incredibly illegal. How can we tell who authorized all of these transfers?"

Harriet shook her head, pointing to the list of transfers that was nearly a page long—the small transfers that added, in total, up to nearly $250,000.

"You want names connected with the actions?" she asked. "These days, it's all done electronically."

"There has to be a record somewhere. I'm going to need that in order to prove any of this."

"My suggestion," she said, "would be to get into the Smythe's electronic banking setup and see if it has a history field. There's usually a code assigned to each transaction."

"Okay, let's do it."

"It's not that simple," she said. "I can't do that here. You need access, code numbers, the right software—"

"In other words, we need to get over to the Smythe offices and do it from there?"

"Exactly."

I hesitated, knowing the last place I wanted to be was back on the road, much less at a familiar place where my tail could once again pick me up and make roadkill out of me. I felt sure we'd be safe in the Smythe offices, though once we left there I wouldn't have taken money on our odds of making it back to the train station in one piece.

There was also the little matter of the cops looking for me. If the Feed the Need receptionist was on the alert to watch for me, I knew the jig would be up the minute we walked into the door. Then this day would be lost for sure, and poor Harriet would end up trapped in Philadelphia just like me.

"Harriet," I said, standing up. "I need you to take off every single item you're wearing that isn't absolutely necessary."

"What?"

"Come on," I said. "Scarf, jewelry, blazer. Let's go."

She did as I asked, stripping down to nothing more than a pair of slacks and a sleeveless shirt. I gave her my navy jacket. Because it was a bit small for her, she hung it down her back and tied the sleeves around the front of her neck.

I, in turn, tied her colorful silk scarf over my hair, loaded on her clunky bracelets and necklace, and slipped my arms into the sleeves of her big purple jacket, buttoning it down the front. Then I grabbed the pile of napkins from the catering tray and began balling them up one by one and stuffing them into my clothes. When I was finished, I stepped back and modeled my new look for Harriet's approval. After a moment's hesitation, she pulled off her rhinestone glasses and slipped them on my nose.

"Oh, goodness," she said, grinning. "From a distance, no one would ever recognize you."

"I hope not," I replied. Though I knew I couldn't carry off this look for long, at least it should get us in and out of the Smythe building without incident.

We quickly loaded up all of our stuff and signed out at the desk. Then we ran to the rental car in the parking garage across the street, climbed in, and headed for Smythe Incorporated.

～

Stepping from the elevator, I led Harriet to the left and into the Smythe offices instead of to the right and into Feed the Need. The first goal was to get to Gwen's office, which spanned the two companies near the back.

"I'm here to see Gwen Harding," Harriet said, just as I had instructed her in the car. "But don't tell her. I'd like to surprise her if I could."

The receptionist, a young man, seemed disinterested at best. He gave us directions to Gwen's office, then returned to the magazine he had been reading when we first came in the door.

So far, so good.

"Swanky place," Harriet whispered as we strolled quickly through the building, my hand at her elbow since she couldn't see that well without her glasses. I was afraid we might run into Alan or Judith, but we made it to the door of Gwen's office without incident.

I turned the knob and swung open the door, stepping inside to find Gwen at her desk, typing away.

"May I help you?" she asked, glancing at us without a break in her typing.

We stepped closer, and I took off the glasses and the scarf.

"It's me, Gwen," I said softly. "Callie."

Gwen stopped typing and stood, looking me over with a smile.

"What are you doing?" she asked with a chuckle. "Is that some sort of disguise?"

I handed the glasses to Harriet and walked toward the desk.

"Someone tried to kill me this morning."

"What—"

"Listen to me, Gwen," I continued. "I don't have much time."

"What's going on, Callie? That nice Detective Keegan called here, looking for you. He said to let him know if you showed up."

"I know. It's a long story. Here's the short version."

"The police are looking for you?" Harriet squeaked, but I ignored her question.

"I'm an investigator, Gwen. Usually, I just investigate companies, but this time I've been investigating a murder. Wendell's murder."

"Oh, my."

"I know there was no building, Gwen. I know Wendell's story about needing a fast $250,000 from the J.O.S.H.U.A. fund had nothing to do with buying some property and everything to do with straightening out the financial mess that had been made with Feed the Need."

Gwen seemed to pale, and she sat in her chair, nodding.

"Talk to me, Gwen," I said. "Tell me what happened here that last day."

I walked around her desk and sat on the edge of it, looking down on her. Though I felt a little ridiculous in the stuffed purple jacket, I knew she was intimidated nonetheless.

"I don't know that much," Gwen said, tears springing to her eyes, "but I certainly know more than I told the police. It's been eating away at me, like a cancer."

I glanced at Harriet, who had taken a seat against the far wall and was watching our interaction with rapt attention.

"Go ahead," I said to Gwen, my voice more gentle this time.

"Oh, Callie, it was awful," Gwen cried. "I don't even know where to start."

"How about at the beginning?"

She wiped her eyes, took a deep breath, and let it out.

"It started about two months ago," she said softly. "Because of his health, Wendell didn't travel much any more, but he needed to go to our factory in Sri Lanka. He took Marion with him, and they planned to end their trip with a few days in Kauai. A little mini-vaca-tion."

"Okay."

"They had a layover in Manila, where Feed the Need has a big district office. Since they had a few hours to spare, they decided to pay the office a quick visit. When they got there, they found that the office was closed down."

I had already heard this story from Marion and had already seen the sign Wendell brought home from Manila with him.

"By the time Wendell got back here, he'd had a lot of time to think about things. He knew that if sneaky stuff was happening in his com-pany, he was partly at fault because he'd been so consumed with his health that he hadn't paid much attention to the business lately. He became obsessed with finding out exactly what was going on."

"What did he find out?"

"That things were even worse than he thought. Five district offices had been closed. Three of the buildings had already been sold. Fifteen people had been laid off from the staff here. All sorts of things to cut costs, right under his nose. Derek was as clueless as his father. In fact, he's still clueless, as far as I know."

I thought about Derek, so consumed with the problems in his marriage that he didn't even see his company was being robbed blind. Suddenly, an idea began to form in my mind. Perhaps Judith had done all of those acts of vandalism against Sidra not out of some demented fury, but as a cold, calculated way to distract her brother from what was going on at his company.

"Had this been a regular business," Gwen said, standing so that she could pace back and forth, "heads would've rolled. Wendell could've tracked down the source of the problem and dealt with it swiftly and severely."

"But…"

"But this was Feed the Need, Callie. This was a nonprofit. You can't just announce to the world that people have been stealing money here. It takes years to build up the public's trust and the efforts of thousands of people to make an organization like this work."

"I know, but—"

"Understand something, Callie. Until this happened, our record was exemplary. We belong to different watchdog groups, and we've met all of the criteria, passed every screening with flying colors. When Wendell realized what was going on, he had a very difficult choice to make. Either he could blow the whistle and destroy the efforts of everyone just because of the destructive acts of a few individuals, or he could deal with it in his own way, quietly: Replace the money, repair the damage, eliminate the troublemakers, and keep our agency's reputation intact. He was doing the right thing. He just didn't have a chance to finish it."

I considered her words, knowing this was a conundrum I had faced often in my years with the J.O.S.H.U.A. organization. Many times I had found an agency or organization that was doing some wonderful things, yet at its core there were serious issues of ethics or improper use of funds. My experience had been that when problems like these existed, the trouble was most often found at the very top with enormous amounts of money going into the pockets of the principals. Just recently I had analyzed a nonprofit that was accomplishing some wonderful things—only to find that the man running the business seemed to have forgotten the "non" in "nonprofit" as he personally received more than a half a million dollars per year in salary and fringe benefits. Then, as always, I had asked myself the same question: Blow the whistle and risk destroying all the good they were accomplishing, or let it ride? Apparently, Wendell had decided to basically fix things and then let it ride.

"This leaves us with one question, Gwen. Who was it? Who was stealing the money?"

Gwen shook her head, her eyes moist.

"I have my suspicions, but Wendell would never say. He told me only that he was dealing with the matter, and when all was said and done, those involved would be out of the organization."

"So whom did you suspect?"

"Alan. And…" she hesitated.

"Judith?" I asked.

After a moment, she nodded.

"Not until yesterday did I suspect Judith," she said. "But then at the funeral it began to dawn on me. She was the only one who had the authority to make the kinds of financial transfers that Wendell had discovered going from Feed the Need into Smythe Incorporated. Only Judith or Derek could've done that. And I know Derek wouldn't rob his own company."

"So tell me about Wendell's last day."

"What can I say? He called me Sunday night and told me about his operation. He also told me he had found an outside source for some fast cash and that he had one day to make everything right. I spent Monday morning rescheduling all of his appointments. He spent the morning trying to redo all that had been undone in Feed the Need."

"But he was a wealthy man," I said. "Why involve my foundation at all? Why didn't he just put up his own personal cash? To someone like him, a quarter of a million dollars couldn't have been all that much."

"Well, he didn't keep that kind of money just lying around, if that's what you mean," Gwen snapped. "His personal fortune was tied up in his portfolio."

"What about getting a line of credit from the bank?"

"It was all a matter of *time*," Gwen replied. "In those last two days, every minute was important. Calling your boss to borrow some of his readily available cash was a lot quicker than trying to secure it other ways. Every minute counted, Callie. Wendell felt he was watching the clock tick away the final hours of his life, and he had to act fast."

I sat back, knowing she was right. The doctors had given him one day to get his affairs in order. He had scrambled to right these wrongs the quickest way he knew how.

"Who killed him, Gwen?" I asked.

"I don't know," she replied, allowing herself to fall back in her chair. "I've asked myself that a million times. I was *right here*. I should've heard something. I should've seen something."

"Do you think it was Alan and Judith?"

She put her head in her hands.

"I don't know, Callie," she sobbed. "I just don't know."

Forty

~

I let Gwen cry for a few minutes; then I handed her a Kleenex and told her that Harriet and I needed to sit down at a computer and go into Smythe's on-line banking system without the knowledge of Judith, Alan, or Derek.

"None of them are here today anyway," Gwen replied, blowing her nose.

"We have the list of bank transfers from Feed the Need to Smythe," I said. "We just have to figure out once and for all who authorized them."

"Yolanda Washington can help you," Gwen said. "I'll take you to her office."

I tied the scarf back on my head, and Harriet and I followed Gwen as she walked us down a short hall until we came to a large cubicle. The woman at the desk was very heavy, in her late 20s, with thick black hair and a dark mole on her chin.

"Hey, Gwen," she said as we peeked into her office. "Can I help you with something?"

"This is Callie Webber," Gwen said, gesturing toward me, "and her associate Harriet Blanchard. They need to find some things out, and I think you're the one to help."

"It's something we need to get to right now," I added quickly. "It's very important. Can you help us?"

Yolanda nodded her head.

"Like what?"

"Financial data," I said, going around behind her desk and pulling a chair up next to hers. Harriet plopped her purse on the floor and looked around for another chair. Yolanda seemed startled. "Tell her we're authorized, Gwen."

"Give the ladies any information they need," Gwen said, coming around to stand behind us.

I pulled a few pages of financial data from my briefcase and skimmed through them. Harriet disappeared into another cubicle and came back with a rolling chair, which she slid into place beside Yolanda.

"You're on a remote internet banking system, I assume," I said to Yolanda. "Pull that up, please. We need to get a look at the history of some of your accounts."

"Okay," she said, typing into the computer. A logo for internet banking appeared on the screen. "What accounts are you interested in?"

I handed the page of numbers to Harriet, and she read off the first account number as Yolanda typed it in. The account came up onto the screen in confusing rows of figures. But Yolanda seemed to know what she was doing. I told her the first transaction I was looking for—a transfer into this account from another account in the same bank—and gave her the amount and the date. She found it quickly and was able to display the authorization code of the person who made the transfer.

"There's your culprit right there," Harriet said, pointing to a number on the screen. "Person number two-zero-two-one. Who's that?"

"That's Judith Smythe," Yolanda replied.

"Judith," Gwen echoed in a whisper behind her.

Harriet and I glanced at each other. Just as we'd suspected. I felt an urgency grow as Harriet read off the next account number.

We worked that way for the next 15 minutes, verifying a series of transactions in the last two months that showed a total of nearly $200,000 coming into the Smythe accounts from Feed the Need. The first few transfers had been done by Judith; the rest seemed to have been done by Alan. Harriet had just read off yet another account number to Yolanda when she suddenly sat up straight and gasped.

"Whoa!" she said, peering intently at the screen.

"What is it?"

"Hold on a minute."

She typed quickly into the computer for a few minutes while I watched over her shoulder, trying to figure out what she was doing. I looked at Harriet, but she just shrugged her shoulders. Finally, Yolanda spoke.

"You see that?" she said, pointing at the screen. "We just pulled that account up a minute ago, and the balance was over $300,000."

"Yes?"

"Now it's under $10,000!"

I sat back in my chair, wishing I knew a little more about banking and accounting.

"Maybe a big check just cleared," Gwen said, but Yolanda shook her head.

"Look. The same thing just happened in this account here."

She typed in some more numbers and a new account flashed on the screen. The account balance was only a few hundred dollars.

"The balance in this account should be about $30,000," she said.

"You're right," said Harriet. "When you had that account up on the screen a few minutes ago, it *was* $30,000."

Harriet and I stared at each other in surprise.

"Where's the money going?" I asked.

Yolanda typed some more, then finally blew out a long, slow breath of relief.

"I found it," she said. "It's just been transferred into a different account."

She brought up that account and we studied it on the screen. The balance was over a million dollars, and a long list of transfers had been made into it in the last two hours.

"I don't get this at all," Yolanda said, watching the screen, chewing her bottom lip. "That's Alan's code number, but I don't know why he's doing things this way. I got a big check out on one of those other accounts that I know isn't gonna clear if he doesn't put that money back where he found it."

I sat up straight, my heart pounding.

"Yolanda," Harriet said. "Can Alan access the on-line banking system from outside the office?"

"Sure, long as he's got a modem."

"Unbelievable."

I reached for Yolanda's phone and dialed the number for Detectives Sollie and Keegan. Though I told the operator it was an emergency, she still put me on hold—and a few seconds of that felt like an eternity. I was still waiting, the phone pressed to my ear, when I heard a disturbance from the front of the Smythe building.

"I'm telling you, he's not here!" a man said loudly. The three of us got up to see what was going on, and much to my surprise Detectives Sollie and Keegan, along with several uniformed police officers, were marching briskly down the hall. I hung up the phone, wondering if they were coming to get me. I pulled off my scarf and jacket, willing to turn myself in as long as they would look at what we had discovered.

They passed me by, however, so I followed them until they reached the end of the hall and Alan Bennet's office, which was dark and empty.

"If you're looking for Alan Bennet, he's not here," I said. Keegan glared at me, anger on his face.

"And where the heck have *you* been?" he demanded. "I got a room full of people who need to talk to you."

By now we had drawn a small crowd. As I opened my mouth to reply, I heard one of the policemen say to another, "He's not here and not at his apartment. Where does that leave us?"

"Are you here for Alan Bennet?" I asked. "Because I don't know where he is, but I sure know what he's doing. I was just trying to call you."

Keegan raised one eyebrow.

"Follow me. Quickly."

I led them back to Yolanda's office, and they crowded around behind her terminal.

"Alan's had a busy day," I said softly, waiting until the police had ushered away the curious onlookers. "In the last two hours, he's transferred over a million dollars into this one account."

"Is he at the bank?"

"No. He's doing it over the internet. He could be anywhere."

I looked at the screen, realizing the balance was even higher now than it had been a few moments ago.

"My guess," I continued, "is that he's pooling money from a bunch of different accounts before going to the bank where he'll either make a giant withdrawal or an out-of-bank wire transfer."

"Get the bank on the phone!" Sollie barked. Yolanda jumped as she reached for the phone and dialed the number with trembling hands. I stepped out of the way, listening as the cops talked among themselves. Apparently, they had come here with a warrant for Alan Bennet to arrest him for the murder of Wendell Smythe.

"What happened?" I asked Keegan, my eyes wide, wondering what piece of the puzzle had clicked for them to point things to Alan. "I mean, how'd you get a warrant?"

"We got the labs back on the print on the syringe and the hair found on Smythe. They both belonged to Bennet."

I told him my theory, the one I had been forming for the last few days.

"It's my opinion," I said, "that Judith and Alan Bennet were both responsible. I think they may have killed Wendell together, and then Alan went out the back way and returned to his office, while Judith stayed there in her father's office until he was dead. I think she was still in the bathroom, cleaning up some evidence or whatever, when I came in. I think it was Judith that I chased down the stairwell."

"We've already sent someone out to pick her up for questioning," Detective Keegan replied, nodding. "But we can't really hold her for murder unless Bennet implicates her. At this point, we have no proof of her involvement in her father's death."

I thought of Alan Bennet, feeling fairly certain he would incriminate his own mother if it made things easier for him.

"We did manage to turn up a few priors on him," Keegan continued. "So we'll see what happens."

"Keegan!" Sollie called, putting his hand over the mouthpiece on the phone. "The bank manager said that that particular account is set up with what they call a 'repetitive wire.' That means Bennet doesn't have to go to the bank in person. He can wire money out of it remotely, just by using a secret code and a telephone."

"On the internet?"

"No. He can move the money around on the internet, but if he wants to wire it to an outside account, he has to do that with a regular phone call."

"What do you mean, a regular phone call?"

"On a Touch-Tone phone. The right code, and the money's outta there."

"You mean you're telling me that with the push of a few buttons, Bennet can wipe out that account right under our noses?"

"That's what they're saying. What do we want to do?"

We all froze, looking at each other. I knew exactly what the two men were thinking: If they stopped what Alan was doing and put a hold on the account, Alan would know they were onto him, and he would take off. But if they didn't put a hold on the account, he might snatch the money out at any minute, and then it would be too late anyway.

"Put on a freeze, and he'll know we know," Keegan said softly.

"Don't put on a freeze," Sollie replied, "and he'll strip those accounts bare."

After a moment, we all spoke in unison. Everyone had a different idea, but my voice was the loudest, and finally they all shut up and looked at me.

"You can trace the phone call," I said, but Sollie shook his head.

"Not if he's on a modem through an internet provider. We had to do that once before, and it took too long."

"No," I insisted, shaking my head. "Right now, he's on the internet, moving money from lots of accounts into one single account. He can move that money around all he wants as long as he's on-line. But when he's finally ready to wire the money out of that bank and into some other private account, he's got to get off of the internet and call in on the telephone. If the bank can intercept *that* call, and you can get a trace on it, then you'll know where he is."

"Risky," said Keegan.

"Riskier than a ribeye in a pen full of Dobermans," Harriet added, "especially if the police can't move fast enough. Then he gets the money *and* he gets out of town."

Sollie and Keegan looked at each other and then at me.

"It's worth a try," Sollie said finally. "Hate to gamble with the money, but I don't want to risk losing our man."

The decision made, they all sprang into action, making phone calls, barking commands into the radio. Meanwhile, Yolanda, Gwen, Harriet, and I continued to tensely watch the computer screen. The balance in that one account had reached nearly 1.5 million dollars.

Finally, the number stopped changing. It just sat there while we watched it quietly. One million, five hundred twenty-three thousand dollars. A nice chunk of change for a morning's work.

"We think activity has ceased," Sollie said into the phone softly, still connected with the bank. "Are we set? Are we ready?"

Keegan was on his radio, saying essentially the same thing. We all held our breath as we watched the number on the screen. Then, suddenly, after nearly a full two minutes of waiting, it disappeared. In an instant, the amount $1,523,000 flicked away.

All that was left was one dollar.

Everyone exploded into noise. Sollie was shouting to all of us to calm down as he listened to the phone.

"Shut up!" he yelled. "Shut up, I can't hear!"

Finally, everyone quieted down and waited as he spoke.

"Yes," he said, listening, "go ahead." He waved for a pen and paper, and Yolanda handed him hers. "Got it. Yes. Okay."

Then he hung up.

"Well?" Keegan asked as we were all waiting, holding our breath.

"They got the number," Sollie replied. "The call to transfer the funds came from a pay phone in Pike Ridge."

"Pike Ridge?" Keegan asked. From what I could recall, Pike Ridge was a small suburb west of the city, not too far from the Smythes' house, about half an hour from where we were. "Have they got somebody on it?"

"Units have already been dispatched to the scene."

"What's in Pike Ridge?" another cop asked. "Besides some expensive houses and a few shopping centers?"

Sollie shook his head.

"I'll tell you what's in Pike Ridge," I said suddenly, thinking of Tom and his trip to the funeral via helicopter. "An airport. There's a small airport in Pike Ridge."

Forty-One

~

The cops drove westward through the city, sirens blaring as they wove in and out of traffic. The detectives had, of course, called ahead to the Pike Ridge police and told them to seize Alan Bennet, probably at the airport. But Keegan and Sollie still wanted to get there as soon as possible themselves to question Alan once he had been arrested. I followed along behind the last cop car, matching their speed in my fancy Lincoln as we flew through the city.

Harriet had opted to take a cab from the Smythe offices to her cousin's house where she would wait for further word from me. I was glad she had some place to pass the time; I knew she had a real aversion for things like high-speed pursuits and apprehending suspects.

As I drove, I thought about Alan, and I wondered if Judith was with him. Despite all the illegal things Judith had done thus far—from diverting funds out of Feed the Need to vandalizing her brother and his wife—I had a feeling that maybe Alan was acting alone in the murder with Monty Redburn as his accomplice. Smythe Incorporated was partly *Judith's* company now, her inheritance. It didn't make sense that she would rob herself—especially not for a paltry 1.5

million dollars. Her stake in the company had to be worth at least ten times as much.

Once I reached the airport, I pulled to a stop in the gravel parking lot, got out of the car, and sprinted closer to the action. There were about seven police cars there now, and most of the cops were braced against them, guns drawn. The guns were all pointed toward a small, private airplane that was parked out in front of the hangar. A man I didn't recognize stood in front of the plane with his hands up in the air. Detective Sollie was pointing a gun at him from several feet away as Detective Keegan headed for the plane itself. As we all watched, he opened the passenger-side door of the plane and then held out the gun, shouting. Slowly, Alan Bennet stepped from the plane, hands clasped behind his head.

I didn't believe it. We had done it! We had caught the murdering thief before he skipped town! I did feel a rush of disappointment that Monty Redburn wasn't also there. The plane had held only two people—Alan and the pilot. That meant Redburn was still at large. And Judith Smythe was nowhere to be found.

Still, a nearly audible sigh of relief seemed to sweep through the waiting policemen as the detective snapped handcuffs on Bennet's wrists. They put down their guns and made jokes and laughed away the tension. I blew out a deep breath myself and headed for the tarmac.

I looked around as I walked, noting that the airport itself wasn't much more than a big open field with one paved runway, a few gas pumps, a hangar, and a main building. There were about ten small private planes parked in a row alongside the hangar, and an old tower out behind the main building. That was about it.

Walking among the small crowd that had gathered, I tried to be unobtrusive but observant, watching as they pulled Bennet's luggage from the plane and listening as they read him his rights. The pilot was claiming that he didn't even know Alan and hadn't ever met him before he was hired to fly him to Vermont.

As they were leading Alan to the car, he happened to look my way. Our eyes met and I held his gaze, thinking how hard it was to believe that I was looking into the face of a murderer, or at least an accomplice to murder.

I noticed movement off to my left, and I glanced that way, stunned to see a dented red pickup truck tearing into the parking lot. It came to a screeching halt, dust flying, and out jumped Monty Redburn, a high-powered rifle in his hands.

"Gun!" I screamed, dropping to the ground and flattening myself against the pavement. I heard a cracking boom and then more gunfire in response. "You liar!" Monty screamed from the parking lot. "You're a liar! A thief and a liar!"

I clutched my hands around my head, too frightened to move. Finally, I heard people running, and I looked up, shocked to see Alan Bennet lying on the pavement, shot in the chest. In the parking lot, Monty had also been shot and apprehended by the police, his own blood seeping onto the leg of his pants as they handcuffed him.

Paramedics were laboring over Alan, who seemed to be unconscious but not dead. A bright red stain radiated from his chest in a jagged circle.

I turned and headed to the parking lot, wanting to come face-to-face with the man who had tried to kill me this morning. Keegan saw me and grabbed the sleeve of my jacket, pulling me back, away from the confusion. He gestured toward Monty, his voice soft.

"He look familiar to you?"

"Monty Redburn," I said. "He tried to kill me this morning in a vehicular homicide. He very nearly succeeded."

"*I* know it's Redburn. But how do you know? What's your connection with him?"

"Before today, not much. He's been tailing me, trying to scare me. Yesterday, he lured me out to the cemetery and then pushed me into an open grave."

"And you didn't report that incident to the police?"

"It's part of an ongoing investigation," I said, shrugging. "I survived. I managed to get his prints, and I asked Duane to run them."

Keegan grunted angrily.

"Sometimes I like to know the identity of the people who are trying to kill me," I added sarcastically. "Surely that's not a crime."

"No," he said. "But avoiding the police when you know you're being sought for questioning isn't exactly what I call being 'mutually cooperative.'"

"You think I've been obstructing justice, Keegan?"

He rolled his eyes and let go of my sleeve.

"I think you've been biting the hand that feeds you," he replied.

Then he stalked off, leaving me to feel guilty, knowing that in a way, I had done just that.

I watched all of the activity for a while, standing on the fringe of the crowd, watching as first one ambulance was loaded with the still-unconscious body of Alan Bennet and then another with the angry and struggling Monty Redburn. Once both vehicles sped away, I sought out Detective Sollie, who was filling out some paperwork near his car. I approached him carefully and apologized for avoiding them the first half of the day. He seemed distracted, but not angry the way Keegan had been.

"Can I ask you a question?" I inquired gingerly.

"Mm-hmm."

"How do you guys know Monty Redburn? Why did his name send off red flags when we tried to run his prints?"

"You're shameless, Webber," I heard from behind me. I turned to see Keegan, hands on hips, lips pursed. He seemed irritated with me, but no longer truly angry.

"He's been fencing some of Marion Smythe's jewelry around town," Sollie replied, obviously unaware of the dynamic between me and Keegan. "Because of his prior criminal history and his connection with the Smythes, he was at the top of the list of suspects."

"Do you think that he and Alan and Judith all worked together to kill Wendell Smythe?"

The two men looked at each other, then Keegan exhaled slowly.

"Redburn's got an ironclad alibi for the time of the murder," Keegan said. "He may have been involved peripherally, but he definitely wasn't there the day the man was killed."

"So it couldn't have been him I heard in the bathroom?"

The men looked off into the distance.

"Nope," said Sollie. "Wasn't there. That's for certain."

Keegan shook his head, confusion evident in his face.

"He's a low-life scum with a long list of priors and a brief work history with the Smythes," he said. "Beyond that, how he fits into this whole thing is anybody's guess."

Forty-Two

I needed to think. All I really wanted was to go somewhere all alone for a little peace and quiet while I sorted out my thoughts. But I still had to pick up Harriet and deliver her back to the train station. Looking at my watch, I decided that if I could find her cousin's house without too much trouble, I would be able to get Harriet to the station in time for the next train, and then I could head for Fairmount Park or someplace where I could take a walk and clear my head.

The cousin lived in a small town in Montgomery County on a main highway. I found the road without too much trouble, and I finally slowed down at the 8100 block, stopping to turn in at a little red mailbox marked 8127.

The driveway dipped down to a small but very pleasant tree-covered lot with a tiny Cape Cod house perched in the center. The front door was wide open, so I parked my car and headed up the walk, noting the lovely geraniums blooming on each side of the front porch. When I arrived at the door, however, I nearly ran right into it. To my surprise, I realized the door wasn't really open at all. It was shut tight and painted to look as if it were open.

My knock brought Harriet to the door, laughing when I told her what I'd done. As she led me into the house, she told me to be careful, that it was only a hint of things to come.

She wasn't kidding. As we walked through a series of tiny rooms, we were assaulted on all sides by a sort of *trompe l'oeil* nightmare. There were "windows" painted into walls, furniture painted to look like animals, walls that seemed not to exist at all. Harriet led me to the kitchen, which was done up like ancient ruins, painted with pillars and statues and crumbling walls, fallen to reveal lovely gardens and more statues "outside."

I suppose it could've been lovely were it not so overdone. But then I looked at Harriet's cousin, the woman sitting at the table, and I realized it probably suited her perfectly. She looked warm and friendly but eccentric in a paint-speckled shirt and overalls. She wore a baseball cap on her head over wiry gray curls, and she had the weather-lined face of someone who had been many places and seen many things.

Harriet introduced Lorraine as her "first cousin, once removed," and the woman rose to shake my hand and offer me some coffee. I glanced at my watch and then reluctantly accepted. We needed to be on our way in ten minutes or so if Harriet wanted to make her train.

"We were just about to get out some of the old photo albums," Harriet moaned when I told her we needed to leave soon. "Some of the family reunion pictures, from when I was younger and prettier, if you can imagine such a thing."

I looked at Harriet, settled comfortably in the warm kitchen of her relative, and felt a twinge of guilt.

"Well, why don't you stay, then?" I said, pulling out a wad of money and peeling off a few twenty dollar bills. "This should cover cab fare back to the station, not to mention a nice dinner."

"If you say so," she replied, grinning, taking the money from me and tucking it into her pocket.

I sat down then and joined them for coffee, thinking I needed to get going. My head felt like it was swirling with unanswered questions, my mind a blur. But it seemed impolite to drink and run, so I allowed myself ten minutes to unwind, sip coffee, and chat with the two older women.

As we talked, my eyes wandered out of the window beside the table. Though houses pressed in on both sides, the backyard was lovely, filled with autumn leaves, shady and beckoning. The end of the property seemed oddly defined until I realized that it backed up on some sort of water.

"Is that a pond out there?" I asked, squinting to look through the bushes.

"A creek, sort of," Lorraine replied. "A branch of the Schuylkill."

"Lorraine's grandson keeps a fishing boat out there," Harriet said. "You can see it, propped up against that biggest tree."

I looked, and sure enough, I could detect the glint of aluminum among the fallen leaves. Suddenly, I felt an urge, stronger than any I'd had in a long time, to run out there, slip that boat into the water, and go for a row.

"Harriet—"

"Oh boy, why'd I even mention it?" Harriet cried. "I can see it in your face already!"

"Just for half an hour," I said, grinning at her. Then I looked hopefully at Lorraine. "You wouldn't mind terribly, would you, if I borrowed your boat?"

It wasn't exactly a canoe, but it would do. After flipping the heavy boat and dragging it to the water through what I hoped wasn't poison ivy, I stood on the bank for a moment and caught my breath. My best canoe at home was a 60-pound, 16-footer. This sucker, though probably the same length if not shorter, surely weighed at least twice as much. Still, a boat was a boat, and I was nearly desperate for some time on the water. I put in one foot, grabbed the sides, and pushed off with the other, settling onto the bench as I quietly sailed forward toward the deeper part of the creek.

I had left my jacket and purse with Harriet so that all I carried with me now was a pair of old wooden oars. I slid them through the oar locks and into the water and gave a stroke, the feel of them heavy but comfortable in my hands.

Ah, blessed water! I looked back at the bank one last time, memorizing the landmarks that would indicate home. Then I took off, rowing even and hard up the creek as fast as I could manage in the unwieldy fishing boat.

I didn't exactly glide, but still it was better than nothing. I found a steady pace and eventually settled into a comfortable rhythm.

The view was lovely on both sides of the bank—modest homes at first, their cluttered yards filled with swing sets and trampolines and sandboxes. Eventually, as the creek became wider, the homes became larger and more luxurious, their manicured lawns sweeping down to the water from ornate stone decks.

Still, for all of the lovely houses, I didn't see any people outside enjoying their yards on this quiet weekday afternoon. I knew they were all out working, just as I should've been. With that thought, I sighted a bridge up ahead and decided to do my turnaround there and head back in.

I rowed at a faster pace all the way to the bridge, working up a sweat, bringing up my heart rate. Then I picked up the oars and held them over the water, gliding as I sailed under the bridge. I looked up as I drew under, not surprised to see what looked like a thousand splatters of bird droppings, several abandoned nests, and a few tiny bats nestled among the eaves. I coasted to a stop about ten feet on the other side, did a careful sweep and brace, and eventually worked myself around toward the opposite direction.

The ride back was slower and more thoughtful as I allowed my mind to turn toward all of the happenings of this day. I had seen two men get shot right in front of my eyes. I wondered when I would finish reeling from the shock of that; I knew wise old Eli would tell me to deal with it right now, right away. *These things can build up in you*, he had told me after my first traumatic day as a detective. *Find a way to let off some steam, or you'll end up going a little bonkers.*

I knew he was right. In the early days, I had taken a tip from my policeman brother and learned to play racquetball, pounding out my emotions on the court. Nowadays, I found better solace in prayer and in canoeing. At this moment, I prayed for Alan Bennet, for his physical health and his spiritual well-being. *How quickly we can move from life to death,* I thought. *How tragic if that happens before our hearts have been sealed for heaven by the Savior.*

By the time I rowed into the shore at Lorraine's house, I felt calm and at peace despite the confusion that I knew would continue to swirl around me. There were still many unanswered questions, still much work to be done—even with Alan Bennet arrested for the murder and Monty Redburn in police custody.

I got one shoe a little wet as I stepped onto the bank, but otherwise it was a clean landing. I dragged the heavy boat up to its tree, huffing and panting until it was safely back in place. It was then that I noticed Harriet running across the lawn toward me, my portable phone in one hand, my beeper in the other.

"Thank goodness you're back!" she yelled, running closer, her breathing ragged and heavy. "They've been beeping you and calling almost since the minute you left."

"They who?" I asked, taking the gadgets from her.

"The Smythe family," she wheezed. "The wife. The son."

"What's wrong?"

"It's the boy," she said.

"Carlos?"

"Yes. Carlos."

"What about him?" I asked, my heart leaping into my throat.

"He's gone," she said, wringing her hands, shaking her head. "Disappeared. They were hoping you might know where he is."

Forty-Three

By the time I arrived at the house, things were in utter chaos with two uniformed cops in the foyer, Derek shouting into the phone in the drawing room, Marion talking frantically on a cellular phone in the front hallway, and Sidra pacing next to Derek, sobbing.

"I don't care about standard procedure!" Derek was yelling into the phone. "I want to know why it took you until 2:30 in the afternoon to let me know my son never showed up for school this morning!"

Sidra grabbed me as soon as she saw me. "Oh, Callie! Where has he gone? Where can he be?"

I had already spoken to her on my cellular phone as I raced back here in my rental car. But seeing her distraught face—seeing the panic on all of their faces—slammed me in the solar plexus like a fist.

"And you are?" one of the police officers asked me, his notebook in front of him for taking notes.

"A—a friend of the family," I managed to rasp. "I haven't seen Carlos since last night."

"She's a houseguest, officer," Marion said, her eyes moist, holding her hand over the phone. "Callie, tell me again, are you sure you haven't seen Judith today? How about Angelina? Our only hope is that he's with one of them."

I shook my head, wondering what they knew of Alan and what had happened at the airport. It was big news, certainly, but it paled in comparison to the knowledge that Carlos was missing.

"Oh, Callie," sobbed Sidra, "I don't know what we're going to do! I watched him go to the bus, but they say he didn't get on. He never showed up at school."

I hugged her, unable to think of any words that might help.

After a few minutes I did, however, pull one of the policemen aside and give him a short version of everything that had happened with the police in Pike Ridge. They got on their radios and talked back and forth while Marion, Derek, and Sidra surrounded me and asked me to repeat the information I had just given the cop. I went into more detail, telling about the bank records at Smythe, the diverted funds, the attempted escape. They were stunned to find out about the theft of Feed the Need funds, but even more shocked to learn that Alan had been shot. I remembered that he had been— until this day, at least—a trusted employee and beloved friend of the family.

"Do you think Alan could have taken Carlos?" Sidra asked. "Like, kidnapped him?"

I was wondering the same thing, but unless Alan had regained consciousness, there was no way to know for sure. I looked at the Smythes, my heart aching for them.

"Where does Carlos go to catch the bus?" I asked Sidra.

"Right at the end of the driveway."

"Show me where," I said.

Together, Sidra and I ran out of the door and descended the front steps, then jogged down the driveway toward the road. We reached the spot where the bus usually stopped. The main road was fairly empty, and I trotted across to the other side.

"Look," I said, scooting down a steep bank to a dry ditch beside the road. "You see the grass here?"

I pointed to where it was flattened against the ground.

"Was Carlos wearing sneakers this morning?"

"Yes. Nike's."

"That's probably his footprint," I said. At the bottom of the indentation in the grass was a clear, child-sized print in the mud where someone was obviously pushing off to climb back out of the ditch.

"It's just my guess," I said. "But I'd be willing to bet he climbed down here and hid until the bus was gone. Then he climbed back out and either took off down the road or headed back home."

"Back home?"

"Have you checked his tree house?"

Sidra shook her head.

"We haven't even tried looking around the house. I just kept thinking someone nabbed him here on the road while he was waiting for the bus."

We ran back across the street, and Sidra took off for the yard, yelling.

"Carlos!" she screamed, her voice carrying the anguish of a mother who's lost her son. "Carlos! You come out right this instant!"

I headed back into the house, and Derek and Marion met me at the door.

"Looks like he hid beside the road," I said. "There's a chance he could be around here somewhere."

"The pool, check the pool," Marion said, clutching at her throat. "He may have drowned!"

She and Derek ran outside. The policemen and I began to search inside the house, and as I was running through the kitchen, Nick came in from outside, carrying a bag of groceries.

"What is going on here?" he asked. I told him as quickly as possible, and he immediately put down the bag and began to help us search the house. I could hear his booming voice shouting for Carlos even when I was upstairs at the other end of the hall.

It wasn't until I went through my own door that I stopped short, my heart pounding. There, on my bed, was an envelope with my name on it, written in what looked like a little boy's handwriting.

I picked it up and ripped it open. Inside was a piece of paper, a typed series of letters and numbers that made no sense at all.

"Carlos!" I muttered under my breath. "What have you done?" Across the bottom of the page he had typed, "Clue to crack the code: Move your fingers to the bottom row of the keyboard."

"Oh, no," I whispered. Carlos' stupid secret code! My computer was in the car. I ran down the stairs and out of the door just as Sidra and Derek were rounding the side of the house.

"He's not anywhere," Derek said breathlessly.

"He left me a note!" I said. "It's in code. I need a keyboard."

I grabbed my computer and ran with it to the table in the drawing room. Derek plugged it in, and I snapped open the lid.

"Angelina's stuff is gone!" Nick cried, running into the room. We all hesitated, looking at him. "Searching for Carlos, I went in her room. Her suitcase and most of her clothes are gone."

We all looked at each other, and I couldn't help but think this all grew stranger by the minute.

"She was not here when I got up this morning," Nick continued when no one spoke. "Today is her day off. I wondered where she had gone, but I did not really think anything of it until now."

The police began asking Nick questions about Angelina. As they did, I turned back to the computer, which was now up and ready to use. I read Carlos' note again, trying to figure out what he meant. *Move your fingers to the bottom row of the keyboard,* it said, so I set the note next to the computer and studied it. The first word was "dqoo83." I put my fingers on the keyboard in the home position, then slid them down one row. I closed my eyes and pretended that my fingers were on the home row. I then typed "dqoo83." When I opened my eyes, I saw on the screen that I had actually written "callie."

"That's it!" I said. Quickly, I typed in the rest of the message. When I was finished I leaned forward and read what I had written.

callie, it said, *i think aunt judith is running away. shes got suitcases in her car and everything. im going to hide in the trunk and see where shes going. ps if i never come back call the police.*

"He's with Judith," Marion said, clutching her chest with relief.

"Derek," I said evenly, "I think you'd better tell your mother about Judith and her little nighttime 'activities' that Carlos discovered."

He spoke quietly, filling her in on the events of two nights before when Carlos and I caught Judith in her vandalism red-handed. Despite all of that, I, too, felt relieved. At least Judith hadn't taken Carlos away intentionally. The greater question remained, however: Wherever Judith was headed, whatever she was doing, once she found Carlos and realized he had been waiting inside her trunk, spying on her—what exactly was she capable of doing to him?

Forty-Four

"This is my fault," I said softly, swallowing hard. "Carlos wanted to be a detective, like me. I told him the situation could be dangerous, but he wouldn't listen."

"But Callie," Marion said. "It's okay. He's with Judith. We'll just keep trying to reach her on her car phone and—"

"No!" Derek and I both yelled at once.

"It might be safer for the time being if Judith doesn't know Carlos is with her," Sidra added more softly.

"What kind of vehicle does she have?" one of the cops asked.

"She drives a company car," Derek answered. "A Mercedes."

"Late model?"

"This year."

The policeman was one step ahead of us, already picking up the phone to dial Mercedes Benz.

"If we're lucky," he said as he dialed, "her car will have a GPS tracking system."

"If you'll give me the plate number and things like that," the other cop said to Marion, "we can put an APB out."

"If he's in the trunk, Carlos may have smothered by now!" Sidra wailed, burying her head against Derek's shoulder. He held her against him like a lifeline, whispering softly to comfort her.

"This way, officer," Marion said, heading for Wendell's study. The cop, Nick, and I followed as she quickly made her way over to Wendell's file cabinet.

"Everything should be here," Marion said as she pulled out a file and laid it across the desk. She read off the plate number to the officer as I paced at the other end of the room.

"I do not believe this nightmare," Nick said, shaking his head. I just walked quietly back and forth, thinking.

When Marion had finished giving the officer the necessary information about Judith's car, he left the room, and she came over to us.

"If only Wendell were here," she said softly, her eyes threatening to spill over with tears again. "He would know what to do."

She walked to the case that held Wendell's antique clothing collection and ran her hand lovingly across the top of the glass. My heart ached for her, and I was about to step closer and put my arm around her shoulder when she gasped.

"The shirt!" she said, bending over to peer into the case. "The Jefferson shirt is gone!"

Nick and I both stepped to the case and looked inside. I realized instantly what she was talking about. The white ruffled shirt from the top right corner of the shelf was missing with nothing but an empty space of black velvet where it had been.

"Could Carlos have taken it?" I asked. "I know he loves this collection."

"Carlos isn't stupid," Marion said. "He knows the shirt is priceless. He wouldn't go near it."

"Priceless?" Nick asked. "Which one?"

Marion waved her hand dismissively.

"One of the shirts from this collection is very, very valuable—and it's been stolen."

"Go get the police officer," I said. "There might be fingerprints."

"I will do it," Nick said, leaving the room.

"Maybe he shouldn't, not just yet," Marion said. "I don't want anything to distract them from finding Carlos."

"But this may be related somehow," I said. "Angelina's disappearance could be, too."

Last night Angelina had a secret, romantic rendezvous with Alan. Was it possible, I wondered, that she was somewhere waiting for him now, planning to be a part of his escape?

"Oh, Callie," Marion said suddenly, one hand to her mouth. "I feel like my whole world is falling apart—first one thing and now another. What's going on? Is God trying to punish me?"

I put my arms around her shoulders and led her to a chair.

"God's not punishing you," I said softly. "He can give you the strength to get through this. He—"

"We found her!"

The policeman was shouting from the living room, and Marion and I both jumped up and ran into the other room. Apparently, the satellite tracking system had located Judith's Mercedes Benz. It was parked just off the Northeast Extension of the Pennsylvania Turnpike toward Quakertown.

Forty-Five

We flew along the Northeast Extension at well over 80 miles per hour, Marion and Nick in my car with me, Derek and Sidra following along in their Jaguar. By the time we reached the exit, it wasn't hard to figure out where the cops had found the Mercedes—there were already at least five police cars surrounding it in the nearby parking lot of a small shopping center. Judith was facing a uniformed policeman, yelling, while another cop seemed to be inspecting the car. A small crowd had gathered along the sidewalk, watching.

"I want a lawyer!" Judith was hollering as we parked and ran up to the scene. Her eyes were wide and furious, and when she saw us she gasped. "What are you doing here? Mother, tell these people that I don't know what they're talking about! I haven't seen Carlos all day! I'm not saying another thing until I'm allowed to call an attorney!"

We all just stared at her, stunned that Carlos was nowhere to be found.

"He's not here?" Derek yelled in horror.

"I'm afraid not," answered one of the policemen.

"*Where's my son, you monster?*" Sidra screamed, and before we could stop her, she had flown at Judith and knocked her to the ground. She pounded on Judith's face while Judith howled in pain. The officers stepped in to pull Sidra off of Judith, but it took nearly a minute of wrestling to get her loose.

Everything was chaos with everyone shouting at everyone else. Judith was sitting on the ground now, yelling loudly. The police had herded Sidra and Derek to a nearby police car where they were trying to calm Sidra down. Nick supported Marion, who stood on the fringes of the crowd looking as though she was about to faint.

"Looks like the backseat latch was broken through from the trunk," one of the officers called out from the car. "The kid must've kicked it out himself, and then climbed from the trunk into the back-seat."

"I don't know what you're talking about!" Judith screamed. "Carlos was never in my backseat!"

"Excuse me," I said finally, stepping over to the officer in charge. "I'm an attorney. May I speak with her privately for a moment?"

"We just wanna find the kid," the cop said, his expression pained.

"Is she under arrest?" I asked.

"Not yet. Right now, we're just trying to ask her some questions."

"I'm very familiar with the situation," I said. "Please. Let me speak with her. Just five minutes."

He looked at me intently for a moment, then down at Judith.

"Five minutes," he said.

He turned and walked away, joining the other cops examining her car. I walked to Judith and held out a hand to help her up. She took it, brushing the dust from her slacks, picking the rocks from her hair.

"Callie, what is going on?" she whispered furiously. "I'm just sitting in there in the coffee shop, minding my own business, when suddenly every cop in Pennsylvania is surrounding my car. Sirens and lights are going, and they're screaming at me to come out of the restaurant with my hands up. I did like they said, and the next thing you know, they're asking things about Carlos and a kidnapping! I don't know *what* they're talking about. I haven't even seen Carlos all day."

I studied her face, looking into her eyes. The skin around the right eye was swollen and already starting to turn a mottled blue. Whether Judith was being truthful about not seeing Carlos or not, I just wasn't sure.

In a steady voice, I explained that Carlos hadn't shown up at school today.

"We found a note he left behind," I said, "telling us that he was going to hide in your trunk. He thought you were up to something, and he was going to spy on you."

"In *my* trunk? Of the Benz?"

"That's right, Judith. You say you haven't seen him, but I don't understand how that's possible, and neither do the cops. Carlos obviously isn't in the trunk now. And yet there are signs that he was at one point. So when would he have gotten out?"

Judith looked wildly around at the scene.

"A cigarette," she said, patting the pocket of her blazer. "I've got to have a cigarette."

She found the pack in her pocket and pulled one out, slipping it between two dry lips. With trembling fingers, she lit it and then took a deep drag, pulling it out of her mouth to exhale.

"I was just going out in the country for a drive," she said, "I never—"

"Don't bother lying to me, Judith," I said tiredly, holding up one hand. "I know everything. I know about your affair with Alan Bennet. I know you've been terrorizing your sister-in-law and attempting to destroy your brother's marriage. I know you've been raiding the accounts of Feed the Need and pulling the funds into Smythe Incorporated. So don't lie to me any more—I know too much. Now, where's Carlos?"

She was speechless, her mouth literally hanging open. After a long pause, she closed her mouth, swallowed hard, then looked at me imploringly, lowering her voice to a whisper.

"Okay," she said. "Alan and I did those things to Derek and Sidra. And maybe I did have a hand in the money issues with Feed the Need. But I would never, ever in a million years have done anything to harm Carlos. He's my nephew."

"Why the vandalism?" I asked. "Why the black roses and the cut up coat and the ruined car paint?"

She hesitated, sucking fiercely on her cigarette. Finally, she blew out a thick stream of smoke and lowered her voice to just above a whisper.

"To distract attention," she said. "It was Alan's idea. He said Derek would be less likely to find out about the accounts at work if he were distracted at home. Once we started, it worked so well, we just kept it going. Derek has been, like, in la-la land for two months. He never noticed a thing."

I just looked at her.

"Okay," she whispered. "I'm not proud of myself. But it was just little things—petty vandalism. Not like kidnapping."

"What about the theft from Feed the Need?"

"We were just restructuring," she said, but when she saw my face she hesitated then spoke again. "Okay, so we were stripping out funds from Feed the Need. It's a matter of priorities. We had to find some low-interest—okay, no-interest—money, to bolster up some of our ventures in the clothing business. We didn't take that much. But Feed the Need is such a monumental waste of money anyway, it didn't seem like that big of a deal. We would've paid it back eventually."

"What about the faked records, the closed-down district offices?"

Judith shrugged.

"Alan handled all of that. I just gave the authority for the money transfers."

"Never mind that by stealing from Feed the Need you stole food from the mouths of starving children all over the world."

"Starving children," she said, rolling her eyes. "Daddy was ready to kiss away his fortune to starving children. Give me a break."

I couldn't even think of a response to that. I wondered what would make a person so totally devoid of conscience.

"That's all I can say, Callie," she told me. "I may have done some dishonest things, but I didn't do anything to my nephew."

"If you're telling the truth," I said, "then answer a few questions."

"Go ahead."

"What were you doing here?"

She hesitated a moment before speaking.

"I was meeting Alan. We were going to the Poconos for the weekend."

"Here? Why meet here?"

"This coffee shop is sort of our 'special' place," she said. "First trip away together and all that. It's right on the way to the Poconos."

"Go on."

"Not much to tell. I went by Alan's house this morning to get him, and he said he had some things to take care of first. He wanted me to go on up to the condo, and he would come later, but I hated the thought of that long drive by myself. So he agreed to meet me here, outside of our coffee shop. We were going to leave his car in this parking lot and pick it up on our way home Sunday."

"Tell me every place your car has been today," I said, wondering where in the chain of events Carlos could've gotten out of the car.

"That's it. From home, to Alan's apartment, to here."

"No other stops, no getting gas, nothing like that?"

"No."

"Did you open the trunk today at all?"

"I don't think so," she said. "I loaded everything late last night after everybody else was asleep."

"Why all the secrecy?"

"Why do you think?" she replied sharply, inhaling on her cigarette. "I'm Alan's *boss*, for goodness' sake."

I had to sigh. The best I could figure, Alan had tricked Judith, sending her off to the Poconos so he could raid her company's funds while she wasn't around. It must've thrown him a little when she showed up at his house early this morning, ready to drive off together. But then he had offered to meet her here, telling her he had errands to run first.

A little more fell into place for me then as all that had gone on before began to make sense. Alan had merely used Judith, preying on her competitive urges against her brother to convince her to steal money from Derek's company and put it into her own. Alan's ultimate goal wasn't to drain Feed the Need or to deepen the coffers of Smythe Incorporated. It was to watch the procedure and obtain the codes so that he could eventually move some money himself, this time from Smythe Incorporated into his own hot little hands.

"How long have you been sitting in the coffee shop, waiting?" I asked finally, my arms folded across my chest.

Judith's face colored.

"A few hours," she said.

"Long enough to realize he isn't coming?"

She took the last puff of her cigarette and tossed it onto the ground.

"So he stood me up," she said, grinding out the cigarette with her toe. "I knew the relationship would burn itself out eventually."

"Stood you up?" I asked, thinking about the airplane he had been on, the 1.5 million dollars he almost stole from her company. She didn't even know yet that he had been running away or that he had been shot. I waved to the cops that we had finished our conversation.

"Oh, Judith," I said before walking away. "You don't know the half of it."

Forty-Six

The police took Judith downtown for questioning by Detectives Sollie and Keegan. The rest of us decided to proceed on the assumption that Judith was telling the truth about Carlos, that the child had had only two opportunities to get out of her car—at Alan's apartment and here. We split up, with Derek and Sidra and several of the policemen and quite a few helpful onlookers deciding to search the parking lot, the shopping center, and the surrounding area. Marion, Nick, and I decided to head to Alan's apartment and see if we could turn anything up there.

Our drive to Alan's was a little slower than the high-speed chase we had taken to Quakertown. As we drove, I went over and over the day's events in my mind. I tried to put myself in Carlos' shoes, tried to think where a boy who fancied himself a spy might have ended up. I hadn't a clue.

My greatest fear was that Carlos had somehow slipped out of Judith's car at Alan's apartment and been spotted by Alan once Judith was gone. By now, I was convinced that Alan Bennet was capable of almost anything. I didn't want to imagine what he might do to a little boy who stood in the way of his well-laid plans.

Once we reached Alan's part of the suburbs, we followed the police car into a large apartment complex where we found an endless series of three-story block-like structures arranged in and around an irregular parking lot. The apartments seemed bland and impersonal, the kind of place where someone like Alan Bennet could live quietly, unnoticed by anyone, while carrying out his nefarious schemes.

"Carlos could be anywhere!" Marion sobbed as we pulled to a stop. The task did seem daunting. Such a big world, such a small boy.

We got out of the car and followed the police to Alan's apartment. There were already a few uniformed policemen there going through Alan's things and packing up any relevant evidence. Marion and Nick both looked bereft as they stood in the middle of it all. One officer assured Marion that they had several officers canvassing the entire complex, looking for the boy, though so far they had no reason to believe he had ever been there.

After we looked around, I suggested to Marion that they didn't need our help here and that we might be in their way. She looked ill and exhausted, and I told her that I thought she might do better to go home and talk more with the police there. Dejected, she let Nick lead her back to the car. Then we all got in and headed for the Smythes' house.

By the time we got there, it was nearly five in the evening. The house was swarming with cops, but there was no sign of Carlos anywhere. They asked Marion for photos, and I overheard one cop say that if they hadn't turned anything up in another two hours, they would try bringing in a K-9 unit.

I found a room that was quiet and empty and pulled out my cell phone to call Detective Keegan. The receptionist wouldn't let me through to either him or Detective Sollie, so I tracked down Duane Perskie. I thought he would be angry with me for not contacting him again after our early morning phone call, but in the meantime he had heard about all that had happened to me today, which sort of let me off the hook.

"So do you know anything at all about the information they're getting from Monty Redburn?" I asked. "I'm so afraid he may have had something to do with Carlos' disappearance."

"Redburn was shot in the leg when they apprehended him," he said. "But they were able to question him a little bit, post-op."

"And?"

"And Redburn's been working for Alan Bennet, first as a plant in the Smythes' home, then lately as a tail on you. But he's a real piece of work, Callie. He denies trying to kill you this morning—said he was just trying to have a little fun."

I felt a surge of anger, remembering the man's glee as he attempted to run me down on the interstate. Yeah, he was having fun all right.

"A plant at the Smythes' home—why?"

"We're not sure, but we think it must've been to steal some item of value from the house. Unfortunately for him, Redburn made the mistake of copping a number of smaller items as well. The Smythes found out and let him go. Bennet didn't want anything more to do with him until you showed up and started digging around. Then he needed some muscle, so he called Redburn back in."

"At the airport, Redburn kept calling Alan a liar. What was that about?"

"Apparently, Bennet's instructions for the day were for Redburn to keep an eye on you at all costs. Redburn knew something big was going down, but in the end, he was supposed to be a part of it. Bennet had promised him that when all was said and done, they would be driving out of town together—but Bennet planned on flying off on his own."

"If that's the case, though, how did Redburn know Alan would be at the airport?"

"He didn't. He was waiting in the Smythe parking lot, hoping to spot you again. He finally picked you up as you were leaving and followed you out there. You led him straight to the airport. Then when he realized what was going on, he acted out of anger. His lawyer's in there right now, talking temporary insanity. But the general consensus is that the rifle he had with him was meant for you. Luckily, he went after Alan first."

I swallowed hard. Real danger had come a little too close.

"What about Carlos?" I asked. "Does Redburn know anything about Carlos?"

"He swears not. And I'm inclined to believe him, though that's one of the few things to come out of his mouth tonight that any of us believe."

We talked a few minutes more, with the only other surprising information being how Alan Bennet and Monty Redburn had met in the first place. Apparently, the two men had been cellmates at Graterford State Prison a few years ago. Seems the police had been able to turn up a much more detailed—and truthful—history of Alan Bennet than I had.

I thanked Duane for his help and hung up the phone. I stared into space for a moment as I continued to piece together the facts in this case.

Alan Bennet had left two people hanging today—Judith Smythe and Monty Redburn—while he attempted to skip out on both of them. That directed my thoughts toward Angelina, yet another person he'd been stringing along. I wondered, had she been in on all of this, or had he hung her out to dry as well?

An idea struck me, and I put away my phone and sought out Nick. He seemed quite agitated, and I didn't blame him. Everyone was concentrating on finding the missing Carlos, but Nick was equally concerned about his missing sister. I told him I had an idea, and I asked him to walk with me to her room.

When we got there, I headed straight for the mirror, pulling down the sexy photo of her smiling at the camera, her hair loose and blowing in the wind.

"Who took this picture?" I asked, holding it out to Nick.

"I do not know," he replied, glancing at the photo.

I showed him the back with the scribbled hearts and the words "our special place." This time, he studied it, frowning.

"I have no idea," he said. " 'Our special place'?"

"Does Angelina have a boyfriend?"

"No. Not that I know of."

He seemed to be telling the truth, which meant he wasn't aware of his sister's relationship with Alan.

"Do you know when this was taken?" I asked. "Or where?"

He handed back the photo to me.

"Looks like Valley Forge to me. The big arch monument there."

"Oh?"

"As for when, it would have to have been some time in the last few months, because she has only been that thin for a short while. My sister used to be heavy, you know. Very overweight."

"I know."

"The stupid kid," he said, going to sit on the edge of the bed. He was quiet for a moment, then he spoke again. "She was fat and homely all her life. Then when she came here…she finally decided to do something about it. Lose some weight. Get in shape. It was a lot of hard work, and it took a long time, but she did it. Look at her now. She is a beauty."

"I know."

"She was easy pickings," he said miserably. "Ripe to fall for the first smooth talker that looked her way."

"You know who that smooth talker was, don't you?"

Nick's eyes met mine.

"Please, do not tell me it was Alan," he said. "Because if he hurt my sister, I swear to you, I will go down to that hospital and finish him off myself."

Forty-Seven

It didn't take long for me to get to Valley Forge. There was a visitor's center near the entrance, and I thought about stopping for directions. But then I looked at the photo of Angelina, and I decided it might be quicker just to find the monument by myself.

Following the road, I steered past the first few buildings and soon found myself driving through gorgeous rolling hills, dotted here and there with antiquated little military huts. There were a few people about, most of them jogging or biking on the roadside trail. I was going to stop and ask one of them for directions when I came around a bend and saw what I had been looking for: Up ahead in the distance loomed a huge monument, looking not unlike the French *Arc de Triomphe. A big arch-like monument,* as Nick had called it.

I found a parking place near the arch and got out of the car. Walking across a cobblestone street, I spotted a familiar figure in the distance. Angelina was there, sitting by herself on a bench that faced the monument.

I slowed as I reached her, noting that she was dressed in a pretty flowered dress with a white sweater, her hair pulled back in a headband, her face streaked with mascara. In her lap she clutched a small brown vinyl purse.

"Angelina?" I said, coming to a stop in front of her. She glanced up at me and her eyes widened. Then she rose from the bench and began walking away.

"Are you alright?" I asked.

She didn't reply.

"Angelina!" I said, grabbing her elbow. "What's the matter? Are you hurt?"

"Go away," she said, in torment. She stumbled a bit on the cobblestones in her heels, righted herself, and kept going.

"Do you have Carlos with you?" I demanded. This seemed to get her attention, and she slowed just a bit.

"What do you mean?"

"Carlos is missing. He hasn't been seen since this morning. Do you know where he is?"

She stopped walking and looked at me.

"No, I haven't seen him since his mother and I watched him go to the bus."

"He never got *on* the bus, Angelina. We think he may have skipped the bus and hidden in Judith's car in order to spy on her and Alan."

Surprise turned to anger as Angelina cursed in Italian, her eyes squeezing into two angry slits.

"Maybe you had better get in my car," I said. "I'll take you home."

"No!" she said. "I can never go back there!"

"Because of Alan and Judith?"

"Because of myself. Because of what I have done."

She burst into tears. I took her arm and led her back to the bench where she sobbed uncontrollably. The few tourists who had been wandering around nearby steered away from our general direction. As Angelina cried, I thought about my hunch, knowing it had been pretty much on track: Alan had arranged to meet both of his women at their "special place." Then, while they waited, he had stolen the money and tried to make his getaway alone.

"Where I come from," Angelina said finally, when she had gotten hold of herself, "we have a term for a man who can lead a woman on. We have a term for a man who tells pretty lies and turns a woman's head and make her do things she would not ordinarily do. The term is *truffatore*. Con man."

"Alan Bennet."

She didn't reply but merely nodded.

"I know the two of you were involved," I said. "What has he done, Angelina? Did he hurt you?"

She shook her head and burst into new tears.

"He broke my heart," she said. "He made me believe things that were not true."

I thought of Judith cooling her heels in a rural coffee shop.

"He stood you up today, didn't he?" I said gently. "He was supposed to meet up with you here, but he didn't show."

"He was going to pick me up this morning between nine and noon. We were going to run away together."

"Where?"

"To city hall, to get married. Then we were going to drive to Florida for our honeymoon."

I sat back, stunned. I could see why Alan had wanted Judith out of town for the morning—so that he could be free to rob her company. But why Angelina? Why leave her sitting in the middle of a national park all day?

"Where are your suitcases?" I asked suddenly.

"Alan came and got my suitcases yesterday when no one was home. That way when I left this morning, even if someone had spotted me, they wouldn't have realized I was leaving for good."

"Why all the secrecy, Angelina?"

She shrugged.

"My brother did not trust Alan. He would not have wanted me to see him."

"But Nick couldn't stop you. You're old enough now to choose your own boyfriends."

"There is Judith, as well," Angelina said, shaking her head. "She has had a crush on Alan since he first came to work for her. He said if she knew he was involved with me, it would cause problems for him at work. So we kept our relationship a secret."

I thought about Alan, marveling at the fact that he had managed to keep two women, both living in the same house, each unaware that he was having an affair with the other. Amazing.

"I waited all day for him," Angelina said. "I thought maybe he got held up at work or something. But then I finally realized he was not coming. He only used me. Nick was right. He said I do not have enough experience with men, that I never learned how to separate the good from the bad."

"I'm sorry," I said. I wasn't sure what else I could say. I was puzzled at Alan's true motivation. He obviously used people to get what he wanted. But what could he possibly have gotten from Angelina that was worth anything?

My heart skipped a beat as I instantly answered my own question: *the shirt!* The shirt belonging to Thomas Jefferson. At first Alan must have planned to have Monty Redburn steal it; that's why he wanted him working in the house. But then Redburn screwed up, so Alan turned to Angelina. He romanced her into thinking they were going to elope; then he got her to steal the shirt and pack it with her own things. He picked up her suitcases yesterday; he probably took out the shirt and discarded everything else. I remembered when Carlos and I had startled Angelina in Wendell's study, the night before. She had probably gone in there to take it then.

"You won't go back to the Smythes because of the shirt?"

She looked at me sharply, panic in her eyes.

"They know it was me? They know I took it?"

I shook my head.

"Why, Angelina? Why would a nice girl like you steal from the family that has been so good to you?"

She cried softly, shaking her head.

"It wasn't any big deal," she said. "Alan loved Mr. Smythe so much, he just wanted something to remember him by."

"So he had you steal a million-dollar shirt?"

"No, it was only worth about a hundred dollars. Alan told me which one to take; he said it was the least valuable part of the collection. He said that if we took it, he would always have something precious to remember his dear friend Wendell by."

I sat quietly and looked around, wondering if all women were suckers or just those unfortunate enough to have come up against the charms of a hunk like Alan Bennet. Poor Angelina, finally slim and desirable after years of being overweight and unwanted; she hadn't stood a chance against a smooth operator like him. What would she do when she realized the item she had stolen was priceless, that the entire reason Alan had romanced her was to get at that shirt?

I didn't know, and I didn't want to know. *But it's better she hear it from me,* I thought, *than from some stranger or on the news.* I took a deep breath and exhaled slowly.

"Well, Angelina," I said finally, gazing out across the gorgeous wooded vista in front of us. "A lot's been going on today. I think there are a few things you need to know."

Forty-Eight

I recapped the day's events to Angelina as she listened, stunned, beside me. Halfway through my explanation, I convinced her to get into my car. I wanted to go back to the Pike Ridge airport; there was a chance, albeit a slim one, that Carlos had climbed from Judith's car into Alan's while they were parked at the apartment complex. If so, then Carlos could have hidden in the back of Alan's car all the way to the airport.

We headed there now, and by the time I was finished with my story, we were pulling into the airport parking lot. As we came to a stop, I spoke sternly.

"I know you're upset," I said. "But the priority for us right now is to find Carlos. There's a chance he's hiding around here somewhere. You need to put all of this stuff with Alan out of your mind and concentrate on the task at hand. Understood?"

"Of course."

We got out of the car and looked around, surprised to see several news vans in the parking lot. The police cars, however, had all left.

Angelina and I walked around to the front of the main building, nearly walking into one newscaster's on-air report. She was standing facing the camera with the runway in the distance behind her.

"...but fortunately for Smythe Incorporated, the airplane's engine difficulties forced a delay in takeoff, giving the police time to reach the airport and apprehend the suspect..."

Angelina and I stepped into the office, making our way through the chaos of reporters and eyewitnesses. I listened to the conversations around us, trying to gather as much information as possible about what I had missed here after I left. Apparently, it had come out that Alan Bennet had hired the pilot to take him to Burlington, Vermont. From there, it was now being assumed, he had been planning to rent a car and drive to Canada, then fly from Montreal to the Caribbean. The money he transferred out of the bank in Philadelphia this morning had gone to a bank in the Cayman Islands, where officials were cooperating with local authorities to secure its return.

I looked around at the room. Probably it was usually a sleepy little airport hangout. The people that were being interviewed were predominately men in baseball caps and grease-stained overalls. The walls were lined with torn pieces of fabric, names and dates written in black marker across them. I was looking at those when a man spoke, standing next to me.

"That's for solo flights," he said. I turned to see a friendly-looking fellow with stark white hair and a toothpick in his mouth.

"Excuse me?" I said.

"Them shirts. When you make your first solo flight, as soon as you land, your buddies tear off your shirttail, write your name and the date on it, and stick it up on the wall. That's mine, there, from back in '72. Martin Van Buren."

"Martin—"

He held up two hands to cut me off.

"I know, just like the president. I've been fighting jokes my whole life. But it tickles my wife. She likes folks to call her the First Lady."

"Nice to meet you, Martin," I said. "My name is Callie; this is Angelina."

"How 'do?" he said, tipping an imaginary hat at us. "You ladies reporters?"

"No," I answered. "We're friends of the Smythe family. We're looking for the boy, Carlos. The one who's missing."

"Yeah," he said, "them cops was out there earlier, looking around for him. They thought maybe they'd find his body in the woods around the field or something. But as far as I know, nobody turned up nothing. Not one sign that he was even here. I think now they're searching elsewhere."

I nodded, thinking this was probably a waste of time. But still, it was worth a shot.

"So who would we see about getting a look inside the hangar, and maybe inside some of those planes?" I asked.

"You have to see the president," he said looking around. "Oh! Martin Van Buren. I guess that's me."

Laughing at his own joke, he led us past the commotion and out of the building, toward the hangar. He brought us inside, letting us look in closets and behind big machines and basically anywhere a small boy could be hiding. A large set of keys jangled from Martin's belt loop, and whenever we came to a door that needed unlocking, he would release a sort of spring catch on the keychain, slide out the key, and unlock it for us. In that manner, we searched the entire hangar and all of the airplanes parked outside.

"Where's the plane Alan Bennet was trying to fly out on?" I asked. Martin brought us back inside the hangar and pointed toward the low-winged plane that was now parked in the service bay.

We went over to it and climbed inside, but it was very small, without a place that even a child could tuck himself into and hide.

"This here's Roy Sullivan's Piper Cherokee," Martin said as we crawled around inside. "A nice little plane. Shame about the engine."

"What happened to it?" I asked.

"It's the darndest thing," Martin said. "Roy pulled the plane up just fine, got 'er all loaded, and then they came inside to fill out the paperwork. When they got back out to the plane and tried to start 'er up again, it spit and sputtered and popped so bad, Roy couldn't even get the dang thing going. He was just trying to adjust the torque on the spark plugs when the police drove up, and then, well, you know the rest. They arrested the passenger, and poor Roy was stuck with no fare and a broken-down plane."

"So is that what it was?" I asked, climbing down out the of plane, then turning to help Angelina down. "Bad spark plugs?"

"Nah," Martin said. "Roy thought so at first. But it turned out to be the gas tank. Darn thing was full of water."

I froze, my heart pounding. *Water in the gas tank.* Where had I heard that before?

"The bus!" I said excitedly to Angelina. "Carlos' bus, at the soccer tournament!"

"What?"

"The bus broke down because there was water in the gas tank! The kids had to spend an extra night in a motel."

"So?"

"So," I said, almost yelling, "if Carlos knew Alan was taking off in this plane—if he knew he needed to somehow stop him—then what would Carlos know to do? He put water in the gas tank! Carlos *was* here, Angelina! He sabotaged the plane!"

Martin and Angelina both stared at me in surprise.

"Where was the plane parked when Alan and the pilot went inside to do the paperwork?" I demanded. "Could Carlos have snuck over and poured some water into the tank while they were in there?"

Martin hesitated, rubbing his chin.

"This plane's got two tanks, one on each wing, both of 'em mighty big. It would've taken five or six gallons each to mess her up that bad."

I tried to picture Carlos lugging gallon jugs of water across the tarmac. I realized that it didn't make much sense.

"Of course, there's the hose," Martin added. "He could've stuck the hose in each tank and let it run for a while. Probably would've been enough time. The passenger held things up for a good while, doing something on his computer, then making a call from the pay phone before he was ready to go."

I took a deep breath, closed my eyes, and said a prayer of thanks.

"Carlos was here," I said softly, opening my eyes. "He's still here somewhere. I just know it."

Martin and Angelina seemed to agree. We headed outside and looked out across the expanse of the runway. It was getting dark now with orange and purple streaks across the western sky. If Carlos were hiding around the perimeter in the woods, soon it would be too dark to find him.

Martin ran off to the building to get flashlights and spread the word. Though I hated the thought of having the press involved, I knew they could be useful. I gave Angelina my phone and told her to call the police while I went over to the small crowd of reporters that was quickly streaming out from inside the building. I waited until they were all out there facing me before I held up a hand for silence. When things were quiet, I spoke.

"We now have reason to believe that Carlos Smythe was here at this airport this afternoon when Alan Bennet was apprehended. The buildings have all been searched as well as all of the planes. Carlos is not there. That means he could be out in the woods or the surrounding area, and we've got to find him."

They all began shouting questions at once, but again I held up my hand for silence. With bright lights shining in my face, I was aware that I was probably being broadcast live on television, and I wondered if Marion was watching, if she knew that, finally, there was some hope of finding her grandson.

"You reporters have lights," I said. "Lights for your cameras, lights on your cars and vans. Mr. Van Buren, here, is going to divide the surrounding area into grids. We need each of you to spread out and start searching, at least until the police arrive and can take over. Hurry up, people. We may not have much time."

Everyone sprang into action at once. And though two of the television reporters chose to film and report on the action rather than become part of the search, everyone else was quite helpful, yelling Carlos' name and taking their orders from Martin.

Soon there were cars parked all around the edges of the airfield, lights shining out at the thick gray pines that marked the edge of the woods. I remained on the tarmac, standing at the center of things, trying to think, trying to decide where a scared 11-year-old spy would go to hide.

Angelina handed me back the phone, and I used it to call the Smythes' house. Marion answered on the first ring.

"Were you watching the TV just now?" I asked.

"My goodness, yes!"

"I think Carlos is here somewhere, Marion," I said. "I think he's scared, and he's hiding. Call Derek and Sidra and tell them to come here. Maybe if he hears them calling for him, he'll come out."

She agreed to call them right away and we disconnected. Glancing to the side, I realized that Angelina was watching me anxiously.

"I cannot believe Alan tricked me into stealing a priceless treasure," she said, obviously thinking again about the Jefferson shirt. "Mrs. Smythe will never, ever forgive me for that."

"At the time, you thought it was nearly worthless," I replied. "A memento for the man you loved."

"I was a fool."

I put my hands on Angelina's shoulders and looked her right in the eye.

"Better a fool who goes to her boss and owns up to her crime and apologizes for it," I said softly, "than a proud but unemployed maid who's been cut off from friends and family over a stupid incident with a *truffatore*."

She nodded and pulled away, wiping tears from her face.

"Maybe you are right," she said.

"Now go help those people find our boy."

"Yes, ma'am."

Angelina ran to join the others as I folded my phone and tucked it into my pocket. I was just trying to decide where to begin my own search when the old tower behind the main building caught my eye, and I stared at it long and hard.

Forty-Nine

The tower was behind the main building, a dilapidated old structure that looked as though it had once been a control tower or a lookout post. Now it appeared to be abandoned. I grabbed a flashlight from the pile and walked closer to it, peering up at it in the near-darkness.

There was a chance that Carlos could've sprinted up these stairs and out of sight after sabotaging the plane. It would've been the perfect hideout, a place where he could observe the action at the airport without being seen. Kind of like the tree house he had used at home.

I was no great lover of heights, but at least these were stairs and not a ladder. I climbed up one flight and turned, climbed up the next flight and turned, continuing on up, counting as I went, until I was five stories up in the air. As I reached the top, I tried very hard not to look down.

There was a door in front of me that opened easily in my hand. I slowly swung it wide and shined the flashlight around the room, expecting to see lots of spiders or bats. Instead, what I found was a little boy, huddled in the corner against the wall, shivering.

I went to him without a word, slid down next to him, and gathered him in my arms. He cried with his head buried against my shoulder as I whispered soothing noises in his ear and smoothed his hair away from his face. We stayed that way for a long time, his ragged breathing contrasting with the distant call of people shouting his name. Finally, I spoke, my voice echoing in the empty room.

"A lot of people have been looking for you, Carlos," I said.

He grabbed my shirt collar into his hands and pressed it against his eyes.

"Am I going to be arrested?" he whimpered.

"Arrested?" I asked. "Why?"

"I don't know," he said. "The police were here all afternoon, and then they were trying to find me. I didn't know what to do, Callie. I was only trying to help."

"Carlos," I said gently, "the police were looking for you because we were worried about you."

"But I ran away and I skipped school and I broke that guy's plane…"

"Thank goodness you did break the plane," I said. "You stopped Alan from getting away."

"But Mr. Bennet got shot," Carlos cried. "That was my fault. If I hadn't messed up the plane, he wouldn't have been standing there, and that guy wouldn't have shot him."

I felt a pang in my heart, knowing that he had witnessed a horrible act of violence, something no child should have to see.

"We're all sorry Alan got shot, honey, but that wasn't your fault. You didn't do anything wrong. In fact, you're a hero."

Carlos pulled back, wiped his nose on his sleeve, then looked at me.

"I am?"

"Yes, you are," I said. "I know Alan is a friend of your family, but he's done some very bad things. By stopping that airplane, you kept him from leaving. You helped the police catch a criminal."

He looked at me, wide-eyed.

"But you've scared your poor parents to death, honey. You've got to come down and let them know you're okay."

"Do we have to tell them about the water in the plane?"

"Yes," I said. "But your daddy will pay the man to fix it, and the people on the news will talk about how smart you were to think of that."

"They will? Are there news people out there now?"

"Lots."

"They got cameras?"

"Yes."

"Then we have to wait a minute before we go down," he said. "I don't want them to know I was crying."

I smiled, watching him rub his face fiercely with his hands.

"Okay," I said. "We can wait a minute."

"Thanks, Callie."

I dug through my pockets until I came up with half of a Kleenex; I handed it to him, and he took it gratefully, blowing his nose.

"Why don't you tell me what happened today, Carlos. Start with when you hid yourself inside your Aunt Judith's car. That was a very stupid thing to do, by the way."

"I know that now," he said. "I got in her trunk, and we drove for a while, and then we stopped. I heard her get out of the car, so I waited a minute, and then I kicked through to the backseat and climbed out."

"She didn't see you?"

"She was already gone. I was in the parking lot of apartments. Then all of a sudden I could hear arguing, and she was coming back. I didn't have time to get back in the car, so I hid behind some bushes."

"She was arguing with Alan?"

"Yeah, they were talking about going on a trip, and she wanted to take his car, and he wanted to meet her later and all this stuff. Finally, she got in her car and drove away. I didn't know what to do, but when I saw Mr. Bennet loading some suitcases and things into his car, I decided to hide in there. He left the hatchback open and went back in the building for a minute, so I climbed in and got under a hanging bag and he never even saw me."

"Were you scared?"

"Petrified. But then I got mad."

"Mad, why?"

"Because when we were driving, the hanging bag slipped open a little and I could see inside. Do you know what he had?"

"The shirt?" I asked. "Thomas Jefferson's shirt?"

"Yes! How did you know?"

"Lucky guess. So what happened when you got here at the airport?"

"I did the same thing. I waited until Mr. Bennet was gone, and then I climbed out of my hiding place and got out of the car. Just in time, too, because the next thing I knew, he had the back open, and he was unloading all this stuff and putting it on an airplane. I wasn't sure what was going on, but I knew something wasn't right. He wasn't doing what he told Aunt Judith he was gonna do. And he had the shirt. I had to stop him."

"So you waited until he and the pilot went inside, and then you stuck the hose into the gas tank."

"I figured if water could stop a bus, it could stop a plane."

"That was very quick thinking."

"Then after I did it, I got scared. So I ran up here to watch. And the next thing I knew, there were cops here and sirens and everybody was yelling, and then they were shooting!"

I could see him tearing up again.

"Don't start crying again, Carlos. We have to get down from here."

He took a ragged breath, staring up at the ceiling, willing himself not to cry.

"I was scared," he squeaked. "Then after they took him away, they started looking for me. I thought they were gonna arrest me, too."

"Didn't you see me down there?"

"Yeah," he said, "At least, I thought it was you. But I couldn't look for too long because I was scared someone would see me. I figured I would come down once everyone left, but they never did. Then when I looked again, you were gone. I didn't know what to do."

I pulled him back in for a long hug. The poor thing. He had spent the afternoon huddled up in this tower, not knowing what to do next, terrified as the long afternoon stretched on into evening.

"I tried to pray," he whispered, "but God didn't hear me."

I pulled away and looked at him, smoothing his hair. He was still a mess, but at least now he could go down and face everyone.

"Of course He did," I replied, smiling. "He sent me here to get you, didn't He?"

We got up off of the floor, and I gingerly walked to the front of the room. It wasn't a window, actually, just a framed-out open space through which I could look down at all of the happenings on the ground.

I shouted and started waving my flashlight. Soon, one person heard me, then the word seemed to spread. Like ants, they all began to head our way.

"Are you ready?" I asked Carlos as I turned from the window.

"Yeah," he said, but it wasn't until I swung the beam of the flashlight toward him that I realized he was hurt, with a makeshift bandage around his leg.

"What happened to you?" I gasped, kneeling in front of him to see where he had rolled his pants up and tied a sock around a wound on his shin.

"I cut myself," he said. "Climbing up here, I tripped on one of the steps. It was bleeding pretty bad."

"Can you walk?"

"Yeah," he said. "No problem."

"Let's get down there, then. We can take care of it at the bottom."

We headed out, Carlos in front, as I shined the light on the stairs. His leg wasn't a problem, but it was slow going for me—much harder than coming up had been. I tried not to look over the edge of the stairs as we walked, tried not to think how high up we were or how unsafe the tower might be. Halfway down, we could hear the shouts of Derek and Sidra from the bottom, and Carlos took off then, running the rest of the way. I stopped and leaned over to the right, training the beam of my flashlight on the stairs in front of him for as long as I could. When he was out of sight, I continued down. Below me, I could hear the joyous shouts of a child reunited with his parents. I continued walking slowly down, my heart light, my eyes filled with tears.

Fifty

By the time I reached the bottom, I realized the airport was once again swarming with cops. This time, however, they weren't holding out guns but handshakes. Legs trembling, I waved off their congratulations and sat on the bottom step, trying to catch my breath.

I let the confusion swirl around me for a while, watching Carlos reunite with his sobbing parents, declining interviews with newscasters who were thrusting microphones in my face. Right now, I just wanted to get somewhere quiet and lie down. Searching the crowd, I caught the eye of Martin Van Buren, who gave me a strong thumbs up. Tears quickly filling my eyes, I gave the same signal back to him as cameras flashed. I had a feeling that's the photo that would make the morning papers.

According to emergency personnel on the scene, the cut on Carlos' leg was deep enough to require stitches. They were also concerned about dehydration and exposure, so they helped him into the back of an ambulance and started an IV as he chattered excitedly about taking a high-speed ride to the hospital. Sidra climbed in next to him, assuring him that they had plenty of time to get there and could go at the regular speed. They were just about to shut the door when Carlos held out his arms, reaching for me. I leaned inside and gave him another hug, opening my eyes to see Sidra over his shoulder.

"Thank you," she mouthed silently, her eyes also filled with tears. We shared a meaningful look, and then they were gone, Derek following along behind in his car.

By the time Angelina and I turned into the Smythes' driveway, Nick and Marion were in her car about to pull out. The police were all gone and the house was dark. I parked the Lincoln along the driveway and walked over to theirs.

"Where's your car?" Nick asked. "Is that a Lincoln?"

"Long story," I replied, thinking that now that all of the brouhaha was over, I would need to get my car over to the police station where Keegan and Sollie could document its wounds as proof of my run-in with Redburn.

"We're headed to the hospital," Marion said, leaning forward so I could see her around Nick. "How did Carlos look?"

"Carlos is going to be fine," I said. "And the cut isn't very wide, just kind of deep. He probably won't need more than five or six stitches."

I could see the relief in her face. I could also see the tension in Nick as I realized Angelina had gotten out of my car and come to stand behind me.

"Marion," I said, "before you go, Angelina wants to talk to you. She has some things she would like to say."

Marion set her jaw and looked straight ahead. I knew she was hurt about the theft of the shirt. I could only hope that the two women could work it out. It seemed a shame to me that a man like Alan with all of his schemes could come in and destroy the warm relationship between them.

For me, I was too tired to try and help them. I looked from Marion to Angelina, who was staring at the ground, red-faced and teary-eyed. This one she would have to handle on her own. Exhaling slowly, I excused myself from the scene in the driveway and headed toward the house. Nick got out of the car and let me in with his key, disarming the alarm for me before turning to go.

I headed upstairs, and when I reached my room, I let myself fall, fully clothed, onto the bed. I was exhausted beyond belief. I closed my eyes, wanting sleep, wishing I could just blink my eyes and wake up in my own bed in my own home. Wearily, I reached for my phone and dialed Tom's number, knowing that his voice was the only one I felt like hearing for the rest of the night.

He was glad I called and said that news of Alan's theft and capture and Carlos' disappearance and recovery had even made a two-minute blurb on the evening news in Washington.

"They showed you climbing down that tower," he said. "They're calling you a hero."

"All in the line of duty," I replied, smiling up at the ceiling. For a moment, I let myself admit that it felt good to save the day.

I asked him what he had heard from the police, and not surprisingly, he was fully informed. After he fussed at me for a while about not removing myself from the case when I realized I was in danger, he calmed down and brought me up-to-date.

According to Tom, Judith was being held by the police on charges of theft and corporate fraud for her part in stripping money from the accounts of Feed the Need.

Alan had regained consciousness in the hospital, though he was still listed in critical condition. He had admitted to the theft from Feed the Need as well as the larger crime of trying to steal more than a million dollars from Smythe Incorporated. But he vehemently denied any involvement with Wendell Smythe's death at all, and now he had changed his alibi. Instead of just saying he was "running errands," at the time of Wendell's death, Alan was now maintaining that on the morning of the murder he had left the office to run to the bank and then the post office; while in line at the post office, he had met a lovely young lady in the line in front of him with whom he shared a cup of coffee and a quick but heated session in the alley behind the coffee shop. He hadn't gotten her name and had no way of knowing how to contact her to prove his alibi. If that were true, I

thought suddenly, at least it would explain his breathless and befuddled appearance the first time we met.

But the police seemed to think they had enough evidence to
convict Alan of Wendell's murder without a confession. Besides the
fingerprint on the syringe in the trash can, they had found his hair
on Wendell's arm. Circumstantial, yes, but when coupled with Alan's
embezzling activities and subsequent attempt to flee, the cops felt it
was an airtight case.

As for Monty Redburn, he had now committed enough crimes to
keep himself locked up for quite a while, and I was glad. With 20
cops as witnesses, getting a conviction on the attempted murder of
Alan Bennet should be a piece of cake.

Needless to say, the J.O.S.H.U.A. Foundation would not be
making a loan to Feed the Need now. Perhaps, Tom said, if Derek
could clear up the mess and demonstrate an ability to lead the company, Tom would consider a future request for funds.

"And, of course," Tom said, "you're almost free to go. As soon as
you go downtown tomorrow morning and give them your full statement, the police will release you from your Pennsylvania prison."

I closed my eyes, thinking how good those words sounded. *Free
to go.* Finally, in the morning, after getting my car and giving my
statement, I would load up and head home. It sounded too good to
be true.

We talked for a moment longer, and then I hung up the phone,
feeling oddly at loose ends. My body was wiped out, but my mind
was now flying. I walked to the window and looked out at the gorgeous moonlit night. This place was so beautiful, the perfect lawn
and stately trees so peaceful.

Finally, unable to resist the call of the smooth blue water below
me, I decided to go for one last nighttime swim in the Smythes'
heated pool.

Fifty-One

Heavenly, I thought as I leaned back in the water, letting my hair float out behind me. *This water is just heavenly.*

Tonight, I decided, I wasn't even going to do any laps. I was just going to lie here and float in the water and relax. After all that had happened, I deserved to pamper myself.

I let my feet rise up to the surface and tilted my head back so that only my face was above the water line. Arms stretched out beside me, I closed my eyes, lying flat in the water, trying to clear my mind of everything but the soft gentle waves that surrounded me.

It almost worked, too. But the longer I floated there trying to relax, the more my mind kept racing back to Alan Bennet, to the moment our eyes met at the airport. The eyes of a killer.

Or were they?

Something about it was bothering me, something about the way that this entire thing tied together. Had Alan Bennet killed Wendell Smythe? For the last few days, I had felt pretty sure that he had. But now, in spite of all that had happened, for some reason I was suddenly doubtful. It was almost as if things had tied together too neatly, too simply, and that bothered me. I just didn't know what to think anymore.

I sat up in the water and swam slowly, going back over the day's events in my mind. I had watched while Alan robbed the company and had seen him arrested and then shot at the airport. I knew he had conned two different women into giving him what he needed and tricked one very unsavory man into trusting him to come through in the end. Even poor Carlos had been caught up in the man's lies, risking his own life to prevent Alan's escape.

Poor Carlos. I thought of the two of us in the tower, of the brave way he had headed down those dark stairs to the crowd waiting below. How odd that this whole thing began—and ended—with me heading down a flight of stairs.

The stairs.

I stopped swimming and stood up in the water. The stairs! Of course! Carlos had run down the stairs of the airport tower ahead of me. He had been going fast, holding onto the rail, and I had shined the light down through the center of the stairwell, so that he could see as he went. I closed my eyes now, trying to picture the stairs in the office building where Wendell Smythe had been killed. The stairs there also ran clockwise as they went down. I remembered my pursuit of the person running down those stairs ahead of me on the day of Wendell's murder. I remembered hearing the sounds of running feet below me, but when I looked down the center of the stairwell, I had seen nothing.

The person I was chasing had been left-handed, I realized! He—or she—had been running down the left side of the stairs, holding onto the left rail. I grew angry at myself for not thinking of this before. I thought back to the coroner's report. Wendell had been injected into the left upper arm, the angle of the needle posterior to anterior. Just the way a left-handed person would do it.

I felt sure Alan Bennet was right-handed. Thinking back to the day we met, I remembered that was the hand he used to carry my printer as he walked me to Wendell's office.

I thought of all the suspects, wondering what was the quickest way to find out who was left-handed and who was right-handed. I closed my eyes, picturing them each in turn, trying to think of some action I had seen them perform and which hand they had been using. All that would come to my mind was Nick, the day I met him, carefully making his pecan tarts.

Nick was left-handed.

"It was *Nick,*" I whispered to myself urgently.

Then I heard an odd sound, like a splash. I opened my eyes and spun around, stunned to see Nick sitting on the edge of the pool. He had taken off his shoes and socks and was resting his feet in the water.

"A penny for your thoughts," he said in his deep male voice.

I swallowed hard, my mind racing, my heart pounding.

"W-what?" I managed to gasp.

"A penny for your thoughts," he repeated calmly. "Wendell used to say that sometimes when he wondered what I was thinking."

He looked at me, his eyes too dark to read.

"I wonder now what you are thinking," he said softly.

I took a step back in the water, trying not to let fear show in my face.

"Why are you here?" I rasped. "I thought you went to the hospital."

He shook his head.

"My sister wanted to talk with Mrs. Smythe. I told her to drive. I decided to stay here, with you."

"I see."

I glanced around, trying to think how I could escape. A quick swim to the deep end, climb out, and run across the yard? He would surely catch me. I looked wildly up at the house, knowing we were too alone, too isolated, for anyone to hear me if I screamed. I thought about Carlos in the hospital having the cut on his leg sewn up. It couldn't take forever. Surely, they would all be home soon.

"I wondered what your plans are now," he said, holding out one foot and tapping it against the water. Ripples rolled out on the surface and rolled all the way to me until they splashed against my stomach and disappeared.

"I'm leaving in the morning," I said lightly, taking another step back. "Now that the killer's been caught, there's no reason for me to stick around."

I could hear my own voice as I spoke, knowing it sounded as fake as it possibly could. What was wrong with me? I was an investigator; I regularly bent the truth for a living. Why now did this one lie sound so pathetic? Had he heard what I said? Did he know what I was really thinking?

He just shook his head, clicking his tongue.

"A penny for your thoughts," he repeated. "Or not. Because I already know what you're thinking. You're thinking Alan Bennet didn't kill Wendell after all."

My mind raced as I tried to fit other pieces of this puzzle together. I thought about Nick's alibi, about the fact that he had been shopping in Philadelphia with Marion at the time that Wendell was killed. I never had gotten around to asking her to clarify that, nor had I inquired as to whether Nick had been with her the entire time.

"Let us not pretend any more, Callie. I just heard you say, 'It was Nick.' You think it was me."

"Why, Nick?" I asked sinking down into the water. "Why kill a man who never hurt anyone, who did so much good in the world, for so many people?"

"Wendell Smythe was a good man," Nick replied, ignoring my question. He reached one hand out to the water and scooped up a handful and splashed it onto his face. The water trickled down across his broad cheeks, moistening his beard, leaving a dark wet spot on the front of his shirt.

"I've already told the police," I said. "They know Alan didn't do it. They know he's not the one who killed Mr. Smythe."

"You didn't tell the police yet," Nick said simply, shaking his head. "You just now figured it out yourself."

I started to speak, but he held up one hand to stop me.

"I was afraid you would figure it out, sooner or later," he said. "So now the question that remains is, what are we going to do about it?"

He stood and took a step forward into the water, the legs of his pants becoming wet. He took another step forward, and the water was now up to his hips. I hesitated, calculating just where I could go if I managed to make it out of the pool. Nick was big, yes, but sometimes big meant slow. Perhaps I could outrun him. Perhaps I could make it into the house, lock the door, and call the police before he could get inside.

"Why could you not just leave it alone?" he asked sadly. "Alan Bennet has been arrested. If he lives, he will go to trial. He will pay for his crimes."

"He'll pay for his crimes, alright," I said. "But should he have to pay for someone else's as well?"

Our eyes met. I saw Nick poised to jump, and I chose that moment to spring backward, diving into deeper water. Heart pumping, I swam as fast as I could through the black water to the other end of the pool. Reaching the cement side, I grabbed hold and hoisted myself out. I was almost up when I felt a hand at my ankle, gripping, pulling, yanking me.

In one motion, I landed hard on the side of the pool and fell helplessly under the water. Then his hand was around my neck. I fought, twisting fiercely, but he was just too big, too strong. He pulled me up out of the water, his arm wrapped around my neck, my back pressed tightly against his body.

"Please," he whispered, his lips at my ear as I gasped for breath. With his other hand, he grabbed my arms and pinned them to my body. "I do not want to hurt you. I just want you to promise you will not tell."

Was he insane? Did I have any hope at all? I thought about us there in the deep water. He was fully dressed, the water in his clothes weighing him down, his legs kicking furiously beneath me. After a while he would begin to get tired. He would lose strength, and then I could get away.

"I won't tell," I whispered. "I promise."

I thought of Angelina, the night I overheard her in the pantry with Alan. *Nick will kill me if he finds us,* she had said. Until now, I had thought it was just a figure of speech.

He changed his grip on me and began dragging me toward the shallow end. He was crying now, his sobs echoing across the top of the water. I wanted to understand why. I just wanted to know what made him do it.

He dragged me all the way to the steps, and then he pulled me against him again, his arm tighter around my neck. I could barely breath. I closed my eyes, willing my heart to slow down, forcing myself to think clearly.

"It'll be our secret, Nick," I rasped. "Yours and mine."

"How can I be sure?" he asked, his breathing heavy, his grip strong. He was rocking us back and forth, still crying. "You should have left it alone."

I didn't know what to do. I felt a wave of dizziness come over me and knew it was the lack of oxygen. I had to breathe. I couldn't breathe.

"Nick, stop!"

The voice of Marion Smythe rang out across the water. She stood at the edge of the pool, watching in horror as Nick's arm pressed more tightly against my throat.

He was startled enough by her appearance that he loosened his grip. I chose that moment to wrench myself away, sprinting from the pool. Feeling him lunge after me, I grabbed for the only thing I could reach—a wrought iron footstool beside the pool—which I lifted and swung around in an arc, catching him sharply on the side of his head.

He went down in a heap, blood spurting from the gash on his head. He was out cold, and for a moment, I was afraid I had killed him.

"No!" Marion yelled, seemingly frozen in place. I knelt down and felt for his pulse, which was strong and regular.

"The towel!" I said. "Hand me that towel!"

After a moment's hesitation, Marion did as I said. She tossed it to me, and I wadded it up and pressed it against the cut on his head. I held it there firmly, trying to catch my breath, watching Nick for signs of consciousness.

"Call the police," I barked to Marion, but she remained frozen where she was.

"You have to call," I said, looking at her. "*Now*, Marion. Nick's the murderer. He killed your husband."

She shook her head, whispering softly to herself.

"No," she said.

"Call them, Marion," I said. "Then bring me some rope. We'll tie him up while he's still unconscious."

"No."

"Marion!" I yelled. She seemed to snap back to attention, looking at me, pain in her eyes. "You *have* to call the police! But get me some rope first."

"Callie," Marion said softly, shaking her head. "Nick didn't kill my husband."

"Yes, he did. And just now he nearly killed me."

"He was only protecting me. He didn't kill Wendell."

"How do you know that?" I demanded.

"Because *I* did it," Marion said. "I killed my husband."

Fifty-Two

I sat in the drawing room with the door tightly closed as Angelina tended to Nick on the couch. He had regained consciousness, and the cut on his head had finally stopped bleeding. I knew he would need to see a doctor soon to get stitches and check for a concussion. For now, he was subdued, his eyes closed, his sister weeping softly as she cleaned the blood from his face and beard.

Marion stood in front of me, holding out the piece of paper that she had sworn would explain it all. I took it from her, noting the wildly shaking fingers and the pale, pale skin of her face.

What she handed me was a suicide note written by Wendell. He had penned it from the hospital bed on Sunday night, the night before he was killed.

> My dear family, I write this with a heavy heart, my sorrow so deep I can scarcely find the words to say what I must say. This is my final goodbye, my suicide anthem. I only pray that one day you will all find it in your hearts to forgive me.

I offer no justification for what I am doing, only the hope that you won't hate me for my actions. Unlike all of you, I witnessed my own mother's demise this way. In my nightmares, I still hear her screams of pain. I cannot and will not let that happen to me. I am afraid of the suffering that begins tomorrow and will only end in death anyway.

My only regret is all of this business with the company and my disappointment with those responsible. I will make things right, and then I will do what I have to do. But once I'm gone, let this weigh on you, Alan, for the rest of your life: I thought you were a trusted friend and employee, but you broke this dying old man's heart.

As for you, Marion, I can only ask for your forgiveness for this, the coward's way out. Surely once the pain of my death has receded, you will understand that it was for the best. You have given me a loving home and family and more wonderful years together than any man has the right to ask for. I love you with all of my heart and always will. Better I die now and leave you with memories of me intact and whole.

Derek, Judith, Sidra, Carlos—I love you. To everyone, I say, God bless you all. You have loved and cared for me for many years, and if the Lord can forgive me for this one final, desperate act, I await that day that we are all joined together again in heaven.

With love and deep affection,
Wendell (Dad and Grandpa)

I looked up, tears filling my eyes. Wendell had been planning to kill himself. He sat in that hospital bed awaiting his operation, knowing it wasn't going to happen, knowing he would kill himself first, as soon as he finished setting things right in his company.

"Nick went to see Wendell Sunday evening after the rest of us had left the hospital," Marion said. "When he got there, Wendell gave him this note in a sealed envelope and told him he was to hang onto it until the operation and then give it to me."

"I didn't wait," Nick interjected softly from the couch. "He was so depressed; I was worried."

"I was worried, too," Marion added. "That it was a suicide note didn't really come as a surprise."

"But Marion—"

"Of course, Nick didn't know what I would do about it," Marion continued softly, sitting next to me dry-eyed on the couch. According to her, she spent that night pacing the floor at home, confused and tormented. In the end, she felt she had no choice but to kill Wendell herself.

"I loved him, Callie," she said simply. "I had to spare him that final act of anguish."

The next morning, after Wendell checked himself out of the local hospital and headed to the office, Marion got Nick to drive her into Philadelphia as well, ostensibly to shop for a robe and some new pajamas for Wendell's return to the hospital. She picked a large department store that was about two miles from Wendell's office, and she left Nick with the car while she went inside. But rather than shop, she simply walked through the store and out the other side, catching a cab to Wendell's building.

She had gone up the back stairs, giving Wendell a pleasant surprise when she came in through the bathroom door. They had chatted briefly, lovingly, and then she had offered to give him his morning insulin shot. Once the massive dosage had been given, she quickly kissed him and left him there to die.

When she reached Nick's waiting car, he had known immediately that something was terribly wrong. Sitting in the car, sobbing, she finally confessed what she had done. Without much thought, Nick drove to the Smythe building and raced up the back stairs, reentering the room where Wendell now lay, dead, on the floor. Very quickly, Nick made sure there was no evidence there to incriminate Marion. He wiped away her fingerprints from all possible surfaces; then, as a red herring, he slid a short blond hair he saw on the floor under Wendell's shirt. Apparently, it was just pure luck that the hair was Alan's and that a needle bearing Alan's fingerprint was in the trash from an insulin dose he had administered to Wendell earlier.

When I had first come into Wendell's office, Nick was still there in the bathroom, trying to wipe fingerprints away from the sink, counters, and doorknobs. Hearing me, he had bolted, but the fact that he was left-handed had kept him safely to the left side of the stairwell, out of my range of vision, as I chased him down. When he reached the bottom, he simply exited the stairwell, walked to the car that he had left waiting in a loading zone around the side of the building, and drove away. Nick and Marion drove around for about 20 minutes before returning to the Smythe offices. This time, Marion came up on the elevator, acting confused about the presence of emergency personnel and feigning surprise at the news of her husband's death.

"When I realized you would be investigating the murder," Marion said to me, "I was worried at first. But then I knew the best way to distract you might be to bring Alan's crimes to light, since that was all happening at the same time anyway. I put the records together in a box and locked it in the safe. I knew the time would come when I could show it to you, and that you would take it from there."

I had bought her story, the day of the funeral, that she had "just discovered" the incriminating papers in Wendell's safe. As Harriet would say, like a bloodhound on the scent of a grouse, I *had* taken things from there, pursuing Alan with a vengeance. Little had either Marion or I known at the time, of course, that Alan hadn't finished yet; his subsequent theft and attempted escape had only helped solidify Marion's plan and my suspicions.

I knew that I had played right into Marion's hands. Yet, oddly, I wasn't as angry with her as I was with Nick. When he realized I was coming too close to the truth, he panicked. Loyalty for his beloved friend and employer had made him act out of desperation.

"I was not going to kill you," he rasped mournfully from his place on the couch. "I just wanted to scare you into keeping quiet."

I looked over at him, thinking that perhaps I would never know for sure. I was going to let a jury decide that one.

"We had no choice, you see," Marion said. "Wendell was planning to kill himself. Better I do it for him, Callie. Better I give him one last kiss and then fill him with insulin and let him die from that. Better his death at my hand than at his own."

"But why?" I asked, struggling to understand.

Marion didn't reply for a long while.

"Because I loved him," she said finally, simply. "I didn't want his life to end in suicide."

And then I understood. Like gears shifting into place, I realized now that almost the entire family had known the true circumstances of Wendell's death—or at least had suspected as much. That explained why they didn't talk about the murder, why they all acted as if he had died of natural causes. Their mother had killed their father to save him from the misery of committing suicide. Somehow, in her mind and maybe theirs, too, the crime was justified.

"You made a big mistake, Marion," I said, shaking my head. She looked up at me through tear-filled eyes.

"Perhaps," she whispered. "But I'm still alive. I still have time to atone for my sin."

"We have to call the police," I said, reaching for the phone. She placed one trembling, manicured hand over the receiver and looked up at me pleadingly as if willing me to understand.

"Don't you understand? It doesn't matter what happens now," she said. "I don't care what they do to me. My punishment is living the rest of my life with the memory of what I did."

"Marion—"

"I loved Wendell so much, Callie," she said, lifting the receiver and handing it to me. "I loved him enough to kill him."

Fifty-Three

In the morning, I went to see Judith.

The jail wasn't nearly as big or intimidating as I had expected. Judith was fortunate that the police were holding her in a county facility rather than the Philadelphia city jail. She was facing charges of theft and fraud, and though I didn't know what would happen to her eventually, I knew she was in serious trouble. The IRS, for one, was none too happy about her using nonprofit money to fund a for-profit enterprise. I thought she might end up doing some difficult time—or at least end up with community service and some hefty fines—particularly as Alan was now trying to push as much blame as possible from his shoulders to hers. We reap what we sow, I supposed.

There were a few chairs lining the walls of the reception area of the jail, and beyond them a window with inch-thick glass and a uniformed police officer sitting behind it. Speaking into a wire mesh rectangle, I told him I was an attorney here to see Judith Smythe. He dutifully wrote down her name before pointing to a door where I was to go in and wait.

It was a small room with four chairs around a table and no windows except in the door. I sat, trying to breathe through my mouth, ignoring the strong smell of cleaning ammonia that permeated the room. The table was scratched and scarred but shining, and I set my briefcase on top of it, thinking about all that I had managed to accomplish in the last 12 hours.

Last night Detectives Keegan and Sollie had come and picked up Marion themselves, treating her as kindly as possible under the circumstances despite the mandatory handcuffs. I had followed along to the police station and stayed with her through questioning until her own lawyer could get there. A high-powered corporate attorney, he seemed fairly clueless about criminal procedure, but he promised to hire her the best criminal lawyer money could buy first thing in the morning.

I had returned to the house late in the night to find Derek waiting up for me. I was afraid he would be angry with me for forcing his mother to turn herself in, but mostly he was just confused. He wanted the whole story, though when it came to his mother's confession, he seemed more sad than surprised. Asking me about her chances in court, I told him I thought they were pretty good. She had turned herself in, after all, and I doubted any judge would have the stomach for the harsh sentencing of a sweet middle-aged lady, however misguided and wrong her actions may have been.

"She'll do some time," I had said to Derek, "but I would hope for the minimum."

Derek, in turn, filled me in on the events at home. He told me that Nick had been taken to the emergency room for stitches and then on to jail, primarily for the crimes of aiding and abetting and obstruction of justice. Angelina was home and had gone on to bed after giving Derek and Sidra a full explanation of all of the events they had missed out on while they were seeing to Carlos' injured leg. They believed her story about Alan's lies that the Jefferson shirt was essentially worthless, and they weren't going to press charges against her for stealing it.

As for Carlos, he was fine after his big adventure, sound asleep in his room in the main house where he belonged. Derek and Sidra were committed to working through the problems in their marriage, he told me, and that began with the three of them living together again as a family.

After my conversation with Derek, I had managed to get a few hours of fitful sleep. Upon awakening this morning, I had packed my few belongings, given the clothes I had borrowed from Judith back to Angelina, and said my farewells. I was sorriest to say goodbye to Carlos, who now looked at me with something approaching hero worship. Not only was I a real spy, but I had managed to save his life and deliver him to safety. I knew I had found a lifelong friend, and I promised to be an e-mail pen pal to him for as long as he wanted.

I left the house and headed to the city. I turned in my fancy Lincoln and picked up my banged-up Saturn and then headed to the police station, where my car was photographed and I was grilled for about three hours by Keegan and Sollie. They had me retrace every step I had made in the last week, and though I left a few things out, I did my best to cooperate. In the end, they let me go with a promise that they would be inviting me back soon to serve as a witness at the various trials connected with the case. The only one of those I looked forward to was the one for Monty Redburn; I hoped to see him behind bars for a long, long time. It wasn't a matter of forgiveness; it was a matter of safety. I wanted him locked away and unavailable. I wouldn't soon forget the grin on his face as he tried to kill me, or the sight of his high-powered rifle aimed in my direction.

Leaving the police station, I stopped off at the Perskie Detective Agency to give Duane a big thanks for all of his help. Then I came here to the jail, my last stop before I headed south toward home. I wasn't sure why I had come; I doubted Judith would be very glad to see me. But I had a few things to say that were weighing on my heart, and at least here she would be a captive audience.

Still, I wasn't prepared for the sight of her as they brought her in. She was wearing a gray jumpsuit, her hair was limp, and her face was tired and devoid of makeup. She seemed subdued and not at all like her usual energetic, feisty self. She let the guard escort her to a chair, and then she simply sat across from me, avoiding my gaze as the guard retreated through the door.

"How are you?" I asked, my voice echoing in the cement room. She nodded, swallowing hard.

"About like you'd expect," she said hoarsely. "The county jail isn't exactly the Plaza."

"I suppose not."

"I should be out on bail in a few hours," she continued. "At least that's what my lawyer told me."

"That's good."

"If you came to tell me about Mom," she said, finally meeting my gaze, "save your breath. Derek was already here this morning. I know everything."

"That's not why I'm here," I said, "but I'm glad he told you."

"I knew it all along," she said softly, shaking her head. "Didn't want to believe it, but in my gut, I knew it."

"I think all of you knew it," I replied.

Judith leaned back in her chair, folding her arms across her chest.

"So why are you here, Callie?" she asked, a hint of the abrupt Judith sounding in her voice. "Come to gloat over the way you managed to solve your little case? Tie up all the loose ends, as it were? I'll give you this, you surprised me. I didn't think you'd be able to do it."

"If you didn't think I could do it," I replied, "then why did you bother searching my room?"

She shrugged.

"Same reason I went through your briefcase. To keep tabs on you. To make sure you weren't finding out anything you shouldn't."

Our eyes met, former enemies surveying the remains on the field from opposite sides of the battle.

"There's just one loose end I'm worried about," I said. "It's from our conversation on Monday when we first met."

"In Daddy's office? What, you want to know what I was looking for in there? Take a guess. I wanted to make sure Daddy didn't have any information about the account transfers from Feed the Need. I'd had a feeling he had figured out what was going on. I just wanted to make sure the cops didn't run across anything incriminating. Not that it made any difference in the end."

"That's not why I'm here," I said, "but thanks for clearing that up."

"What then?"

"I'm talking about the part where you told me that you didn't believe in God. That Christianity wasn't for you."

"Ah," she said slowly, leaning forward to rest her elbows on the table. "First my missionary brother and now you. Why, today, is the whole world suddenly so concerned about my soul?"

Much to my amazement, I thought I could see a hint of a tear glistening in the corner of her eye. I took a deep breath, praying that God had used this difficult time to prepare her heart.

"Because we know that deep inside you're searching for something. Something we've already found."

"I've heard this sermon all my life. Why should I choose to listen to it now?"

"What's wrong with now?" I replied. "Jesus is right where He's always been, Judith. Standing at the door, knocking. Waiting for you to let Him in."

Our eyes met and held. Watching her, I could see that years of angry defiance were melting away from her face. She was a strong person, full of resolve, finally brought to her knees by her own misdeeds. Perhaps she was ready to take that next step.

"How could you not want what God has to offer you, Judith? Peace. Forgiveness. Love."

"Peace? I don't know what that is."

"All you have to do is accept Christ," I said, "and you'll know. The Holy Spirit will fill you with a peace like you've never felt before. He'll carry your burdens for you, Judith. He'll help you through this difficult time."

Judith ran a hand through her hair, her expression wavering.

"How can I believe in something I can't see?" she whispered. "How can I know something is true that I have no proof of whatsoever?"

"You grew up in a Christian home," I replied. "You've seen the works your father has done, the love that was shared between him and your mother, the love of your brother despite what you've done to his company. How can that not be proof enough?"

"We're talking about a big decision here," she said. "If I believe Jesus was the son of God, then I have to buy the whole package—that He died, was buried, and rose again. All just to save me from my own sins."

"He did, Judith. For me. For you. Why is that so hard to accept?"

"I need *proof.*"

"Is that all that's stopping you?" I asked, smiling. "As Jesus himself said, 'Blessed are those who have *not* seen and yet have believed.' Accept Him on faith! He's ready to bless you, Judith. I feel sure He sent me here to tell you just that."

She studied my face for a long time, a hunger burning somewhere behind her eyes. I knew that expression; I had seen it the few times I had led others to Christ. She was open. She was in need.

In her heart, she was ready.

"I'll say the prayer if you want," I whispered. "You can just repeat it after me."

She looked down, shaking her head.

"I was brought up in the church," she said. "I know what to say."

She bowed her head and closed her eyes and was silent for a long time. I, too, closed my eyes, silently asking God to surround us with His love, to surround us with His guiding hand. Finally, after a long while, I heard Judith murmur a soft amen.

"Amen," I repeated, and opened my eyes. I wanted to tell Judith not to expect some sort of miraculous change right away, that salvation isn't always as much an emotional experience as it is an intellectual one. But one look at her, and I knew I didn't have to say a word. In her eyes, on her face, it was there.

Judith Smythe had finally come home to God.

Fifty-Four

My house smelled musty, of course, as it had been closed up for days. I put my bags down in the kitchen and then walked around and opened every window I could easily reach. Almost instantly the breeze swept in and cleared the trapped air.

I walked down the quiet hall to my bedroom, unbuttoning my blouse as I went. I was weary but in desperate need of some physical activity after the long drive home. Though it was too late to take the canoe out, it looked like there would be just enough light left for a quick jog to the post office, the dog sitter, and back.

Opening the drawers of my bureau, I pulled out sweatpants and a sweatshirt, sliding them on and exhaling deeply from comfort. What a pleasure to have my own clothes back again! I quickly slipped on my running shoes, did a few stretches, and headed out the front door.

In my rural area, I was safely able to leave the windows open and the door unlocked. I jogged down the front steps and hit the driveway, breathing in my precious Chesapeake air as I ran. *There truly is no place like home*, I thought to myself. The peculiar salt marshes and high river grasses weren't for everyone, but to me they were like pieces of heaven. I reached the main road and then stepped off onto the bike path, enjoying the high grass surrounding me on both sides, insulating me from everyone and everything but the well-worn path under my feet and the setting sun ahead of me on the horizon.

As I ran, I thought of Bryan and how much he had loved it here, how he, too, saw it as our little haven of rest. Then I thought of Tom, and I wondered if he had ever been to a place like this, if he knew the difference between things like cattails and wild rice the way Bryan had.

I reached the post office and though the window was closed, I could still get into my box. It was completely full. I pulled everything out, flipped through it, found nothing important, and then tucked it all into the drawstring bag at my waist. On the way back, I circled around by Lindsey's house and collected my dog Sal—short for La Salle, the French explorer who once traveled a journey of about 3000 miles by canoe.

"She missed you," the teenager assured me, leaning against the front porch rail, watching as my little doggy trembled in excitement from head to toe. I put Sal on the ground and let her dance around, reaching out to collect her leash and her bowls from Lindsey. I paid the girl for all of the pet-sitting, plus a ten-dollar tip for washing the dog. I didn't comment on the purple toenails peeking out from Sal's fur. If Lindsey wanted to play beauty parlor with my dog, it was okay with me. She was a sweet girl, and she provided a good "second home" for my pup.

Sal and I jogged the rest of the way home together, and as we ran up the steps, I could hear the phone ringing inside. I grabbed the portable just in time; it was Tom, about to hang up.

"I see you made it home okay," he said.

"I was just picking up the dog," I replied, still out of breath. As we talked, I went to the cabinet, pulled out a strip of beef jerky, and gave it to Sal. She took it gratefully and carried it to her favorite spot by the sliding glass door to settle down and munch.

Tom said that he had just spoken at length to Derek. After some anguished soul-searching, Tom said, Derek had decided to step down as CEO of Feed the Need. Apparently, he and Sidra had been doing a lot of talking about their current lifestyle, and they had reached a compromise: Though Derek had no desire to reenter the foreign mission field, he did feel compelled to move into home missions. They planned to start some sort of local ministry together—something on a much smaller scale than Feed the Need.

"Of course, he'll remain on Feed the Need's board of directors and continue to serve in a consulting capacity," Tom said, "but the day-to-day operations will be overseen by the new CEO."

"Who's that?" I asked.

"Gwen Harding!" Tom laughed. "Apparently, that was Wendell's directive, and Derek is in full agreement. He said that Gwen was a bit shocked when he first told her this morning, but she's been warming up to the idea all day."

"Strike a blow for secretaries everywhere," I said, smiling. "They practically run their companies anyway."

I grabbed a bottle of water from the fridge and headed out to the deck. Sliding the door shut behind me, I turned to face one of the most gorgeous sunsets I had ever seen. Of course, I thought almost every sunset on my inlet was the most gorgeous I had ever seen, but this one seemed especially beautiful.

"You'll be glad to know that Derek and Sidra are going to go to counseling," he continued. "The events of the last few days have really made them both take stock. But Derek said you started it all with a good tongue lashing—one that made a lot of sense."

I smiled, picturing myself fussing at Derek in the diner.

"Yeah," I said, "as Harriet would say, I really gave him 'what-for.'"

Tom laughed the easy, warm laugh I knew so well.

"I wish you could see the sunset right now," I said, sitting in my favorite deck chair. "It has the most incredible colors, and every one of them is reflected in the water."

"Sounds gorgeous."

"It is."

He was quiet for a moment, and I closed my eyes, trying to picture him here with me, wondering if it was a place he could ever belong to.

"For what it's worth," he said now, "I'm sorry I brought you in to all of that mess. If I had had any idea how it would turn out…" He let his voice trail off.

"It's okay," I said. "Good for me, in a way. Made me confront some things I've been needing to deal with for a while."

I thought of Marion, of her dilemma over her husband's suicide.

"Let me ask you something, Tom," I said. "Do you think a person who kills himself automatically goes to hell? I don't. I was always taught that when we accept Christ, *all* of our sins are forgiven—past and future."

"I'm not sure what I think," he answered. "The nature of forgiveness is a very difficult concept to grasp. I've never thought about suicide in those terms. But I know a lot of people who believe the way Marion does, that if her husband had died by his own hand, he would've automatically been condemned for eternity."

"Don't you think the Lord knows the anguished heart of a man contemplating suicide? Don't you think He takes that into account on judgment day?"

"I don't know, Callie," Tom said. "I do think that sometimes God forgives our sins *long* before we are able to forgive ourselves."

I thought about that for a moment, hearing something in the somber tone of his voice. It wasn't the first time Tom had spoken this way, had spoken of the need for self-forgiveness. I wondered about that, wishing I could understand the burdens he carried.

A penny for your thoughts, Nick had said to me the night before. I thought that now, about Tom. How little I knew about him, really, when it came down to it.

"You struggle with forgiveness, don't you, Tom," I said, unable to help myself, knowing that his life—his sins—were his business and not mine.

"More than you know, Callie," he answered after a long pause. "More than you could ever know."

We hung up a few minutes later, but I stayed there on the deck, looking out at the sun and the river, listening to Sal grapple with her favorite chew toy at my feet. I thought about Tom and his private struggles, about the Smythes' great wealth and their heartaches, and I knew I had them all beat hands down.

I couldn't bring Bryan back, but I could live a life that honored him. I could protect his image in my memories. And I could maybe, just maybe, learn to let go and give love another chance.

For the time being, I thought it might be time to take it all to the Lord in prayer. I sat there on the deck and bowed my head, thanking God for the beauty of nature surrounding me. I prayed for Judith and her newfound salvation, for Marion and her pain, for the souls of all who were lost. I prayed for myself and my future. I prayed for the starving children who were saved through outreach programs like Feed the Need.

Mostly, I prayed for Tom, for a healing of whatever burden of forgiveness that he carried. When I was finished, I sat on the deck in the gathering darkness and listened to the sound of the crickets in the grass. I sat there until the last speck of light had left the horizon. Then I picked up Sal and went inside, grateful for the night and the sweet, relaxing sanctuary of my home.

Join Callie on her next investigation
in The Million Dollar Mysteries series

Don't Take Any Wooden Nickels

One

I heard the gunshots from a distance, sharp and loud in the cool November air. A few seconds later there were more gunshots, then more, then all was silent.

Quickening my pace, I rounded the corner and stepped through two large stone arches into the Glenn Oaks Cemetery, a beautiful, shady old graveyard on the outskirts of Nashville, Tennessee. I had timed this just right, because I didn't really want to get there until the funeral was finished. Now that the honor guard had fired three volleys, I knew it was almost over.

I found the gravesite and waited a respectful distance away, noting that there were about ten people in attendance and a minister, plus seven older men in dress uniforms with rifles, and two other younger military representatives. I didn't know who the deceased was, only that he had been a naval chief petty officer in his youth and that his family had wanted him to have a full honor guard burial.

From a distance, I watched as the two younger soldiers carefully folded the flag that had been draped over the coffin. Finally, as they presented the flag to the woman I assumed was the widow, one of the older men lifted a bugle to his lips and lightly sounded out the notes for Taps. The simple tune, always so mournful, sounded especially sad in the middle of this Tennessee graveyard.

Ordinarily, I think, the whole scene would've brought me to tears. Even though I didn't know the deceased or his family, I had been widowed myself only three years before. Since then, it didn't take much to get me going at a funeral. Today, however, I was thankfully distracted by other matters. Today I had an exciting event of my own that kept my mind from becoming too absorbed with what was unfolding before me.

Once the service ended, I watched the tiny crowd. The seven men I was here to see turned and walked in the opposite direction from me, somberly shouldering their rifles as they headed toward a row of cars. I tried to catch up with them but the ground was muddy, and the heels of my Joan & David pumps sunk into the ground with the first step. Fortunately, storing away the bugle and the rifles took a few moments, allowing me time to walk around the perimeter on the sidewalk and reach them before they drove away. All of the other mourners had already gone by them, leaving only the seven men crowded into two cars and me.

I waved at the driver of the front car and he rolled down his window and smiled. The second car must not have noticed me, for they pulled into traffic and headed off, I assumed back toward the veterans center.

"Can I help you, young lady?" the man in front of me asked, perfect dentured teeth showing in a tanned, wrinkled face. He looked to be in his late 70s, weathered but still handsome in a crisp white naval dress uniform. I guess to him I *was* a young lady—though, in my early 30s, I didn't feel all that young.

"I'm looking for Commander Davis," I said.

"That's me," he replied. He opened the door of the car and stepped out, closing it behind him as the other men peered curiously from inside.

"Callie Webber," I said, reaching out to shake his hand. "It's a pleasure to meet you, sir."

"It's my privilege, ma'am," he replied, glancing down at the envelope I held in my hand. "Thanks aren't necessary. It's part of the Greater Nashville Honor Guard Society service. No charge, please."

I realized he thought I was connected to the deceased and that I was here to thank him and to pay him for the military send-off. I smiled. I *was* here to give him some money, but not for the reason he thought.

"That's a beautiful service you provide," I said. "Very dignified and touching."

"It's our opinion, ma'am, that every veteran deserves full military honors at his or her funeral."

"Yes, I agree," I said, aware that although the government mandates supplying a burial flag and two military representatives at veterans' funerals, it's up to volunteer groups like this one to flesh things out by giving a full military sendoff, including the firing party and a live rendition of Taps. I thought their group provided a valuable community service, and I was happy to be the bearer of good news on this sunny autumn morning—despite my distracted mind-set and the grim surroundings of a cemetery.

"'Course," he said, "our job is a lot easier on a gorgeous morning like this. Two days ago, we were out doing this in the pouring rain."

I smiled, agreeing that it was, indeed, a lovely day. Unbeknownst to him, I had observed his little group of veterans at that rainy funeral—though at a distance and from the warmth of my rental car. In fact, I had been in town now for three days and had spent the majority of the time discreetly examining his organization. As an investigator for a charitable foundation, it was my job to scrutinize the finances and activities of certain nonprofits, awarding grants to them if they passed our rigorous screening process. This gentleman's application had struck me as particularly charming, and I was glad that after a little digging around I had been able to determine that his group was, indeed, a legit bunch doing good work and that a grant would be a big help for them. The handing over of the money, like now, was the fun part that always came at the end of a successful investigation.

For me, however, an even more fun event awaited at the conclusion of this particular investigation: After a lot of frustration and much anticipation, I was finally going to meet—face-to-face, for the first time—my enigmatic boss, Tom. I couldn't wait. Though we had spent countless hours on the phone and on the internet, we had never actually met in person. Today, however, we were finally going to get together—albeit briefly, and only in an airport.

Our meeting was just about all I could think of. All morning, I had been trying to put it out of my mind and attend to the task at hand.

Focus, Callie, I told myself. *Focus.*

"I would imagine you have a lot of expenses associated with something like this," I said, giving my attention back to Commander Davis.

"Well, the government provides the blanks for the M-1s," he replied. "Other than that, it's just your basic stuff, transportation to the funerals, maintenance on the rifles, things like that."

I nodded, thinking back over the information he had supplied in his grant request. I especially liked the section he had written under "Additional Needs:" *I guess we could use a few bugles and some bugle lessons,* the application had said, *'cause right now the only one in our group who plays the bugle is Charlie Goodall, but he wants to move to Memphis to be closer to his daughter, not to mention that his emphysema keeps acting up, and when it does he can't really get enough breath to play good.* I smiled now remembering it, thinking that Charlie *had* sounded a little breathless when he tooted out Taps today.

"I suppose I should tell you," I said, "that I'm from the J.O.S.H.U.A. Foundation."

"The grant people? Yes, ma'am, I sent in an application a while back."

"Well," I replied, "it made its way to me, and I'm happy to say we will be awarding you a small amount of money for your bugles and bugle lessons."

I handed him the envelope, inside of which was a check for $5000 made out to the Greater Nashville Honor Guard Society. I could see a slight disappointment flash across the man's face, sorry that he hadn't received the money for his primary request, which was $11,000 for a used transport vehicle to carry their small group back and forth to all of the funerals they attended in the region.

"Well, that's good news, that's very good news," he said finally, tucking the check back inside the envelope. "We sure do appreciate that. Old Charlie, especially. Thanks."

Old Charlie waved to me from the back seat, obviously hanging onto every word of our conversation.

"The best way you can say thanks," I replied, repeating the little speech that always accompanied the handing out of a donation, "is to take that money and use it to further your mission as outlined in your grant proposal. The foundation believes strongly in what you're trying to accomplish, and we just wanted to have some small part in furthering your efforts."

"Well, that's real nice," he said, reaching out to shake my hand. Similar sentiments were expressed from inside the car, which I accepted on behalf of my employer. I told them I understood if they needed to get going, and I waited until Commander Davis got back into the car before I leaned over and spoke again.

"Oh, and on your way," I said, "you might want to stop off at Henderson Motors."

"Henderson Motors?" the commander asked, concern wrinkling his brow. "Do we have a flat tire or something?"

"No, sir," I replied with a wink. "But they'll have your new Transmaster Eclipse twelve-passenger van ready for you in about ten minutes."

"What?" he asked, his eyes wide with excitement.

"It's all yours, gentlemen, compliments of the J.O.S.H.U.A. Foundation."

Mindy Starns Clark's plays and musicals have been featured in schools and churches across the United States. Originally from Hammond, Louisiana, Mindy now lives with her husband and two daughters near Valley Forge, Pennsylvania. Visit Mindy's web site at www.mindystarnsclark.com.

Mindy's fast-paced and suspenseful inspirational writing—with a hint of romance and a strong heroine—are sure to make this exciting new mystery series one that will delight readers everywhere.

Coming soon in the series are *Don't Take Any Wooden Nickels* and *A Dime a Dozen*. Look for them soon at a local Christian bookstore near you!

Harvest House Publishers
For the Best in Inspirational Fiction

Introducing...

CHAMBERS OF JUSTICE

The Resurrection File

by Craig Parshall

—⚍—

A Respected Professor...

A Slash-and-Burn Lawyer...

A Small-Time Preacher...

Who Is Telling the Truth?

Depressed, down on his luck, and dropped by his law partners, Will Chambers is an attorney whose troubles are starting to exceed even his considerable talents.

When Reverend Angus MacCameron asks Chambers to defend him against accusations that might destroy not only the man's ministry but the very foundation of the Christian faith, everything in Chambers' nonbelieving heart says "run away."

But Chambers can't resist the preacher's earnest pleas, the presence of his lovely and successful daughter, Fiona, and the chance to go up against high-powered attorney J-Fox Sherman.

Quickly caught in conspiracy involving terrorism, top-level government intrigue, and wild legal maneuvering, Chambers is in for the ride of his life—a ride whose destination he never could have imagined.

—⚍—

The Resurrection File is a legal thriller with tightly drawn characters, page-turning twists and, at its core, a compelling story of one lawyer's discovery of the truth and power of Christ's message.